Stupid Magical Love

OTHER TITLES BY AMY BOYLES

ROMANCE

How to Fake it with a Fae

How to Outwit a Wizard

COZY MYSTERY SERIES

Sweet Tea Witches

Magical Renovation Mysteries

The Accidental Medium

The Withering Mysteries

Southern Belles and Spells Matchmaker Mysteries

Southern Ghost Wranglers

Bless Your Witch Mysteries

Southern Single Mom Paranormal Mysteries

For a full list of books, visit Amy's website:
http://www.amyboyles.com

Stupid Magical Love

AMY BOYLES

This is a work of fiction. Names, characters, organizations, places, events, and incidents are either products of the author's imagination or are used fictitiously. Otherwise, any resemblance to actual persons, living or dead, is purely coincidental.

Published by Montlake, Seattle
www.apub.com

Amazon, the Amazon logo, and Montlake are trademarks of Amazon.com, Inc., or its affiliates.

EU product safety contact:
Amazon Media EU S. à r.l.
38, avenue John F. Kennedy, L-1855 Luxembourg
amazonpublishing-gpsr@amazon.com

ISBN-13: 9781662531743 (paperback)
ISBN-13: 9781662531736 (digital)

Cover design by Hang Le

Cover image: © VasjaKoman / Getty; © mountain beetle, © Dumith Pramodaya, © i_fleur / Shutterstock

Printed in the United States of America

To Mark, Harper, and Briar—for always letting me work on "just one more chapter"

Chapter 1

There's a saying in my little town just outside Mystic Meadows, Georgia: *Bad luck begets more bad luck. And if you're Rowe Wadley, you won't just* attract *bad luck—you* are *bad luck.*

Nasty, right? I mean, it must be pretty terrible to be this Rowe Wadley person.

"Today is going to be great," I announce with gusto, to no one.

Well, "no one" unless you count Buster the Cat.

Buster the Cat is a plump red tabby whose main form of morning exercise is sitting on the bathroom sink and batting at the sticky notes I read my morning affirmations from.

I pull my dark hair over one shoulder and braid it while repeating the sentence penned on the wrinkled paper that's attached to the mirror. Months of shower steam have softened the note and eaten at the glue, causing it to peel away from the reflective surface. I rub the top back down and glance at the next affirmation, one sticky note down from the first.

"'I got this!'" Chest up. Head high. My gaze falls to the final note and the uplifting words on it. "'Greatness is within me!'"

I smile. Wide. Feeling the greatness. I'm feeling so much greatness that my chest is going to explode. Or maybe my bra's too tight.

"You hear that, Buster? Greatness is within me."

The cat meows like he doesn't believe a word.

"Don't be such a Debbie Downer." I boop his nose with my finger. "We've got this. You're going to be my right-hand cat when Mom leaves today. I'll be counting on you to help feed the pigs and collect money from the tourists."

All the tourists I'll somehow pull out of my butt, that is, since we literally don't get a single one. Not like we used to.

But hey! I got this! "It's just gonna be you and me."

Buster the Cat meows again.

I mock-gasp at his perfectly normal feline tone. "Don't even pretend that you don't love the pigs like I do. I see how you look at them when you think no one's paying attention. You love their sweet little pink snouts and their tiny little hooves almost as much as you love Meow Mix with cream on top."

The cat stares at me as if he does not, in fact, adore livestock.

Don't let him fool you. He's a big ole puddy tat around them. "Your secret's safe with me. No one will ever suspect how you really feel—undying love and all."

He stretches and jumps down from his perch, terminating our morning talk. And just when I was getting warmed up.

As the cat exits the room, tail swishing, my gaze drifts to the window. Outside, the faded-red barn sags like the Leaning Tower of Pisa. The gray fence surrounding the place isn't much better. It looks like it's made of splintered toothpicks instead of thick planks that are constantly having to be propped back up thanks to the rotting wood.

I sigh. Six months. I've got six months to get this place fixed up so that when Mom returns, she'll see a whole new farm—one brimming with life instead of one dying the agonizingly slow death of a Victorian-era courtesan succumbing to tuberculosis.

This is gonna be fun.

I head downstairs, grabbing hold of the banister my grandfather hand-carved, and whip around in a half circle, sliding into the kitchen in my socked feet.

The smell of fresh coffee fills the room, which is covered in wallpaper that features blue-feathered roosters. Matching porcelain cookie jars with removable rooster heads are sprinkled across the counter and built-in desk. Not only that, but rooster place mats sit on the table beneath plates stamped with, you guessed it, more roosters.

The entire room suffers from a fowl explosion.

"Good morning," my mom says, sweeping in beside me, wavy, gray hair billowing behind her like a cloud. She's wearing her bright-orange kaftan. A moonstone necklace dangles from her neck, and shining silver rings twinkle on her fingers.

"Morning," I say as she pours a cup of coffee. "Today's the big day. You excited?"

With her back to me, she finishes pouring and shoves the carafe into place. "I'm not going."

I must be hearing things. I tug on my ear and laugh. "That's funny. I thought you said you're not going."

Mom turns around and stares at me, hard. "I'm not."

The laugh stutters and dies in my throat. Then, to add insult to injury, a gob of my own saliva strangles me.

I finish choking and wheeze out, "What do you mean, you're not going? Mom, this is what you've been wanting for ages. You and Bill are heading out on the road. You've been *dying* to follow the Happy Clams around the country since before I was born. I should know. You've told me this like *a thousand times*." She glances bashfully at her feet. "Mom, I love you. You need to do this for yourself. Besides, you've been planning this—*your dream*—for a year."

Her eyes flash up. "But who's going to take care of you?"

"I don't need to be taken care of," I say defensively, slumping onto one of the frayed chairs that surround the farm table. "I need for you to go and do this. I mean, don't you think you've been through enough?"

She gives me a pitying look as if I'm keeping a secret only she knows the truth about.

I ignore her expression. "Is this because of Dad? Is that what's brought on this change of heart?"

"No, no." She presses one hip against the counter. "No. It has nothing to do with Dad. I just . . . it's just . . ." She releases a long exhale. "There's something I need to tell you."

Oh, God. From the look on her face, it must be bad. "Are you sick?" My chest tightens so hard I can barely breathe. "You're not sick, are you?"

"No."

Air rushes from my lungs in relief. *Thank the Lord.* I can't lose another parent. Losing one was enough to last me a lifetime. "Then what is it? Is it me?"

I bet that's it. My mom still thinks I'm sixteen and smoking pot in the back of the pickup. Why do parents never think you grow up? If anyone's smoking pot *now*, it's her. For goodness' sake, she's leaving to follow her favorite *jam band* around the country. If that doesn't scream *CBD-fueled midlife crisis*, what does?

"Mom, I'm perfectly capable of taking care of the farm. I know you're worried that I can't handle it, but I've been in charge since Dad died. I'll be fine," I say staunchly. "I don't need help."

Besides that, I have plans. Things I'm going to do. Things she always says are too expensive, can't be done—all of that. There's always an excuse.

"I know you don't need any help, hon. It's not that. It's . . ." Her gaze swivels around until it finds the *rooster* clock on the wall. "Oh, would you look at the time? There's something important happening upstairs."

She moves to go past me, but I grab the giant cuff of her kaftan. "You're not getting away that easy. What is it? What's going on?"

She presses the back of her hand to her forehead in resignation. "Well, you see—"

Just as she's about to word-vomit all over me, the phone trills on the wall. When I release her to rise and grab it, Mom takes the opportunity to shuffle out of reach. "We're not done with this conversation," I say sternly.

She looks relieved as she slips out of the room. "Of course not. We'll finish it . . . later."

I scowl at the wall she disappeared behind and bring the slick-surfaced, puke-green phone to my ear. "Hello?"

Heavy breathing answers. What now? A phone-sex call? Isn't it a bit early for that? It's probably one of the Collins boys. Everybody knows all five of them are jonesing for girlfriends. But if those teenagers think they have a shot at twenty-seven-year-old me, their mama's going to get an earful.

The person finally speaks in a thick Southern accent. "Rowe. Wadley."

Right. I may have forgotten to mention that I'm Rowe Wadley—*the bad luck* in my town.

And my bad luck just got worse.

Because the sound of that voice makes the last slice of happiness die inside me. Unfortunately, this is not the Collins boys attempting to woo me with early-morning, bad-breath phone sex, and now I kinda wish it was.

I twirl the cord around my finger. "Why, Sally Ray, to what do I owe the *displeasure* of a call so early in the morning?"

"Cut the crap, Rowe. Your stupid pigs are on my property."

"No, they're not. I mended the fence yesterday."

I glance out the window above the kitchen sink. The sun breaks through the trees, smearing cotton candy and blue raspberry across the horizon. Cardinals sing. The piggies graze in the yar—

Wait a minute.

The pigs are not grazing. They're not even in sight.

They're not rolling around on the scraggly grass that lives in bundles of tufts, nor are they stampeding past the tractor, which has hay creeping out around the tires.

There's not a piggy in sight.

I groan. *Great.* Just *great.*

"You don't see them, do you?" Sally says victoriously.

My jaw clenches. What a way to start the day—first Mom and now this. "I don't appreciate you calling my pigs 'stupid.' They are highly intelligent."

"Who gives a crap? If you don't get your ass over here right now, I'm going to shoot 'em. One by one. Little piggy by little piggy."

She wouldn't! But then again, Sally very well *would.* "Don't you touch one hair on their heads," I fume.

"I got rights. They're on my property, destroying it."

There is a special place in hell for murderers and Sally Ray. She is the blight on my potato, the absolute worst person in the world. Imagine a small Southern woman with big hair and an even bigger attitude, and you've *almost* got Sally Ray. Now add *evil villain* onto that, and you've got her pegged for sure.

My gaze skims the room, looking for my dad's old boots. As if my thoughts were heard, an ivy vine shoots out from under the floorboards, scoops up the boots from where they sit on the other side of the room, and deposits them beside me.

I jam my feet into them and say to Sally, "If you hurt even *one* of my drove, I swear you'll regret it for the rest of your life."

"Like hell I will, Rowe. I'll be eating bacon for months."

I suck air. "You wouldn't dare!"

"Just try me," she says nastily. "If you don't get these damn piggies off my property in five minutes, they'll become feed for my *unis.*"

She pronounces the word *uu-nee.*

"Making bacon's a new low even for you, Sally."

"You don't *know* low, then, Rowe."

The line goes dead, and I have no doubt she'll keep her promise and start shooting in less than five minutes.

"Who was it?" my mom shouts from upstairs.

"Sally Ray! The pigs are out!"

Mom's face appears on the stair landing. Her wavy, gray hair is now pulled back, and her necklace dangles over the railing. "You need me to call the sheriff?"

"No! We don't need the law getting involved." Last time they showed up, we nearly got fined for the pigs being out. Not our fault, I explained. Bobby John, the one and only deputy in town who does anything, barely let us off the hook. I had to promise him it would *never* happen again.

And now *it is* happening, it is *very much* happening, and Sally's about to make bacon.

My arms shoot out. "Don't call anybody! I'll be right back."

I dash onto the back porch and head straight for the bag of feed. The pigs won't come home by themselves. They'll take one look at me, stick their pink snouts in the air, and prance like ballerinas in the opposite direction. Which means I have to lure them.

But the fifty-pound brown sack is down to crumbs. Crap. Why don't we have their feed? Why are we out? Mom was supposed to buy it.

There's no time to point fingers; I've got piggies to save. I stuff what looks like cereal crumbs in my pockets and charge out.

I sprint across the two-lane highway and climb over Sally's pristine white wooden fence. Just before I'm clear, my jeans catch on a nail. I yank to pull free, but the fabric rips.

I hiss as the nail rakes across my inner thigh. When I'm over the fence, I inspect the damage. A triangle of denim has been torn away, and there's an angry red scratch swelling on my thigh.

Ouch! And dang! These were my good jeans.

"Just great."

I race past the sign that reads **Dancing Trails Farm** and run to the top of the hill, where the house sits. I'm winded, and my side's killing me. I pause just long enough to rest my arm on the side of the house. That is, until I hear a—

BOOM.

Fear rushes through my bloodstream, making my heart convulse.

Oh no. Sally's killed one of them!

"Stop! I'm here!"

I wave my hands in the universal sign of surrender as I plow down the hill and finally get a good look at what's going on.

Sally's in her pasture, raising the gun and kicking the air in an attempt to frighten the pigs, who are paying her absolutely no mind, not even after the shotgun blast. *That* was apparently a warning shot, as no piggies have been injured.

Thank God.

Behind her, more than a dozen unicorns watch the scene with silky black eyes. They stand tall and magnificent, white coats shimmering in the early-morning sun. Shoulder muscles ripple. Delicate golden horns dazzle. Right on cue, a breeze ripples through their rainbow manes, making the creatures look picture perfect.

I can't help but stare at them for a brief moment before my gaze falls on the piggies. As opposed to the unicorns, they are not picture perfect. Their spindly legs and round bellies make them look like potatoes stuck on toothpicks—potatoes that are currently invading the unicorns' feed trough like ants at a picnic.

This is Sally's beef, and I can see why.

Almost two dozen of them surround the feed bin. Several piggies scramble to jump into it, launching themselves like dogs trying to land on a couch. Most don't make it. One, however, does catch the edge with its front legs. The pig struggles to climb inside, but it can't get its hind legs up under it. In the end, it slips, landing on its back atop the grass below before flipping over and trying again.

Some pigs never learn.

Others have been more successful in their jumping attempts. A few stand in the trough, foraging the feed like they're plowing farmland, and in the process, nosing it over the rim. Grain falls in a glittery shower that creates small piles on the dewy grass. There, the piggies who've given up trying to get in are greedily munching. Eager to eat as much as possible, half a dozen of them shoulder and shove one another aside, accidentally bumping the trough.

The trough takes a hit and rocks back onto the fence. Neither the pigs nor Sally notice that the contraption is balancing precariously.

"Sally," I yell, racing toward them.

She looks up just as the pigs slam into the trough again, this time from the opposite side.

And that's all it takes to bring the whole thing down.

The piggies squeal in fright, racing to get out of the way as the wooden bin falls. The ones inside the trough are smart enough to stay put. When it hits the ground, they roll out, riding the feed like surfers as a wave of grain spills out onto the grass. I groan as a piggycorn slides on her rump atop the grain, coming to an abrupt halt when she bumps into my foot.

She blinks up at me, looking adorable and guilty at the same time.

"Tallulah, what have y'all done?"

Sally marches toward me, glowering. Her unicorns stamp and blow in annoyance. Meanwhile, the piggies are now free to eat as much feed as possible, seeing as how it's now all over the ground. None of my drove are hurt, and they snort happily as they gorge themselves.

Sally is still waving the gun.

"Don't you do anything stupid," I snap.

She lifts the barrel, pointing it to the sky, and yells, "They destroyed my property. Those pigs ain't nothing more than a nuisance. The whole lot of them should be made into sausage!"

My heart's racing as I reach the rest of the drove. "Y'all stop eating that and come home. Look, I brought your feed."

The pigs recognize my voice and look up. Tallulah, who's right on my heels, is the smallest and my personal favorite. She takes a step toward me and presses her snout in my hand, sniffing. Her face drops enough that the small golden horn protruding from her head brushes my arm. Then she looks up and returns to the mess of feed.

Which I now recognize as the piggies' favorite.

"What gives, Sally? Why do you have the piggycorns' food? That's why they're here." I throw up my hands. "They probably smelled it from across the road. You know how good their noses are."

Sally pulls off her ball cap and rakes a hand through her messy blond hair. Her face is all sharp angles, like she only eats protein, and as much as I'd like to say she's ugly, Sally's the kind of pretty that's enviable.

She snickers. "My unis like it, too. There's no law that says I can't give the unicorns the same feed."

I glance up at the pasture full of unicorns—beautiful, majestic creatures that are as awesome in person as they are in fairy tales, even if they aren't born with magic anymore. Even powerless, they're still more popular as pets than piggycorns.

I should know. Sally mentions it every time I see her.

I'm surprised she doesn't say it now.

"You gotta get these piggycorns out of here, Rowe. I've got a family coming to pick out their uni in an hour. If they see these nasty swine, they'll turn and leave. No one buys stupid piggies anymore—not since the price of unicorns came down."

Oh, wait. I spoke too soon. There she went, getting in her dig. And it's barely even six a.m.

But she's right. It used to be that everyone wanted a piggycorn for a pet. They're very doglike in demeanor—friendly, lovable. They're the perfect companion animal. Or at least, they were, back in the early days, when magic still flourished in our town. But now the magic is gone, having up and left for reasons unknown, and as the luster faded, so, too, did interest in piggycorns.

I move to fix the trough, but she waves me off. "I'll do it. You'll probably just break it worse." When I scoff, she adds, "All you're doing is catching flies with your mouth hanging open like that, when you should be catching swine and vacating my property."

"Fine, I'll get them out of Your Highness's way," I say, snatching the ball cap from her head.

"What're you doing? Give me back my hat."

I grin at her. "You said you wanted the piggycorns gone. Well, I'm getting them gone, Sally. You never said how, and seeing that you have their favorite food, I need some of it so that they'll come with me."

I fill the hat with feed and push it under the piggies' noses. "Come on, y'all. Let's go. We know when we're not wanted."

They slowly start to follow, tails swishing, grunts of happiness filling the air.

Sally sneers. "Never mind. Keep the hat. I've already taken something of yours, anyway."

Her eyes slide to the mammoth red Tundra stationed in the driveway. My heart *pound-pound-pounds* against my chest at what she's implying.

She doesn't mean the truck. Sally's referring to its owner, Luke.

I force myself to smile tightly. "You'll find your hat in the mailbox. Unlike you, Sally, I don't steal other people's property."

Her jaw drops as I lead the piggycorns off.

So yes, piggycorns. It's a creature that is exactly what it sounds like: a pig with a unicorn horn. They're small, about the size of a pug, and are also adorable. Many people love them—except for Sally. The only thing she loves is money and unicorns. Maybe money more.

Definitely money more.

The pigs understand we're going home, and they prance out in front of me, crossing the road as they head toward the farm.

Sally calls out, "Hey, Rowe!"

I turn to see her standing on top of the hill, fists on her hips, lips twisted diabolically.

"Won't be long until I don't have to worry about you and those stupid piggycorns much longer anyway."

Then she smirks and storms off, the shotgun tucked under her arm.

What is she talking about?

I'm about to call her back when the sound of screeching tires grabs me by the throat. A murder of crows lifts from an oak tree as I turn around, just in time to see a black SUV heading straight for my pigs.

Chapter 2

PANE

"When are you coming hoooooome?" my little sister whines through the SUV's Bluetooth. "Greta made me practice piano for half an hour yesterday, and it was tooooorrrturrrre!"

I chuckle, envisioning ten-year-old Natalie throwing herself on her bed and burying her face in the pillows.

"She tortured you?" I feign shock at the horror of piano lessons. "Did your hands fall off? No, let me guess—your fingers dropped onto the keys and you couldn't reattach them no matter how much superglue you used."

She cracks up into a fit of giggles. "Paaane! Don't be silly! Nothing fell off. My hands still hurt, and I think they're going to hurt foreverrrr."

I tsk. "It's no good having hurt hands. Maybe you should stop using them. Don't eat—no more ice cream cones, lollipops, tacos."

Beside me in the passenger seat, my brother, Stone, plays up a huge sigh. "It's not that bad, Nat. You should've been around when Pane and I were little."

"That's right." I tap the steering wheel for emphasis. "Nanny Edith was worse than Greta by miles."

There's a pause that suggests she's sitting up now, curious. "How?"

"Well, first," I explain, "she was at least a thousand years old."

"Nuh-uh."

"Oh yeah." Stone grins. "And she was so wrinkled that we were convinced she was a mummy come back to life."

She laughs. "Stop it."

My sister's giggle makes me smile. "Stone's telling the truth. You don't know how good you've got it with Greta. Just play the piano when she asks, and everything will be fine."

My little sister falls silent for a moment as she considers this. "When are you coming back?"

I exchange a glance with Stone. We don't actually know, so this is a best guess. "Today, maybe? Probably later. I'll have to catch a flight."

"Can we have ice cream?" she asks, her voice lifting in excitement. "When you get home?"

"Absolutely. All the ice cream you want. But remember, you've got to mind Greta."

"Okaaaaay." I can tell she doesn't want to, but I know she will. "I promise."

"Pinkie swear?"

"Pinkie swear."

"Love you, Natalie."

"Love you."

"Hey." Stone slaps a hand to his heart. "What am I, chopped liver?"

"No, you're *hot dogs*," she teases, knowing full well that my twin hates them.

"Yeah, yeah, I know you love me," he grumbles playfully. "See you soon."

"Bye!"

"Bye," I tell her before hanging up the call and settling back into the driver's seat. Green hills roll past as I maneuver us down the two-lane road. "So, we're in Georgia," I murmur.

"We sure are," my brother confirms. "You know, I can't remember the last time I was this deep in the South."

"I can," I reply tensely, squeezing the steering wheel so hard my knuckles become pale peaks.

"When was that?" he asks absently, before realizing the answer and exhaling sharply. "Right. Sorry. I forgot. Should have remembered."

"You're a terrible twin," I joke, because Stone is great and he knows it.

But still, my brother grimaces. "Guess I dropped the ball on that one. But to be fair, last time you were here, we were seniors in college, and that was over ten years ago."

"It *has* been a long time."

An uneasy silence ignites in the cabin until Stone nods toward my wrist. "Is that a new Rolex?"

He's trying to change the subject, to get me to stop thinking about what happened back then. It works.

"Yes. A gift."

"Oh? From whom?"

"Han Joon-Seok," I say very slowly, pronouncing each syllable. Georgia is sweltering, especially in late summer. Even though the sun isn't up yet, the outside temperature is still high, and the sticky humidity only makes it worse. I punch up the air and exhale as a cool blast hits me in the face. "The Korean businessman."

"It's a very nice watch," Stone murmurs. "Why did he give it to you, exactly?"

I shift in my seat, settling back. "The hotel hosted his daughter's wedding last month. Everything was smooth sailing until the groom's ex-girlfriend showed up trying to crash the ceremony. We were able to get her out of the hotel before she could make a scene."

Stone makes a sound of mock disapproval. "And all you got was a Rolex?"

He's joking. It's a big gift, obviously. But I can't let this opportunity pass by. I drag my gaze away from the road to give him a pointed look. "The watch was his *second* offer. His first was one of his Ferraris."

Stone gulps. "And you didn't take it?"

"Didn't seem appropriate. I told him the Rolex was enough thanks."

My brother tugs at his collar. "It does pay to be a Maddox."

"That, it does."

My brother settles back into the passenger seat and scrolls on his phone. After a few moments he comes out with, "Sylvia's giving it to me, you know."

Like hell she is. "Why would she give it to you, when you've been on the West Coast doing nothing? We both know that the East books more rooms, fills more restaurant seats. I'm the golden child here, the prodigal son."

"You realize the prodigal son abandoned his family so that he could party his life away."

"Only you would bring that up." I glance over and we both laugh. If there's one thing my twin and I are good at, it's friendly ribbing—no harm intended and none taken. "The point is, when we see Mom, she'll announce that she's giving it to me."

He throws his head back and chuckles. "Oh, how naive my twin can be." Even I bark out a laugh at that. "Don't worry. I'll take care of you, *little* brother."

I roll my eyes. "Five minutes does not a little brother make."

"To me, it does," he says in a chipper voice.

"Keep dreaming." The laughter rumbling in my chest dies down, and I say, "How much farther is this airport?"

He checks his phone and, a moment later, comes back with, "Fifteen minutes out."

"Good."

"What? Too many cow pastures for you?"

"If I never see another one, I'll be grateful."

Not only does the countryside resurrect memories I'm not interested in reliving, but it also offers something else—allergies.

Unluckily for me, plants grow like jungle weeds *everywhere*. There are more trees than I can count, meadows the size of the Mediterranean, and fields filled with small bushy plants that look as if they may be some sort of food.

"*Why* is Mom here again?" I ask.

"Sylvia"—Stone always calls her by name—"wanted to visit a small town in the area. Mystic Meadows. There are ley lines here, or something like that. Supposed to be unicorns." Before I can ask my brother what "ley lines" are—and did he say *unicorns*?—his phone pings with a text. "There she is. She needs to be in the air in twenty. I'm telling her that we'll arrive in ten."

"Neutral territory," I murmur.

"What's that?"

"That's why she brought us here. We're on neutral territory, where neither of us has the upper hand."

"Yes, because she's picking me."

"She's not picking you," I snap.

He rakes his ash-blond hair away from his face. We're twins, but not identical. Stone's got lighter hair and a golden complexion. I've got dark hair. He tans at the beach. I burn.

If being twins isn't already enough to *almost* hate him for, just that fact is enough.

"Wait." Stone does a double take out the window. "What is *that*?"

He points to a faded-gray sign attached to a scraggly-looking steel-colored fence. I squint. "It says—"

"Look out!"

I whip my head back toward the road, and in that instant my mind races to catch up with my eyes. Because between the moment I looked away and when I now glance back at the road, a herd of small pigs has stopped directly in front of me.

And I'm going seventy miles per hour.

My heart flies into my throat as I hit the brakes. The SUV lurches, tires screaming violently. My automatic seat belt snaps tight, slapping me backward.

As the tires squeal, a woman wearing a T-shirt and ripped jeans jumps in front of the pigs, throws out her arms, and yells, "Don't hit my piggycorns!"

The SUV screeches to a shuddering halt just inches from crashing into all of them.

My stomach fills with acid, and the taste of metal bleeds over my tongue. I curl my hands into fists as anger fills me.

I'm not in the mood for inconveniences today.

My gaze lands on the woman, whose eyes are brimming with thanks and something else. Anger? Can't be. She should be grateful that I didn't run over her and the small creatures that *look* like pigs but, at the same time, don't.

I turn to my brother. "You okay?"

"Yeah, I'm good."

"What *are* those?" I growl, furious that I was inches away from plowing them down.

Stone drops a hand from his chest and exhales. He limply points to the faded-gray sign sagging from the weathered fence that reads **Wadley Farms: Home of the Piggycorn.** "Piggycorns."

That was the word the woman had screamed, a word I'm not familiar with. "What is a piggycorn?"

"Pigs that have a horn like a unicorn," my brother expertly points out.

I spot it then. Every pig that is now sniffing the front of the SUV, instead of moving across the road, has a golden horn protruding from a small tuft of pink fur atop its head.

Never in my life have I heard of such a creature. "Are those real?"

"Oh yeah," my brother confirms, like horned swine are an everyday occurrence. "They appeared after the first unicorns showed up—something to do with the ley lines in this town, I think." *There's that phrase again.* "But I haven't heard of them in years. Not after all the supposed 'magic'"—he makes quotation marks with his fingers—"dried up. I didn't know people still sold the creatures."

I shake my head. "I didn't follow any of that. Unicorns aren't real."

"They're real here, just without magic." He shoots me a hard look. "Do you live under a rock?"

"No. It's just that I don't have time for fairy tales and fantasy." I cock a brow in disbelief. "I'm sure the *unicorns* that appeared are nothing more than horses with horns sewn on."

"Your heart is truly black."

I smirk. "No. It's truly black and white. I see things for what they are. But those swine—they need to go."

I get out and come around to the front of the vehicle, where the woman attempts to shoo the pigs across the road.

"What are you doing?" I demand.

She tosses out her arms. "Throwing a block party! What does it look like? I'm trying to get them across. No thanks to you and your reckless driving."

Excuse me? "I was going the speed limit."

"Sure you were. If the speed limit was a thousand miles per hour."

This is the gratitude I get for *not* flattening her into a pancake? "Get your swine out of here."

Her cheeks, pink with frustration, puff out. "Why don't you get your SUV out of here?"

"Because I'm legally allowed to be here."

"Well, so am I," she sasses, hand on her hip.

She points off somewhere in the distance, but my eyes don't follow. In my world, one snap of my fingers and people fall in line. This woman isn't falling into anything, and my brain can't seem to wrap itself around the fact that she isn't *thanking* me for not killing her.

Who is this woman, with pink lips that form a perfect bow and dark hair that's woven into a messy braid? She's got this whole girl-next-door vibe—prim and proper, easy and carefree. Sassy in the bedroom.

A primal urge erupts throughout my body. The desire to wrap my fingers through her hair and claim this woman nearly knocks me over.

"The sign," she grinds out.

"I'm, um . . ." My brain's fogged up. Can't think. Can't form words. This experience is so out of my norm that frustration gushes through my bloodstream, which actually helps my focus return. "The sign . . . ?"

She jabs the air. "The one right there."

I tear my gaze from her warm brown eyes to the yellow road sign stamped with the black silhouettes of two horned animals—a pig and a unicorn—with the word **XING** printed at the bottom.

A long exhale helps finish the job of getting my head screwed on straight. "Sorry," I growl. "I didn't see the sign because I was too busy trying not to kill you and your mutant swine."

Her jaw drops and she sucks in air, her expression one of sheer disbelief that I would dare insult the small creatures she's Little Bo Peep–ing across the road.

"Piggycorns," she corrects, clearly flustered. "They are called *piggycorns.*"

Our gazes lock, and one side of my mouth ticks up into a smirk. "Mutant. Swine."

She bristles, her hackles lifting like the delicate pink mohawks striping down the swines' bodies. "They are not mutants. For your information, piggycorns are a rare breed of pig that just so happen to have a horn."

I sense a sore spot. "Someone being mean to your piggies, Sunbeam?"

"What did you call me?"

"I called you Sunbeam."

"Why?"

"Obviously because of your radiantly sweet personality," I reply sarcastically. "Do your swine grant wishes?"

"No," she grudgingly admits. "But they are adorable, and plenty of people love having them as pets."

"What do they do? Retrieve your phone?"

"Very funny." She folds her arms and juts out her hip. "They do not bring you objects. They do other things."

"Like?"

"Like . . ."

She clears her throat, her cheeks red from embarrassment as she desperately tries to come up with some sort of fantastic answer. It's cute, her floundering.

Shut up, Pane. She is *not* cute.

"I'll tell you what they do," she finally says.

"Please. I'm on the edge of my seat."

She shoots me a quick look, acknowledging my sarcasm and frowning. "Piggycorns snuggle with you, cuddle, and lick your feet."

"And this is supposed to *sell* me on them?"

She throws her hands in the air. "Would you just help me get them across?"

"As you wish."

She pushes one swine gently, walking away, giving me a great view of her ass, which leaves me spellbound. It must be the pollen in the air that's causing me not to think straight. I'm supposed to be on my way to securing my family's company, but here I am, being enchanted by a pig herder. *Herdess?* Is that a word?

Definitely not a word.

She turns back to me, her braid whipping over her shoulder. "Well? Are you just going to stand there? The sooner we get them across the road, the sooner you can get going."

"Right. And you move them, how? By pulling on their horn?"

I reach for one, and she slaps my hand away. "No, that's a terrible idea. Are you trying to hurt them? They can't lose their horns."

"But the horns don't do anything. Are they even real?"

"Of course they're real." Sunbeam scoffs while rolling her eyes dramatically. "Oh, I get it. You're one of those people who don't believe in the unicorns."

"Why should I?"

"I have no interest or time to debate the magic of unicorns with a man in a three-piece suit." Her gaze slides up and down my body. "Besides, I don't care what you believe. Just help me. Shoo them. Like this."

She taps one on the haunches, but the creature shows absolutely no interest in doing anything except sniffing the dead dragonflies on the SUV's grille.

Oh, wait. One of the bugs moved its head. It's not actually dead, just stuck.

I pull it free and release it into the air as she snaps her fingers. "You know, it would be great if you'd help. It's the least you can do for almost killing us."

Oh, *now* she's asking for it. "For your information, *you* were standing in the middle of the road right after I rounded a curve. If I *had* hit you—and I didn't—it wouldn't have been my fault because your pigs weren't moving *then* and they're not moving *now*."

She nudges another one, who holds its ground surprisingly well for a creature no larger than a small dog. "They just need a little encouragement. Listen, whether this gets done today or tomorrow, it's got to get done."

My brain misfires as if I've heard the sound of a record scratching.

Every cell in my body hardens into a wall of steel. "What did you say?"

She shrugs. "Whether it gets done today or tomorrow—"

"I heard you." I pinch the bridge of my nose. "Don't say that again. *Never* say that."

She shakes her head at the piggycorns, who are now plopped in the middle of the road like it's break time. "You don't get to tell me what to say. You don't own the world."

Hmm. Maybe not the whole thing, but a decent chunk of it.

Then, on top of that, she sasses back, "I'll say whatever I want."

"Fine. Just don't use that phrase."

She scoffs. "Hurry up, and I won't have to."

I glare at her, but she just tosses her farm-girl braid over one shoulder and turns her attention to the piggycorns. "Who's a sweet little piggy? You are!"

I am officially in hell.

When I bend over to shoo the animals is the moment my allergies decide to flare up. After several violent sneezes, when I finally stop, I have an audience of piggycorns staring up at me, pink snouts lifted in the air, eyes glittering with curiosity.

And the moment I stop is when they up the ante, no longer content with simply fixing their attention on me.

One rubs against my leg, wiping what I hope is mud on my suit pants. I push it away, but several others circle like Komodo dragons going in for the kill. Either that, or the pig that rubbed against me wiped its scent on my pants, signaling to the others that I'm now one of them, ready to be smeared with war paint.

That must be the case, because before I know it, they're tangled in my legs.

"Tallulah, stop," Sunbeam says. "Y'all get off him."

The swine are literally swarming. I can't move without crushing them. One lifts up on its hind legs and places its front hooves on me, pushing me into another who's behind my calves.

I lose my balance and drop onto the road. Next thing I know, small pigs are crawling over me, sniffing my arms, foraging under my knees. What the hell?

"Get off him," she commands, more annoyed than worried.

I push them off and get back on my feet. *Screw this.* I hoist a pig under each arm and haul them to the other side of the road. Miraculously, the rest of the creatures follow.

"There." I set them down gently and gesture to the farm. "Take your pigs."

"Piggycorns."

"Same thing."

I look down and notice the smudges of dirt that line my sleeves and three-piece suit. It looks like I've been rolling around in mud. Fantastic.

She brushes dust off her hands. "Thank you."

It's the first nice thing she's said, and it makes my chest swell with pride.

So I ignore it.

Sunbeam tips up her face and smiles. This woman really is stunning. And frustrating. And aggravating. But she also smells really, really good—like wildflowers on a cloudless day.

Her warm eyes hold mine for a breath before she blinks and looks off, taking in my shirt and suit, which are ruined. "I'm so sorry," she says, panicky. "Your clothes. Let me get you something to change into."

I smile grimly. "Overalls? No thanks."

She frowns, which makes a divot pop between her brows. "I'm sure I can find pants and a shirt."

Then her gaze rips from me to the fence and house. The fence is splintered, and the house looks the same—old and tired. She draws her eyes away from the home to my cuff links—hammered gold, from Milan.

She nibbles on her bottom lip in an expression I've seen before—the realization that I've got wealth.

And she hungers for it.

Yet surprisingly, the longing vanishes and is replaced with unease. She seems to shrink right in front of me, tugging on the collar of her thin white T-shirt and tucking one booted foot behind the other.

"Goodbye and good luck," I tell Sunbeam before jogging back to the SUV.

When I get in, Stone coughs into his fist. "You stink like a pig."

"As if you know what one smells like."

"I do now."

I roll my eyes. "You could have helped."

"And miss out on watching *you*? No way. That was a memory worth imprinting on my brain forever." I put the SUV in drive and hit the gas. He watches the farm as we roll past. "Did you get her number?"

I bark out a laugh. "No."

"Why not? Maybe she's not a social climber."

"As far as a Maddox is concerned, they're all either social climbers or fortune hunters."

"So Sylvia says," Stone says bitterly. "I don't know. Looked like the two of you were hitting it off. Oh, wait. Maybe I'm thinking of the pig that was climbing all over you. Let me know when you plan to introduce your new girlfriend to the family. Does she have a special diet? Slop, maybe?"

"You are hysterical," I say dryly.

"I looked up the farm while I had all of eternity to wait for you. It's a petting zoo. You can also buy a piggycorn, but from the looks of the place, no one's visited in the last decade. Not like that unicorn farm over there."

He nods to a glossy, white-washed fence. The whole place practically glows, it's so beautiful—green meadows, frolicking unicorns. Allergy attacks.

"Why don't I have one of those?" he says. "I would love a unicorn. Look how cool that is."

I eye a white horse with a golden horn poking out of its head. "Too common for folks like us."

My brother smirks. "Does nothing impress you?"

"No."

"Pane, your black heart will one day be softened."

"Doubtful."

"I suppose you're right." He wags a finger in the air. "If unicorns and piggycorns can't melt you, nothing can."

As we drive off, my gaze flicks to the rearview mirror, where I get one last glimpse of the brunette as she disappears behind her fence.

Just thinking of what she said—*Whether it gets done today or tomorrow, it's got to get done*—pisses me off all over again.

Good. Stay pissed off. I don't have time for fortune hunters in my life. Don't let the country-girl persona fool you—where money's concerned, she's like all the rest, willing to lie, cheat, and steal to get it.

Stone's phone rings and he puts it on speaker. "Hello, Sylvia."

"Boys, where are you? The plane leaves in fifteen minutes."

My shoulders tense. Thanks to Sunbeam, I'm all worked up, and I have to bite back the growl in my voice. "We're on our way."

"Good," my mother replies just as sharply. "Because I'm about to choose the next president of the Maddox Hotel Group. It's going to be one of you. But which one?"

Chapter 3

ROWE

As they drive off, the SUV's tires kick up a cloud of dirt that smacks me right in the face.

Thank you, horrible man with the knee-quaking green eyes (not that I noticed), who assumed the only clothes I own are overalls.

One glance at my ripped jeans explains why he thought that. Perhaps I shouldn't be too hard on him.

As I choke on grit from the dust cloud that keeps on giving, I decide that, yeah, I should be hard on him. He looks like the kind of guy who'd get you pregnant and then leave you.

I don't need that happening to me.

So I spit out my dirt breakfast.

I swear, if this day gets any worse, I'm going to scream.

Just as I'm turning into the yard, following the pigs, who are prancing off as if they didn't almost *just* get killed, a tractor sputters up.

"Morning, Rowe." Clarice Sinclair waves.

My seventysomething neighbor grins widely as she bounces atop her slow-as-molasses John Deere. Today, Clarice is wearing a frayed straw hat and a baggy lime-colored shirt over jeans that are rolled up to her calves.

"Morning," I volley.

Every day without fail, Clarice drives her tractor into town to grab breakfast at Hardee's with her friends. Several years back her driver's license was suspended, seeing as how she went legally blind for a minute (or three) and ran into several buildings—buildings that belonged to her then-husband. Luckily, no one was hurt in the rampage.

Even though Clarice swore up and down that the blindness was temporary, and had only surfaced because her husband of fifty years had left her for a woman half his age, the judge (who also happened to be *his* cousin) was not swayed in his decision to ban Clarice from operating fast-moving vehicles.

However, he did say she could drive her tractor. He said it as a joke, most likely. But that is not how she took it. So now, good old John Deere is her main form of transportation to and from town.

"Who was that man you were talking to?" Clarice asks as she snails by.

"I don't know."

"Some fancy car."

"Yep."

"From where I was sitting, looked like he had a cute butt."

I bust a gut, laughing. "Yeah, he may have had that."

He *may* have had that? *May* have? Who am I kidding?

The mystery man who despised overalls was *hot*. Superhot. Straight-off-the-presses hot.

Not that it matters, because I'll never see him again.

"He had pretty hair, too," she continues, like an undersexed geriatric who just arrived on the doorstep of an assisted-living facility ready to meet the octogenarian of her dreams.

The worst part is, she's right about the stranger.

His dark hair was wavy and just long enough to kiss the spots behind his ears. His jaw was straight, and his green eyes reminded me of sage grass—a beautiful color, when he didn't have that smug smirk on his face. Which was the whole time I talked to him.

Also, as much as I hate to admit it, his neck was football-player thick, and it got all corded and muscle-y when he was annoyed.

Which *also* happened throughout our entire conversation.

My mind flashes back to how he accused me of trying to get myself killed. He was the one going a gazillion miles per hour. The nerve of him, mansplaining where I can stand in the road.

Hmm. I wouldn't mind him mansplaining what to do in the bedroom.

Oh my gosh. *Quit it right now.* You're never seeing his hotness again, Rowe. Cool your jets.

I mean, what sort of person blames the almost-victim for being run over?

A seriously privileged jerk.

"Did you get his number?" Clarice calls as her tractor tires keep spinning way too slowly down the road.

"No, I sure didn't."

"Huh." She picks at a spot on her chin, which may or may not be growing a hair. "Maybe you can catch up to him in your truck."

I laugh again. "I'm not getting his number. He wasn't from around here. He didn't even know what a piggycorn is."

"*Who* doesn't know about piggycorns?" she says, voice overflowing with disbelief. Then she considers her statement and backpedals. "Besides us, I mean? And a lot of the world, I guess." Clarice scratches her chin. "Does anyone in the outside world know or care about piggycorns?"

"That is beside the point," I snap.

"Well"—she cups a hand beside her mouth and yells loud enough for folks one county over to hear—"maybe you still got a chance with those Collins boys. Everybody knows you've got cobwebs growing in your coochie, Rowe. You gotta get back out there and find you a man."

Uh. It's official. Worst. Day. Ever.

When a geriatric, tractor-riding farm woman tells you that your vagina is atrophying, the day officially sucks.

I back up into the yard, trying to put as much distance between me and Clarice as possible. "Great seeing you, Mrs. Sinclair!"

"Maybe one of them Collins boys will take you. Rhett's acne ain't as bad as it used to be!"

"Bye, now!"

I shut the gate behind me and quickly pinpoint the piece of fencing that the pigs squeezed through.

"You little weasels. Y'all need to stop getting out."

They snort in reply, foraging through the brittle late-summer leaves that blanket the yard.

I push the fence back into place and head inside, scrubbing my feet on the doormat and slipping out of my boots.

A new vine emerges from under the floorboards, picking up the old shoes and depositing them in the corner where they belong.

If there's one perk to living on top of magical soil, it's that the vines outside the house tend to do nice things for you.

"You are never going to believe what happened," I start, charging into the kitchen and slapping Sally's hat on the counter.

I don't expect my mom to be in there, figuring she's still hiding upstairs to avoid talking to me. But when I enter the rooster-decorated room, she's sitting on a stool at the counter, phone in hand, talking to Bill, whose face I see on the screen.

"You've got to tell her," he says.

I fold my arms and frown. "Okay, what is it? What's going on?"

"Swing the phone where I can see Rowe."

She does as Bill says, and there he is, his bright-white teeth smiling at me. They nearly glow against his dark skin and the ivory beard that covers his jaw and mouth.

"Hey, Bill. You about to head over?"

He's standing beside his silver Airstream, which looks more like a bullet than it does a camper. Bill claps a hand against the metal side. "I'm ready to go live the jam band dream."

A hearty, soul-cleansing laugh lifts from my throat. Bill's a good guy. We've known him for years—he was one of Dad's best friends. After he died, Bill became like a second father. He had lost his wife a few years earlier and understood the pain of losing someone who's vital to your life.

In the months following Dad's burial, Bill would drop in to see how we were holding up. He helped around the house, brought us supper. It was a couple years before he and Mom started dating, and when they did, I was glad for them. Really, truly happy that *she* was happy again.

Mom smiles brightly. It's a fake smile, the one she puts on when her world's crumbling into an ash heap. "Rowe, you've got to smell this new tangerine candle I made."

She plucks a glass jar off the counter and pops the lid. Inside, hardened orange wax climbs the walls of the container as if it's trying to break free. My mom loves to make candles, though the final product often turns out messy.

She lets me sniff, and it does smell good—citrusy, homey, like a kitchen on a spring morning.

Mom hugs it to her chest. "I burned it during my meditation, and the scent put me in the zone to receive blessings, Rowe."

"Sabra," Bill says sternly to Mom, because she is clearly stalling.

Her face crumples and she shakes her head. Okay. So she's not sick. Does that mean *Bill* is?

"Bill, are you okay?"

He pats the air. "I'm fine, Rowe. This doesn't have anything to do with me. This is something your mom needs to tell you."

She slumps back on the stool, and I can't help but feel pity for her because of everything she's been through these past few years. But still, whatever it is, she needs to just say it.

"Spit it out, Mom. I'm already done with today, and it's not even lunch. So whatever you've got to tell me, spill it. Yank off the bandage, because you're not doing me any favors by keeping quiet."

"Go on, Sabra," Bill says gently.

He has a very understanding but firm presence—what comes to mind when I think of what a man should be like. Quiet but kind.

He reminds me a lot of my father, and I'm grateful for that.

Mom mutters behind her hand, "Meer woosing de furmmm."

"I don't speak German, Mom. What did you say?"

"Sabra," Bill scolds. "We're leaving in an hour, come hell or high water. I'm loading up the last of my things in a minute, and then I'm heading your way. We've got to get on the road if we're to reach Orange Beach in time for the concert tonight."

Mom inhales deeply. "Okay. Here it is. Rowe, you know that ever since Dad died, things have been tough. That we've had bills." A bitter laugh slips from her mouth. "What am I saying? Of course you know. You left school because of the cancer."

Just thinking about it makes my throat knot up. I'd been an English major, but when Dad got sick, Mom needed extra help around here. Everything happened at once—the cancer diagnosis, people not buying piggycorns (which, to be fair, had been rapidly declining for years). It was one thing after another, all of it compounding so that by the time he died, she was using all their savings to pay his medical bills.

The farmhands were let go, and I never returned to school. I was simply too heartbroken from losing both him and Luke to muster up the energy to get my degree.

Plus, it wasn't like I could abandon my mom in her time of need. Leaving her alone in this big old house with the piggycorns and Buster the Cat didn't seem right.

So I stayed.

"You were only going to be here for six months," she reminds me, her eyes full of sorrow. "I'm sorry about that."

"Hey." I swing my arm like it's no big deal, like I'm ready to give life the good old college try. "I wouldn't trade the time that I've spent here for anything else. Besides, I've done just fine. I've managed to get some side gigs designing landscapes."

All the extra money I've brought in has gone directly back into the farm—food for the pigs, paying bills.

She licks her lips. "Right. About that. When Dad was in the thick of his illness, I took out a second mortgage to pay for the chemo. The thing is, since no one's bought a piggycorn in a while—well, we're struggling, Rowe."

My heart breaks for her. She's so worried, but it's all gonna be fine.

I rub her arm in reassurance. "I know that. But I don't want you to worry about this place. I've got a little money in the bank. While you're gone I'm gonna fix up the farm, make it so shiny and new that for the first time in years, we'll be real competition for Sally Ray."

Her gaze drops. "I'm afraid . . ."

She trails off, and Bill sighs quietly. "Just tell her."

"What, Mom?" She's very quiet. Deathly quiet. Now I'm getting worried. "What is it?"

My mother swallows loudly and lifts her gaze, and when she pins it on me, sorrow brims in her eyes. "Rowe, we've already lost the farm. It's in foreclosure."

Chapter 4

PANE

"I need you to strip, sir."

I blink. "Sorry? What was that?"

My mother's assistant takes hold of a slick black suitcase and rolls it toward me over the jet's carpeted floor.

When he speaks next, his voice is slow, deliberate, as if he's explaining to a child why it's *not* okay to play with matches. "Mrs. Maddox has requested that you change out of your suit and put on the clothes that you will find in here."

I frown so hard that my brows pinch together. "Why?"

He purses thin lips that match his even thinner face. "She didn't say why, Mr. Maddox."

"What's this?" Stone says, entering the plane.

I point to the case. "Mom wants me to change clothes."

My brother snorts. "She must've heard you smell like a pig."

The assistant produces a matching case and wheels it toward my brother. "Sir, your mother has requested that you, too, change out of your clothes and into the ones provided in here."

Stone scoffs. "This can't be real."

"Oh, it's real," I counter. "What was all that about her having to leave in ten minutes?"

The assistant shrugs. "I believe she's extended her trip."

Great. Mom's decided to make us play dress-up instead.

The assistant gestures to the lavatory. "It's free for you, Mr. Maddox." To my brother, he points to the rear of the plane. "The other lavatory is also free. Mrs. Maddox will see you both in her office after you've changed."

So I guess there's no getting out of this, though I don't mind changing out of my mud-smeared suit. Since I'm about to become the next president of the Maddox Group, it's best not to accept the position looking like a farmhand.

I take the suitcase and enter the lavatory. Unzipping it reveals a few pairs of jeans, some casual shirts, underwear, socks, and a toiletry bag. Why are there so many articles of clothing if I'm only changing into one of each?

But I simply do as instructed, leaving my suit on the hangers provided.

When I exit, the assistant is waiting for me. "One last thing, sir. Your accessories."

"Accessories?"

His gaze falls to my Rolex.

"You want my watch?"

He nods, and a bitter laugh escapes my throat. This is too much. What is Mom playing at? But whatever. I hand it over. I'm about to pass by when the assistant blocks my path.

"Your wallet and phone, too."

"I'm not going to record anything. Why am I handing over my phone?"

"You will receive a new one, Mr. Maddox, as well as a new wallet."

This whole thing is beginning to feel like some sort of setup. After a pause, I sigh. "Fine."

I slip both from my pockets, and the assistant hands me a new phone. I open it and find that there are no contacts.

It's a blank slate.

He then gives me a new wallet, which holds my picture ID and some cash. That's it. No credit cards.

The assistant takes the suitcase, watch, wallet, and phone. My gaze tracks his every movement as he stows them in a box before locking it in the plane's safe.

What is going on?

"Your mother will see you now," he says with a hand flourish, gesturing to her office.

Finally.

As I enter, the smell of the cabin hits me—bergamot and cotton. It's clean, comforting, warm. I should know. I created it, making it the signature scent for all the Maddox hotels.

My gaze follows my nose. Inside the cream-on-white office space, my mother sits like a queen behind her ivory desk—shoulders high, chin lifted. Her dark hair is pulled back into a tight bun, and her white pantsuit is immaculate. The only piece of color on her is a sapphire brooch pinned to her lapel.

Stone's already seated across from her on the pale couch. He's dressed similarly to me and looks uncomfortable, irritated, as his foot bounces atop his knee.

"Pane," she says in greeting.

I lean over and kiss her cheek before taking a seat beside my brother.

"It's good to see you," she tells us in her cold, affectionless voice. "Thank you for coming all this way to meet me."

"You're welcome," Stone replies with forced cheer, foot still bouncing.

He's worried, same as me.

This feels like a trap, but I can't predict what's going to happen next.

"Before we begin, Pane, I heard there was a scuffle this morning."

My gaze slides to Stone, who pretends to pick lint off his jeans.

"No scuffle," I tell her.

Her left brow lifts in a calculated look. "You're sure? We don't need any more Georgia scandals."

An old pain hits me in the solar plexus. My jaw flexes as I work out, "There won't be any scandals."

"Good." She leans back in her ivory chair and taps her lacquered fingernails on the slick surface of her desk. "Nor do we need any fortune hunters. Your father was quite enough."

Beside me, Stone tenses. He scrapes the backs of his fingers down his cheek. "Can we move on from Dad?"

Mom's eyes flash on him. We never refer to our father as *Dad*. We don't refer to him at all.

Instead of questioning Stone, she shoots me a pointed look as if I'm the one who made the mistake of marrying our father instead of her.

"No scandals. No fortune hunters," I assure her.

"Glad to hear it. Now, on to business." Dramatic pause. When neither of us interrupt, she continues. "As you know, I'm retiring. For these past few years, as vice presidents in the company, you've done amazing work. Pane"—her laser focus lands on me—"with you guiding the East Coast, we've seen a renaissance. During a tumultuous economic time, not only has our flagship hotel remained steadfast in terms of profits, but your idea to create a competitive rewards program, along with focusing on wellness vacations, has benefited our other locations. In short, you've done an exemplary job and have exceeded my expectations."

A compliment from the ice queen? I'll take it. "Thank you."

"And Stone," she says, and he puffs up his chest like the peacock he is. "Under your tutelage, the West Coast hotels have increased their market share by twenty percent."

He flashes me a wink but says to her, "Thank you."

"You're welcome." Her cool gaze shifts from my brother to me. "But you both know that only one of you can be president."

"And that's me," we say in unison.

Stone said it because that's what he believes, and I said it because I knew that Stone would.

He smirks at me and I grin smugly in response.

Mom clears her throat. "I'm sure you're wondering why I had you change clothes and hand over your phones."

I scrape a thumb over my bottom lip. "It did occur to us."

Mom leans forward and folds her hands. Her knuckles turn white as her grip tightens like she's trying to contain her excitement. I'm glad *someone's* excited.

"Starting now, you are no longer Pane and Stone Maddox, heirs to the Maddox Group of hotels," she explains.

My brother and I exchange a confused look. For a long moment neither of us speak.

It's Stone who hesitantly pokes the bull—I mean, my mother. "Then who are we?"

Mom leans back and grins widely. "You are Pane and Stone Maddox, big nobodies."

What is she talking about? "What do you mean?"

She clicks a button on a remote, and a screen buzzes down from the ceiling. She opens her laptop, presses a few buttons, and a PowerPoint begins.

The first slide reads WIN THE MADDOX GROUP.

Win the Maddox Group? "Are we supposed to play some sort of game?"

Stone's foot pops off his knee and he sits up. "What is this?"

Mom points to the slide as if that will explain everything. "You see, boys, I thought I'd made a decision, but when I rechecked the numbers, both of you were too close in terms of profits for me to confidently pick the next president and CEO. So we're doing it this way."

My stomach drops. The rug has *more* than been pulled out from under me; it's been tossed into the ocean, where it's drowning in a whirlpool. The company should be mine. *Mine.* I've worked hard, given up my life for the Maddox Group. Stone's worked hard, too, but he hasn't sacrificed his personal life.

"What is 'this way'?" I growl.

She clicks a button on her computer, and the next slide appears. My mother explains what it says, so I don't bother looking at it. Besides, all I can see is red, as her frivolous decision to make us play some sort of *game* feels like a betrayal of how hard I've worked, a betrayal that sinks deep into my bones, crystallizing and petrifying.

"From tomorrow forward," she explains with delight lacing her voice, "you each have sixty days to resurrect a dying business. This business must be on the verge of collapse, with no hope of recovering. In two months you must whip it into shape so that when the time frame is up, your venture has a higher valuation than your brother's."

A headache blooms behind my eyes as I wrap my mind around what she's saying. "You're telling me that I have to find a business and make it more profitable than Stone's, and I have sixty days to do it."

"Yes." She smiles like a satisfied cat. "Exactly."

"And I'm also a big nobody."

"That's correct." *There is way too much glee in her voice.* "The only things you now own are the clothes in each of your suitcases, the money in your new wallets, and a vehicle that has been picked out for you."

Stone scrubs his fingers through his hair and laughs bitterly. Then he sits back and folds his arms. "So when you say that we're nobodies, you really mean that."

"Correct. You're not allowed to use any of your resources—no business contacts, no bank accounts," she clarifies in a voice that suggests she thinks this is fun. "You are completely cut off, and must win the company *alone*—without help from me or each other."

Well, there went the millions in investments that I could have used.

"And if I find out that you *do* access your funds, you are automatically disqualified—*unless* you have my approval and the funds aren't going toward the project," she adds, eyes flashing from me to my brother.

"There goes cheating," Stone half jokes.

"In the end, the venture with the highest valuation will also receive a one-time bonus from the Maddox Group. A gift, if you will, of one hundred thousand dollars."

My brother turns his head right and left, popping his neck, a tic he only does when he's angry. "Can anyone know who we are, or do we need to keep our identities a secret? Like, should I just introduce myself as Mr. Nobody?"

Her eyes narrow and he mumbles an apology. Stone's as pissed as I am that we've been bamboozled. We were supposed to walk onto this plane and find out who was the next president and CEO. But instead we've been handed a nasty joke.

"Your identity is on a need-to-know basis. You may tell people who you are, but pick accordingly. Your celebrity status could get in the way, and if that happens, you will be—"

"Disqualified," Stone mumbles. "Yeah, we get it."

"What else?" I growl, tired of this nonsense. "Have you picked our businesses for us? Is that in the presentation, too?"

"No." She rubs her hands with glee. "This is the best part."

"Doubtful," Stone mutters.

"You will pick Stone's business, and he will pick yours."

"What?" my brother says, jumping up from the couch. "He's supposed to pick mine? Who knows what sort of sadistic business Pane will pick for me?"

"It'll be just as sadistic as the one you choose for me," I remind him.

"Oh, right. You've got a point." He palms the back of his head. "Maybe this is actually the one good thing in this entire game."

"It's not a game," our mother corrects. "This is a competition, one that will sow the seeds of your future. Pick wisely for one another."

Great. Stone will pick the absolute worst business for me, as I will for him. This is survival of the fittest, brother against brother.

As I watch my mother swivel from side to side in her chair, it's hard to remember that somewhere deep in her soul, I'm sure that she loves me. The only thing is, I've no clue where, or *what*, that love is.

"And"—she glances at her watch—"you've got one hour to find a project for each other. Starting . . . now."

Stone snaps his fingers. "I don't need an hour."

She stops swiveling. "You don't?"

His mouth splits into a wide grin, which he focuses on me. "Can someone say, 'Little pig, little pig, let me in'?"

As soon as he mentions pigs, a dozen images of that woman, Sunbeam, brighten like a solar flare inside my head, taking up space rent-free. I'm subjected to her warm brown eyes, her friendly smile—*when* she smiled—and her wildflower scent.

I'm also subjected to a memory of her ridiculous use of platitudes.

My head snaps up. "No," I snarl. "No. I'm not going there."

Stone tsks. "You have to, brother. I get to choose, and that's what I choose for you."

Shit. This is going to be harder than I thought.

In front of us, Mom claps her hands. "Wonderful! May the best Maddox win!"

Chapter 5

ROWE

It feels like the entire world has tipped over and I'm falling off it. "The farm is in foreclosure?"

Mom presses her lips together as her eyes well up with tears. "Honey, I would've told you sooner, but I just couldn't."

She looks so shattered. I get it. I completely understand why she didn't say anything before.

But it's more than a blow. My head's swimming. My stomach's done up in knots. I'm going to be sick.

"You're green." She comes over and takes me by the arms. "Let's sit you down."

I let her guide me to a chair, where I sit and slump over, placing my head between my knees and taking in deep gulps of air.

We've lost the farm. What will we do? Where will we go? What am I going to do with my piggycorns? Where will I take them?

A light bulb pings, and I lift my head. "Maybe I can buy the place, or at least pay some of what's owed."

She shakes her head sadly, making her big hoop earrings swing from side to side. "We owe over forty thousand dollars."

Now not only has the earth tilted, but I'm floating lifeless in outer space. "Forty thousand?"

I can't even wrap my head around that. I have some money saved, but not much. It's certainly not forty thousand dollars.

The doorbell rings. In my delirium, all I can think to say is "Bill's here so fast. When did you get off the phone with him?"

She glances down at her cell. "I have no idea who it is. But I'll go see."

I groan. "It better not be Sally Ray or the sheriff."

In case it's the sheriff and I have to beg him not to ticket me for this morning's piggycorn fiasco, I follow Mom to the front door. Soon as she swings it open, I suck in air.

There stands all six foot three of Luke Preston. His hair is clipped short on the sides, and a rolling wave of a pompadour rests on top. He grins his snakelike, thousand-watt smile at Mom and pulls a wad of hundreds from his front pocket.

"I'm here for the furniture."

What?

Mom glances nervously over her shoulder at me. "Um, Luke, you were supposed to come just before the sale."

He slaps the money into the palm of his opposite hand. "Well, I'm here now with cash."

I step between them, focusing on Mom, who looks super guilty. "What's he talking about?"

She rubs her forehead. The easy breezy new age person inside her doesn't want to talk.

"Mom," I urge her. "What is this? Why is he here?"

"He's going to buy some of Grandma's old furniture." My mother shoots laser beams of fire from her eyes at Luke. "But he wasn't supposed to do it until just before the foreclosure went through."

Luke waves the money around like it's his first time in a strip club and he just can't wait to slide dollar bills into panties. "Like I said, I'm here now with the *cashola*. Take it or leave it."

I want to slap the smug smirk right off his face. "Mom, you can't let him do this."

"We need the money, hon," she tells me, clearly resigned to this horrible situation.

"I'll be quick, Sabra. Just want the pieces we talked about."

Mom moves out of the way, and Luke sidesteps her, aiming to breeze his ass into *my* house and take stuff that doesn't belong to him.

I block his path. "There's no way in hell you're coming in here and taking anything."

"Rowe Davenport Wadley, watch your language," Mom snaps.

I throw up my hands. "I'm sorry, but this situation calls for it."

Luke scoffs in amusement at our kerfuffle, but I stand firm. He's not getting by me.

My ex slicks a hand down his beard and studies me like I'm a rabbit he's about to shoot and kill. "This doesn't concern you."

"The hell it doesn't." I flash my hand toward Mom. "Again, please excuse the cussing." Then I turn on Luke. "You can't charge in here and take things that don't belong to you."

He takes an intimidating step forward and glares down his nose at me. I lift my chin defiantly.

"Your mom and I have an agreement."

"Well, you can just have an *un-agreement.*"

"Rowe," Mom says, moving toward me.

I drag my gaze away from my second-to-worst enemy (Sally Ray is my absolute worst) to fix it on my mother. "What?"

"Rowe," she scolds.

"Sorry. *Ma'am?*"

Even in the heat of an argument, no Southern mother will allow a child to forget their manners.

"Since Luke knows about the foreclosure—"

I sneer. "Of course he does. Seeing as how he runs the bank."

Her jaw clenches. "He offered to buy some furniture to give us money."

"I'm sure he did," I boom so loudly that it's surprising the glass in the windows doesn't blow out. "I bet he's happy to take Grandma's antique French sideboard off our hands so that he can give it to Sally Ray, who's wanted it forever. Not to mention the horsehair chaise that's been in the family for a hundred years. Yep. I just bet you're happy to help out us poor folks, aren't you, Luke?"

He gives me a long look before tearing his gaze away and turning to Mom. He slaps the wad of bills in her hand and says over his shoulder, "Come on, Sims."

Ronald Sims, an old high school friend and newly minted *traitor*, enters the house. He takes off his baseball hat and crushes it between his hands as he stares at the floor. "I sure am sorry about this, Rowe."

"You should be, helping out the enemy."

"He pays good," Ron whimpers.

Ron's a neighbor who also works at the feedstore. I've known him my whole life, and I'm good friends with his wife, too. Jennifer's the town pharmacist.

"Let's grab the couch," Luke says, giving me a chilly look before heading into the living room, his boots thudding against the floorboards.

No way will Luke Preston take family treasures from my home.

Before Ron can reach the chaise, I throw myself on top of it starfish-style and clutch the sides in a death grip. I really hope this doesn't tear the upholstery.

"If it goes, I go with it!"

Luke sighs in annoyance. "Get off the couch, Rowe."

"It's a chaise—and no!"

I peek over my shoulder to see him drop his hands to his waist and shift from hip to hip. "You're being childish."

"I don't care. You're not taking it." I tighten my grip. "How much is he paying you, Mom?"

"Well, I don't, um . . ."

"I'll pay whatever he is." I pop up to see if my bribe is affecting her. Mom scratches her head, thinking about it. "I'll double it!"

"Get off the couch," Luke snaps. "It's mine. Not yours. I paid for it. Come on, Ron. Let's get it up."

"I don't know, Luke. I hate to hurt Rowe."

"Rowe won't be on it." Luke lifts the chaise from the bottom and tips it in a vain attempt to dislodge me.

Clearly, he does not know the power of a determined female. He's just lucky I don't have children to protect. If that were the case, his eyes would've been scratched out minutes ago.

I clutch the fabric harder. "I am not leaving, no matter what you do."

"That's it." Luke tugs me by the waist, trying to pull me off.

Desperate times call for desperate measures: I begin licking the chaise. No, this isn't my finest moment. Obviously. But sometimes you gotta do what you gotta do.

"I'm spreading my germs all over it," I say between licks while Luke tries to detach me from the heirloom. "I'm calling Sally Ray first thing and telling her what I've done. She won't want this now, not after I've licked the whole thing."

"That's right disgusting," Ron agrees. He cocks an eye at Luke. "You sure you want this?"

Luke drags a hand through his hair. "Let's grab the sideboard instead."

If he thinks I'm going to let him have my grandmother's sideboard, he's an even bigger idiot than I thought.

I catapult off the chaise and scamper around him.

Soon as I'm off, he turns back to the chaise. "Let's get it, Ron."

I watch in horror as Luke and Ron walk the chaise out the door.

"Mom," I beg.

"We need the money. I can't ask you to give up what you have."

"But I would," I whimper.

She pulls me into a hug. "It's just furniture. It's just things. It's not *people*."

I almost crack at that, but when Luke, boots thudding on the sidewalk, heads back this way, lava boils in my gut.

I rush back over to the mahogany sideboard and throw myself on top of it.

I clamp my arms on the sides. "No."

Luke ignores me. "Grab the other end, Ron."

"With her on it?"

"With her on it." I look up to see him nod stiffly. His pointy beard makes him look like a sinister villain in an old cartoon. "At some point she's bound to get off."

"I will not."

"Rowe, be reasonable," Mom pleads.

"I will not be reasonable. There's nothing reasonable about handing over family heirlooms to them. Don't you remember what he did to me, Mom?"

"Of course I do."

Luke rolls his eyes. "Get off, Rowe."

"And what if I don't?"

He leans down and whispers in my ear, "Then I'll drive with you on top of this cabinet all over downtown for everyone to see. They already know about the farm. What are they going to think when they see you hanging on to this sideboard?"

"They'll think I've got principles," I spit.

He shakes his head. He's so close that the blackheads on his nose wave to me. "They're gonna think, 'Poor Rowe Wadley, all that bad shit she's suffered has finally got the best of her and her brain broke.'"

I hate him so much.

It's not just that Luke left me. He took a part of me with him, and now he wants to take *pieces* of my life. I simply can't allow that.

"Mom, I'll give you everything I've got," I shout, "if you won't sell to him."

"Let's go," Luke tells Ron.

They lift the sideboard and proceed to walk with me leeched on top of it.

Mom looks terrible as she watches me act like an oversized toddler. "You're gonna need your savings, hon. Please, just get down and let him have it."

As soon as Luke's through the doorway, I throw out my arms and grip the doorframe. Luke's thievery comes to a halt as I hold on to the wall with all my might.

He sighs like I'm nothing more than a pesky mosquito. "Release it."

"No." I glance back at Mom. "Whatever he's giving you, I'll triple it!"

No clue if I have that much money, but it's worth a shot.

"Rowe, please. We need this. *I* need this."

It's the *I need this* that does me in. It feels like I'm stealing from the one person who's only ever wanted to provide for me.

That's what finally makes me drop my hands and whisper in defeat, "Fine. Take it."

I slide off the sideboard and watch with tears as they load it up into the bed of his truck. When Luke returns, I figure it's over, but when he also grabs my grandmother's antique hurricane lamp, two side tables, and a matching pair of mission lounge chairs, I stop watching.

My heart can't break anymore, I think. It just can't.

"Please don't hold this against me," Ron begs, looking pathetic with his shoulders slumped.

I shake my head. "Jennifer and I are too good of friends for that. You gotta do what you got to."

When Luke's finally heading out the door, I slink over and start to throw it closed.

"Good riddance."

But his foot shoots out, blocking it. I gasp as my ex pushes the door open and sticks his head in. "Learn your place, Rowe. You didn't win this battle, and when the war comes to your front door, you'll lose again. This house will be foreclosed on, and I'm going to get every single piece of it that I want."

A chill winds like a ribbon down my spine and snaps tight. I can't believe that there was a time when I loved this man. *Loved him.* Desperately. With all my heart and soul. I would have given him everything—and I did. Or almost did.

"See you around, Rowe."

He releases his hold and I shove the door closed.

It's when I hear him walking down the porch steps that I venture a look at the living room. There's nothing left except for my dad's old, frayed recliner. Everything else is gone.

Anger gurgles in my veins. There's no way in hell I will ever let Luke Preston get hold of this farm.

I'll die before that day comes.

Chapter 6

ROWE

"Bye, Bill! Bye, Mom."

I pull my mom into a hug and inhale the scent of patchouli that clings to her hair and skin. It is the most calming fragrance that I know and love.

"I'm sorry about earlier," she says.

"It's fine." Once Luke left, she explained that after the foreclosure had become binding, he had offered to help by buying a few pieces of furniture.

I bet he had, I thought. But I didn't tell her that.

My mom is such a free spirit that she generally thinks most people are out to do the right thing. Most people except Luke, that is.

There's no point in blaming her for it. My relationship with Luke was over years ago, but boy, does that breakup still sting.

Especially since I see either him or Sally Ray every day, given that they live right across the road. It also doesn't help that they have a super-popular unicorn farm that currently has an almost-full parking lot, while we have a dying piggycorn farm filled with rolling tumbleweeds.

Bill buzzes down the window of his truck. "You coming, Sabe?"

She twists toward him and waves. "Coming." Then she claps my shoulders and studies me with a wobbly smile. "You sure about this? That you want to try to take this on?"

"Mom, by the time you get back, I'm going to have saved our home. I swear it."

The look on her face suggests there's no way I could do that. But I'm determined. The last thing Luke said really knotted my knickers. He wants more than just the furniture—he and Sally Ray want to claim the house for themselves.

The people who ripped my life apart are not allowed to have my home.

"Everything you need is in the office," she says. "All the financials."

"Thanks. Now, get out of here. Bill's about to blow a gasket from waiting."

Bill is ex–armed forces and likes his life to work on a very succinct schedule. He's not at all like me and my messy existence.

I give Mom one more hug and watch as she gets into the truck and Bill backs out of the drive with the Airstream behind them. My arm hurts from waving by the time they're on the road and out of sight, and tears prick my eyes.

I'm alone. For the first time in my entire life, I'm all alone. Literally, truly alone.

Tallulah pads up beside me and presses her pink snout into my leg.

"I know." I sigh. "You're out of food. Let's go into town."

"What do you mean, there's no credit left, *Ron*?"

I drop my purse on the counter of Mystic Meadows Feed and Tack and glare at Ron, who, only two hours ago, helped Luke steal my furniture.

Even though there was money involved, yes, I consider it theft.

Ron's gaze drops to his hands as he nervously organizes and reorganizes a box of various seeds.

"Ron?" I repeat. "What's going on?"

He grimaces. "I'm sorry, Rowe, but your credit's been cut off."

"Cut off?" I yell.

Shoppers turn in my direction and I drop my voice. "Cut off?" I hiss. "What do you mean? We pay our bills."

"I know, but I guess with the whole"—he waves his hand, clearly meaning the foreclosure, and I can't help but roll my eyes—"Sally had you cut off."

Today just gets better and better.

Sally Ray owns the feedstore and Luke manages the bank. Together, those two are going to squeeze every drop of blood out of me.

"Fine. I'll pay for it." I open my purse and slap down my card. "Here."

He runs the card and frowns.

"What?" My nerves are fried. I feel a migraine coming on. "What is it?"

"The card's declined."

"*What?* There's money in the account." Frustrated, I dig my fingernails into the top of my purse. "Try it again."

Ron slips the card into the reader, and it beeps angrily at him. "Sorry, it's still not working."

"Try this one."

He does and that card doesn't work, either.

Two words hit me in the head: Luke. Preston.

"I'll be right back," I growl, yanking the card from Ron's hand.

"I'm sorry, Rowe," he says feebly.

"We'll see who's sorry," I mutter.

I barge outside. Soon as I'm in the blistering sun, the Georgia humidity hits me like a wall. It's so thick that it's clinging to the air like yesterday's panties on a hooker.

Drops of sweat sprout on my forehead and upper lip. I swipe them off with the back of my arm.

Even though it's gonna be a hot fall, my town is adorable. It's unicorn themed, so all the storefronts have charming scrollwork, and the names of the stores reflect the whimsical feel. There's the Prancing Pony Café and Twilight Treats Ice Cream, among others.

There's also a bridge where you can hang a lock after you place your and your lover's name with the words *4 eva* on it. After snapping the lock on to the wire fencing that runs the length of the bridge, you toss the key into the river, where it will be swept away, ensuring that you and your partner will be together *4 eva*.

Yeah. Luke and I did that. You see how our relationship turned out.

And today, Luke is apparently the undesirable gift that keeps on giving, because Mystic Meadows Savings and Loan is directly across from the feedstore. Soon as I walk in, the tellers duck in their seats.

"We don't want any trouble, Rowe," one says.

Ha. So they already know why I'm here.

"Is he in?" I say, not bothering to wait as I head to Luke's office.

"He's busy," replies another teller.

"Not anymore." I throw open Luke's door and stare him down.

He's cleaned up since this morning—put on a suit and tie.

My ex shoots back in his rolling chair and pretends to look surprised. "Rowe. Two visits in one day. To what do I owe this pleasure?"

"Cut the crap, Luke." I stomp over to his desk and drop my hands on it, leaning over as far as I can without falling on top of the slick surface. "Give me back my money."

One side of his mouth ticks up in a smug smirk. "I have no idea what you're talking about."

"You disabled my credit and debit cards."

"I would never do such a thing. But since you've got a problem, let me refer you to Member Services."

He reaches for his desk phone, but I slap his hand away. "I don't want Member Services. I want my money!"

He drops his voice. "If you continue to yell at me, I'll have to call the sheriff."

I. Hate. Him. So. Much.

After forcing a smile that's tighter than a virgin's butthole, I grind out, "Why aren't my cards working?"

"Well, Rowe, let's take a look."

He pulls his chair back up to his desk and punches some keys on his computer. He frowns and shakes his head before swinging the computer screen around for me to see.

"Looks like there's been suspicious activity on your accounts—both your credit card and your personal checking."

"Suspicious activity?" Shock rocks through me. "What?"

He nods. "For your own security, your accounts have been frozen until an investigation is completed."

"For my own . . . ? *Bullshit.* That's bullshit, Luke." My heart becomes as hard as stone. "What suspicious activity?"

"It doesn't say." His voice is tinged with fake sympathy. "All it says is that they've had to deactivate your cards as well as freeze the money while the investigation is being completed. Everything should be cleared up in a week or two."

"A week or two! What am I supposed to do about feed?" I shove my finger under his nose. "And don't think I don't know that you had Sally Ray cut off my line of credit at the store."

He pushes my hand away. "All I know about is the bank. I don't regulate what Sally does over there."

"Horse manure."

"You have a lot of fecal references today."

I'll *show him* fecal references. In fact, I'll shove them right up his rear end. "What am I supposed to do about money in the meantime?"

He sits back and taps the tips of his fingers together like a greedy oil baron about to con a small-time farmer out of the petroleum pools under his land. "I'm sure there are more things to sell in your home—antiques you've got hidden upstairs. As memory serves, I gave your mom a wad of cash this morning."

I lean in until we're nose to nose. "Let me make this crystal clear for you, Luke, since you and Sally Ray don't seem to understand: There is no way in hell that y'all will get one more piece of my property."

"Sixty days," he sneers. "You've got sixty days until you and that shitty little piggycorn farm of yours are out on your ass, and that property will belong to me—I mean, the bank."

We stare at each other for a couple of beats before he breaks the contest first. And yes, it was a contest, and yes, I won.

He riffles through papers on his desk. "If there's nothing else that I can do for you, I need to get back to work."

"Sure. Get back to work."

My world is melting faster than a snow cone on a summer's day, and he needs to get back to work.

Without a word, I turn on my heel and storm out of the bank. I head over to my truck—an early-'80s Ford F-150 with a diesel engine. The thing is so well made that it'll probably outlive me.

I slump against the door and drop my head to the window. What am I going to do? All my money's tied up in that bank.

Maybe there's some in the house that I'm forgetting about. There's probably enough for a few groceries, but not enough for the piggycorns' feed.

Their sparkleberry food is expensive, and it's the main staple of their diet. But maybe the ones that I'm trying to—

"Rowe!"

Ron peeks out from behind the feedstore, motioning to me.

"What now?" I grouch.

When I reach him, he pulls me around the corner. "I feel awful bad about what happened in there and for everything that went on at your house earlier." He rubs the back of his neck in embarrassment. "So here."

He moves aside, unblocking from view a fifty-pound bag of feed. My heart leaps into my throat.

I throw my arms around his neck. "Ron! You are my hero! Thank you so much!"

"Now, don't get excited," he tells me, pulling back bashfully. "You'll have to repay this pretty fast. Sally Ray keeps a keen eye on inventory, and if she notices that it's missing, I'll be fired."

"Okay, I promise. Soon as I get home, I'll take a look and scrounge up all the money that I can."

"You don't have to get it back to me *that* fast. You've got at least a week."

By then my accounts might be accessible again. "Thank you. Now. Can you help me load this up?"

He nods. "Drive around back here so nobody'll see."

"And here we are—that's been my entire day, and it sucks," I say, my voice echoing in the now-bare living room.

I'm lying on a pile of quilts I brought down from upstairs. There's a margarita in my hand, and I'm successfully wallowing in the evil I've endured in the last twelve hours.

Cristina, my ride-or-die, walks over and pours more frozen mango margarita into my green-speckled party-for-one glass. "Congratulations, my friend. You've officially had the shittiest day ever, and I'm pretty sure I have no interest in beating it. Though, when I think about it, the day that you had to give Stella to Sally Ray may have topped this one." When I shoot her a look, she scoffs. "What? That was a bad day, too, though not as bad as when Tyrell left me by the side of the road after prom. Now *that* was bad."

"I'm not gonna disagree."

She crosses back to my dad's old recliner in her eggplant-colored jammie set trimmed in pink feathers.

She looks around the room and sits. "I have to admit, the place does feel empty."

"That's because it is," I announce, listening as my words bounce around the empty room.

Cristina lifts her glass. "Cheers to things looking up!"

"I'll second that."

Every Wednesday, one of us hosts Margarita Night. Tonight was my turn, but when I called Cristina and told her how awful today had been, she insisted on making the drinks for me and coming over. We usually watch a movie in our pj's and then call it a night before she heads home.

The only movie that could possibly make me feel better is *Titanic*, as it's a worse disaster than what I'm living through. Unfortunately, the love story kills it for me. A romance like Jack and Rose's doesn't exist.

Cristina smacks her lips. "Have you looked over the financials?"

I point to my mom's office, where her laptop sits on the desk. After I got home from town, I started poring over spreadsheets. I'm no accountant, but even I could tell that we are so far in the red that we're now approaching the crimson gates of hell.

"Yeah, I looked. We're screwed."

Cristina passes me a bowl of chips. She's on this new no-seed-oil, no-flour, and no-corn diet, so the tortilla chips are made from black beans and cooked in avocado oil.

I take one and drag it through homemade guacamole. It's pretty good. Not gonna lie—I miss the corn, but these will do.

"Maybe there's a way to salvage—" she starts.

"There's no way."

I throw out my one arm that's not holding the margarita. No way am I risking any of this yummy goodness being spilled on the floor. With all the money I *don't* have, no food can go to waste, margaritas included. The last thing I need to add to my humiliation is hunkering over the floor and using my hands to scoop my slushy alcoholic beverage back into my glass.

"Even if there was a way to save the place, I don't have the money to pay someone to look through things. Luke made sure of that."

"What about the money he paid your mom?"

"She took it, and I wanted her to. She doesn't need to sink more of her cash into the house."

My bestie rakes her long, dirty-blond hair over one shoulder. "I hate Luke so much. Did you know that?"

"I do," I reply with a giggle. "But I doubt you hate him as much as I do."

"Hmm. It might be pretty close." She tucks her long legs underneath her and swirls the orange liquid in her glass. "I could slash his tires for you. If that doesn't work, I could shiv a dick."

I choke on the margarita, I laugh so hard.

"I don't mean literally slash his nuts off," she confirms. "Only *he's* a dick, so I'll cut him for you. But not *in* the dick, because that's horrible. Even I wouldn't do that."

When I stop wiping laughter-tears from my eyes, I croak out, "It's fine. I'll figure out a way through this. I can take care of myself. After all, I took care of myself just fine when Luke dumped me." I prop up a bunch of pillows and lean on them. "I just don't understand why they're both doing this."

She pokes the air with her glass. "Ah, you forgot the important ending to that sentence—why are they doing this *to you*?" She bites into a chip and adds, "Because they can."

"Because they hate me."

"They're evil, is what they are." Cristina makes a little whimper of sympathy in the back of her throat. "I can loan you the money."

"No. Absolutely not. I don't want or need your cash. Besides, you're saving it."

"I am, but that doesn't mean I don't have some stashed away for you."

"No. That is my final answer."

Cristina's a massage therapist. She works several towns over and is trying to buy a home.

"You need a miracle," she tells me before sucking the dregs of her drink through the straw. "Really. That's what you need. You need some extraordinary thing to happen so that you can save the farm."

"You mean like maybe piggycorns will somehow turn out to be magical and they'll kick the unicorns' butts?"

She grimaces. "Since unicorns aren't born with magic anymore, I doubt that piggycorns ever will be."

"But they were magical once," I say, sounding pitiful even to myself.

"I know."

It's true. When the unicorns first appeared on Sally Ray's grandfather's farm fifty years ago, they had magic. Lots of healing magic. Heck, the whole town was magical—at least, that's what my dad always told me. But he also explained that Sally Ray's grandfather got greedy and began overbreeding the unicorns. Their magic slowly dwindled—and so did the town's power—until they became nothing more than a horse with a horn.

Cristina nibbles on a chip, studies it, and nibbles again. "These aren't bad."

I take one and eat it in one bite. No point in saving calories. Any diet I might have had when I woke up was shot to hell by six this morning.

"Oh!" She covers her mouth with a hand, still chewing. "I saw Clarice Sinclair today. She said that you met some hot stranger. Tell me everything."

"There's nothing to tell." I drop a finger into my drink, swirl the liquid around, and suck it off. Turns out, the margarita is just as good from my finger as it is from the glass.

I must be drunk if that's as deep as my thoughts are getting.

"What do you mean, 'nothing to tell'?" she prods.

I drop a hand down beside me and coax Tallulah over. Yes, the piggycorns sometimes come into the house. They're trained, thank you very much. Except for that one time when they got into some old cabbage that may or may not have accidentally been left in their trough by accident when I was in a rush to head into town. Other than that, they've never had an accident.

Ever.

I rub the sweet piggycorn under her chin. She snorts happily before curling up at my feet and letting me run my fingers down the soft pink mohawk that hugs her spine.

The rest of the piggycorns who wanted to come inside lie on a quilt in the corner, huddled together, the sounds of their light snoring filling the room.

"Just what I mean—nothing to tell. This morning the piggies got out, and some guy in a big black one-hundred-thousand-dollar SUV almost killed them."

She whistles. "And was he hot?"

"*No.* Yes. Very hot. Very rich. He looked at me like I was a dirty farm girl."

She pumps her eyebrows suggestively. "You could be, given the right man."

I toss a pillow at her. She catches it to her chest and chucks it back. "Well, what? You could be. You haven't been with anyone in years, Rowe. I bet those Collins boys are looking good right about now."

"Oh my God, I'm going to kill you if you say something like that again."

She laughs. "All right, I won't. But it wouldn't hurt to smile a little bit at a man. I mean, what else have you got to do besides save your family farm and destroy Luke and Sally Ray?"

I burst into laughter just as the doorbell pings. Cristina's eyes flare. "Are you expecting anyone?"

"No. But I wouldn't be surprised if it's Luke with a moving truck ready to take everything."

"Shut up. Maybe it's that hot guy from today." She inhales, getting excited. "Maybe he's back and wants to date you. Maybe he couldn't get enough of your whole farm-girl-thing and hasn't been able to put you out of his mind."

"Stop it. It's not him."

"Well, whoever it is, don't leave them waiting." She flicks her hand, and the feathers glued to the end of her sleeve slowly wave through the air. "Hurry."

The doorbell peals again, and I hoist myself up from the mound of quilts. "I'm coming!"

As I shuffle toward the door, the room tilts. I grab a wall to steady myself. Perhaps Cristina made the margaritas stronger than normal.

Good. Now I'm loose. If it's Luke, I'm ready to tear into him. What am I saying? Of course it's Luke.

The pealing doorbell woke up the piggycorns, who are now up and stretching, eager to greet our new guest. They bunch around my legs as I leave the room.

I nudge piggycorns out of my path and yank open the door. "Listen, you, I've had just about enough of—"

And then I blink. Because it's not Luke standing on my front porch.

No. It's the man from earlier today. The one in the SUV who almost killed me.

He smiles grimly and says, "Hello. My name is Pane Maddox, and I'm here to save your farm."

Chapter 7

PANE

When Sunbeam tugs open the door, I don't expect my heart to jump. But it doesn't just *jump*—it catapults into a different dimension. I frown, pushing the fluttering organ and tidal wave of feelings away, and remind myself of a few simple facts.

Sunbeam is a distraction. Sunbeam is a fortune hunter. Sunbeam is nothing more than a business venture.

But my heart must not get the message, because one look at her nearly knocks me back. Her hair is out of its earlier braid and now cascades in waves over her shoulders like a waterfall. Her breasts are high and round as she inhales deeply.

And the way she smells—wildflowers on a cloudless day. I cannot get enough of her scent.

She thrusts a finger at me and slurs, "Listen, you, I've had just about enough of—"

And then she stops. Leans forward. Squints. Her gaze picks me apart, starting at my face and then darting down to my dress shoes. She takes her time coming back up for air, lingering on my thighs, my chest, my eyes.

I take the moment to memorize her face. Just so that I can describe her to my sister, obviously. Not for any other reason.

Freckles constellate her cheeks and nose. Her face is scrubbed clean, and she looks like she should be picking daisies in a field instead of being cooped up in a house.

Even though I've got my script down pat, now that she's staring at me with those doe-brown eyes that resemble polished wood, shooting me a look that suggests she can either take me or leave me—mostly *leave* me—the outer layer of iron that I've built up around me starts to crumble.

Like hell it will. I've got a job to do, an empire to win, and I'm not going to let this woman get under my skin.

"Hello." I give her my handsomest smile, the one that melts hearts. "My name is Pane Maddox, and I'm here to save your farm."

She laughs, and the scent of tequila smacks me in the face. It doesn't quite mesh with the whole wildflower vibe she's got going on. "What are you talking about, *save my farm*?"

"Exactly that. Your front signage is old and faded. No one's visited the place in years." Probably. It's a guess, but a decent one. "Your business needs help."

Sunbeam slumps against the doorframe. "Why would you help me? You couldn't get out of here fast enough this morning." She jabs a finger in my chest, then drops her gaze to said finger and pokes me again. "Are you wearing armor?"

She's definitely drunk.

Switching focus away from my chest, she snarls, "I offered clothes when yours were ruined, and they weren't good enough. And look what you're wearing now—jeans and a shirt. Oh, how the mighty suit man has fallen. How'd you get those? By stumbling into the one Hugo Boss store in Atlanta and snagging them?"

My blood churns in irritation. I'm here to do *her a favor*, and she's insulting me? "This morning I was running late for an appointment, and I couldn't have shown up in jeans or *overalls*. Not that it's any of your business, seeing as how you're a complete stranger—a stranger whose piggycorns I had to get across the road. Which you barely thanked me for."

She steps forward and peers up into my eyes, silently challenging me. "May I remind you that you almost killed me?"

I take another step and now we're nose to nose. "*Almost* isn't the same as doing."

The closeness of our bodies seems to charge the air. The humidity thickens, and the hairs on my arms prickle to attention. Sunbeam must feel it, too, because she shivers and retreats a step.

"And what sort of appointment were you late for?" she asks, flicking her hand in dismissal.

"I was meeting my mother."

"In a suit?"

"In a suit."

"What kind of mother makes her son meet her in a suit?"

"Mine. Listen"—this conversation is incredibly exasperating—"I can tell you everything if you'll let me come inside."

"Let a complete stranger into my home?" She scoffs. "The sun's setting. You might have a gun. You might want to rob me. Yes, you looked wealthy this morning, but you could be a grifter. That suit could have been stolen. You might even be after *the silver*."

"Do you have any silver?"

"No," she says, swaying. "Wait. That's not your business."

I lift my arms, gesturing toward the farm. "I'm a thief, and I've picked *your* house to rob? Not the home across the road with the unicorns?"

She smacks her palm against my chest to punctuate each word. "That's. Right."

Oh. My. God. I rake a hand roughly through my hair. "Look, I'm not a thief. My family owns a line of hotels. You can look me up. Surely you've heard of the Maddox Hotel. It's famous."

"I don't know." She sucks her teeth and puts on a hard Southern accent. "Us country bumpkins don't know nothing about you big city slickers. We ain't got 'nough sense to use that there internet."

There she is, getting amusing again. Smarting off with a mouth that's just begging to be tamed. I scratch my temple, unable to keep the wry smile from my lips. "Somehow I think you've got plenty of sense."

"Listen . . ." Fire dances in her eyes. "I've had a hell of a day, and the last thing I need is you pulling a practical joke. Did someone set you up to this? Let me guess, my not-so-nice neighbors. Did they follow you out of town, tell you that they'd pay you to pretend to help me? Are they watching this whole thing?"

Where in the hell has she jumped to now? Fairyland? "What?"

She clasps her hands and presses them to her chest before batting her eyes like a damsel in distress. "Don't tell me—you're here to be my knight in shining armor. Wow. Thank you so much. You're everything that I've always wanted—tall, with a complexion that probably turns golden in the sun, and handsome. And rich, you say? Wow. Please, help me, sir."

She drops to her knees and tugs on my pants. I would stop her, but it's way too tempting to see where this might go. Not to mention, she's in the perfect position to unzip my jeans.

"Please," she mock-begs. "You are the miracle we've been waiting for. Now the farm won't go into foreclosure because, what? You're going to buy it? Of course you are!"

She throws her hands up and rises, glaring at me. "I know your grand plan. You buy my farm and then turn around and sell it to Luke and Sally Ray." She jerks toward the road and yells, "Your plan isn't going to work, Sally! You'll have to pry my dead body off the floor to get my property!"

This is . . . more than I was planning for. "Listen, I think there's been some kind of misunderstanding."

She whirls on me, all wide-eyed, her words slurring just enough so that I know she's at least three drinks in. She's small. It wouldn't take a lot to get her tipsy.

She waves a finger around. "There's been no misunderstanding, Mr. Richie Rich. You can get the hell out of here. I can smell a setup when I see one."

A piggycorn peeks out from behind the door.

The door.

Which means the swine is inside the house. Of course it is. Who am I kidding? She probably hides piggycorns in her back pocket.

The swine wiggles through the gap and another one pops up behind it, taking its place. That one wriggles through the space, and suddenly a dozen piggycorns are charging toward me, running at full speed.

The horde slips and slides over the planks, their hooves scrabbling for purchase. The first comes to a stop by sliding into the toe of my shoe. Behind it, one after the other, each pig skates into the one in front of it, coming to rest on their rumps until there's a pile of piggycorns at my feet.

"Y'all!" Sunbeam shrieks. "Get off him!"

A dozen piggycorns gaze up at me. Tongues loll from mouths. Eyes blink. Tails wag.

The woman's gaze drops down, and she says, "Go back inside, y'all. I'll only be a minute."

When the swine don't move, she taps her foot impatiently.

That's when a tree branch shoots out from nowhere, scoops up the piggies like a giant hand, and deposits them inside.

I jump back. "Whoa."

Did I just see what I thought I did?

Maybe there *is* something to this whole "ley line" thing.

Awe fills my voice. "The land around here *is* magical."

"Yeah. And if you're not careful, it'll get you," Sunbeam threatens.

If the land is as scary as her—and she's about as terrifying as a kitten with tiny claws—I'll be just fine.

She wags a finger at the tree, which has now pulled its branch back in so that it looks normal again. "Where were you today when I needed you to stop Luke?" Before it can answer—do they do that here?—Sunbeam lifts her hand in a stopping motion. "Forget it." Then she turns back to me. "I don't know why you're still here. Go home."

"I'm not leaving until I have an answer."

"About what?"

I extend a hand. "I want to help your business."

"Didn't you hear what I just said?"

"I don't know anyone named Sally. She didn't send me."

"That's exactly what a spy would say. Listen, *spy* . . ." She cranes her neck and comes in very close, tapping my chest with all the confidence tequila can give a person who doesn't know who I am. "Get off my land before I pull out my shotgun."

Things weren't supposed to go like this. She was supposed to smile prettily and say, *Of course you can help me. Wow! Where did I get such luck that one of the most famous families in the country would want to help me? This must be a dream!*

But for some reason none of that has happened, and my patience is gone.

I smile tightly. "We've gotten off on the wrong foot. I'm here to save your farm. Can we discuss that?"

She sucks in her cheeks, shoots me a hard look, and says, "No."

Then she slams the door in my face.

Chapter 8

ROWE

"Who was that?" Cristina asks when I swagger victoriously into the living room.

"No one."

Tallulah glances up from her spot on a quilt. There's a lot of hurt feelings in her eyes. She wanted to let that *liar* pet her, and she's mad I wouldn't allow it.

"Traitor," I mumble.

The nerve of my favorite pet, approaching my newest enemy like he's her friend.

"Rowe?" Cristina asks.

I plop back on top of the quilts. "Yes?"

"Who *was* that?"

I wave away her question and turn back to my margarita, which is now melting into a sad, sloshy mess. "I don't know. Some guy who said he wanted to help me with the farm."

She sits up quickly, which makes Buster the Cat, who's been lying at her feet, flinch. "What?"

"Don't get excited. He was obviously a spy sent by Sally and Luke."

A wrinkle worms its way across her forehead. "What if he wasn't?"

"Oh, he for sure was."

"What was his name?"

"I don't know. Maddox something. Pane Maddox? Something weird like that. Said his family's famous."

Cristina's eyes nearly pop out of her head. "Pane Maddox? Like, from the Maddox Hotel family?"

"Maybe?" I say around a yawn.

She grabs her phone and starts typing. A moment later, Cristina shoves the device under my nose. "Was this him?"

The phone is way too close. I push her hand away and squint at the image. It's a picture of a man leaving a restaurant with a woman on his arm. He looks to be in his early thirties, and he's got the same dark hair and knee-buckling green eyes as the man from the front porch, who is now officially the third person on my shit list, right behind Luke and Sally. Wait. Those two are tied at number one. Okay, stranger is number two.

"Um. Yeah, that looks like him."

Her jaw drops. "Rowe, this is *the* Pane Maddox from the Maddox Hotel chain. He's, like, superrich. What's going on?"

I blow my bangs out of my face. Man, does my breath smell like alcohol. "First of all, he's the guy from this morning, the one who was so rude and awful."

"You didn't say anything about him being rude and awful."

"Well, he was. And he was snobby."

"Of course he was snobby. He's, like, a gazillionaire." She straightens, looking down her nose at me. "So what did he want?"

"Just what I said—to help the farm."

There is an incredibly long pause, which makes me think that Cristina has forgotten how to talk. "You are kidding me."

"No."

"Oh my God! Go back and get him!" She grabs my arm and pulls me up. I barely have time to save my margarita before it sloshes over the side of the glass. "Now! He's your miracle!"

"No, he's not, and I don't need a miracle."

"You will excuse me if I completely disagree with you." When I don't move to run after him, she says, "If you're not going to get him, I will."

Before I can argue with my best friend, she races to the front door. Wait. She cannot. I mean, she cannot be seriously thinking that the guy on my front porch is this Pane Maddox guy. No way. Probably a stunt double. Or just a guy who looks freakishly similar and who goes around impersonating him so that he can swindle unsuspecting women out of their hard-earned money. Well, I am not unsuspecting. I am *trés* suspecting, thank you very much.

Cristina's got the door open. "Wait!" she yells.

No! She's really doing it. She's really getting this guy back. He's so horrible. Awful. He called my piggycorns *swine*.

Though, technically, they are, but it was the *way* he said it, with his nose lifted and his voice sounding all snotty.

I reach the front door and grab Cristina's arm, yanking it down to her side.

Pane Maddox is bent down at the fence, arms extended. I charge out in my hot sauce–themed fluffy slippers. "What are you doing?"

He lifts a piece of rope. "Securing this so that your pigs don't get out."

My gaze drops to where he's tightened the fencing. He's done a decent job of it, and my chest squeezes around my heart at this random kindness. "Thank you."

He cuts the rope with a pocketknife, rises, drops the extra in his back pocket. "You're welcome."

Cristina runs down the steps. The feathers attached to her jammies wave in greeting. "You have to excuse my friend. She's had a terribly hard day, and even though *she* doesn't know who you are, I can see that you're obviously Pane Maddox. Rowe said something about you wanting to help?"

He eyes me coldly. "If she'll let me."

"Of course she will." Cristina grabs his arm and drags him up the steps, elbowing me so hard that I wind up in the bushes. "Come inside. Let's hear what you have to say."

The bushes spit me out. Twigs poke through my hair and into my face. I pull out the sticks and drop them to the ground. "Hold on a second. I'd like to see some identification. Make sure that you're really who you say you are."

He pulls a wallet from his back pocket and fishes out an ID. "Both of you know who *I* am. Whom do I have the pleasure of speaking with?"

He's talking to her but looking at me. When I don't answer, my bestie rolls her eyes. "I'm Cristina, and my silent friend is Rowe Wadley."

"Nice to meet you," he says.

"Pleasure's all mine," Cristina says, smiling brightly.

He hands the ID to Cristina, who stares at the picture for way too long.

Oh, I get it. Not only is his face pretty, but it's irresponsible the way he fills out his clothes, making us stare at his steely thighs and well-defined pecs.

After a long moment, Cristina rips her gaze from the pic and hands the ID to me. According to this, Mr. Donalpane Aloysius Maddox is six two, weighs 190 pounds, has green eyes, and is . . . thirty-five years old. He's not smiling in the picture, but there's a sparkle of smug arrogance in his eyes that he has even now.

I really don't like this man.

"All right. You appear to be legit. Why this farm? Why now?"

He takes the ID and says gruffly, "Let's talk in the house."

Soon as Pane steps inside, my home seems to shrink around this man as if he's too bulky to contain. It's like the house can't breathe because he's sucking up all the space.

Cristina seems oblivious, jumping into action as she plays hostess, ushering us into the kitchen. As we make our way there, Pane sneers at the sight of Tallulah lying on the quilts. Her brothers and sisters are piled up on both sides of her, aimlessly kicking as they've fallen back asleep. Pane also takes a long look at the rooster decor, and I swear his mouth dips into a scowl.

One that, yes, he does eventually direct toward me.

While the coffee brews and Cristina bounces around grabbing mugs, cream, sugar, and placing them all on the table, I focus on the man sitting across from me.

"You've got five minutes to tell me the whole story about why you're here. And don't think that I'm going to believe that when you spotted me this morning, you decided to take it upon yourself to be my Prince Charming."

Pane drums his thick, masculine-looking fingers on the table.

They're really very nice fingers—strong and lean.

What is wrong with me? When did I get a finger fetish?

Right about now, it seems.

"My mother is retiring from the Maddox Group."

"She is?" Cristina asks, clearly startled by this revelation about a woman whom neither she nor I know personally. "But she's run the company for, like, forever." I shoot her a look and she shrugs. "What? Of course I follow them."

I shake my head. "Go on."

Cristina hands him a cup of coffee. He looks up and smiles grimly, as that's the only emotion he's intimately familiar with. "Thank you."

I tap the table impatiently. "Your mother?"

"Right." He waits until my bestie gives me a cup of coffee, which I doctor with cream. My mama raised me right, so I push the pot toward him, but he waves it away.

Apparently, the man likes his coffee like he likes his attitude: strong and bitter.

"It's between myself and my brother as to who becomes head of the company, and my mother can't choose."

"Can't or won't?"

He drags his gaze from his coffee to meet my eyes. "I don't really know."

The way the skin around his eyes tightens makes me think there's something he's holding back. But whatever it is doesn't concern me.

I sip my drink—noting scornfully that the world is spinning less than it was when I was happily slurping down a margarita—and listen as he continues.

"Since my mother can't choose between me and my brother, she's decided to hold a competition. Whoever saves a business from near death, and does it the most successfully in sixty days, will become president and CEO of the Maddox Group."

Cristina plops in a chair. "The whole thing? Like, the whole company?"

"The whole company," he corroborates.

"Wow." She sips her coffee. "So that's why you're here."

He sighs, scrubs a hand down his face. "My brother had to pick the business for me, and I had to pick his. After seeing the farm this morning, he decided this would be a good challenge."

"He's right about that," Cristina says. I clear my throat and stare at her. She shrugs. "What? He *is* right, Rowe. Even you can't disagree."

Of course I can. "What business did you give to your brother?"

"A hot dog restaurant. He hates hot dogs. But to be honest, I think we've got the most potential here."

"Great!" Cristina claps her hands. "How much money are you planning to put into the place? I mean, you're rich, after all. You throw several thousand dollars at Wadley Farms, and Rowe will be able to get out of foreclosure."

His head swivels to me. "What?"

I cringe. "Yeah. My mother told me that this morning before she left on an extended vacation. We've got two months before the bank takes it."

He exhales, absorbing that. "So if I can't save the place, you lose it," he says, for the first time sounding something other than insufferable.

"Right. We lose it all, down to the last piggycorn."

Cristina claps her hands again and announces like a cheerleader, "Isn't this great? The two of you have a common goal. Like I said, how much money can you put into the place? It needs new fencing, paint, and a new sign. You also need someone to take over marketing, to show the tourists that there's more to Mystic Meadows than just the unicorns across the road. Rowe hasn't had time to focus on social outreach, as she's been doing day-to-day tasks, and her mother, great as she is, isn't a social media maven. Oh, and then there's the unicorn presence in town. You've got an uphill battle there." She waves her hand dramatically. "Those creatures are everywhere. You know, there's the unicorn water park and all the unicorn-themed stores in town, and then the streets are named after the creatures." She deflates as she appears to realize the stronghold that we're up against. "There are a lot of unicorn things."

"But there isn't a big piggycorn presence," he tells us quietly, with this whole silent-warrior vibe he's got going on.

"How much money will you put into it?" Cristina asks again.

"I don't have any money."

And the shoe just fell off the other foot. "Excuse me?" I ask. "All your talk about changing the place, making it awesome and better, and you don't have any money? I'm confused."

His scowl deepens. "That's one of my mother's stipulations. We can't use our own funds."

I laugh. Really toss my head back and laugh like a maniac two seconds short of sticking her finger in an electrical socket.

Just kidding. I would never do that.

I slap the table. "Well, guess what? I don't have any money, either. So what you're talking about—this dream where piggycorns are the best of the best—it's going to cost money, and I'm dead broke. Unless you can pull some cash out of thin air, I thank you for your time. Have a great life."

I push the chair back and rise, but his hand shoots out, covering mine. I jolt as a tsunami of heat winds around my wrist and snaps me in place.

Pane's eyes are on my wrist, and when he looks up, it feels like my rib cage shatters. I can't breathe. I can't think. I'm in his grip, and for the smallest flicker of a moment, I don't mind his presence.

His voice rumbles from the center of his chest. "Have you ever wanted to be more than where you came from?"

My jaw unhinges slightly. "What?"

"Have you ever felt *trapped*?"

His voice is low and sultry. The question feels intimate, like we're standing on a deserted beach at night with a crescent moon lighting a trail of breadcrumbs that connects us to one another.

His sage eyes hold mine, and my insides quiver. "Have you ever felt like a prisoner to your family's legacy? My whole life, all I've ever wanted is to be more than the Maddox name, to be better than my . . ."

Who? Better than who?

He doesn't continue the thought. Instead, he looks away and inhales, and when he pins his sage grass eyes on me again, my pulse flutters at the base of my throat.

"People see me coming and they sum me up in two words: rich brat."

Pane sinks back in his chair, releasing my wrist, and I immediately covet the heat he took with him. "Becoming CEO of the group was supposed to be my chance to change that, to prove that I'm more than a man born into a life of luxury. I always thought the company would be my ticket in doing that, but it's not. It's *this*—your farm. Your business is not only *my* future, but it's yours as well. You can understand that, can't you?"

The way he's looking at me makes a boulder tumble into my throat. He doesn't wait for an answer, which is great because I don't have one.

"You're from a small town where people pigeonhole you, the same as they do me. This is your shot at proving that they're wrong about you, that every small belief they've ever held about Rowe Wadley is incorrect. You're bigger than Mystic Meadows, and I want to help you show it."

I'm speechless.

"Holy shit." Cristina clearly isn't.

He leans in. "I'm more than the prejudices the world has saddled me with. Are you?"

He looks at me and it's like he can see my soul, like he's reading me right out of a book. "Yes," I find myself whispering. "I am. I want to be."

And it's true. I've been seen as sad little Rowe Wadley for forever—a piggycorn farmer, a woman who can't keep a man and whose lot in life sucks. My one chance to fix up the farm was stolen by the bank.

But maybe there's a shot with Pane Maddox.

I lean in toward him until only inches separate us.

"What do you want for this place?" he asks. "What's your vision of its future?"

I lick my lips. His gaze darts to my mouth, and my cheeks heat. "I've always wanted this farm to beat out Dancing Trails across the road. For my parking lot to be filled, while theirs is dwindling. For people to see that piggycorns are what I've always known—that they are the perfect companion pet. Sweet, loyal, smart. They're like dogs, except cuter, cuddlier, with big personalities and a curiosity that makes my heart swell." And it does. There's no better feeling in the world than having a piggycorn sit beside me and put its chin on my lap. "They are kind, gentle creatures that don't get the credit they deserve."

A smile lifts one side of his mouth. It's a nice mouth. One that's begging to have lips brushed against it.

Wait. Where did that come from?

"That's what I want for your farm, too. If you let me help you, if you will put your trust in me, I will work day and night to save this place and turn it into every dream you've ever wanted."

Cristina mumbles, "Is it getting hot in here?"

I have no idea what she's talking about, but Pane Maddox is magnetic. He's all supercharged positive ions and I'm negative, drawn to him. His speech not only ignites a fire in my gut, but it also starts a fire in my panties.

He leans in one more inch. "I will win your farm back for you."

I believe him. Every inch of me believes this man as he stares at me with eyes as green as brilliant glass marble.

"So. What do you say?"

Before I can stop myself, I give him my answer.

Chapter 9

PANE

"Yes," she murmurs. "I say yes."

Rowe leans in to me. I lean in to her, too, and it feels like the world has disappeared, like we're the only two people who exist.

Heat fills her eyes before she blinks and shakes her head, making it vanish. Then she slumps back onto the chair.

"You can help me," she confirms icily. "But there will be rules."

Rules. Good. I like rules. Rules keep people in their place. Rules separate the wheat from the chaff. Rules remind me that I'm not here to get lost in her eyes or her luscious scent. I'm here to win.

And I'm also not here to discuss my personal life. The fact that I almost told a stranger who I want to be better than, is ridiculous.

Keep your thoughts in check, Pane.

I drum my fingers on the table. "Agreed. We need rules. Tell me everything you've got."

"Well . . ." She scans the room as if there's a sheet of bylaws taped to the fridge. After a moment she says smugly, "You have to run all ideas past me first."

Sunbeam, who's all of five two, studies me like I'm the big bad wolf, like she can protect a village of piggies all by herself when trouble comes.

She's disconcerting. Everything about her has me in knots. What is wrong with me? I've only just met the woman, but she's different . . . sassy, determined, and she doesn't give a flip about who I am.

And let's not forget that she's also broke.

If there's one thing my mother taught me, it's that the Maddox family does not need a fortune hunter in our family—and what else would a broke woman on the verge of losing everything be, but a desperate digger of wealth?

I repeat her first rule. "I have to run all ideas past you? Deal." Rowe blinks as if she's surprised I gave in so quickly. "I'm not here to make your life miserable. We have to work together for this venture to be a success."

She shoots a look to Cristina, who shrugs. "Don't ask me. This is your whole thing. I'll clean up the kitchen. While I do that, why don't y'all talk somewhere else so that I don't distract you."

Rowe narrows and un-narrows her eyes, sharing a silent conversation with the woman who is clearly her best friend.

Cristina waves her off. "I'll be right here."

In case I try to murder Rowe, no doubt. Somehow I manage to not roll my eyes. If I wanted her murdered, I would obviously pay someone to do it. It's not like I'd get my own hands dirty.

But I would never kill anyone, just to be clear.

Sunbeam exhales an exasperated sigh. "Let's talk outside."

I follow her through the kitchen—which, for some reason, is infested with ceramic roosters and living swine.

We step past a pile of piggycorns smooshed together on a dog bed. "They're not going to lick my feet?"

Rowe glances over her shoulder, brow lifted delicately. "Normally, they would. Your feet must smell bad."

I bite down the chuckle that rumbles in the back of my throat. *Tit for tat, this one.*

The back porch is small, decorated with a grill and a table for two. Rowe crosses to the railing, faces me, and folds her arms, which I'm quickly learning is her fighting stance.

I, on the other hand, lean against the tall balustrade, eyeing her with curiosity. What happened to this farm girl for her to be so on edge?

I mean, besides the whole foreclosure thing?

Don't get personal, Pane. This is a job. This is my future. That's what I have to focus on.

But why do I suddenly care?

I don't care, just to be clear. I'm only curious.

She shoots a quick glance out toward the farm, and I follow her gaze. At night, the place is stunning. The moon bathes the grass in a silvery light, grass that unfurls to a fenced pasture that gleams almost ethereally.

Wait. It doesn't *almost* gleam. It *does* gleam.

As I watch, a breeze washes over the grass, and as the blades bend, the earth beneath glows as if it just became activated.

I've never seen anything quite like it. For as many places as I've traveled—all over the world—this swatch of land is magical.

"It's the ley lines," she says, yanking me from my thoughts.

I drag my gaze from the pasture back to her. She's not looking at me. Instead, she stares into the night.

"Sorry?" I ask.

"The ley lines. They're rivers of power that exist in the land. That's why Mystic Meadows is—or *was*—magical. At least here it still is, somewhat." She tips her head back and forth as if chewing on a thought. "But anyway, you can see the power on the farm because this is where the ley lines are." She nods toward the meadow. "The land glows."

"It sure does," I reply, enchanted.

For as beautiful as the land is farther out, the stuff closest to the house is scrubby, as if the magic doesn't quite reach it, like there's an artery blockage stopping the power from seeping through.

"I also get final say in all things," she murmurs, still looking away.

"Good. I was beginning to think you didn't have any more rules."

Her gaze snaps on me. "Oh, I have more rules."

"I would expect nothing less."

"Are you making fun of me?"

"Absolutely not, Sunbeam." On hearing her nickname, she physically bristles, her back going ramrod straight. "All I'm saying is that based on our encounters so far, I have no doubt you've got a list of rules inside that complicated head of yours."

She frowns. "I'm not complicated—and yes, I do."

Okay, sure. Not complicated.

She shifts her weight and returns her gaze to the land, giving me a perfect view of her profile. She leans over the railing, and moonlight splashes on her skin, making her glow just like the rest of the earth.

Whatever magic hangs in the air, it's shrouded her, and I don't think she has any idea that it's happening.

She looks like an angel.

Of death.

For me.

Keep thinking that way, Pane. You've got sixty days to win an empire. Not sixty days to lose your heart.

"You get final say," I repeat. "So even if I have an idea that I know will make you money—"

"You won't do it unless I give my approval."

"No."

She balks. "What?"

I give a single hard shake of my head. "You need me a lot more than I need you. I can find another business to save. You can't find anyone else to salvage this farm, or else you already would've done it."

"You are so—"

"Arrogant? Yes, I know. I've heard it all before, and it's true." She glowers, and I roll my eyes. "You don't get final say, but I will ask for your opinion. How is that?"

She scoffs. "Are you always like this?"

"Yes, I am. Now. Any more rules on your exhaustive list?"

"It's not exhaustive . . . And yes, there's one more."

"Only one?"

"I'm not as uptight as you seem to think."

"That remains to be seen."

She smirks. "You're not sleeping in the house."

"I didn't even ask if I could stay here."

She tips her head back and laughs. "You're a billionaire short on cash. Where else are you going to stay?"

Good point. "Where will I sleep, then? The barn?"

God, not the barn.

"I'm not that terrible." She shoots me a look so scalding that it could burn the hair right off my head. "My mom's she shed. She uses it to make candles. There's a bed in there, and it's temperature controlled."

I frown. "Are you also going to lock me in at night?"

"Don't tempt me."

Her mouth curves lusciously when she says it. So I look away.

I lean my shoulder against one of the porch's posts, and her gaze lingers on my arm before darting back to the landscape.

"So to recap, your rules are"—I tick them off on my fingers one at a time—"I have to run everything past you, you get not-quite final say in all decisions, and I have to sleep in a she shed."

"It's more like a *shamper*, but yeah, that's right."

"Done."

She balks. "Really?"

"Did you actually think that a few rules would make me say no?"

She eyes my shirt, which is rolled up to the elbows. "To be fair, I thought the shamper might break you."

"Hardly." She extends her hand to shake on the deal, but I stop her with, "I have a few rules of my own."

Her shoulders tighten. "*You* have rules?"

"If you get them, then so do I."

"It's my house, so it makes sense that I would have them."

"And I'll be doing a lot of work so that in two months you can sail off into the sunset of financial freedom. At the very least, I'll have a road map and a staff for you."

"A staff?"

"You can't do this alone. You'll need people. I'll get them."

"I can do things on my own."

My gaze scours the wrecked farm before landing deliberately back on her. "Of course you can do it alone."

She hears the sarcasm in my voice, but the only hint that it gets under her skin is when she folds her arms. "Fine. Tell me your rules."

I lift my finger. "Rule number one—should we write these down?"

"Are there a lot of them?"

"No."

She taps her temple. "Pretty sure I can remember, even if I do own overalls."

I tear my eyes away from her smirking mouth. "Okay. Even if you don't like an idea of mine, we're still going to try it."

"But what if—"

"What if, *what*? It makes you a million dollars?"

She scrapes her teeth over her bottom lip. "Fine. What else?"

"Next rule"—I hold up two fingers—"no piggycorns in the house."

Her jaw falls. "What? You're not *sleeping* in here. What does it matter?"

"I will be working in the home, and those are farm animals. They are not cats or dogs. Or even chinchillas. They are swine, and this is a business. We don't know how we'll be using the house yet, and it might come into play." I create an X with my forearms. "No swine inside."

She makes a little whimper in the back of her throat. "But what about—"

"No," I say sharply. "None of them. Not even your favorite. They stay outside while I'm here. In two months, you can do whatever you want. But absolutely no piggycorns inside for the next sixty days. Got it?"

She tips her face to the sky. Moonlight bounces off her features, making her brown hair a silvery gold. "Fine. No piggycorns in the house. You better be all that you're cracked up to be," she mutters.

I prowl over, and her eyes flare in surprise as I drop my mouth to her ear. "You have no idea how amazing I am."

Rowe stiffens, and the air between us electrifies to a crackle. Then she leaps back and scoots away, putting a good five feet between us.

She swallows and her throat bobs. "Any more rules?"

"Just one."

"And that is?"

I tap my knuckles on the railing. "I'm here to help this farm. Unless I'm doing so because there's a need, I will, under no circumstances, be asked to feed an animal or perform farm chores."

"God forbid you do an honest man's work," she snarls. "Don't worry. I'm more than capable of taking care of this farm, and myself."

"Good. Because I'm not trying to take care of you. I'm trying to take care of me."

"Good."

"Great."

"Wonderful!" She throws up her arms. "Is that it? Is there anything else you'd like to say, Your Highness, before I show you to your penthouse suite?"

I pause. "By that you mean the shamper, right?"

"Yeah, the shamper."

I straighten and stretch my shoulders back. "Nope. That'll be all. Show me to my bed, and tomorrow we'll get to work."

"*This* is the shamper?"

For the second time since I've met her, Rowe is genuinely smiling. I glance away in disgust and focus on the posters lining the small camper, my new living quarters.

Every inch of wall space is covered in pinups featuring '80s pop artists. Some of the posters are sun bleached, but many of them look brand new, like Rowe's mom kept them rolled up and hidden away for years before deciding that her candle-making haven would house them.

It's a study in the feminization of men. Every man wears makeup, yet they all look masculine. There's Duran Duran, the Thompson Twins, Culture Club, Adam Ant—and so many more.

The only reason I know their names is because they're printed at the bottom of each poster.

Even the ceiling is covered.

"Home sweet home," she says brightly. "If there's anything you need, let me know. There's a bathroom that's hooked up to its own septic. The water works." She points to a window unit. "There's the heat and air. You should be good to go."

"One more thing."

She rolls her eyes. "What?"

"Don't tell anyone who I am. Word will spread anyway, but I'd rather it do so in a trickle instead of a deluge. If my mother finds out and thinks that it gives me an unfair advantage, it will ruin our chances of saving this farm."

"You mean winning your company."

"That, too."

She mimes locking up her lips and tossing the key. "Your secret's safe with me."

I nod in thanks.

"If there's nothing else, I'll leave you to it. Good night."

"Good night."

Without another word she exits, and the next thing I hear is the door clicking.

Son of a—

I try the knob, but it's locked.

"Okay, so I decided to lock you in," she yells from the other side, "in case you're a murderer. Don't worry, I'll let you out early enough."

"What time?" I demand.

"Hmm. I'll have it unlocked by six."

"Five thirty—and I take my coffee black."

"Maybe I'll be here by then, and maybe I won't. Good night!"

The sound of her sassy mouth lights my insides on fire. When I'm bringing in money hand over fist for this place, we'll see how much backtalk she gives.

I drop my suitcase on the floor and survey my new home. "Well, guys, I guess it's just the fifty of us."

The camper is small, and there's not much to explore, but I do have clothes to put away. The first cabinet I open is filled with smelly candle things that immediately make my allergies flare. After a head-pounding sneezing fit, I forego putting anything away, strip down to my briefs, and collapse onto the bed.

The mattress feels like I'm being punched in the back by a thousand fists. This is going to be a long night.

Just as I'm about to snap off the light, my new phone rings. I recognize the number. It's from my mother's house. "Hello?"

"Pane," Natalie whimpers. "You're not here. When are you coming home?"

I sigh. "It might be a while, kiddo."

"But what about my bedtime book?"

I pinch the corners of my eyes. "I'll have to grab a new one for you tomorrow. I don't have anything tonight."

"But how will I sleep?"

"What about a story? One that I make up."

"I don't know."

Her voice makes me grin. "You'll like it."

"I'd better."

Time to put my money where my mouth is. It takes about half a second before I'm spitting out, "Once upon a time, there was a princess named . . . Sunbeam, and she smelled like wildflowers."

I pause to gauge whether she likes the beginning, and when she prods me with, "Go on," I continue.

"And this princess was the biggest pain in the neck you've ever met. In fact, it was her nickname—Princess Pain-in-the-Neck."

The earth underneath me rumbles as if it doesn't like me calling Rowe a pain in the neck. Too bad. It'll just have to get used to it.

Through the phone's speaker, Natalie giggles. "Tell me more about this princess."

Chapter 10

ROWE

"So, how was it?" Cristina asks when I'm back in the living room.

I drop onto the quilts and exhale the curtain of bangs from out of my eyes. "This is either the smartest thing I've ever done or the stupidest."

"It might not be the stupidest, but it's by far the craziest."

"Thanks," I say sarcastically.

She stretches her legs out in front of her. "I don't know what you're so upset about. The hottest, richest guy *ever* shows up to help you like he's a gift from God, and you're mad about it?"

"He definitely *thinks* he's a gift from God."

"He sort of is." She glances up from her phone. "Are you going to tell your mom?"

"No. At least, not for a few days. No point in getting her hopes up in case this falls through."

"Don't think like that. Think positively. Heck, it would be my dream to snap my fingers and have some hot guy drop onto my doorstep." She pauses. "Think it'll work?"

"No." Tallulah pads over and snuggles against me. I stroke her and murmur, "He says no piggycorns in the house."

"That hot brute," my bestie says with a dramatic eye roll. "What other torture did he make you agree to? Being chained to the bed while he runs a feather over your naked body?"

I explode with laughter. "No. Nothing like that. I locked him in the shamper. Don't look at me like that. I have to make sure he's not dangerous."

"The first hot guy to come around in forever, and you lock him up with posters of eighties pop bands? Are you trying to torture the man?"

"Maybe."

"Good God, what am I going to do with you?"

"I don't know."

"That's it!" She throws her arms up. "You officially need a reeducation on men. I mean, you can't deny that he's good-looking."

I shrug. Of course I don't deny that. But he's also smug, arrogant, horrible, conceited, privileged—all things that I can't stand.

"Do you think he wants us to tell anybody that he's here?" she asks.

"No. Since he's trying to win his family's company, it might give him an advantage if word gets out. This way it's more fair if he wins."

"Not if, Rowe—*when*. *When* he wins. When he wins and you get to keep the farm and give Luke a huge middle finger."

I hope so. But every time I think about Luke taking my farm, my stomach gets all knotted up. So, for that reason, I shove the thought away and stroke Tallulah's head. "Pane said to keep his identity a secret—as best we can."

Her mouth makes this part-grimace, part-cringe thing. "But people will ask who that hot man is."

"Then I'll let *him* tell them."

Now Cristina full-on grimaces.

"What? Have you already said something?"

She pulls her feet up to her chest. "I may have told a few people about him. Don't panic. Not many. Just a couple."

That could mean Cristina has only shared this with a few people. Or she could have told *more* than just a few people. It could also mean that the people she told will blab to *all the wrong people*, and word will spread faster than a fire doused with gasoline.

My phone starts vibrating.

When I open it, there are messages from friends, acquaintances, people I hardly know, and even Clarice Sinclair, all asking about Pane Maddox.

And the messages keep pouring in.

Dread pools in my stomach. "What did you do?"

She cringes. "I may have posted about him on social."

"Cristina!"

"What? How was I supposed to know? In the kitchen, he didn't say anything about *not* spreading the news. But don't worry, I'll take the post down right now. Hopefully that will stop this from traveling any farther than town. But I mean, hey, you put him in a plaid shirt and tight jeans, get him working around the farm, and women will pay to see that. *I'll* pay to see that."

"Stop turning him into a sex object."

She frowns. "It's really hard not to. Impossible, actually. The man can't help it. He oozes this whole sexy vibe. Really, Rowe. If you don't jump on him while he's here, I'm going to be very disappointed in you."

"And you need to stop talking as if having sex with random men is something that I do."

"That's true. It's not."

As my phone continues to ding, panic scrambles up my throat, throwing me back into the problem at hand. Oh no. This isn't good. This isn't good at all.

Pane Maddox is going to be pissed.

Well . . . what else is new?

Chapter 11

ROWE

"Good morning," I say cheerfully, holding a cup of coffee as a peace offering. "How'd you sleep?"

Pane frowns, which makes a dimple snap, crackle, and pop below the apple of his cheek. "As best I could, considering there was an audience."

A night of rest did nothing to improve his mood. If he's this ticked now, he's really going to be mad once he figures out that half the town knows of his presence.

I gesture toward the old Toyota Tacoma he parked in the drive. "Well, you could always sleep in there." He takes the coffee with a grunt and sips. "Ready to get to work?"

He gives a curt nod. "I need to look at the P and L statements."

"The what?"

"Profit and loss."

"Right. Those'll be on my mom's computer. I'll set you up."

After getting him logged on to the computer, I start breakfast. The animals have been fed, but you wouldn't know it by how the piggies are sitting on the back porch, snouts pressed to the screen door as they eye me accusingly. No doubt they're wondering why I've locked them out and replaced them with a stranger.

After an hour I knock on my mom's door. Pane glances up from the computer. His third cup of coffee sits neatly atop a coaster beside the laptop. He took his refills by walking in and grunting like the brute he is.

Lucky for him, I speak grunt.

"Breakfast will be ready in ten minutes."

He drops his gaze to the screen. "Thank you, but I'm good."

"You sure? The eggs are fresh."

"From chickens?"

"Actually, from the octopus I keep in an underground aquarium."

"I've actually heard good things about that," he jokes dryly.

I rest my shoulder on the doorjamb. "I'm only going to make the offer once."

"Fine." He drags his eyes from the computer and rises, stretching his arms over his head. This morning he's wearing a tight burgundy popover shirt, which is a cross between a Henley and a button-down. He's pairing this fashionable ensemble with pressed jeans and dress shoes.

"You need boots," I tell him as he approaches. "My dad has an old pair. They might fit you."

"First, I need a tour of the house. Then breakfast."

I roll my eyes. "Fine. Boots can wait."

Said tour takes all of five minutes. I cringe when we reach the living room, which is a carpet of quilts and naked flooring. He studies it carefully, his gaze scraping over the empty boards, some of which are sun bleached from where antique furniture once sat—as of yesterday, in fact. But luckily for me, Pane doesn't comment on the lack of furnishings.

When we reach upstairs, he spots my sticky notes on the bathroom mirror and inspects them with a sharp eye.

"I like your aspirations."

I sweep past him and rip the notes off the mirror and dump them in the garbage. "They're not mine."

He lifts his brows but doesn't say anything else. As we head to the stairs, Buster the Cat darts out of my bedroom and follows us.

The whole way to the kitchen, Pane types on his phone, barely bothering to look up as he maneuvers steps and turns.

To give the hotel heir a true Southern welcome, I've made the breakfast to end all breakfasts—scrambled eggs, bacon, biscuits, and gravy.

While he refills his coffee I build his plate, cracking open a biscuit, slathering it in butter, and drowning it in white sausage gravy.

He stares at the plate when he sits down. "What is that?"

"What?" I lick a splotch of gravy from my thumb. He stares at me for a second before pinning his focus back on the meal. "What's what?"

"The white stuff."

"It's gravy."

"No, it isn't."

"Yes, it is. It's not beef gravy. It's white sausage gravy."

"What's it sitting on?"

My gaze swishes from side to side. Am I on a revamping of the show *Punk'd*? Is someone going to jump out and tell me that this is a joke?

But when Pane studies me expectantly, I reply slowly, "It's a biscuit."

"The white thing is a biscuit."

"Yes, and that's sausage gravy on top of it."

"Is it good?"

"No, it's awful," I deadpan. "That's why I'm feeding it to both of us."

His eyes narrow before he picks up his fork in his left hand and glances at the spot on his right. "Where's the knife?"

"The knife?"

He nods, very serious. "Yes, the dinner knife."

I've never used a knife at breakfast, but there's a first time for everything. "Do you mean a butter knife?"

"No, not a butter knife."

"A steak knife?"

"No, not a steak knife." He rises. "Where's the cutlery?"

I blink, trying to wrap my head around this weird conversation. "The *silverware* is in that drawer."

"Thank you." He drops his napkin on the table, gets the *butter* knife, and sits back down.

I point to it. "That's a butter knife."

"No. It's called a dinner knife. Butter knives are smaller."

Well, you learn something new every day.

I watch with fascination as he holds his fork in his left hand, the hilled side pointed toward the ceiling. Then he cuts the biscuit with the *dinner* knife (what a peasant I am for not knowing this) in his right hand. The fork enters his mouth with the wrong side facing up, and I can't help but be mesmerized by this way of eating.

My trance breaks when Pane closes his eyes. "Oh my God."

"What? Is it bad?"

He slowly shakes his head. "What is this amazing meal?"

Really? Is this a trick question? "It's called a country breakfast. They serve it at Cracker Barrel."

"Please don't talk. I need to focus on the food."

"You just asked me a question."

"That's beside the point."

Okay, Mr. Grumpy. He takes another bite, closing his eyes again and this time, moaning as he chews.

The moan makes a tingle tumble willy-nilly down my spine and straight to my crotch.

I gulp down a bite and keep my eyes on my own breakfast, doing everything in my willpower not to focus on Pane and his orgasmic-sounding eating.

When I dare glance up, he's inhaled the entire biscuit and gravy. The man releases a satiated sigh, sits back, and studies me. "That's a biscuit?"

"Have you never had one before?"

"No."

I nearly fall off my chair. "What?"

"We don't serve this in the hotels—but my God, that was amazing." He sits up eagerly, a surprising look of childlike excitement scribbled across his face. "Is there more?"

I push the basket of biscuits toward him. "Help yourself."

"How do you make it?" he asks, picking up a small one and pulling it open, watching as steam uncurls from the hot dough. "It's so flaky," he marvels.

Is he putting me on? Did the shamper full of posters damage his brain? "Well," I say slowly, "it's pretty standard breakfast fare in the Southeast. It's just flour, salt, fat, and buttermilk." I study him, trying to figure out if he's being serious. All signs point to yes. "You've really never had one?"

"Never." He shoves one half in his mouth. "Wow."

I grab his wrist, and a jolt of lava hits me in the solar plexus. Holy cow. I drop him as quickly as I took hold, chalking the shock up to static electricity.

"Put butter on it. It's better."

He scans the table. "Where's the butter knife?"

"Just use your dinner knife. That's what us poor people do."

"Sorry," he mutters.

I cock my ear toward him. "What was that?"

He gives me a withering look. "*Sorry.* I'll use whatever knife you give me."

Then he slathers the rest of the half in butter and eats it, moaning again. After he swallows, he says, "It's better with the gravy."

Which he then pours on his plate and dredges the other half through it, finishing it in two bites.

I think I've created a monster.

Pane slurps coffee and swallows before explaining, "We don't have any hotels in this area; that's why I don't know about this food. But this is amazing. May I have another?"

"Have as many as you want." He takes one and now has his routine in place—butter, gravy, eat. "What do you usually have for breakfast?"

He finishes chewing. "It depends on where I am. In New York, the hotel serves eggs and bacon. In Paris, it's salmon and caviar. In Tokyo, it's grilled fish and miso soup." He shrugs like waking up in Paris or

Tokyo is an everyday occurrence, which I suppose it is for him. "Like I said, it depends."

I frown. "It sounds like you live in a hotel."

"I do."

My eyes nearly pop from my head. "Why?"

"So that I can be close to work. Traveling takes time, and I like to start early." He swipes a napkin over his mouth. "What is it?"

I speak after downing a bite of eggs. "It just doesn't sound very warm to live in a hotel. Like you'd be surrounded by beauty, but nothing cozy. It would be so sterile."

Pane shrugs. Who he is, how he presents himself, begins to make sense. I wonder if his lack of warmth is because he grew up in such a cold place. After all, his mother expected him to wear a suit to their meeting, even though his was ruined. Is she cold, too? Just like an antiseptic hotel lobby?

He eats a fourth biscuit, moaning through every bite in a way that snares my attention. It's impossible to do anything but stare as this beastly man takes pleasure in a biscuit.

A biscuit, y'all.

After voicing his gratification so loudly that a blush rises to my cheeks, Pane wipes his mouth and nods firmly. "Thank you. If you keep feeding me those, I'll be your servant forever."

"I'm sorry, what?"

A ghost of a smile graces his full lips. "It's a joke."

"Oh." I laugh. "That's good, because I was inches away from asking what kind of servant."

"Not a sex servant, if that's what you were hoping."

His knee-quaking green eyes spear me so hard that I can't breathe. My gaze starts to plummet to my lap from embarrassment, but I stop myself. There's no way that Pane's allowed the last word.

"Nope. I wasn't thinking of that kind of servant at all," I squeak.

"Good." He whips his phone from his pocket and opens it. "Now. Let's talk about the farm. I've checked the P and L's."

"How were they?" I ask dismally.

He grunts.

"That bad?"

Another grunt. "How many visitors do you get on a daily basis?"

"None. The unicorn farm across the road takes all the business."

He frowns. "You don't even get spillover?"

"Sometimes."

"That seems odd." He frowns and types something in his phone. "How busy is it this time of year?"

"Since kids are back to school, it's slowing down except for weekends."

"But fall is almost here."

"And tourists will come to see the leaves changing color."

He considers this. "Fall also brings festivals. Any of those?"

"No, there are none in this area."

A flash of movement outside the window grabs my attention. I spot a green tractor topped with one Clarice Sinclair. She's puttering in front of the farm.

In fact, other folks are also driving by. Wait. Not driving—*crawling* in a conga-sized line of vehicles.

Oh, crap. Even though Cristina deleted her post about Pane, apparently the news about my guest has circulated, and the townies are now vying to get a glimpse of the billionaire.

"What is it?" he asks, turning toward the window.

I slap my hand over his and his head snaps back, his green eyes turning dark with irritation.

"Oh! Thought I saw a mosquito on your hand. Die, mosquito! You don't want West Nile, do you? I just did you a favor."

Pane slides his hand away and eyes me uneasily. "Um. Thanks."

As discreetly as possible, I fire off a quick text to Cristina, begging her to get her butt out here and break up the welcome caravan.

Me: SOS! Pane's fan club has arrived! Get them gone before he sees.

Cristina: I'm on it!

Me: Also, he's never eaten biscuits before.

Cristina: What? Was he raised in a barn?

Me: No. In a gilded cage.

Cristina: Oh, right. Of course. I'm such a peasant.

Me: That's what I thought, too!

He waits for me to finish texting before returning to our conversation, pelting me with questions. "So, no festivals? Not even nearby?"

I tell him what I can, completely distracted and barely listening to myself as I give long, elaborate answers so that I can buy any and all time possible. Cristina doesn't live too far away, but it will take her a few minutes to get out here and break up the brigade.

While talking, I keep one eye on the traffic, which is now rush-hour heavy. People hold signs out their windows that read **WELCOME PANE MADDOX! WELCOME TO MYSTIC MEADOWS! WE LOVE YOU, PANE!** There's even a **MARRY ME** sign.

That one has a bunch of hearts under it. Oh, wow. If these people knew what he was like, they'd change their tune lickety-split. They'd be locking him up in *their* shampers just to get a break from his sour attitude.

Pane rises and stretches, dragging me back to our conversation. "Well, that's all I need here."

I rise, too. Must keep him away from the window at all costs. "Great. What's the first step in saving Wadley Farms?"

His eyes narrow as if he's smelled a rat. "You excited to get started? Quite the reversal from yesterday."

"Well, I had time to sleep on it," I lie. After Cristina went home I tossed and turned, burning up about the fact that Pane Maddox had arrived to save me. I don't need saving, as I've mentioned.

But the fact is, even if *I* don't need anyone, the farm does. The farm needs a big heaping dose of assistance if it's to remain in our family.

He crooks a brow. "Is that all? You just slept on it?"

He's fishing for some kind of epiphany—a deep truth sitting at the bottom of the ocean, just waiting to surface. "I slept on it and realized that I could have been"—it takes great effort for the words to come out—"nicer . . . to you."

I exhale. There. I said it. And being nice to Pane didn't kill me.

Yet. There could be a delayed effect.

He smirks. "Great. Now that we're on the same page, let's head into town. We need supplies."

Outside the window, there's now a 4Runner rumbling by with a sign that reads **LIFETIME MEMBER OF THE PANE MADDOX FAN CLUB!**

Wow. Just wow.

Where is Cristina? Oh, there she is! I spot her driving on the road's shoulder, honking her horn. The other cars chime in, until there's a cacophony of horns blaring outside the farm.

My body goes still as Pane frowns. "What's all that noise?"

Oh no. He can't look!

He starts to move toward the sound, but I grab his sleeve and tug him back. "Supplies? What else do we need?"

His gaze brushes my hand and lingers there for a moment before his eyes flick to mine. Whenever he places his whole focus on me, it feels like I'm shrinking, like I'm falling into a deep black hole. He sucks me in and I can't think.

I blink to shake off the feeling as he explains, "We also need man power. That's on the list." A truck honks loudly, and Pane's shoulders tighten. "Why are those cars honking?"

He begins turning again, but I pop up in front of his face, diverting his attention. "How do you plan to get this man power, exactly?"

"I'll tell you on the drive to town." The honking gets louder and he snaps, "What's going on outside?"

He starts to whip toward the window. He'll see the signs, the cars, and he'll be pissed—so pissed that he'll probably leave right here and now, and I'll lose my last shot at saving the place.

I can't endure that. There's no way to tell my mom that we had a miracle standing in the middle of our rooster-infested kitchen and I let it get away.

As Pane pivots, time seems to slow to an absolute stop. Outside, the green leaves on the trees shimmer and the scraggly grass seems to grow. The whole place inhales and whispers to me. Whispers for me to save it, to keep this land and this place that I love.

And it tells me how to stop Pane from seeing every car and truck that's rolling out the red carpet for him.

So as he turns, my arms reach out.

I should not be doing this. He will kill me for this. But it's a risk that must be taken.

I take the hotel heir by the shoulders and spin him around to face me. Then I grab him by the face, push myself up on my tiptoes, and kiss Pane Maddox.

Chapter 12

ROWE

He is for sure going to kill me.

But even though death is upon me, it's impossible not to notice that Pane's lips are soft, yet firm, as I press my mouth to his.

He's the last man I want to kiss—other than Luke. But desperate times and all that.

I keep my mouth glued to Pane's and venture opening one eye to check Cristina's progress. My bestie's getting the car line dismantled. Yay! Give it just a few more seconds, and the last folks will be moving on.

And I'll be able to disentangle myself.

But before that happens, Pane tears away from the kiss and rears back, chest heaving.

"What are you doing?" he demands.

Oh, crap. I'm in deep trouble now.

His eyes blaze with rage. His nostrils flare. His cheeks are streaked with red as he glowers at me.

Before I can come up with an answer, he rushes forward, cups the back of my head with one hand, and slides his other hand around my waist.

Then Pane Maddox lays one on me.

In other words, he kisses me back.

And what a kiss it is.

His lips are full and soft as they take me, prod me, devour me. My eyes flutter shut and I melt against him, forgetting for a moment that I'm kissing enemy number two.

He has obviously also forgotten our mutual dislike of one another, because his tongue slips past my teeth and tangles with my own.

Whoa. I am not expecting this.

He tastes like coffee and butter. This strange medley is suddenly my new favorite flavor combination. I can't get enough of it.

His hand on my waist drops to my hip and squeezes. Even through my clothes, the heat of his touch scalds my flesh, creating a fire that erupts in my core and floods every cell in my body.

I want to drown in him. Clearly, I've lost my mind, am definitely experiencing temporary insanity.

Worse, I'm . . . moaning!

I'm moaning into Pane Maddox's billionaire mouth and his fingers are hooking into the loops of my jeans. He tugs me to him so that my chest is flat against his. His stubble scrapes my skin, making my face tingle. My nipples are diamond-hard. My panties are soaked, and every nerve ending in my body screams with pleasure.

My knees are Jell-O, and when he deepens the kiss, I can't believe that it's even possible. This is bliss. Pure, absolute ecstasy. I haven't kissed anyone like this in, maybe—ever. Not even Luke.

Our tongues are in sync now, like it's a competition of who can deep throat the other person the best. Okay, that sounds kind of gross. Perhaps not an accurate description.

It's way better than I can describe. The air around me is charged with energy. The glass in the windows rattles. The floorboards jump.

Wait. Is the magic infused in the earth responding to our kiss?

There's no time to ponder, not when I'm deep in the best. Kiss. Ever.

I tangle my fingers in his silky hair and inhale his scent. Pane smells good—like juniper . . . and something else that I can't place and don't want to right now. It's bright and masculine. I could swim in his scent.

My mind goes numb as his hand slides up my side, getting dangerously close to the rim of my breast.

That's when my brain snaps back into place.

What am I doing? Am I really allowing myself to be felt up by some *rando* I met yesterday after a four-year dry spell? Have I lost my mind?

I jump back, breaking the kiss.

Pane's pupils are blown, and his eyes are overflowing with lust. Same as mine are, I'm sure.

He blinks, shakes his head as if surfacing from a trance. "W-what the—" he stammers, stepping back. "That was completely unprofess—"

"Thank you," I spew out. "For liking the biscuits. No one's ever liked my cooking so much, and I got carried away. Just felt the urge to kiss you. It's a thing we do here in Mystic Meadows." I continue to blab, coming up with a terrible lie. "We kiss people as thanks. Sometimes. Not all the time—and certainly not married people, unless it's on the cheek, and definitely not during flu season because that would be spreading germs."

"That was *you* thanking me for liking a biscuit?" He scrubs a hand down the stubble peppering his chin and takes a step into my space, towering over me like a beast. "What if *I* want to thank you for feeding me the most delicious meal I've ever tasted?"

The glint in his eyes is dangerous, and my brain screams at me to run and hide in a cave—a dark cave, with very little flickering light so that all I can see are shadows when Pane sneaks up on me, grabs me by the waist, and—

Stop fantasizing about the evil, grunty man.

I fold my arms. "Don't get used to it."

He chuckles bitterly. "Shouldn't that be the other way around? *You* shouldn't get used to kissing *me*. I get it. I'm the whole package—rich, successful, handsome. A lot of women have thrown themselves at me. You wouldn't be the first. In fact, you're not."

Why, this smug jerk. He thinks he's got some sort of power over me? That I just can't help myself? Oh, he is so, so wrong.

He shoots me a sympathetic look. "Let's not do this, okay? We both know you're in trouble financially, and I'm very good at spotting women who want to take advantage of me."

I scoff. "Are you calling me a gold digger?"

"We prefer the term *fortune hunter*."

Is he for real? Pane Maddox thinks I'm trying to use him for his money? I throw my head back and laugh. "Trust me, the last person I'm interested in is you. I'm sure where you come from, the only thing people value is your money and the social status that being linked to you will get them. But that's not how we do things here in Mystic Meadows. We judge people by their character. Money isn't the most important thing to us—or *me*, for that matter. So let's get that straight. I might be broke, but I'm not interested in you or your cash. You are the very last person on earth I would ever be with—rich or not. So you can put a pin in that inflated head of yours."

With that, I toss a glance toward the window. The line of cars is nowhere in sight. Neither is Cristina, for that matter.

Good. Because I don't want to be cramped in this house with Pane Maddox for one minute more.

I grab my purse and sling it over my shoulder. "Let's head into town and see if your *social status* can help my farm."

"By the way . . ." he adds as I'm halfway out the door.

"Yeah?" I halt, and the screen door whacks against my arm. "What?"

It takes him so long to talk that I glance over my shoulder to see him standing with his arms crossed, a smug smirk slapped across his face.

"Rule number four," he announces. "No kissing."

Chapter 13

PANE

Sunbeam kissed me for liking her biscuits?

Wonder how she'll thank me when I praise her pot roast.

Will clothing come off?

Stop it, Pane.

There will be no further thoughts of tongues, lips, or other body parts.

Because now I know who she is. The only reason a person kisses a man they just met is because they're either starved for love, or they're a social climber.

Rowe wants to use me. This is an old game. Her plan is to see if she can seduce me into handing over half my fortune. She'll play coy for two months until I'm tied up in knots over her. Then it won't matter if I save the farm, because in sixty days I'll be proposing. She'll have landed a prize much better than her home.

Me.

Well, it's not going to work.

My heart thuds against my ribs as I drive us into town. It hasn't stopped pounding since we left the house. It feels like my chest is too small for my heart, like it's going to pop right out of my rib cage.

Worse—with it comes all these strange feelings. Tangled and knotted desires that sink into my bones. Rowe's wildflower-and-sunshine scent permeates the truck's cabin, smothering me.

Thoughts of plucking flowers and giving them to her pop into my head.

What is wrong with me?

Must be the magic in the land or something, because I am not, I *will* not be taken in by a fortune hunter.

I won't be fooled again.

My fingers tighten on the steering wheel, and I shove all these strange emotions away and focus on the drive.

"Turn left up there," she says from the opposite side of the bench seat. Rowe's squeezed her body into the smallest pretzel possible as she sits pressed against the door.

She hasn't looked at me once since we got into the truck. I've returned the favor.

As we enter town, my gaze sweeps over Mystic Meadows, and I can say with complete certainty that I've never seen anything quite like this before.

It's as if a unicorn caught a violent stomach flu and *vomited* grimy rainbow sparkles over every building.

The facades—once white, I assume—are now streaked with years of neglect. Instead of the polished, gleaming surfaces I expect from a town that supposedly thrives on tourism, every inch is coated in a dull film of grime, as though dark ash has settled deep into the pores of the wood.

Swinging placards creak overhead, weathered by time and indifference: Mystic Sweets. The Enchanted Café. The Horned Hat Boutique. Most of the businesses cling to the unicorn theme, though their names do little to distract from the chipped paint and sagging awnings.

The central square is *technically* busy, though it has the energy of a party long past its prime. A few sluggish tourists drift near a massive unicorn statue, snapping pictures more out of obligation than excitement. The statue itself—rearing back on its hind legs, front hooves pawing the air—hasn't escaped the decay. Its once-shimmering surface has been dulled by time, its proud horn chipped at the tip.

I spot a billboard advertising **The Unicorn Water Park!**, complete with faded cartoon drawings of prancing unicorns. Another sign boasts **Unicorn Zip Lines!** And then there's **Unicorn Mountain!**

Mystic Meadows certainly knows how to commit to a theme.

We cross a wooden bridge, the tires of my truck rumbling over the worn planks. Below us, a creek snakes through the landscape, leading toward a waterfall in the distance.

I glance down, expecting to see glistening water.

Instead, I see sludge.

I do a double take. Surely I'm seeing this wrong.

But no—the water is a murky brown, thick and lifeless. Even the waterfall looks, for lack of a better word, *sad*. It doesn't cascade with the sparkling brilliance I'd imagine—it dribbles down the rocks like it's lost the will to fall.

And the worst part? There's a sign boasting **Inner Tube Rides! Fun for the Whole Family!**

I stare at it, incredulous. Who the hell would voluntarily sit in that mess?

Fingers drumming against the steering wheel, I exhale sharply. "*What* happened to this town?"

Rowe, who has been mindlessly scrolling on her phone, finally glances up.

"Interesting that you would ask."

"I doubt it."

She shoots me an unimpressed look. "Well, if you *must* know, the shops *have* been painted. They get a fresh coat every year. But within a few months, they all end up looking *like this* again."

I frown. "I *know* I'm going to regret asking this, but . . . why?"

She shrugs, stretching out her legs and crossing her ankles like she's about to deliver the world's most casual doomsday prophecy. "Because the town lost its magic. No one really knows *why*, exactly. Some folks think it's because the unicorns were overbred—Sally Ray's grandfather is the one they blame for that. According to my dad, Mystic Meadows didn't used to look like this. When the magic first appeared, everything sparkled—the water, the trees, the buildings. People came from all over to see it."

Her voice is matter-of-fact, but there's something almost wistful beneath it.

I glance down again at the sluggish, brown water beneath the bridge, my stomach twisting. "And now?"

She gestures vaguely at the dreary town around us. "Well . . . more unicorns kept being born. But with every generation, they had less magic. Until eventually . . . there was none left. And the town started fading."

I let that sink in. The whole town, its entire *existence*, was built around magic—real, undeniable, tangible magic. And when that magic started to wane, the town did, too.

We rumble over the last stretch of the bridge and into the heart of downtown.

"So you're saying the unicorns were overbred, their power got diluted, and that somehow caused the town to lose its sparkle?"

She tilts her head. "I mean . . . *maybe*. It's not like there's a scientific study on this." She huffs. "All I know is that unicorns aren't born with magic anymore. Not like they used to be."

I shift my grip on the wheel. "And I'm supposed to infer that this town is still desperately clinging to the *idea* of its magic, trying to keep tourism alive . . . but since the unicorns have lost their luster, no one's coming anymore?"

She meets my eyes. For the first time since Rowe got in the truck, she looks serious.

"Exactly. The world has forgotten about us. People in Atlanta don't even visit the way they used to, like when I was a kid. One thing led to the other. The magic died here—except for in a few places, like my farm—and because that magic died, people said the unicorns were nothing more than horses with horns sewn onto their heads. They said the same thing about my piggies."

A ripple of guilt hits me, because that was what I had thought, too. But Rowe, for as frustrating as she is, seems honest and forthright. "So not only is your offseason slow, but your busy season is slow, too."

"Right."

I nod, beginning to understand what I'm up against. This isn't just about one farm. It's about the entire town. "So those who do visit, what happens? They see a unicorn once and that's it? All the luster's worn off?"

"Pretty much. Once you've seen them, what else is there?"

"I don't know. I haven't seen one."

She frowns. "You haven't? What am I saying? Of course you haven't."

"It doesn't sound real," I murmur.

"What doesn't?"

I wave my hand in demonstration. "Magic being here. Unicorns. All of it. I mean, I know that I've seen what your plants can do. It's just a lot to take in."

She props her arm on the door and rests her temple on her fist. "Just because you can't hold magic in your hand—just because you can't *buy* it—that doesn't mean it doesn't exist."

"Oh, I could buy it."

She snorts. "You can't buy the magic in my land."

"People would pay a lot for it, especially since it appears to be the only magic around. At least, from what you're saying. And that's, *why*?"

"First of all, not selling," she snaps. "Secondly, I think the reason why my property still has some power is because the ley lines are so close by. And third, seeing a unicorn—a real one, one with power—is an experience."

I quirk a brow. "I thought you said they don't exist."

"There may be one or two left."

We reach a stoplight and I take the opportunity to turn to her. "How so? Tell me, Miss Wadley, how is seeing a unicorn an experience like no other?"

She thinks about this, tapping a finger against her phone as she figures out a way to explain it. "You know how piggycorns are just cute?"

"No, I don't." The light turns green, and I rip my gaze from her back to the windshield. "Explain this mystery."

Rowe shakes her head in annoyance. "They *are* cute. It's just that your cute button is broken."

I scowl. "My *cute* button?"

"Yeah, the button inside a person that makes you want to watch adorable animal videos and say things like, *Ah, that's so cute. Now I want a sugar glider.*"

"I don't have that."

"No kidding. Anyway, where piggycorns are cute, seeing a unicorn for the first time is mind-blowing, to put it mildly. There's something ethereal about looking into the eyes of such a mystical creature and wondering if you're worthy of it."

"*Worthy* of it?"

"Yeah, to stand in front of it and feel its power, or be healed if the creature thinks you're deserving. There are a few that can do that. But those are rare, and they don't just heal anyone—and before you ask, you can't take some of their DNA, spin it down, and extract the gift from them, either. In case you were thinking of doing that."

As if. "Why would I do that?"

"Obviously because you're rich and money corrupts."

This is news to me. "Money would make me want to map a unicorn's DNA?"

"Yes."

"Huh. I'm not only rich, I'm also an evil scientist."

"You see how this goes." Our gazes lock, and for a brief second a smile flickers on her lips before she turns it into a frown. "But anyway, that in a nutshell should answer your question about the tourists and why they fizzle out in the fall and are pretty lacking in the summer, too."

It did, and a plan begins to slowly form in my mind.

But first things first. I need supplies if we're going to make Wadley Farms a business that has a chance at surviving.

And that's what I'm concentrating on as we pull into a parking spot in front of Mystic Meadows Hardware.

"Do you want me to come inside?" Rowe squeaks as if she's hoping I'll forget she exists. "Need any help?"

I smirk. "No." My gaze drills into her. "I don't need any help."

She's not even looking up from her phone. "Let me know how it goes. Coleman Barrier can be kind of a human splinter, so watch out."

I lean in to her. She glances up, her eyes widen, and she sinks deeper into the valley between the seat and the door.

"Don't worry," I growl. "I can handle him."

"Great," she whispers, dropping her attention back to the lit screen. "I'm going to call my mom while you're inside."

My gaze falls to her mouth. It's so plump and glossy, like a waxed apple—perfect for biting into.

I rip my eyes away and they land on two men walking by. They spot Rowe, who sits oblivious in the passenger seat as these two Neanderthals ogle her, eye-fucking her at the same time.

I get out and slam the driver's-side door. The men glance at me, note the scowl on my face, and speed into the shop, their proverbial tails tucked between their legs.

That's right. Keep moving.

No one's allowed to eye-fuck Rowe except . . . except . . . I don't know who.

As I make my way down the street, there are clusters of locals outside, walking into stores. For as gray as the exterior of Mystic Meadows is, the people are drab, too. Their clothing is colorless—dingy whites and faded blacks, sorrowful slates and muted creams.

It's almost as if the decline of magic that Rowe told me about didn't just affect the town structures, but the people as well.

I tuck that info away and head inside the hardware shop. There, the men who leered at Rowe are nowhere to be seen, and a few folks browse the aisles. The store's nice. It's well lit, and a quick glance reveals that they sell everything from paint to camping equipment.

Just as I turn toward the tents, I hear them.

Voices—gruff, agitated, and just loud enough to snag my attention.

Up at the counter, three men stand with their arms crossed, their postures stiff with frustration. They're dressed like every contractor I've ever met: baseball caps pulled low, mud-stained jeans, and yellow construction boots that have seen their fair share of jobsites.

One of them, the clear ringleader, plants his hands on the counter and levels a glare at the man behind it. His voice is as sharp as a handsaw.

"I'm sick of this, Coleman. Every time I buy lumber from you, K-Yard advertises a better deal. Every time. Now, I like your lumber, but your prices are just too high."

"Yeah," mutters the man beside him.

"Damn straight," adds the third, his drawl thick with irritation.

Well, well, well. What's this I hear? A problem? A negotiation standoff?

This might just be the opportunity I need.

Behind the counter, Coleman Barrier—store owner and, as Rowe so lovingly put it, "human splinter"—stands like a stone pillar. His thick forearms are crossed defensively over his chest, his flannel shirt untucked, black-rimmed glasses perched on his nose. He doesn't budge, but his jaw tightens.

"Now, hold on," he says, voice steady but firm. "I give y'all the best deal I can. You know that, Chandler."

Chandler, clearly the man in charge of this contractor trio, snorts and slaps a sheet of paper onto the counter. "This is the deal K-Yard has running right now. If I do the math, going with them on my next job will save me thousands."

Coleman wipes a hand down his face, exhaling sharply. "I can't force y'all to do business with me."

"Oh, but you can," a voice calls from the back.

Heads turn as a woman peeks out from behind a shelf, one manicured hand braced on the edge. She wears a low-cut white blouse with ruffles at the sleeves, big hoop earrings swaying as she leans forward. Her hair is teased up high, and dark liner circles her sharp blue eyes.

"Hilary," Coleman warns.

She purses her lips like she's about to spit fire, but instead she just lifts a knowing brow and disappears behind the shelves again.

Chandler picks up the flyer and shakes it at Coleman. "If you can't match these prices, I'm walking."

The other two men grumble their agreement, shifting like they're already halfway out the door.

And that's when I step in.

"Now, hold on just a second."

The room freezes.

Coleman shoots me the pointiest who-the-hell-are-you look I've ever been thrown. Chandler and his men turn, sizing me up like I just strutted into a lion's den wearing meat-scented cologne.

"What?" Chandler says flatly.

I pluck the flyer from his hands and scan it. It only takes about three seconds to find what I'm looking for.

I flip it back around, tapping a finger at a line buried in the fine print. "You're being cheated."

Chandler blinks. "Excuse me?"

"This." I slide my finger under the text. "See this part? After the first fifty boards of lumber you buy at a discount, K-Yard hikes up the price. By a lot. They charge extra after that. You're getting lured in with a flashy deal, but the second you need more material, you're paying more than you would here."

Chandler snatches the flyer back, and the three men huddle over it, reading. The silence stretches as realization dawns.

Coleman's gaze snaps to me, sharp and suspicious. I flash him a wink.

Chandler exhales hard. "Well, hell."

"I told you last time that place wasn't all it's cracked up to be," one of the other men mutters.

I take the opportunity and push forward. "Look, you know the quality of lumber here is better. It's why you're still buying from Coleman in the first place. That means in the long run, you'll need less to get the job done. And if you place an order today, I'm sure Mr. Barrier will be willing to offer a small discount, plus a guarantee that your next lumber order will be in stock. Right?"

Coleman's eyes widen slightly, his mouth parting like I just hit him over the head with a two-by-four.

Chandler turns to him expectantly. "A small discount?"

Coleman clears his throat and nods, recovering quickly. "Yes. A small one. And guaranteed stock when you return. Absolutely."

Chandler rubs a hand down his stubbled jaw. "You got what I need today?"

Hilary pops her head out from behind the shelves again, a wide smirk on her lips. "Oh, we got it."

"Then let's do this." Chandler claps Coleman on the back and motions for the others to follow.

For the next fifteen minutes, I browse the store while Coleman handles the transaction. But I don't miss the way he keeps cutting glances at me, his expression unreadable.

It's only when Chandler and his crew are heading out the door that Chandler looks back at Coleman and jerks his chin toward me.

"I don't know who that new employee is," he says, "but you need to keep him."

As soon as the contractors are gone and the store's empty, the store owner comes out from behind the counter, crosses his arms, and scowls at me. "I'd like to know who this new employee is, too. Though I suppose I should thank you for saving those customers for me."

I extend my hand. "My name's Maddox. Pane Maddox."

After all, my mother didn't say that I had to keep my name a secret. She just told me that I'm a big nobody. That's me—Pane Maddox, big nobody.

"What's your angle, Maddox?" Coleman's gaze sweeps up and down me, pausing at my dress shoes. "You don't look to need a job."

"No, I don't need a job. I'd like to do some business with you."

He snaps to attention at that. He's practically got dollar signs in his eyes. Even his tone is softer. "What sort of business?"

"I'm fixing up a property here in town. This is the kind of project that, once it's completed, will bring attention to Mystic Meadows. Contractors like the ones who just left, along with investors, will sit up and pay attention. They'll want to build here. They'll want to invest in the future. They will see this town in a way that it's never been seen before. And the best part? They're all going to need supplies. That's where you come in."

"I'm listening," he says.

"So am I," parrots Hilary, who's come out from the back.

Coleman thumbs toward her. "My wife, Hilary."

I give her a nod. "Nice to meet you."

"What were you saying about building?" Coleman prods.

"Right. As soon as I've completed my project, you'll have orders coming out of your ears. But the thing is, right now I'm lean on funds." He frowns. I push on. "I'm looking for a line of credit. Now, you're taking a chance giving it to someone you don't know. I realize that. But for taking that big chance, you'll see an even greater reward. Imagine it, more business than you know what to do with—orders flooding in, and no one's talking to K-Yard. They're all dealing with you."

Hilary pokes him. "You need to listen to him, Coleman. I been wanting a trip to Paris. You been promising it to me. You can get the money and I can have my trip."

He studies his wife before focusing back on me. "And how are you going to do all this? Have you seen our town? Few visit Mystic Meadows anymore. Once the magic dried up, the whole town fell apart. Hell, I'm lucky to have the business that I have."

Here's where the Maddox determination floods through me. Even though I'm going out on a limb, I believe every word of what I'm about to say. I don't know how, but it's a feeling bubbling deep inside me.

"This town is going to come back, and the first property that's going to be part of this renaissance is the one I'm working on."

"And what property is that?"

"Wadley Farms."

There's a beat where Coleman looks at me and blinks. Then he tosses his head back and laughs. "That old place? That farm ain't worth two pennies. How are you going to make it anything?"

My chest constricts. He just insulted my business, and by doing so, he also insulted Rowe. "I don't appreciate being laughed at," I growl.

"I'm sorry, but there isn't hope for that property. You tell me that you're going to fix up the ice cream shop and I'd believe you, think maybe you'd be on to something. But the Wadleys'? Forget it." He turns his back to me and walks off. "Good luck, city boy."

No.

No way am I leaving without this man's partnership. I storm up to the front counter, which he and his wife are back behind, still laughing.

My next words are spoken around the gravel in my mouth. "What would it take for you to do business with me? To help me out?"

One side of Coleman's mouth ticks up into a smirk. "I'll tell you what it'll take."

Coleman points. "You see all those trees over there?"

"Yes, sir. I do."

We're out in a lumberyard behind the hardware store. One side is filled with treated and cut planks. The other is filled with uncut logs.

He points to the mess of haphazardly stacked logs. "I need those cedars cut into poles. We got a big order going to the off-grid yurt community that's just outside town. All my workers are busy on other projects. If you can get those cut, then we'll talk."

Why do I have the feeling this test isn't about whether or not I'm a successful person, but whether or not I'm a man?

"I'll be happy to cut them."

"You ever worked a chain saw before?"

Once, a long time ago. And it was only the one time. My uncle had us up at his cabin, and he was cutting away at a tree that had fallen.

That was also twenty years ago, and as much as I'd like to say that the hotel business requires regular maintenance with chain saws, it does not.

"I've, um . . ."

"Great," Coleman says, slapping me on the back. "Just make sure that you cut where the logs are marked, straight down the center. You'll find safety gear there." He points to a shed. "If you need anything, just give me a holler. Get to it, and let me know when you're done. Good luck, kid. May you be able to put your money where your mouth is."

Before I can say anything else, he disappears inside the store.

A chain saw. I've got to cut cedar posts with a chain saw. This is definitely a test of my manhood.

I flip back through my memories, trying to quickly recall everything my uncle taught me—keep your hand steady, watch for kickback, don't let the chain touch the dirt. That seems about it.

I rub my hands together. This is going to be a piece of cake.

Chapter 14

ROWE

"How are things going, honey?" Mom asks.

"Oh, pretty good." *I suppose, considering I've been accused of having the hots for the cockiest jerk ever.* "How was the concert last night?"

"It was great," she gushes. "There's one more tonight, and then we're heading north."

"How's Bill?"

She flashes the phone's camera to Bill, who's lying in a hammock he's hooked up between the camper and a tree. He's got an open book propped up on his legs.

He waves. "Morning, Rowe!"

"Morning!" I eagle-eye the colorful cover. It's clearly a thriller, so I tease him with, "Is that the latest Abby Jimenez romance you've got there?"

"What?"

"Never mind. Hey, don't let my mom boss you around too much."

He chuckles. "Oh, I let her do it just enough so that it's cute."

I can't fight the grin that takes over my face. "Well played, Bill. Well played."

"Honey," Mom says, "Clarice Sinclair called me this morning and said something about a man living at the house."

Wow. She waited all of two minutes before starting in on the gossip.

A deep divot creases the space between her brows. "What's going on?"

My stomach ties up in knots. How do I make this sound awesome and not insane? *Here goes nothing.* "Okay. So this is crazy, but bear with me."

I tell her everything—about us being cut off from the feedstore, about Pane. Everything but the kiss, that is.

Oh, *that kiss.*

It can't be pushed out of my mind fast enough, no matter how hard I try. I thought for sure he would bring it up in the truck, but he didn't say one word.

Not one.

I'm scared. I don't know if that's good or bad.

Bad, probably. He probably hated every second of it.

So why'd he break it off and then *launch* himself at me?

Instinct, obviously. When someone kisses you, of course you want to take it to the next level and tongue them.

Unless you're smooching family members.

But Mom must not sense any emotional turmoil in me, because all she says is "Honey, that's great! Is he nice? Do you think he can save us?"

"I don't know. He's talking to Coleman Barrier right now. But I'll keep you posted."

"Do we need to come home?"

In the background, Bill looks up from his thriller and frowns.

"No, Mom. I've got everything under control. Just enjoy yourself. I'll keep you posted."

She works her top teeth over her bottom lip. "If you're sure. I want to make certain that you're okay. If this Pane guy is bad news, I don't want him anywhere near you."

"It's totally fine. No worries."

"Okay." She sounds and looks unsure, but since I'm tossing out my thousand-watt grin, she has no choice but to keep on keeping on.

"Call if you need anything. It doesn't matter what time it is. Just pick up the phone."

"Will do. Love you." I toss out, "Love you, Bill!"

"Love you, Rowe!"

After hanging up, my phone's silent for about half a second before it screams to life. Cristina's video-calling.

I accept the call and see her gorgeous face, blond hair spilling over her shoulders. She's sitting in her car, in what appears to be the drive-thru lane of Creature Comforts Coffee.

Cristina leans into the camera, eyebrow lifted. "Rowe. What is going on?"

"What are you talking about?"

"First, I save you from the parade of cars in front of your house, which is my fault. So. *Apologies.* Next thing I know, Pane Maddox is about to work a chain saw at the hardware store."

"What?" The phone slips from my hand. I scramble to grab it before the device plops onto the floorboard. "What?" I screech again when I've got Cristina's face in view.

"Yes. It's all over the group chat."

"What group chat?"

She rolls her eyes. "The one that the old ladies have. You know, Clarice Sinclair started it so that she and her friends could dish about single men. They wrangled me in because I'm the only one who could set up the group."

"Why haven't you left?"

"Because." She sighs. "They ask for my opinions on the eligible bachelors who are of a certain age, if you know what I mean."

"And you've been keeping this from me?"

Her gaze drops. "It is my shame—and mine alone—to bear."

As hysterical as it is that Cristina is part of an older-woman group chat, the idea of Pane Maddox working a chain saw makes acid surge up the back of my throat.

He'll kill himself.

He's not even wearing the right shoes.

"Gotta go," I tell her.

"I'm coming, too. I want to see this."

Before there's a chance to tell Cristina not to head over, she hangs up and I'm throwing myself out of the truck.

That's when I spot it. To the side of the hardware store sits a wooden fence. Standing in front of the fence is what appears to be half the town.

Oh no.

Pane's going to kill me.

I slam the door and rush over, squeezing between Ron from the feedstore and Clarice Sinclair.

"'Bout time you showed up," she huffs. "The show's about to start."

I slip my sunglasses to the top of my head and zero in on Pane. He's positioned in the middle of the lumberyard wearing head-to-toe neon-orange safety gear, which includes leg chaps, a vest, a visor and helmet, and protective earmuffs that are pushed up above his ears, so they are literally offering no noise protection at the moment.

He's got all this on, plus his tight popover shirt and *polished dress shoes.*

Oh no. This looks so bad, like a-pretty-boy-city-slicker-attempting-to-mount-a-bull-at-a-rodeo bad.

In this moment, I sort of, *almost* forgive Pane for being such a jerk about the kiss—a kiss that he was into, by the way.

"What's this all about?" I ask, trying to bite back the fear that has a stranglehold on my throat and is threatening to squeeze all the air from my lungs.

Ron nods. "Apparently, Coleman told that man— What's his name?"

"Pane Maddox," Clarice and I say at the same time.

I shoot her a dark look. "No one's supposed to know he's here, Clarice."

She splays her arms and scans the audience. "Half the town's here. There's no keeping this secret any longer. He's good-looking. Rich, too." All four foot ten inches of Clarice Sinclair squints up at me. "You jumped him yet?"

About a dozen heads turn in our direction. I grit my teeth and grind out, "No, Clarice. For your information, there will be no jumping."

"You're missing out on a fine piece of ass."

"He does have a good ass," Ron concurs. "Not that I would jump it. I'm just saying—as one man admiring another's physique, it's nice."

"Good grief, Ron. I know you're married. You don't have to explain yourself to me."

On my other side, Clarice elbows me. "Scoot over, Rowe. I cain't see." I do as she says, and then she scans the street behind us. "And where is Cristina with my mocha?"

"Your mocha?"

"Yeah, I gotta have snacks for the show."

I roll my eyes. "The show," as she calls it, is gearing up. Pane makes his way over to a row of cedar logs. The branches have been sawed off, leaving only the long, straight trunks with their bull's-eye-red centers.

My throat shrivels to the size of a pea. Does Pane know how to use a chain saw? What if he cuts his leg off?

"Be right back."

I squeeze through the fence and speed walk toward him. Pane spots me and lowers the saw.

"Hey," I say brightly.

A quick glance at the crowd confirms they are watching this exchange with rapt attention. All they need is popcorn and 3D glasses to complete the experience.

Pane shoots me a bored look. "Yes?"

I grin, trying to look like this is no big deal, that I'm not freaked out about this entire, potentially lethal situation.

"What are you doing?" I say, still grinning so that the crowd doesn't suspect the peril.

He points to the logs. "About to use a chain saw."

Still grinning. "Do you know *how* to use one?"

He pats the air and replies with the arrogance I'd expect, "I'll be fine, Sunbeam. I've worked one of these before."

My smile dims. "Do you maybe want some pointers?"

"From whom?"

"From me. Would you like pointers from me?"

He chuckles. "No thanks. I'll be just fine."

I drag my bottom teeth over my top lip to tamp down how insulting it feels that he so easily dismissed me. "I can help you."

"I don't need your help." He moves away, showing me his back. Then he pauses, glances over his shoulder, and shoots me a pointed look. "Or your thanks."

Heat immediately flares on my skin. The nerve of him, bringing up that kiss right now.

"Fine," I snap. "Good luck. Don't cut off your leg."

I storm back across the yard, fists clenched to my sides, wolf whistles from the crowd filling the air.

I squeeze back between Clarice and Ron. Clarice eyes me carefully. "What'd you tell him, Rowe? You're as red as a beet."

"Nothing. I didn't tell him one single thing."

That man can cut his leg off for all I care.

"Have I missed anything?" Cristina asks, appearing with four coffees hugged by a cardboard holder.

"Nothing yet," Ron says.

"Here's your coffee, Clarice."

"Come to Mama," the older woman says, greedily taking the cup from my best friend.

"And one for you, Ron."

"Thank you."

I pause to stare accusingly at the woman who's been my bestie since fourth grade, when her family moved to town. "You stopped to grab coffee for everyone?"

"Well, no. I was already there, and when Clarice told me about it, I said I'd get her one."

"And then I overheard," Ron admits sheepishly. "And you know I just can't pass up a great cup along with good entertainment."

Screw me.

"Don't be jealous. Besides"—Cristina hands me a sleeve-wrapped cup—"I got one for you, too. I figured you'd need an extra-salted caramel mocha to deal with this."

She's not wrong. I take the mocha and sip it. It's basically flavored sugar swirling in what is probably coffee, but it tastes like chocolate and caramel.

I thank Cristina as Ron nods toward the lumberyard. "Looks like he's about to start."

All heads swivel to Pane. I hold my breath as he tugs the pull start. The machine glugs for a second before dying.

"He's gonna have to yank harder than that," Ron murmurs before sipping his coffee.

"Work those arms," Clarice yells.

Pane glances over, and even behind the visor, I see him frown.

"Put your earmuffs on!"

He awkwardly tugs down each side with one hand. Well, at least he took one suggestion from me. He then prepares to yank the pull start again.

Even though I'm pissed at him, I still cross my fingers. *Please let him get this*—for the sake of the farm, obviously.

After three attempts to start it, the chain saw finally sputters to life on the fourth pull.

Everyone cheers.

"I was afraid I was gonna have to go in there and help him," Ron mutters.

My face flares so hot that it feels like my skin's about to burn off. Right now Pane Maddox is an extension of me. If he fails, I'll never live this down.

"Maybe your bad luck's turning, Rowe," Clarice says brightly. "Let me know when he gets in your pants."

I. Just. Want. To. Die.

One good thing: Pane's positioned himself correctly. Thank God for that. I hold my breath, praying he doesn't sever an artery.

He approaches the first log and immediately lowers the saw. It cuts the wood, but once it's through, the saw kicks back.

I gasp as the bar, whirling teeth attached, jumps up, aiming straight for Pane's face. Just before the saw pierces his helmet, the chain brake activates and the engine dies.

I exhale. Oh, that was so close. Thank goodness for the chain brake. Otherwise, Pane would've sawed into that arrogant head of his.

After two tries, he gets the engine started again.

"This is more interesting than being at work," Ron yells over the sound of the motor. "You may have to get in there and help him, Rowe."

"Nope," I say tensely. "He's doing just fine."

Cristina's face scrunches in disbelief. "'Just fine'? He almost decapitated himself."

"Nah, it's got a safety," Clarice informs her. "He's doing good for a Yankee."

Cristina and I exchange a look. Technically, her parents are Yankees, and she didn't move to the South until she was ten. She still doesn't have much of an accent, but my friend has lived in town long enough that no one calls her a Yankee anymore.

At least not to her face.

"He's going in for the second cut," Ron announces.

Pane lowers the bar to the log, but he makes a mistake with his technique and I cringe, anticipating what happens next. The saw glides through the wood, but it stops halfway when the log pinches around the bar. Pane keeps the chain going, but it doesn't move.

He stops the chain saw and yanks the machine until it finally breaks free from the cedar.

"He's gonna keep having that problem," Clarice murmurs.

Pane gets the saw going again, but I can see the frustration on his face. My heart pings. I know how hard this is, and I also know how much is riding on his success.

Worse, a quick glance at Coleman Barrier, who's standing on the other side of the yard, tells me that he's enjoying this. He doesn't bother hiding the smirk plastered across his smug face.

The only thing that would make this situation nastier was if Sally Ray and Luke were here. One glance around the crowd tells me they're not.

Oops. I spoke too soon.

Luke enters the crowd. His eyes flick toward me, and my gaze darts away before he can see me looking at him.

The anticipation in the air is thick. Folks won't leave until Pane either succeeds or fails miserably, and no one will help him. They're too curious about the rich man doing everyday work. They want to see where this goes. Worse, from the looks on some of the people's faces, it appears they want him to fail.

That's just wrong.

I cross my fingers again, hoping Pane will succeed this time. Once the saw starts, he begins cutting, but the log, which is sitting on top of another one, shifts and closes in on the bar. The saw is pinched, and Pane kills the motor. But instead of pulling up, he wiggles the saw from side to side, bending the bar too far to the righ—

Snap.

There's a collective exhale among the crowd.

Oh, crap.

Pane just broke the chain saw.

Chapter 15

PANE

I am so screwed.

"Don't worry about it," Rowe tells me on the way back to the farm. "We'll figure out something else."

"There's nothing else to figure out," I snarl. "There isn't time to run around the countryside begging store owners for help. And on top of that, I made a fool of myself in front of the entire town." My head snaps in her direction. "How did they wind up there? Does word about newcomers travel that quickly?"

"You know, it must," she says, sounding mystified. "No clue how that happened."

Rowe looks out the window, avoiding me. She's lying, but I don't know why.

I'm too pissed off to care anyway. Dammit, I need the wood, paint, and hardware if I'm to have a fighting chance at winning this competition.

My stomach knots in anger. Un-fucking-believable. Stone probably has half of Boston eating hot dogs by now, and I'm still scrambling to get a plan together. *Thanks, Mom.* You wanted to challenge us—well, you've got your challenge.

Sunbeam glances back my way and says in a soothing voice, "Don't worry, Coleman yells at people all the time."

An image flares in my head, one of Coleman, arms in the air, glasses askew on his face, and spit flinging from his mouth as he screamed—*at me*—from the top of his lungs.

"Thank you for the reminder," I say, my voice sounding cold even to me. "That's a memory burned into my brain forever."

"I told you he could be something else."

"You didn't say that he'd be evil."

"Did he even *ask* if you could run a chain saw?"

"Yes."

"And what did you tell him?"

I pause. "That I could."

"Then you have no one to blame but you. You got yourself into this mess—"

"And I'm going to get myself out of it," I bite back. "Thank you for the useless platitude. You want to add more to it? Something like, *Whether it gets done today or tomorrow, it's got to get done*?"

From the other side of the truck, I feel her glaring at me. "What's your problem with sayings?"

"*Everything.* Nothing. Never mind. It doesn't concern you."

"Good. I'm glad it doesn't. I don't want anything that deals with you to concern me. But unfortunately"—she tosses out her arm—"you've shown up promising to help me, so I'm stuck with you."

We reach a stop sign and I slam on the brakes. "Trust me, I wouldn't be here if I didn't have to be. I don't want to be with you and all your"—I wave in her general direction—"*stuff.* You're nothing but a little sunbeam, and I'm not interested."

"Great! Neither am I!"

"Me neither."

A car behind me honks, and I gas the truck through the intersection. "I'm stuck with a dying farm and no prospects. On top of that, I get to sleep in a shamper with men staring at me."

"Don't you touch any of those posters."

"Don't worry, I won't. But maybe I'll take out my sexual frustrations on them."

Her jaw drops in horror. "You wouldn't dare."

"No, I wouldn't, because I don't swing that way. I'm just pissed off right now, and you're not helping."

I drive in silence for a few minutes, until Rowe meekly ventures, "What will you do now?"

"I don't know."

I swing the truck onto the farm's gravel drive. It tosses from side to side as we make our way to the front of the house. In the far yard, piggycorns race to greet us, kicking up their squatty hind legs in excitement.

There are maybe twenty of them, all white bodied, with golden horns that glisten in the sunlight and pink fur topping their heads. "Why are there so few pigs?"

"What?" she asks, facing me.

I throw the truck into park and kill the engine. I nod toward the swine. "Them. I thought pigs had huge litters. Why do you have so few?"

"I watch when a pig's in heat, and I separate her. No use in having too many if no one's buying. Besides, their feed's expensive."

"Huh," is all I can think to say.

I'm numb, my confidence shattered, my plan burned up, and all hope gone.

"You know," she says quietly, watching me closely with those soft brown eyes of hers, "if you're nice—and *only* if you're nice—I *can* show you how to work a chain saw."

"I'm not nice."

"I know that. But I do know how to work one. Not that I enjoy watching you eat crow. Oh, who am I kidding, of course I enjoy that." And then, as if it's a side note, she adds, "However, my dad taught me."

So Rowe *does* know how to use one—and I laughed in her face at her first offer to help me, an offer that would have saved me in front of this entire town.

The guilt I now feel rolls over my bubbling anger like a creek over rocks, extinguishing it.

There's a long, drawn-out moment before I quietly admit, "So you *can* run a chain saw? You? Sunbeam?"

She wrinkles her nose in distaste. "First off, I don't like that nickname. It doesn't sound genuine. Secondly, yes. My dad was a champion chain saw carver. There used to be competitions around here. He won ten years in a row."

This gets my attention. "Do you think that if I can go back to the store . . . ?"

"I don't know." She shrugs noncommittally, tipping her face toward me. But her brown eyes spark with possibility. "Coleman Barrier has a heart in him—and to be honest, what he had you do wasn't fair, and I think it may have been because . . ."

Rowe shoots me a look full of uncertainty, and I know what she's going to say. "Because he wanted to see what kind of man I am?"

"Yeah."

"My thought, too."

"Don't worry, we won't all make you jump through fiery circus hoops."

I give her a wry look. "You're not going to put the hoop over a pond of water filled with spiky objects and sharks?"

She tips her head back and laughs. "Look who's read *Matilda*."

The smile on her face makes my rib cage tighten. "Not only have I read it, but I've watched it." Her smile threatens to be infectious, so I tip my mouth down into a frown. "Too many times to count."

"Really? You don't strike me as the type to enjoy children's literature."

I glance out the windshield. "I read to my younger sister sometimes."

She's quiet now. Sunbeam must be shocked that I've got a sister, and that I'd do something as humane as help piggycorns cross a road *and* read a book to someone else.

She clears her throat. "I'm sorry about what happened. That Coleman Barrier put you through that."

"Some people just want to knock others down a notch."

"I don't think he meant it like that." She places a hand on my arm. She's warm, and an inferno flares to life on my skin, winding its way up my shoulder, threatening to overtake my chest.

I shift uncomfortably and she pulls back. "Like I said, I don't think that's how Coleman meant it. I do think that he wanted to test you, but I don't think he thought you'd be—"

"Humiliated?"

"Yes. But just so you know," she adds quickly, as if trying to soften the blow, "half those people literally have nothing to do all day, and most of them wanted you to win."

"And you?"

Why am I asking this? Obviously it doesn't matter if she wanted me to win. This is a business arrangement, and you don't have to like who you're in business with—you only have to tolerate them.

But there was something about seeing her out there, looking worried, that got under my skin. Maybe because it was unclear whether she was concerned for me or for her farm.

Not that it matters. Isn't this settled? She's a verified fortune hunter. End of story.

"Well, of course I wanted you to win." She says it to the window, like it's painful to admit. She gestures to the farm surrounding us. "Without you, we're . . . we're done."

Well, it's settled. She was worried about the farm. That pisses me off, too. Everything's pissing me off today—her being a social climber, the chain saw breaking. It's one big mess.

Rowe's gaze drifts from my drumming fingers up to my face. Color dots her cheeks, and she unstraps her seat belt.

"But I'm guessing," she tells me, "that if you show back up there, unfazed by Coleman firing you, and prove that you can cut those posts, he'll be impressed. Heck, the whole town will be." She tugs on the door handle and opens it slightly. "So what do you say? Will you let me teach you a thing or two about working a chain saw? Or are you going to pretend to know everything?"

I swipe a hand down my face in exhaustion. Seeing as how I've got a company to win, I may just have to be willing to take lessons from anyone I can.

"Sure. Why don't you show me a thing or two about chain saws?"

She slowly grins like this is a victory. "Great. I thought you'd never ask."

This is something I never thought I'd say—watching a woman work a chain saw is about the sexiest damn thing I've ever seen.

We're in Rowe's dad's shop, which is covered in vintage product signs—from Coke to Pepsi to Shell to Castrol. They're all neatly hanging on the walls, and most of them look brand new. They've been cared for, revered.

There is also just about every tool a man could need, as well as half a dozen chain saws.

I run a finger over the smooth surface of a Husqvarna. "These are your dad's?"

"*Were* his," she clarifies in a hard voice.

"He collected them."

She glances up from the smaller STIHL chain saw she's holding and says with surprise, "Yeah, he did. I never thought about it much, but yeah."

"I can appreciate a collector."

"Oh? Do you collect things?"

"Vintage Land Rovers," I tell her. "The older, the better. The rougher, the better. There's nothing like finding an old Discovery 1 series and rebuilding the engine."

Her jaw drops. "You can fix a truck?"

"I'm not just a pretty face," I growl. "I do have talents that don't include playing golf and investing money."

"And eating caviar," she tosses out sarcastically.

"And that." I glance up around the barn, noting the patchwork of different-colored wooden boards that line the ceiling and walls. There are shades of gray, brown, and tan, all lined up on top and beside one another, creating a symphony for the eyes. "This is a nice space."

She shrugs. "Yeah, I guess."

The nonchalance in her stance doesn't hide the pain in her voice. A moment later, she shyly glances at a tall blue-enameled tool cabinet with longing and sadness.

"You don't come out here much, do you?"

"Not really. My mom does, though."

I walk my fingers over a table and approach her. Rowe's gaze darts up to meet mine before it flutters back down to the chain saw in front of her. She takes a cloth and dusts the top.

"Why don't *you* spend time here?"

She keeps her eyes on the saw. "I don't know. It's too hard, I guess." She looks up into the rafters and around at the signs. "Some people want to visit where their loved ones spent all their time. Me? I just like to wear my dad's old boots. Being in here reminds me that he's really gone, that I'm actually on my own."

I work my jaw at the realization that her dad's deceased, and her parents aren't simply divorced like mine. "I'm sorry for your loss."

"It's okay."

The sadness in her voice rocks me to my knees. My heart cracks in two, and in this moment, I feel closer to her than I expected after what happened this morning. I also sense that she doesn't want to keep talking about her dad.

So that's why I whisper, "Why'd you kiss me? Really? It wasn't about biscuits."

Her eyes are glassy, about to spill with tears. She blinks and sighs. "Why'd you kiss *me*?"

Well played. "You first."

Sunbeam grimaces. "Promise you won't kill me?"

"Kill you? No. But I might spank you."

Her eyes bulge.

I round the counter and come to stand directly in front of her. The energy between us buzzes. Outside, the wind picks up and branches smack against the roof.

She tips her face up to study me, obviously hoping I'll keep my promise to lightly punish her.

Just kidding.

Maybe not.

"It got out about who you are," Sunbeam explains. "It wasn't my fault. Cristina posted it on social media before you told me not to reveal your identity."

"Ah." Now it all makes sense. "That's why I had an audience at the hardware store."

"That's why."

I frown. "But that still doesn't explain the kiss."

She grimaces. "This morning there was a line of cars going up and down the road. People were holding signs out of their windows welcoming you."

A laugh rips from my throat. "Really? So that's why you kissed me? So that I wouldn't see?"

She swallows loudly. "That's why. You told me the whole thing about losing."

"Yeah, as long as the press doesn't show up, we'll be fine."

From my angle, this small firecracker of a woman looks so fragile, so in need of protection. Though I should be angry that my identity got out, I can't be.

It's impossible to be frustrated when my chest is squeezing my heart like I'm about to suffer from cardiac arrest.

The wind blows in through the open door, and it pushes me toward her. She edges forward at the same time, as if she's also being manipulated by the elements.

Rowe licks her lips, and my gaze drops to her mouth. "So why'd you kiss me again?"

I tap the chain saw with my fingers. "I think it's time I learned how to use this properly, don't you?"

"Are you avoiding the question?"

"Pretty sure I've already answered it."

"No, you haven't. So why'd you do it?"

Because in that moment, all I wanted was to lay my mouth on yours and taste you again? Because I felt the need to own you? Because you wind me up and knock me down in a way that I haven't experienced?

"I don't know," is all I say.

She cocks her head and studies me as if learning my face. "Okay," she says huskily, moving on. "Let me show you chain saw basics. Grab that Husqvarna."

The tension between us breaks, and my brain snaps back into working mode. For the next few moments, Rowe teaches me correct chain saw posture. Then we move outside, where there's a small tree. "You're going to cut that down, and I'm going to talk you through it."

Sunbeam instructs me on how to fell a tree like an expert, cool and calm, correcting me every step of the way.

It's sexy as hell.

On top of that, she's wearing a white jean skirt and cowboy boots. My God, who thought a woman in a visor and earmuffs, wearing a skirt and walking me through the correct way to use a chain saw, would be *hot*?

And when she puts a hand on my arm, silently asking me to pause, my cock just about bursts through my jeans.

Once the tree's down, she shows me how to cut it so that the bar doesn't get pinched, and as she closes in, her scent fills my nose. It's light, feminine, and uniquely hers.

She instructs me to make circular cuts around the log instead of pushing straight down. Otherwise, the bar that the saw is wound around will get caught. If the tree's flat on the ground, then I can slice through it. In that position, the wood won't collapse around the bar when I'm cutting, thus pinching the saw.

Simple. Easy.

And Rowe . . . she's so patient. There's no judging, and she's lost her snark. She's a calm presence as she guides me, never once getting frustrated or treating me as if my money makes me useless.

And for the first time today, I'm not *feeling* like a useless rich guy whose only talents lie in managing people and money, seeing someone's weakness and figuring out how to turn that into their strength.

I'm being useful in a real and existing way. If a tree fell in front of Rowe's house, now I could cut it up and move it myself. I wouldn't have to wait for anyone.

This moment brings back memories of my childhood. It reminds of the summer I spent with my uncle, when he taught me how to use a chain saw. My brother and I stayed in his cabin, and it was the first time in years that I'd felt loved by someone, that someone told me they were grateful that I existed.

I'd felt love and it had warmed my heart.

Now my heart's doing strange things again, thumping and pulsing every time Rowe smiles at me or whips her hair over her shoulder.

Maybe it's early signs of that heart attack I mentioned earlier.

I clench and unclench my left hand. Everything feels good and seems to be in working order.

After an hour, Rowe pulls off her safety goggles and grins—*really* grins—at me. My stomach coils as she tips her shining, girl-next-door face up at me and says, "You did great! I think you're ready."

I turn off the chain saw and rest it on the ground. My arms and back ache from the labor, but it's a good pain—the kind filled with a sense of accomplishment.

She slips a pair of work gloves off her hands. "I don't know about you, but I could use some lunch. What do you say?"

I hoist the saw off the ground. "I'm starving. After lunch, let's see if I can win us some supplies."

Her gaze darts to my feet. "But before that, you need a pair of boots . . . And I know just where to find them."

Chapter 16

ROWE

Pane's wearing my dad's old boots. They fit him like a glove. Well, at least that's what he says. But personally, from the way his voice sounded pinched when he told me, I'm pretty sure they're too small.

Too big on me and too tight on him. Those boots only fit one man, and he's gone.

But there's no time to dwell on the past, because Pane's standing in the lumberyard of Mystic Meadows Hardware, geared up and ready to saw.

Again.

My heart's thundering. The entire town's back, holding their collective breath in anticipation. Even Coleman Barrier's watching the spectacle from start to finish.

I cross my fingers, praying that Pane knocks this out of the park.

He takes up position, grabs the chain saw's pull start, and yanks it hard. My heart leaps into my throat.

Please let it fire up on the first try.

It does.

The chain saw rumbles to life. Clarice Sinclair elbows me in the arm. "He's off to a good start."

Don't ask me how these people organize so quickly. But however they spread messages—group chat, carrier pigeon—whatever it is, it works.

Cristina is the one person who isn't here, though. She had errands to run. But she made me promise to keep her posted on Pane's progress.

Speaking of which, he moves to cut the first log. The hairs on the back of my neck prickle to attention. It takes a minute to realize my physical response isn't from nerves. It feels like someone's watching me. I snap my head to the right and stiffen.

Luke's here, and he's got Sally Ray beside him. He sees *me* see *him*, and his gaze zooms away, back to Pane.

"What're they doing here?" Clarice sneers.

"Whole town showed up. I'm sure they heard about him through the grapevine," I grumble.

But it does tick me off that Luke's hovering about like a mosquito, just waiting to stick his little needle mouth into my farm and suck it dry.

"There he goes," Clarice says.

Ron, who's on my other side, edges closer to me.

"What are you doing?" I ask.

"Trying to make sure Sally Ray don't see me. If she knows I left the feedstore for this, she'll have my ass."

"It's not like anyone's gonna be buying feed right now anyway," Clarice tells him. "Not when we got entertainment like this in front of us—strapping young man about to cut some logs." She pumps her brows. "If you know what I mean."

That may have been the grossest sexual innuendo I've ever heard. "I don't know what you mean, Clarice—oh, here he goes."

Pane's chain saw slices through the first log like it's a hot knife sliding through butter. A dinner knife, to be exact.

He does the same with the second log. But the third one is tilted, and I hope he remembers what I told him about pinching.

But Pane must be feeling invincible, because he begins to saw straight down.

The bar's going to get pinched, I just know it. Please, please, I don't want Pane to snap another chain saw, and I don't want to witness Coleman Barrier flipping out again.

There will be no third chance if that happens.

He lowers the blade, and for a moment it stops moving. But then, behind Pane, another log lifts slightly, raising the cedar he's cutting through and releasing the stress on the chain saw.

Holy cow. The magic in the land just saved Pane Maddox's butt. Wait . . . *the magic in the land* isn't here. It doesn't exist *here* anymore.

What is going on? How did that happen?

Before there's time to question what I just saw (perhaps it was my mind playing tricks on me?) the chain saw cuts all the way through the log, and I exhale, relieved. I glance over at Luke, who's scowling. If nothing else good happens today, just seeing him annoyed that I'm winning, that I may have a shot at keeping the farm, is enough to boost my spirits.

Twenty minutes in, and half the logs are cut.

Forty minutes in, and Pane kills the saw, every log now a cedar post.

I'm biting my lower lip, I'm so nervous. Surely Coleman Barrier has to see how awesome this is, that Pane is deserving.

"Wonder what Coleman's gonna make him do now?" Clarice says. "Swing from a tree?"

"Don't joke," Ron tells her, his tone serious. "I've seen him put new employees through a rigorous physical workout that included monkey bars."

"He's going to give him what we need," I murmur. "He will."

"Long as that Rowe Wadley bad luck doesn't set in," I hear someone in the crowd say.

Pane yanks the helmet off his head, and his eyes instantly latch on to mine. I smile and give him a double thumbs-up.

I must be losing my mind to congratulate such a pain in my butt.

He begins stalking forward, his gaze zeroed in on me, and it feels like the world's shrinking, like Pane Maddox is the only person who exists. He's even shut out thoughts of all my cute little piggycorns. Really, when they lick your feet it's the best. Feeling. Ever.

Pane's smiling now, *really* smiling, and I don't think I've ever seen a man look so handsome. His eyes sparkle with joy. His lips are spread wide, revealing those perfect teeth.

He's almost to the fence when Coleman steps out. "Finished, huh?" he says, all burly and manly, like he doesn't take crap from nobody. "Let me have a look."

"Yes, sir," Pane says as Coleman sweeps past him and inspects his work, one painstaking log at a time.

The crowd remains quiet. All of us watch in anticipation as the hardware store owner's gaze brushes up and down the logs in search of any nitpicky thing he can use to prove that Pane doesn't deserve praise.

Even from this distance, it's obvious the hotel magnate has done a fantastic job, one to be proud of.

When Coleman's finished inspecting, he makes his way back to where Pane's been standing quietly. He's taken off his gear and piled it up beside him. Now he's just in his jeans, a tight shirt, and my dad's boots.

"Well? What do you think?" he asks.

Coleman slides a hand down his face in thought. "You did a pretty good job."

"I cut on every mark."

"Sure did. It almost makes up for the bar you broke."

"Well, sometimes you must destroy in order to create. What I'm trying to do here in Mystic Meadows is new. Like I told you before, the project I'm working on will attract investors to the area."

"How can you be sure?" Coleman taps his fingers on his belt impatiently. "That farm out there's a mess. People pass by the Wadleys' and head right on to Sally Ray's because it's nicer."

Everyone in the crowd looks at me. My cheeks burn from shame. It's one thing to *know* my farm's a mess. It's another to hear it from a local.

"Don't you listen to him," Clarice whispers. "He's just a mean old coot whose wife only screws him when she wants something."

I bite back a laugh. The thing is, Clarice is probably right. She knows a lot *about a lot* in this town. I give her shoulder a friendly squeeze in thanks.

I feel eyes on me and look over to see Luke staring and scowling. Oh, does this not play into his plans to steal my life? How unfortunate for him.

Pane nods to Coleman. "My vision is to change the public's perception of not only the Wadley Farm but also this town. To do that, I'll need supplies, and a lot of them."

Coleman shifts his weight. "And you're lean on cash," he says, his voice dripping with sarcasm. "So how am I supposed to get paid? You don't have money. As far as I'm concerned, maybe I'll pay you for half a day's work and that's it."

The entire crowd gasps. Except for Sally and Luke, that is. From their direction, the sound of snickering wafts through the air. They think they've won.

And from the satisfied smirk on Coleman's face, it appears they have.

Even though I believed in the billionaire, what he needs seems as flimsy as paper in the face of reality. How can he ask Coleman for supplies when he literally has nothing to offer other than his name—one he's trying to keep a secret? Even if Coleman knows who he is, people around here don't care about the clout of a name. It's what's inside you that matters.

Pane slowly nods, and when he speaks, we all watch with bated breath, leaning in to catch every word.

"Mystic Meadows is less than two hours from Atlanta. My vision for the Wadley Farm will have everyone in the city clambering to come here, to fill every bed-and-breakfast in the area. They won't be staying for the day. They'll be coming for the weekend. To house all of those people, hotels will need to go up. Contractors will need lumber. Mystic Meadows Hardware will supply that."

There's a definite shift in Coleman. He's listening with interest, but his body's still stiff with disbelief. He shakes his head. "And what can *possibilities* do? What does all that conjecture and fantasy have to do with me?"

Pane smiles confidently. "When I'm finished, my phone will be ringing off the hook. I have friends in this business."

He places both hands on his hips. "Why don't you get them to help you?"

I cringe. Coleman has Pane. What will he say?

But the billionaire doesn't miss a beat. "What I'm doing here needs to stay quiet until it's ready. But I have a lot of connections, wealthy men and women whose expertise is in development will be calling, wanting a point man. That point man will be you." He shrugs. "If you want the job, that is. But if you don't think it'll be worth it, then I'll keep looking until I find a hardware store owner who *is* willing to take a small risk up front in order to reap benefits that will last . . . *years*."

My jaw is on the ground from watching Pane suavely outmaneuver the arrogant Coleman Barrier. It's funny—Coleman walked up thinking he held all the cards, but Pane has quickly shown that he possesses the power in this dynamic, and even Coleman seems to feel it.

The owner of Mystic Meadows Hardware sees the carrot Pane's dangling in front of him, and he seems to want to take the bait, but his pride stops him.

He sinks back on his hip and shakes his head once more. "I need more than that."

"What do you mean, you need more than that?" Hilary shouts. She runs up and grabs Coleman by the sleeve. "The man just said that you'll be rich and famous! What more do you want?"

"Dammit, woman, I'm trying to negotiate here."

Hilary points to Pane. "He's done all the negotiatin'. What else you expecting?"

Yeah? What else is he expecting?

But Pane, who hasn't even broken a sweat through this whole thing, leans in to Hilary and whispers something only she and Coleman can hear.

"Really?" she says to Pane, excitement filling her voice.

He nods. "Really."

Half a beat later, she throws her arms up and yells loud enough for all downtown to hear, "You've got a deal!"

Chapter 17

ROWE

As soon as Pane shook hands with Coleman, everyone cheered. Folks surrounded the billionaire, congratulating him before dragging him down the street to celebrate.

Which means we're currently at Sparkle Bar, a local watering hole on the far end of downtown that specializes in craft brews.

Right now, Pane's sitting at a table with Coleman, I assume going over the details of what he needs for the farm. He and the store owner are nose to nose, with a piece of paper situated between them. Every few minutes, Pane scribbles something on it and Coleman nods or shakes his head, making adjustments.

"So what did he whisper to you?" I ask Hilary.

Hilary snatches a handful of roasted peanuts from a bowl and shells them, tossing the waste over her shoulder. The floor is littered with shell casings, and more than once I've seen Pane glance at the debris with distaste etched across his face.

Yeah, this place is for sure lowbrow compared to what he's used to.

It's fascinating to watch this man who'd never eaten a biscuit see what the real world is like. Yes, there are peanut shells on the floor in a small-town bar. If he waits long enough, maybe he'll witness someone drinking a beer from an actual bottle instead of a frosted glass.

Hilary smacks loudly. "What did *who* say?"

"Pane, when he whispered to you. What made you take his offer?"

"Oh, that." She waves at me to come closer. Her eyes are hooded. Hilary needs more than a handful of peanuts to soak up the shots she's done. She leans toward my ear and drops her voice to a whisper. "He said that we have a free place to stay in Paris. He's going to put us up at some hotel, a place called the Maddox." She pauses, scrunches up her face in thought. "Didn't he say that was his last name?"

"I don't think so," I lie.

She shrugs. "Anyway, he said we could stay ten whole days. Can you imagine? I don't know how he's gonna pay for it, but for some reason, I believe that guy."

Oh, I know how he's going to pay for it.

Hilary leans in, and the stench of beer fills my nostrils. "He also said that we could take advantage of the spa. I plan to." She grips my arm, the alcohol making her body sway before she straightens. "Do you know about this place, the Maddox Hotel?"

For some reason, my stomach clenches with guilt. "No, I can't say that I do."

Why should I feel bad? The man showed up at my house yesterday. Cristina's the one who vetted him. Why should I look into his life filled with luxury hotels when he won't be here in a few weeks?

Besides, the only reason I helped him today was to save the farm. I'd sworn to never touch those chain saws unless absolutely necessary. Keeping my dad's shop in good condition means something to me.

And I never *thought*—scratch that, *never believed* I'd let a stranger use one, *plus* show him how to work it.

But Pane needed help, and so does the farm. So I did.

The surprising thing was that he didn't act like an arrogant brat when I showed him how to work the saw. He listened and was respectful.

It did, I admit, throw me for a loop.

Pane glances up and sees me staring at him. My cheeks flush hot, and I look away.

I don't know why I was looking at him. Our lives exist on two different planes. Planes that don't intersect. They won't ever converge, and the only reason why they're sliding up to each other right now, for this brief period, is because he's trying to become head of his company.

In a few weeks he'll be gone, and I'll still be here.

Hilary continues, snapping me from my thoughts. "You should look up that hotel. There's more than one, even, and all of them have spas. Not only that, but they give you those waffle robes to wear in your room—for free! There's room service, of course—and the menus. Oh my gosh. They have the most amazing restaurants, many of them Michelin starred. There are also golf courses. I don't play golf, but apparently they're award winning. Like I said, I have no idea how he's going to pay for it, but his shoes are nice, so I figure he'll be good for it. Either that, or Coleman'll have his kneecaps broken."

Well, that's one way to make sure you get what you want.

Then Hilary slumps into my arm and laughs. "I'm just kidding. Coleman wouldn't do that."

"Oh, that's good to know."

As my gaze drifts over to Pane again, it hits me—he hasn't talked about the hotels. I mean, he introduced himself as being part of the Maddox Group. Otherwise, I would've thought he was some sort of crazy person and I wouldn't have listened to him. Of course, he *mentioned* his family's business but Pane never went into specifics.

He never bragged.

He also didn't boast when he told me about his usual breakfast. It was simply put. I'm the one who jumped to conclusions about the snobby caviar and elevated his daily meals above mine.

Pane didn't.

Besides, he loved the biscuits. Devoured them. He didn't look down his nose at them.

It was for all of those things—the biscuits, the failure with Coleman, the need to save the farm—that I took him to my dad's shop and helped him.

I dare to sneak another glance at Pane and watch as he pushes back his chair and stands, shaking Coleman's hand. His shoulders strain against the rugged shirt he's wearing. The cotton hugs his broad shoulders and defined pecs. I'm sure plenty of women are ogling him behind their beer bottles.

Pane glances up, spots me, and heads in my direction.

Those knee-quaking sage eyes of his make my stomach flutter.

Wait. No, they're not.

That's the alcohol that I've downed. I haven't eaten in hours, and that's why my stomach's currently engaged in a double Dutch jump rope contest.

Though all that's true, I find myself being drawn to Pane. Something about him pulls me in.

After excusing myself from Hilary, I drift toward him as he does the same, our gazes never straying from one another.

That kiss jumps into my head, and it's impossible not to stare at his lips. They're thick and luscious, looking like they ache to be smooched again.

What is wrong with me? Some guy cuts some logs, and I'm suddenly unable to think straight?

Apparently so, because I'm still inching toward him like he's a magnet.

When we're only a few feet apart, Cristina jumps in front of me. "Hey, I heard about the log-cutting. You should have called me. I would've given anything to see Coleman Barrier taken down a notch."

My gaze flicks to Pane, but he's already got company. Ron's peppering him with questions, and Pane listens intently, arms folded.

I give Cristina my undivided attention. "Yeah, it was quite the spectacle."

"How'd he learn to work a chain saw so fast?"

When I don't answer, her jaw drops. "No! You showed him? On one of your dad's? I thought you said that you'd never—"

"I know what I said," I say tensely. "But he needed help, and we've got to have the supplies. I don't know what for, other than slapping a coat of paint on the house and fixing the farm, but we need them."

She eyes my nearly empty glass. "Want another?"

"No, I'm okay for now."

Cristina glances around the room. "Where is Pane?"

"Behind you."

My best friend discreetly glances over her shoulder, looks him up and down, and then turns to me. "If you don't hit that, Rowe, I'll never forgive you. I mean, what man can make a popover shirt look sexy? I didn't think that was possible."

"Me neither."

She grabs my arm. "Come on. Let's sit at the bar."

As she drags me to the bar top, I toss one last glance at Pane, who's still in conversation with Ron.

One gin and tonic later, and Cristina's deep in her cups. "All I'm saying, Rowe, is that it's a tough dating pool out there, and you've got to look past Mystic Meadows."

"I know. You're right."

She runs a finger over the rim of her glass. "You can't let one breakup ruin all men for you. You just can't—even though what Luke did is shameless. And I'm not just talking about the cheating." She shoots me a pointed look before her phone beeps. Cristina glances down at it, sighs, and looks up at me.

"Anything good?"

"No, just Jace's mom asking me when I'm going to take back her son. The woman won't give up." She cringes. "I picked up the last of my things from his place a few days ago. Did I tell you that?"

I frown. "No, you didn't. I would've gone with you to get them."

She waves me away. "It's fine. Totally fine. He was really nice and I was really nice. There wasn't any drama." She picks up her glass and shakes it, clinking the ice together. "I'm hungry. I'm going to head next door for an empanada. You want one, or three?"

"Not now. Maybe later."

Cristina slides off the barstool. "I'll be over there. Or I might bring it back here and eat." She lifts her glass. "Can I get a to-go cup?"

Isaac, the bartender, approaches. His long, dark braids land in the middle of his back, and his earrings are black-rimmed gauges. He flashes a wide smile—a set of perfect ivory teeth against deep brown skin.

"Cristina, you're not going to get in your car, are you?" he asks, grabbing a Styrofoam cup.

"No, no. I'm just going to Gloria's to grab something to eat. You want something?"

"Oh yeah, will you grab me a Cuban sandwich?"

She mock-gasps. "Not an empanada?"

"Not tonight."

"Sure." He pours iced tea from a pitcher into the cup and pushes it toward her. "You know we don't do alcohol to go," he reminds her gently.

She pouts. "I know. But I was hoping." Cristina raises the cup and takes a long sip, ending with a satisfied smack of her lips. "This will do. Be right back."

As soon as she's gone, my attention falls to my empty water glass, which Isaac swiftly removes.

"What're you having?" comes a husky voice to my right.

My stomach does an entire gymnastics floor routine before I manage to calm it down with, "Whiskey sour."

Two of the most masculine fingers that I've recently found myself obsessed with lift. "Whiskey sour and a scotch, neat."

Isaac nods and begins making the drinks as Pane sits. He smells musky, of scents that I can't place but want to devour. I inhale to drink in more of him, then look up.

His gaze is unapologetically leveled on me. A shiver shoots down my spine, and my eyes dart away to lock on anything besides his.

"Congratulations," I murmur.

Isaac sets our drinks in front of us. Pane lifts his to me. "I couldn't have done it without you. To us."

I smile as we clink glasses. "To us." Movement to my right catches my attention, and I watch as Coleman Barrier escorts a very tipsy Hilary from the bar. "So. Did you get everything squared away with Coleman?"

Pane sips his scotch, watching as the couple exits the bar. "Even after all that, he still tried to weasel out of a few things. But I got him. We'll have everything we need. Plus a new set of boots for me."

That makes me laugh. "You need them, if you're going to be working construction."

He rests an elbow on the table and leans a cheek on his fist. It is literally the most relaxed position I've yet to see him in. "About that. I have an idea for the farm."

"Oh?"

"Yeah. We make it a spa."

I choke on the whiskey sour, sputtering.

Pane sits up and rubs my back in slow, luxurious circles. "You okay?"

His concern is disconcerting. "Yeah, I'm fine," I tell him, waving off his worry and his hand from my back. "For a moment there I thought you wanted to turn my farm into a spa."

"I do."

My jaw falls. "Are you out of your mind?"

He sips his drink and frowns. "Not last I looked. However, I did learn how to use a chain saw today from a woman who owns a piggycorn farm. She was also wearing a jean skirt, I might add."

Pane's gaze drops to my legs, and he unabashedly studies my thighs.

My neck flushes with heat. "Whoever this mystery woman is, she must be very accomplished to use heavy equipment in such fashionable clothes."

"Apparently, she's much more accomplished than I thought."

He watches me, and my throat shrivels. I manage to squeak out an, "Ah, I see," while ignoring the Tilt-A-Whirl my stomach is currently riding.

I take a second and allow my gaze to drift around the bar. I've been in Sparkle Bar maybe a hundred times, but for the first time, I'm seeing it with new eyes.

The faded outer exterior has seeped inside. The whole bar looks worn, tired—like a seventy-year-old barfly who can't seem to pull herself away from the sticky countertop. It's not just the peanut shells on the floor. It's more than that. It's an ambience that pervades every nook and cranny. Even if the bar top was polished to gleaming, it would still have a dull coat on it, like all the chairs, tables, walls, and doors do.

It's like there's a layer of sadness dusting all of Mystic Meadows.

How have I not seen this until now? It's like I've had scales on my eyes and now they've fallen away.

Pane knocks his knuckles on the bar top, bringing us back on topic. "There's nothing enticing people to Mystic Meadows this time of year—other than the fall leaves, that is—and there should be. Atlanta's two hours away. We need to tap into that market, convince people that Mystic Meadows is the retreat they've been searching for. They can pet piggycorns and relax in luxury."

"But this is a family destination."

He lifts a finger. "But it could also be a girls' weekend."

I ease back and eye him suspiciously. "Who are you?"

"Your knight in shining armor."

The words hit me hard because he looks like a knight—sexy, a pouty mouth, a bit of stubble. Rugged but refined.

Yet I don't need saving. Okay, maybe I do. To clarify, the *farm* does. Not me. "How are you going to turn the farmhouse into a spa?"

"Here. I did this to one of our hotels, focusing on a luxury-spa experience."

He pulls out his phone and taps a few buttons, and seconds later, I'm watching a virtual tour of a signature Maddox Hotel, living the experience as two immaculately dressed men in crisp red coats with gold buttons open elaborate, gilded glass doors that lead into a marble-lined grand entrance with smiling attendants. I'm given a tour of suites accessorized in rich navy and silver, and finally I'm shown the spa—which is sleek, minimalistic, gorgeous, and finished in pale jade stone.

Oh my gosh. This is where the man comes from? I'm *so* out of my league.

While I'm mesmerized by the tour, Pane goes over details, walking over the layout of the house and what he can do. After watching the video and listening to him, I admit his plan is pretty mind-blowing. And also terrifying.

"What if it doesn't work?"

"What if it does?" he counters. "You have a spa during the day, and at night people can walk through the mystic gardens."

I frown. "Mystic gardens?"

"Your backyard. The way the grass lights up. There, customers will be enchanted by the piggycorns. They'll also get to relax with a massage and a facial during the day."

"Where am I going to live?"

"Upstairs. The spa will take up the bottom of the house."

"And you think that you can get the place booked?"

He laughs. "More than book it. We can fill the farm to capacity, and then some. With the right marketing, your small place could become a tourist destination. Just you. Just Wadley Farms. Want to escape? Book a facial. Need to relax? Play with the piggycorns. People pay to play with kittens all the time. They'll definitely hand over cash to pet horned swine that they've *never* heard of."

"*I've* heard of piggycorns," I reply, feeling insulted that Pane would correctly assume that no one besides a handful of people believe in my favoritest pet on the planet.

"Rowe, you need to accept the fact that you're one of the only people in the world who knows how special they are." He lifts his hands as if waving a flag of surrender. "Even though I realize the farm used to be successful and you sold th— *Wait.* You *sold* them, didn't you?"

"We did," I admit with a hearty sigh. "But people couldn't breed them because we never sold in pairs, and the piggies don't mate outside of the farm." I use my finger to iron a wrinkle in my skirt. "They're funny about that. They're like animals at a zoo that don't like to breed in captivity. Same type of thing. So anyway, what I'm saying is that the ones we sold eventually died, and the magic died, too, so . . ."

"The town died," he finishes.

"Right, and then magic-less unicorns were born, so the price came down, so people stopped caring about piggycorns. I've even posted videos and photos, but no one seems to notice—or they reply that the piggies aren't real and have fake horns sewn on their heads. A few folks may visit our town, visit the farm on occasion, but it's just not enough." I shake my head, hoping that I'm making sense. "When the magic died in Mystic Meadows, it dragged all of us down with it."

Pane thinks about that and nods. "Then let's change it."

Before I can agree, the bartender approaches, wiping down a glass with a rag. "Another round? This one's on me."

"Just water," Pane tells him.

Isaac glances my way.

"Ditto."

"But thanks for offering the free round."

Isaac grins. "Anyone who can beat mean old Coleman Barrier deserves to have the red carpet rolled out. Congratulations, by the way."

"Thank you. Pane Maddox."

"Isaac Granbury." They shake hands. "Welcome to Mystic Meadows."

"Happy to be here."

I thumb toward Pane. "Don't believe him. He hates our town."

"No, I don't." Pane glances around. "Everyone's been really nice."

"Yeah, Rowe, we're friendly," Isaac gently chides. "Listen, man, I don't know if you like poker, but a few of us have a game once a week on Wednesday nights. You're welcome to join. We play here."

"Thanks, I might do that."

But from the way his mouth is set, I can tell that Pane won't. This town still isn't good enough for him.

Isaac sets down our drinks. "See you then. Let me know if you need anything."

As he wanders off, the jukebox starts up, playing Ray LaMontagne's "You Are the Best Thing."

Pane slips off his stool and extends his hand. "Care to dance?"

I stare as if he's holding out a snake.

"I don't bite," he says, annoyed.

"Are you sure?"

A smile twitches on his lips. "Well, I might do other things."

Like what? Don't ask, Rowe! He probably means something dirty, something that Clarice Sinclair would approve of. "I don't think we should."

He drops his mouth to my ear and whispers in a husky voice, "Why not? If we dance one song and no one joins us, then we'll stop. But if other couples start, then I get two dances out of you."

"The Sparkle Bar, contrary to its name, isn't the type of place where people dance." I point to the pool tables and dartboard. "It's more like that."

He straightens. "So we start a trend." Pane flexes his fingers. "Don't be chicken."

I scoff. "I'm not a chicken."

"Then prove it."

I shake my head in annoyance. "Fine. Just one song."

"Unless—"

"Yeah, yeah, unless others join."

I down the rest of my water and let Pane take my hand. When he does, fireworks explode up my arm. I grind my teeth to keep from flinching, yet I can't help but wonder what kind of nuclear-level electric shock that was.

Pane scowls as if he felt it, too. However, that's also the billionaire's normal expression, so it's impossible to know if he experienced what I did.

He leads me to the center of the room and wraps an arm around my waist. He's so tall that I have to tip my chin way up to make eye contact.

When he pulls me close, his exotic scent hits me hard, and I blurt out, "What are you wearing? I have to know."

He smirks. "Is that a compliment from little Sunbeam?"

I roll my eyes. "I know how to give a compliment."

"Apparently. I just heard one from you."

I squint up at him and he glances down, stone-faced. "Are you teasing me? Trying to prove that you're actually human?"

He chuckles. "Last I checked, I'm very, very human."

Is it just me, or was there some superstrong sexual innuendo in that sentence? Another wave of his musky scent hits me, and his aroma is so amazing that I want to douse a cozy blanket in it, wrap myself up, and drink some hot chocolate.

"Seriously, though. What cologne is that?"

"It's mine."

"I know it's yours. What's it called?"

"Pane Maddox. It's my scent. I had it created."

My feet get gummed to the floor. "What?"

He smiles bashfully. "Last year I worked with a perfumer to create a signature smell for the hotels. While we were at it, I had one created for me, too."

"Are you blushing?"

"No. It's hot in here." He glances away, looking annoyed. "Are you going to start dancing again? Or keep standing there?"

"Sorry."

We start back up, and after a few seconds, he murmurs, "I don't really talk about this."

"You mean, talk about the fact that you have your own scent."

"Yes."

This is so fascinating. "What's in it?"

He shakes his head. "You don't want to know."

"Oh, I for sure want to know."

He's quiet for a moment before admitting, "It's dry gin, rosemary, and sandalwood."

"I knew I smelled juniper," I reply, feeling very smug. Then I show no shame and sniff his shirt. "The sandalwood really comes through, and now that you pointed it out, I can also smell the rosemary. But it's the dry gin—the juniper—that's the one that makes the whole bouquet stand out." I sigh wistfully. "It is so good. You should sell it."

"No."

"Why not?"

"Because then it wouldn't be mine. I share enough with the world."

He sounds bitter. Maybe his life isn't as rosy as I assume it is. Before I can ask him about it, he shifts the conversation. "Tell me three things about you. Besides the fact that you let piggycorns lick your feet, I mean."

"Even though you're saying that sarcastically, you just wait until it happens to you. You'll love it."

"Absolutely not."

"We'll see about that."

When I don't answer, he gently squeezes my hand. "Three things."

I frown up at him. "Why?"

"Because I'm living in your shamper and I'd like to have something to talk to you about other than piggycorns."

"They are a great conversation piece."

His nose wrinkles in distaste. "Not for me."

"Fine." I sigh dramatically. "Three things. Okay. I went to Auburn but dropped out, and when I have spare time, I design landscaping. I know you'd never know it by looking at the farm, but I'm really good."

"Did you study horticulture?"

"No. English."

He waves around the hand that's gently cradling mine. "How did you get from English to landscaping?"

I shrug. "I couldn't figure out a major and I always loved to read. I guess that I just wanted to live in fantasyland and read books all day."

"Hard to pay the bills like that."

"You're telling me." I laugh bitterly. "But a few years into college, my dad got sick. So I left to come home and help take care of him, and . . . I never went back. So now I spend my time between the farm and piddling with plants, which I've always enjoyed."

A line of concern worms its way across his brow. "And your dad?"

"He passed away from stomach cancer."

"I'm sorry." Heaviness blankets the conversation until a flirty smile flits across his lips. "So you love plants *and* animals."

My heart expands under the weight of the flirtatious look on his face. I find myself grinning back. "Yeah, plants and animals."

"That's two things." He holds up the same number of fingers. "What else?"

"Oh! When I was a kid, I loved *The Dark Crystal.* I watched it with my dad over and over."

"What is that?"

I roll my eyes. "We've got to get you out more." He smirks, not unkindly. "Well, that was my three. Now it's your turn."

He thinks about it by pursing his lips, which makes that dimple in his cheek snap. "You know that I fix old Land Rovers. I also like to run. I do it almost every day, which means I'll need to track down some sneakers. Some might say that I'm running from my past, but I simply like to go far. It forces me to work my way back home even when I don't want to."

I laugh. "So you're saying there's no deeper meaning there."

"Absolutely right." We lock eyes and laugh. There's a strange new feeling that's taken up residence in my chest. It's like butterflies are banging around in there, trying to get out. "I also call my sister every night, no matter where I am, to tuck her in."

My heart implodes.

"And what else . . ." He glances up at the ceiling in thought. "Oh, and my superpower is that I can see a person's potential and help them grow into it."

"That's actually really nice."

"See? I'm not the demon you think I am."

He twirls me around, which makes me laugh. When he pulls me back in, I say, "So why all the questions? I mean, apparently I recite useless sayings."

He lifts his chin, nodding in realization. "Yeah, about that . . . I'm sorry."

I cup a hand to my ear. "Wow. I've gotten two *sorry*'s out of you, and you've only been here for one day."

It's Pane's turn to roll his eyes. "I may have overreacted." He glances up, giving me a superb view of his amazing jawline. "I don't like platitudes. People say them as if they have deep meaning, but they usually don't. People also use them to ingratiate themselves."

"An apple a day is supposed to ingratiate me to you?"

He shakes his head. "It's hard to explain."

"I'm all ears."

He sighs. "My dad always made a big game of reciting sayings. He'd start one and have me finish it."

"And that's bad?"

There's a thick, hairy pause before Pane finally answers. "He abandoned us."

My stomach bottoms out. What? Who could do that, and why? Why would he abandon his kids?

My heart hurts for this man, who's holding me so gently, like I'm something precious that could fall and break.

"I'm so sorry," I tell him.

"There's nothing for you to be sorry about, Sunbeam." The song ends, and Pane glances away from me, smirks. "There's another couple out here with us."

Ron and Jennifer have taken to swaying. She glances over and grins at me. Surprisingly, I don't want to leave Pane's arms.

"Looks like you get one more dance."

Chapter 18

ROWE

"So why do you want this?" I ask, hoping to change the subject from Pane's dad to something else. "To win the company? Yesterday you said that you wanted to be seen as more than just Pane Maddox. Why?"

He quirks a brow. "Now *you're* asking questions?"

"Knowing four things about you gives me an advantage."

He barks a laugh before pulling me into him as "Careless Whisper" by Wham! begins to play.

"Ah, George Michael," he says. "One of the many faces I see before bedtime."

"I'm sure George is lovely."

He studies me for a moment before sighing. "I'm not ready to tell you my reasons for wanting to win the company."

"What? That's no fair."

He drops his mouth to my ear. "You haven't earned the right to that knowledge—not yet."

I bristle. "I'm helping you win the competition."

"There's a long way to go before we win, Sunbeam," he tells me before proceeding to spin me out.

He pulls me back in and tugs me close so that every inch of my torso is pressed to his. Sparks ignite in my body, torturing me as they fire off. Just when I think I can't take it anymore, he swings me out again, and I can finally breathe.

That's before I'm pulled back in and the cycle starts all over.

As the song continues, his movements slow. He holds me in a way that makes my brain scream, *Run!*

This whole dancing scenario has destroyed my notion about who this man is. For as sarcastic and grunty as Pane has been, he apparently also has a softer side.

"Speaking of scents . . ." he says, lifting his hand and spinning me. He reels me back in effortlessly. "You smell like a bouquet."

"You're joking."

"I would never joke about such a thing."

The way he's staring down at me makes a lump clot up my throat. Somehow I manage to talk past it. "How do I smell? Could you bottle it?"

"Oh, I could bottle it," he growls.

The heat in his voice sends hormones flooding through my bloodstream. My panties are now soaked through. Thank you very much, hormones. *Must not think about wet panties.* "So, what is the smell?"

"It's . . . wildflowers."

"Wildflowers?"

"On a cloudless day," he muses.

Our gazes latch, and I blink in a pathetic attempt to claw my way out of the hole I've plummeted into.

"Tell me . . ." He nods toward the crowd. "What's the dating pool like here?"

"It's a small town. What do you think it's like?"

"Tiny."

We both laugh and it feels good. Right. *Lawd, have mercy.* I must be losing my mind to think that.

This is not supposed to happen. This is a business relationship, and I must remember that.

"Since you know everyone in this town," he continues, "I assume that means you're also privy to their secrets. I'm guessing that means you're—"

"Not interested in dating any of them."

He hitches a brow in disbelief. "Never?"

"Never."

Pane's hand on my back tightens. "Which means one of them broke your heart."

I stiffen. This is not the time to spill about Luke. Not now, and not with Pane. No matter how fabulous he smells.

My heart immediately throws up walls around itself. "Why are you asking? Wondering if I've almost nabbed other rich men?"

His expression falls. "If your dating pool is small, mine is, too."

"How could your dating pool be tiny? You can date the whole world."

"But does the whole world want me? Or does it want something else?"

My heart stutters at what Pane's suggesting—that woman only date him for his money.

I've been staring at him, and it's getting hot. Or I'm feeling hot. "Can we sit down?"

"You okay?" he asks, concern etched on his face.

"I'm fine. Just tired."

I don't like the look on his face. Our relationship was better when we hated one another. This is new. Confusing. Strange.

He escorts me back to our barstools and we sit. My water is empty now, which makes me sad. Pane sips his drink and swivels his barstool around to face mine, giving me his undivided attention.

"Another water, or whiskey sour?"

"I'll take a whiskey sour."

When the drink is in my hand, I suck it down in an attempt to fog up this new feeling for Pane. I'm working really, really hard to not like him, but here he is, steadily watching me. Pane Maddox is acid, slowly dissolving my resolve to continue hating him.

"May I ask . . . where is your mom?"

"Oh, her." I grab a handful of peanuts and slowly shell them, popping each in my mouth as I explain. "She is living her dream and following her favorite jam band around the country, alongside her boyfriend."

"People do that?"

"They do. There's a whole community of retirement-age folks who follow bands in their campers." I chew and swallow a peanut. "My dad's death hit her pretty hard, and it was years before she and Bill started dating. She deserves to have some fun and not worry about all the mess that's going on here."

Pane taps my wrist. "How long have you been back from college?"

I hold up both hands. "Six years."

"Which would make you . . . ?"

"Twenty-seven. And you are?"

"Thirty-five."

The alcohol is now flooding my system, and Pane's face is swimming. I squint to keep it steady. "That's why you've got that gray."

He pats his hair and frowns. "I don't have gray."

"No, you don't. But I made you think that you do."

He smirks. "And you haven't dated anyone the whole time that you've been home? Six years?"

I exhale, annoyed. "So many questions about dating. Yes, I dated. I brought a man, Luke, home with me from college, but we only lasted about a year before he dumped me for Sally Ray, my neighbor who owns the unicorns. Now they're married and are living happily ever after."

"Luke," he murmurs darkly.

"Don't worry. You shouldn't have to meet him. He works at the bank. Besides him, *I have* dated a few guys, but nothing serious. Probably because they lack my love of piggycorns."

"How evil of them."

"See? You get it." I lightly poke his shoulder for emphasis. "Now it's my turn to pepper you with questions about your love life."

"Shoot. I'm an open book."

"Do you have a girlfriend?"

"Absolutely not."

I frown. "You say that so emphatically."

"What kind of man would be dancing with one woman while dating another?"

"Good point. But I saw a picture on the internet of you with a blond woman."

"Ah, you're an internet sleuth."

"Not me. Cristina."

"Well, that was an old picture." He folds his hands. "I've dated women on and off, none of them seriously."

"Why not?"

He cringes. "The women who run in my circles are socialites. Their concerns are different. Don't get me wrong—they're smart, educated. Even if they weren't educated, they'd still be smart. But they're just not my type."

A knot jams up my throat. It *should* be jammed up, because he's talking about how sophisticated the women he dates are. Sophisticated enough to know the difference in knives. But the way he's looking at me makes it very clear: *Those* women might not have been his type, but *maybe* . . . Nope. Nope.

Not going there.

Love leads to heartbreak. Love leads to relying on other people—people who do things like die or dump you.

I clear my throat. "Well, the woman in the photo was certainly beautiful."

"There are other, more beautiful women in the world," he says with hooded eyelids.

No, no, no! There will be no flirting. I jump out of my chair. "Are you hungry?"

He pats his flat stomach. "Starving."

I cock my head toward the door. "Great. Want to grab something to eat?"

Chapter 19

PANE

One step inside the restaurant and I know Rowe made the right decision, because the place smells like heaven.

It's definitely cleaner than the bar. Who wants to walk on broken peanut shells? But the place was welcoming, even if it did make me wonder whether or not my tetanus vaccine is up to date.

A woman in her sixties with short, gray hair enters from the back of the restaurant. She wipes her hands on a towel and gives us a warm smile.

"Hello, my darlings. What can I get for you?"

"Gloria's from Cuba," Rowe whispers loudly behind her hand.

Sunbeam's adorable when she's a little loose.

"My dear, do you have a new friend?"

Rowe steps forward, tugging my hand. She stares down at where her finger is curled around my pinkie and drops me like I'm made of ice.

"Gloria, this is Pane Maddox. He's amazing with a chain saw. Pane, this is Gloria. She is amazing with empanadas."

I take the hand she offers. "Pleasure. Do you need any work done that I can use a chain saw for?"

The woman roars with laughter.

"Of course she doesn't." Rowe slaps my chest and whips toward Gloria. "Please excuse him. He doesn't know how to act around normal people."

"Welcome to Mystic Meadows," Gloria says in her thick Spanish accent. "You'll love it here. There's no better place on earth." Then she gives us a big smile. "Okay, my darlings, what can I get for you?"

Since this is Rowe's jam, I let her do the ordering.

Then we sit in the waiting area while Gloria disappears in the back to make our food.

"We can take it with us to the bar," Rowe explains. "Isaac won't care. Plus, Gloria doesn't have a dining room, as you can see." She gestures to the small waiting area that's decorated with four chairs. "It's purely a to-go establishment. But it's the best," she gushes excitedly. "You're going to love it, as long as you enjoy meat and pastry."

"I think I proved that this morning," I reply, eyeing her mouth.

She licks her lips—whether consciously or unconsciously, I don't know—and it about drives me out of my mind.

Rowe leans in. "Can I tell you a secret?"

"If it's not good, I'm never going to speak to you again."

"You—" She straightens, frowns at me. "Are you serious?"

"If I am?"

"You *have* to talk to me. We're saving my farm. Plus, I like you." She elbows me before her gaze darts to my arm. She quickly backpedals. "Not *like* you, like you. But you're okay."

"I'm 'okay'? That's all? I can't do better than that?"

She shrugs. "For now, you're okay."

"That's it," I announce emphatically.

"What?"

"I'm going to prove to you that I'm better than okay."

"I don't think so."

My jaw drops. "Challenge accepted. You are definitely going to like me by the time this is over. Or at least tolerate me."

"Do you mean *like* you, like you?"

"Of course not." My heart does this strange bird-wing-flapping thing that I strongly disapprove of. "That would be unprofessional."

She frowns. Does that mean she wants me to *like her*, like her?

Sunbeam drops one leg atop the other and bounces her foot. "Don't you want to know my secret?"

I swipe a hand down my face. *All this topic-swapping is going to be the death of me.* "Tell me."

She whispers in my ear, so close that I wish she'd bite me. "You . . . are a great kisser."

My entire body freezes. "Why, did Rowe Wadley just give me a compliment?"

"Don't get used to it. But you are. I didn't expect you to use tongue." She sits back and studies me. "Why'd you do that?"

Oh, shit. This woman. "Um, well, you know—someone kisses you, and . . ."

She nods. "It's instinctual."

"Unless it's family."

"Obviously."

"That's disgusting."

"Oh yeah. Or if it's flu season."

I slash the air with my hand. "Let's be clear: I never would've done it if it was January."

"I never would've let you." She sits back. "How old is your sister?"

"Well, that's a conversation jump." I quirk a brow. "Why are you suddenly asking about her? Because if you're insinuating that I've Frenched my sister, then—"

Her eyes flare in fear. "No, no. We were just talking about family and not kissing them. So that's what brought it to mind."

"Do you have any siblings?"

She opens her arms wide like she's giving the room a hug. "No, just my piggycorns."

Of course that's her answer. "My sister's ten."

"So your mom remarried?"

"Yes, and divorced him, too. My brother and I look over Natalie as much as we can." I drop my elbows to my knees. "She needs a father in her life."

Rowe's silent for a long stretch before replying, "Yeah. We all need a dad."

"I agree."

A side door opens and out walks Cristina, mascara running down her face. She's holding a bag of food.

Rowe pops up. "What're you doing back there?"

Cristina's eyes are red and puffy from crying. "Oh, nothing. It's just . . . I ordered some food, and while I was waiting for it, I DD'd."

"You drunk-dialed Jace?"

Cristina slaps a hand over her forehead. "What's wrong with me?"

She hunches down like she's going to cry again, and Rowe wraps her best friend in a hug. "Come outside. Let's talk."

Rowe shoots me a look that says everything—she needs to be with her bestie. I nod, silently telling her to go on, that I'll wait for the food.

Gloria appears with our order a few minutes later. I pay with the little cash that I have and frown. I've got to find a way to put money in my pocket. Maybe I'll take Isaac up on that poker game after all.

The restaurant owner hands me the bag of empanadas. "Miss Rowe is a good one. You two seem cute together."

"Oh, we're . . ." I start to gesture toward the front door Rowe disappeared through, but drop my hand. "She *is* a good one, isn't she?"

"Enjoy your empanadas, my darling. We'll see you soon."

I take the bag, wondering why I didn't correct Gloria about Rowe and me being a thing.

Maybe because my head was still spinning from Rowe questioning whether or not I'm likable. What did I even mean when I said that by the time this is over, she'll like me?

In bed. She'll like me in bed.

Stop. Don't make this complicated. Rowe and I have to get along for the next two months if her farm is to succeed.

Which means she'll have to like me. Hey, I'm likable when I want to be.

Not if you ask her, though. The way Rowe talks, I'm a horrible grouch.

Perhaps that's because I am.

But deep down, I'm likable. At least, I *can* be. And I plan to prove it.

That's it. By the time I'm out of Mystic Meadows—in two months—Rowe Wadley will like me.

Not *like me*, like me. But like me.

Or maybe I'll wind up liking her.

Outside, Rowe and Cristina are sitting on the curb with their heads together. When I walk up, Rowe rises. "Can we drive her home? Are you sober?"

"I haven't had a drink in a while."

"So you *can* drive us?"

"Sure."

"Wait." Cristina lifts a bag. "It's a Cuban sandwich for Isaac. Can you give it to him?"

"Absolutely." I hand Rowe the keys to the truck and walk back to the bar. Inside, Isaac is washing glasses. "This is from Cristina."

"Ah, my Cuban. I was beginning to think she'd forgotten."

"Nope."

"Thanks, man." He points at me. "Don't forget, this Wednesday. I expect you to show up."

"I'll be here."

As I'm heading out, Ron stops me. "See you tomorrow, Pane."

I shake his hand. "Thanks, again. I appreciate everything."

He gulps. "Sally Ray's going to be pissed, but what you're doing is important."

"I think so."

Back outside, Rowe has walked Cristina to the truck, but Cristina's shaking her head. "I can't get in, Rowe. My legs don't move like that right now."

I frown. "They're not moving how?"

"You know." Cristina opens her hooded eyes. "Up and down. They're broken."

Rowe cocks her head toward her friend. "She's pretty buzzed."

"Let me help you, then."

While Rowe holds the door open, I hook my arms under Cristina's legs and slide her into the truck.

"Jace used to hold me like that—once upon a time. Ah!" She flops down on the back seat. "He used to love me!"

She begins wailing as I close the door. Rowe grimaces. "Sorry."

"It's fine. I love taking drunk ladies home. Haven't done it in years."

Once Rowe and I are inside, Cristina's blowing her nose into the long sleeve of her shirt. "I'm so sorry that you have to see me like this, Pane. This is not my normal. Tell him, Rowe."

"This is not her normal," Rowe deadpans.

Cristina's head pops up between us. "See? I'm not like this at all. I'm a very put-together person. I'm a massage therapist and I travel to people's homes—but only if I trust them. I can't be showing up to some rando's place. Rowe, remember the time I went to that man's house and he had all those women's shoes hanging from the ceiling? I didn't stay. Ugh. I really need my own space to work."

She does, does she?

Rowe and I exchange a look.

Cristina keeps talking. "But that man's house wasn't anything like Jace's, which seems empty now that my stuff's gone—and tonight I had all those drinks and my brain went haywire. His name just appeared on my phone out of nowhere, and I pushed the button."

She holds up a wrapped empanada in a bag. "I even got him food! Why did I do that, Rowe?"

"Because you're not over him. Give me that."

She takes the empanada, rolls down the window, and flings it outside.

Cristina gasps. "That's his food. What's Jace going to eat now?"

"Bugs, for all I care."

There's a pause before Cristina whimpers, "But we were so good together."

"You were good until he decided to be a royal jerk. There are tons of other great guys out there whose names aren't *Jace*."

Cristina groans and slumps back on the seat. "I don't want one of the Collins boys."

"Collins boys?" I ask Rowe.

She shakes her head. "Don't ask. Oh, make a right at the next turn."

We stop outside a small apartment complex. "We're here." She glances over her shoulder. "Cristina?"

Loud snoring comes from the back seat.

"She's passed out," Rowe confirms. "What do we do?"

I unsnap my seat belt and kill the engine. "I'll carry her in."

"You don't have to do that."

"I don't mind."

With Rowe leading the way, I gently take Cristina from the back seat and carry her up the stairs and into the apartment, which Rowe unlocks with a key from Cristina's purse. It's neat. Tidy. Smells like citrus. Rowe leads me to the bedroom and pulls back the sheets while I gently lay Cristina down.

One of her eyes opens a slit. "You're a good one, Pane Maddox. Rowe, you really need to hit that."

I cough into my fist.

Crimson explodes across Rowe's cheeks. "I'll get you a glass of water. Be right back."

I wait outside until Rowe appears and gently shuts the door. "Thank you."

"You're welcome."

She sinks her teeth into her bottom lip. "Sorry about that back there."

"What's there to be sorry about?"

She rolls her eyes. "You know about what."

"No, I have no idea what you're talking about. Unless you mean the whole hitting—"

"Yesthat'swhatImean," she says in one breath. Then she exhales. "Let's go home and eat."

We eat in the gazebo overlooking the rolling meadow behind the house. The moon is high, washing the farm in its milky glow. Neither of us says a word as we unwrap our dinners.

I bite into my empanada and groan. "Oh, wow. I've had plenty of picadillo empanadas before, but this is amazing."

Rowe grins from behind her meat pie. "Plus, you don't need a knife. Not when you eat it with your hands."

I chuckle. "That's definitely a perk."

"I knew you'd like it. I mean, you have to be lacking taste buds to hate these." We're silent for a few moments before she quietly adds, "Thank you."

"For what?"

"For helping with Cristina."

"You've already thanked me."

"I know, I just wanted to say it again."

"So, this Jace guy. Has he made the rounds in Mystic Meadows, breaking hearts?"

Has he broken yours? If so, where can I find him and break his face?

She eyes me shyly, as if deciding what to say next. "They dated for a couple of years. At first everything seemed good—normal, even. But then Jace started acting like a jerk. He told her that she could become his first wife."

The empanada almost falls from my mouth. "He *said* that?"

"Told you he's a jerk."

"He *is* a jerk. Sounds like he wanted her to break up with him."

"He did. He was just too afraid to do it himself."

I'm quiet for a moment, staring down at my food. When I look up, Rowe's watching me thoughtfully. "What is it?" she asks.

I shake my head. "Some men don't know what they have. They think that love is a drama—or it's all high-riding emotions, that initial thrill and nothing more. But that's not what love is. It's the settling of the emotions, the depth of knowledge, the ease of it all that makes it worth it. It's being with someone day in and out, loving them through the good and bad until you finally fall into that comfortable place."

"Yeah," Rowe whispers. "I guess it is."

The air between us shifts, and my heart throbs. It feels like it's cracking. That just being around Rowe Wadley has broken something open inside me.

She looks up at me with those doe-brown eyes of hers—eyes that brim with sadness.

Her dad died. Her boyfriend dumped her. This woman has spent years having her heart shredded by those she loved.

I'm not staying around, either. In two months, I'll be gone, abandoning her like everyone else.

She smashes the empanada wrapper between her hands. "Ready to be locked up in the shamper?"

I give a curt nod. "Lead the way."

As I follow her, I make a decision right then and there: Even if I want her to like me, she can't.

Rowe Wadley must not, under any circumstances, fall for me.

And I must not, under any circumstances, fall for her.

Chapter 20

PANE

For the next week and a half, I'm busy making plans and having supplies delivered. Every idea goes through Rowe, who gives me very little pushback. We discuss design, layout, and the flow of the house.

She has keen insight, and is really good at identifying future problems, for which, with both our heads put together, we work at finding solutions.

Between talking about the new business, she shares information about her mom, who is apparently a hippie; her mom's boyfriend, Bill, who likes to read; and her deceased father, who loved this old farmhouse.

I can tell—the workmanship inside is gorgeous. He thickened the ceiling molding, added new windows, and refurbished the wraparound porch.

I tell her things about my life, too, sharing what I do on a daily basis. I explained to her that when I started working in the hotel, I was put on housekeeping duty. For some reason, Sunbeam thought that was hysterical and couldn't stop laughing about it all day.

I didn't mind.

I also tell her about the books I've read to Natalie and how Stone is my best friend.

But for as much time as we spend in one another's orbit, and for all the breakfast biscuits I've been eating, there's been no more kissing.

But, man, do I want to.

I really, really want to.

I know what I said about not falling for her. That hasn't changed. It's just hard to look at Rowe and not imagine my mouth on hers.

But sadly, all-you-can eat biscuits and a lack of kissing don't change the fact that I'm low on cash, and the little money in my pocket is dwindling rapidly by the time the weekly poker game rolls around Wednesday night.

"Hey, how's it going?" I say to Isaac when I enter Sparkle Bar.

The peanut shells have been cleaned up, thank God. The place even has a nice smell to it—pine. It doesn't have the wastewater scent that many bars do.

Isaac gives me a wide smile and takes my hand. "Good to see you. We were just getting started. Have a seat."

He points to a table where Ron and another man are already settling down.

I nod to Ron as I pull out a chair. "You didn't tell me you'd be here tonight."

He grins sheepishly. "That's because I wasn't sure."

"Ron's wife doesn't know that he comes," Isaac informs me, sitting on Ron's other side. "He has to pretend that he's out hunting."

The fourth man, who's wearing a plaid button-down shirt, snickers. "What season is it again, Ron?"

"Grouse?" he suggests.

The three roll with laughter. Isaac slaps the table. "There hasn't been a grouse in this area for years. He might as well be telling Jennifer that he's hunting unicorns."

"*Piggy*corns," Ron corrects.

I smile, worried that all these men will talk about is hunting and fishing—two things I know little about.

These aren't the kinds of guys who talk about their yachts and their mountain vacation homes. Not sure what we'll have in common. This might be a long two hours.

Isaac makes introductions. "Pane, that over there is McCauley." He points to the man in the plaid shirt. "He's our resident lawn-care guy. Does all the yards in town."

"I bet that keeps you busy," I say.

"It does." He brushes dark hair from his eyes. "I tell you what, a while back I tried to hire Rowe to help me with some of the landscaping design that folks want, but she wouldn't do it. Said it would take her away from those piggycorns."

"She does love them," Ron whimpers. When the two men stare at him, he shrugs. "What? They're cute. I can say that. They're like puppies."

Isaac grabs a pile of cards and begins cutting. "That why you quit the feedstore? So that you can play with piggycorns?"

"Ron's been a huge help," I tell them. "Without him, I wouldn't know where to start. You should see him with a sander and a measuring tape." Ron puffs out his chest with pride, and I add, "In fact, I could use another set of hands if you've got time to spare."

Isaac lifts his brows. "What do you need?"

"What *don't* I need? We're turning the place into a spa."

Isaac and McCauley exchange a look. McCauley speaks first. "A spa? Like, where women go?"

Ron scoops up a handful of shelled peanuts and drops it into his mouth. "There'll also be couples' massages."

Isaac looks up from the deck of cards he's shuffling and laughs. "I can just see Jennifer going for that. She'll be dragging you in there by your ear."

"And some guy named Lance'll be oiling down your legs," McCauley adds.

I bark out a laugh as Ron's face turns red.

"What're y'all over here jabbering about?" comes a voice from behind us.

Up walks an old woman who's got to be in her late seventies. She's wearing capri pants, sneakers, and a Braves ball cap over a mop of curly, silver hair.

She places a tray of drinks on the table. Isaac quirks a brow. "Mojitos, Clarice? Really? You said you were making something special."

She frowns. "This is special. When I'm working the bar, I get to pick the drink, and I picked mojitos. Do you want me to stay, or would you rather I go home and make you quit your poker game?"

"No, no. Don't do that." Isaac takes the drinks and hands them off to each of us. "Pane Maddox, allow me to introduce Clarice Sinclair. Clarice, Pane is helping out Wadley Farms."

She pumps her brows behind thick-lensed glasses. "I know all about Pane Maddox. Watched you with that chain saw, and you did pretty good."

"Thank you."

She works her jaw, and it appears that she wants to ask a question, but when a customer enters, she waddles off back behind the bar.

As soon as she's gone, I say, "Isn't she a bit old to be working so hard?"

"Nah," Ron says. "She likes to gripe and complain, but this is the one night she gets out, and Wednesdays are always dead."

"Yeah. Folks know to go easy on her," Isaac tells me.

"All folks except Luke Preston," McCauley adds.

Ron and Isaac groan.

"Don't jinx it," Ron says. "Just saying his name may conjure him up."

"Luke," I murmur. "Is that . . ."

"Rowe's ex," Isaac informs me stoutly. "He used to play poker with us when we played on Tuesdays, but he always won."

I quirk a brow. "Always?"

"Yeah. No telling how many thousands he got out of us." Ron knocks back his mojito. Ice clinks as he lets the glass hit the table with a thud. "We could never figure out how he cheated, but we know he did."

"So instead of firing him, we changed nights." McCauley raps his knuckles on the table. "Speaking of, are we playing or not?"

"Texas Hold'em. Fifty-dollar buy-in," Isaac announces.

I peel open my wallet and swallow a knot in my throat. I'd better do some winning if I'm going to make this back and then some. Otherwise, I'll be begging on the streets for food.

I toss my fifty into the middle of the table. "I'm in."

Two hands in, and I'm up. I don't even feel guilty about it. The guys are nice, and they don't treat me like I'm a fragile rich boy.

The bar, even for all the stuffed bucks and coyotes on the walls, is beginning to grow on me.

Ron's about to deal the next round when the front door opens. "Well, well, well. So this is what happened to poker night."

The three men around the table freeze. In unison, they slowly turn their heads.

A guy with thick, dark hair and a well-oiled beard rolls up the sleeves of his white shirt.

"And here I thought y'all had given it up."

He swaggers over, grabs a chair from a nearby table. Its feet scrape across the floor as he pulls it up to us and wedges it between Isaac and McCauley.

When neither man moves, he growls, "What gives? Y'all not letting your friend Luke play?"

If I'd had any doubts before about his identity, they're gone now.

"Sure thing," Isaac says, scooting over. McCauley moves slower, sliding the chair inch by inch.

Luke's face tenses, and he matches McCauley's pace, wedging his seat closer to the table every time McCauley moves.

"Come on, man," he mutters.

"Sorry. My hip's been bothering me. It's hard to move that way."

Isaac drops a hand over his mouth to cover a laugh.

When Luke's finally seated at the table, he extends his hand to me. "Luke Preston."

"Pane Maddox."

"You're the one who's helping over at the Wadleys', right?"

The three men go quiet. Eyes are glued to cards. Fingers twitch.

That tells me everything I need to know about what's going down.

I remember several things about Luke: He broke Rowe's heart, he lives across the road, and he works at the bank.

All three make me instantly dislike him. "That's right, I'm over at the Wadleys'."

He scratches his beard. "What brought you here?"

It's no one's business why I'm doing what I am, just that *I am*. "It's a little project I'm working on."

Luke turns to Ron. "You gonna deal or what?"

Ron starts shuffling nervously. "Yeah. Fifty-dollar buy-in."

"Make it one hundred," Luke counters.

Ron swallows nervously. Isaac and McCauley both glare at Luke. They're probably thinking he's going to cheat again, and he knows he's going to win. Otherwise, he wouldn't bother coming in high.

It's Isaac who tries to make things reasonable. "Come on, Luke. A hundred?"

"Fine. Keep it at fifty."

The men's shoulders soften, and Isaac smiles. "Maybe Pane'll be our good luck and we'll beat you this time."

Luke winks. "I sure hope so." After Ron deals us in, Luke talks as he stares down at his cards. "So, what're you doing over there at the Wadleys'?"

Luke is trying to sound nonchalant, seem uninterested in the answer, but he's got something up his sleeve. The man oozes snake-in-the-grass like no one I've ever met.

"He's turning the place into a spa," Ron blabs.

McCauley shoots Ron a look and Isaac scowls.

"Is that so?" Luke says, tossing away a card. "You know it's gone into foreclosure."

"I'm aware."

"Let's play, y'all," McCauley growls.

Luke wins the first game with two queens. It's uncanny that he'd wind up with such a winning hand, but it could also just be luck.

Clarice delivers another round of drinks. "Mojitos again?" Isaac grumbles.

"You better be glad that you got one," she snips.

Luke glances up. "Where's mine?"

"It's up your ass, is where it is. You know I can't stand you."

He scowls. When she leaves, he mumbles, "She's just pretending to hate me."

"No, I ain't," she calls with her back to us. "Not after what you did."

His face flushes red, but he quickly turns his attention back to the game. "So, you and Rowe . . ."

I glance over my hand at him. "Me and Rowe?"

"Are you two, you know . . . together?"

"What's it your business, Luke?" Isaac asks after sipping his drink. "The two of you aren't a thing."

"No reason. She's just one you wouldn't want to be with."

"Can we play cards?" McCauley says impatiently.

Ron folds. Isaac folds. McCauley and I stay in, but Luke wins. Again.

How is he beating us?

I lift my drink to take a sip, trying to wrap my head around what he's doing. There aren't any trick cards, he's not pulling anything out from his sleeves—but the man is cheating, I have no doubt.

Just as I think that, the glass rumbles in my hand. I put it down, at first wondering if we're experiencing an earthquake. But the chair's not shaking. The building's not moving.

Only my glass is quivering on the table.

The men aren't paying any attention. They're focused on McCauley as he deals the next hand.

As the glass quivers, the mint begins to spin like the hands of a clock, twirling and twirling, until all of a sudden, it stops. There's a pause; then the three green leaves come together, making the shape of an arrow—an arrow that points at Luke.

Wait. I'm seeing things. Mint can't point, and mint from a town that's lost its magic *really* can't point.

I squeeze my eyes shut, pinching them with my fingers. Maybe it's the alcohol causing hallucinations.

When I open my eyes, the green arrow dives down into the glass, between two ice cubes, and begins curling and uncurling like an accordion, still aimed at Luke.

Maybe it's not the alcohol after all.

The mint is frantic, pointing down.

Does Luke have something under the table that's helping him?

I move the napkin to the right of my hand until it falls. When I lean down to get it, I take a good look at Luke.

Spilling out of his pocket is what looks like rainbow hair.

Not hair—*mane.*

Unicorn mane.

Luke Preston's been stuffing magical unicorn mane into his pocket in order to win at poker.

That's how he's been cheating.

An idea snaps in my head. "I'm out this game, but count me in the next one."

As I rise, I hear Luke murmur, "Must be getting tired of losing. Maybe he's not as rich as we think."

My back snaps tight and I turn around. "I'm not a liar."

Luke levels his gaze on me. "Didn't say that you were."

"Yeah, you did."

He winds a finger around his ear. "Hanging out at the Wadleys' has probably broken his brain."

I curl my hands into fists. "No. More like playing poker with you is making me dumber by the minute."

Before he can answer, I'm at the bar, pulling Clarice aside. "I need you to do me a favor."

"Does it have to do with Rowe?"

"No, it has to do with dropping Luke down several notches."

"I'm in."

"Luke, I made you a Long Island iced tea. How's that sound?"

Clarice waddles up holding a tall glass filled to the brim with brown liquid.

Lust fills Luke's eyes.

"Why, thank you, ma'am. See?" he says to us. "I told y'all that she likes me."

Right when Luke reaches for the drink, Clarice drops it in his lap.

Luke jumps up and his chair crashes to the floor behind him. "Dammit, Clarice!"

"I'm so sorry! Must be my old hands!"

She makes a big show of dabbing his front pocket with the napkins she brought, but he snatches them from her. "Get away, woman," he shouts. "Get!"

"I'm sorry," she mumbles.

"Damn!" He shoos her off. As Clarice passes me, I extend my hand and she drops the unicorn mane in my palm.

"Gentlemen"—I shove the mane in my pocket—"let's make this our last game. I'm getting tired."

The men grumble in agreement as Luke blots his soaking crotch with the napkin.

A few minutes later I announce, "All in," pushing every dollar bill I've got into the pile.

Luke lifts a brow. "You got that good a hand, huh?"

"You'll find out."

He tries to hide a smile, but he can't. He's got this one in the bag, he thinks. "What the hell. I'm all in, too."

Luke drops all the cash he stole onto the table, plus everything that's in his wallet. It's a good three thousand dollars. He sits back with a satisfied smile.

"I'm out," Ron declares.

"Me too," says Isaac.

"Me three," adds McCauley.

Luke smirks. "Let's see if that Rowe Wadley bad luck is rubbing off on you."

"What's that?"

"Nothing." He scratches his beard. "Just that folks in town say Rowe's bad luck."

"She's not bad luck," I snap, glaring at him.

"Hey, don't kill the messenger." He lifts his hands in surrender. "I'm just saying what everybody else knows."

"Everybody but me."

Isaac raps his knuckles on the table. "Show 'em if you've got 'em."

Luke drops a straight, and begins to gather the money with a cocky smirk when I say, "Hold on."

His expression falls. "What do you have?"

I place my cards face up one at a time. "Ace, king, queen, jack, and ten of spades. Royal flush."

His jaw drops. "You can't— That's not possible."

"Oh, it's possible."

Isaac nods to me. "Pane's the winner of this round."

I pluck cash from Luke's hand and drag the pot of money toward me.

Luke checks his pocket and sees that the mane is missing. He jumps out of his seat and towers over me, eyes bulging, neck veins popping. "You had Clarice . . ."

Then he stops, because he can't admit that he's been cheating.

But this jerk's not getting off that easily.

"I had Clarice, what? What did I have her do?" I rise slowly, putting the bills together and folding them over. Ron, Isaac, and McCauley stare at each other in confusion. "What were you going to say, Luke?"

He jabs a finger at me. "This isn't over, Maddox."

I hold his gaze and lean forward. "I don't expect that it is. Now, get out of here before you do something you'll regret."

Rowe's ex studies me for a long minute. Then he pulls his lips back and sneers, "No matter what you think you're gonna do to fix up the Wadley place, it won't work. What's out there, it's *used up. Wasted.* And I'm not talking about the property."

One word flashes through my mind:

Rowe.

Before I can think, I grab two fistfuls of his shirt and back him into the wall. He hits it with a hard thud.

"What did you say?" I demand.

Instead of answering, Luke pulls back his fist and slams it into my jaw. My head snaps to the right and pain blooms, but there's no way in hell I'm going to let this loser win.

I refocus, pull him forward, and shove him back again, making sure his head smacks the wall—*hard.* Above us, framed pictures and buck trophies shake, threatening to fall.

Luke groans and sags against the wall.

"You got something else to say about her?" I growl.

Luke blinks, shakes his head.

I toss him to the right. He stumbles, throwing out his arms and using an empty table to break his fall. He slowly straightens, and when he turns around stiffly, Luke says, "You don't know who you're messing with."

"Neither do you," I reply, fists tight by my sides.

He stares at me for a beat longer and then storms out. As soon as he's gone, everyone goes quiet for a moment as all of us exhale.

"Holy shit," Isaac says, clapping me on the back.

"How'd you do that?" McCauley asks, picking up the money I dropped on the floor when I grabbed Luke. "Not scare Luke—that was awesome. But how'd you beat him?"

I pull the piece of mane from my pocket. "This is how Luke's been cheating. Saw it in his pocket." I rub my sore jaw. "Come on. Let's divvy up the money. Y'all deserve to get back everything he stole from you."

They protest, but I'm not keeping the cash. For all the times that Luke cheated them, these men deserve some sort of compensation.

Clarice walks up while I'm putting the last of the money in my wallet and pats me on the arm. "You made yourself an enemy tonight."

I hand her a hundred and wink. "I sure did, and I couldn't have done it without your help."

"Kid, before you know it, you're gonna become a local."

"I doubt that."

"She's right about Luke," Isaac says while slipping on his jacket. "You'd better watch your back."

No. He'd better watch his, because if Luke Preston tries anything against Rowe, I'll destroy him.

And that's a promise.

Chapter 21

ROWE

"What happened to your face?" I ask Pane the next morning when he enters the foyer, a pencil behind his ear, tools threaded to his belt, new boots on his feet, and a tight shirt on his torso.

The man could make a blind woman swoon.

Except for the knuckle-length bruise that runs just under his left cheek.

He touches it and winces. "There may have been an incident at poker last night."

"An *incident*?"

He sucks in air through his teeth. "Yes."

"With whom did you have this 'incident'?"

"A fist." His gaze flicks to the driveway, where Cristina's pulling in. "Ah. Coffee delivery."

He moves toward the door, but I dart in front of him, pointing my dry paintbrush at his chest. "Not so fast, mister. You're not getting off that easily. I still want to know what happened to your face."

"Are you showing concern for me, Sunbeam?"

"No. *Yes.* I mean, if you get hurt, it'll ruin our progress."

Keep telling yourself that all you care about is progress. Maybe you'll start to believe it.

Inwardly, I sigh, because to be honest, these past few days I've learned that Pane Maddox is smart, dependable, and not nearly as snarky as when I first met him.

I do actually like him.

Not *like him,* like him. But you know what I mean.

He studies me, the corners of his eyes tightening, but all he says is "Right. Me getting hurt will mess up our progress."

Then Pane sidesteps me and opens the screen door for my best friend.

Did I say something wrong?

But before I can ask him, Pane puts on a big smile. "Cristina, just the woman I wanted to see."

She enters the house holding a cardboard container full of coffee and looking confused. "Why? Did something happen? Is this about the other night?" Her gaze frantically searches mine. "What did I do? I didn't try to kiss him, did I?"

A belly laugh rolls out of me. "No, you were a good girl. Except for Jace's food."

She groans. "Don't remind me. But anyway, leaving the past in the past, here's a salted-caramel mocha for you. Three shots of espresso for you," she says to Pane. "And a latte for me."

She takes a long sip and smiles at Pane. "Now that I'm caffeinated, why are you so excited to see me?" Then her eyes pop wide. "And what happened to your face?"

"That's what I want to know," I say, folding my arms.

She glances at me. "So you didn't do this to him?"

"No, of course not."

Pane pulls the coffee cup from his mouth and pats the air. "Can we please discuss my face later? For now, let's discuss business." He looks at me and smiles. My knees wobble. "Do you want to tell her?"

"No, no. It's your idea."

"Well, somebody better tell me before I explode. What is it?"

Pane drapes his elbow on the molding leading into the living room. "How would you feel about having your own permanent space for massages, facials, and whatever else you want to do?"

Her gaze swivels from Pane to me. "Rowe, what's he talking about?"

I gesture to the house, which is covered in drop cloths and lined in painter's tape. "He's talking about turning the farm into a spa, a place that caters to couples and girls' weekends."

Her jaw drops. "Oh my God. It sounds fabulous. It would be a dream come true. But can you do that? Do you have time?"

Pane nods out the front door, where Ron, Isaac, and McCauley the lawn guy are all in the midst of putting up new fencing. "We have time. We're only renovating a few rooms downstairs, plus the bathroom, and painting the others."

Cristina squeals. "Yes! Show me everything." Then she turns around. "Oh, wait. Your piggies followed me up. They want in, too."

Ten of them sit in front of the screen door, watching us with dark eyes full of questions and hope—hope that they will once again be able to pile up on quilts at my feet.

Pane thuds over in his heavy boots, shakes his head, and says, "Go on. You aren't allowed in here."

"Pane," I scold.

"What?" He turns and shrugs. "They know the rules."

They do. In fact, Tallulah leads them off, making a point to lift her tail, showing us her rear end.

Oh yeah, they have an opinion about Pane, all right.

I stifle a laugh before grabbing Cristina by the arm. "Come on. Let me show you what we're thinking."

A few minutes later, I've gone over Pane's concept and talked to Cristina about her role in the business. I've pitched the nighttime walks and the option for people to play with piggycorns as a stress-relief activity.

"I love it," she tells me. "It's absolutely brilliant. Why didn't you think about it before?"

I rest my shoulder on a doorframe leading into what will become Cristina's studio. "I don't know. Maybe because we were too close to all the sadness."

"These are good things, Rowe. Really good things. So"—her mouth pinches into a tiny *O*—"how are things with . . ." She nods toward the front of the house, where Pane is working.

"I kissed him," I whisper.

"What?" she shrieks.

I press a finger to my lips and shut the door. "I had no choice in it because that was the day all those cars were honking and coming by."

"Oh my God!" She grabs my sleeve. "How was it?"

"So good!" I then tell her how he broke away and then kissed me again, and the use of tongue, and then I finish with the whole no-kissing rule.

She exhales in disappointment. "No! Not another rule."

"It's fine. We need it. I can't get attached. He's leaving."

"He is, but you can have fun while he's here."

I sip my coffee and rest my back against the closed door. "Right now, the best thing is for me to focus on the farm."

"Well, if you find yourself lonely one night, you might just want to walk out to that shamper. I bet he'd let you in with open arms."

I smirk. "I'm not going to find out."

"I don't know," she chirps. "I see chemistry. There's something in the way he looks at you."

"He's not looking at me in any *way*."

"Could've fooled me."

Outside, a truck engine rumbles loudly, the noise so jarring that I immediately know who it is.

Luke.

"Sounds like trouble," Cristina murmurs.

"Agreed."

We head into the hallway, where Pane's looking up from the tape measure he's holding to the foyer floor.

"It's Luke," I tell him.

His face darkens as he rises. "I'll deal with this."

I frown. "Do you . . . Have you two met?"

"We may have had a run-in."

My gaze drops to his bruise, and my jaw drops. "That's not from . . . You didn't . . . *What happened?*"

Pane's jaw clenches and unclenches. "I beat him at poker."

"Oh, you beat him at— Wait. What?" I can feel a line forming between my brows. "He hit you because you won?"

"Not exactly."

"Wow," Cristina chimes in. "Everyone knows he cheats. How'd you win?"

Pane's face darkens. "I found out his secret."

"Well, don't keep us in suspense. How does he do it?" she asks. When I shoot her a hard look, she mutters, "It's an honest question. We all want to know."

"He'll explain later," I grind out.

Luke exits the truck, jerking his long limbs like he's trying to shake something off him. Either he's ticked, or a fire's been lit under his ass. Thanks to Pane, my bet is that he's ticked off.

Luke spies all his ex–poker buddies working on the fence, shakes his head in disgust, and approaches the house. He's wearing his bank clothes—button-down shirt, gray suit pants, hair slicked to the side and his beard oiled.

He's carrying papers.

His gaze drinks in the new lumber and the mended fence before he takes the porch steps two at a time.

"Morning," he greets us through the screen door, his attention landing on Pane for all of half a second before he focuses on me.

"Morning," I say icily.

"May I come in?"

Pane folds his arms over his chest. "No."

Luke tugs at his collar. "Last I checked, this wasn't your house, Maddox."

"Last I checked, it wasn't yours, either."

Cristina whispers in my ear, "Is it sexy that they hate each other, or is it just me?"

I shoo her away. "Whatever you want, Luke, you can say it from there."

Luke waves at the lumber and tools lying around. "Looks like you're doing some improvements."

"Um, yes." I slip my hands into my back pockets. "We've got plans for the farm."

"So I've heard. People in town can't stop talking about what's going on out here." Luke cranes his neck to peek inside. Pane steps up and blocks his view. "Looks like it's going to be nice."

"Is this an official visit, Luke? Or are you here to grab more furniture?"

He snickers. "Just wanted to have a glance myself to see if Ron and everyone else is telling the truth. Had to make sure."

"Make sure of what?"

The hand holding the papers snaps out. "That you're in violation of the foreclosure proceedings."

My mouth dries. "What?"

He nods toward the papers. "In accordance with the contractual terms of foreclosure, there cannot be any major changes to the property during the foreclosure time period. If major changes are witnessed by a bank official—who would be me—then the date wherein which the property returns to the bank is changed."

"Changed?" Pane opens the door and snatches the papers from his hand. "How is it changed?"

Luke slips his hands in his pockets. "The time period just got cut short by two weeks."

"Two weeks?" I blurt out. "Luke, you've been driving by. You've seen that we've been working. Why'd you wait—"

Until now to do this, I was going to say. But from the way Pane and Luke are glaring at each other, I know why Luke's doing this now.

He hates Pane, and Pane hates him.

"As an officer of the bank, it's my duty to do what's right," he tells me.

"Bullshit," Cristina coughs into her hand.

Luke slowly backs away from the screen door. "Thirty-five days. That's all you've got until the place goes to auction." He glares at Pane, a victorious sneer slapped across his face. "Good luck."

Chapter 22

PANE

"So now I've got less time," I explain to Stone later that night. "Can we move the deadline up?"

In the background, I hear someone barking orders. Stone breaks through the intrusion with, "So now you want me to have *less* time to beat you. Is that it?"

"Technically, it's less time that it'll take for me to win—and yes, that's what I'm asking."

My brother laughs. "So smug. Tell you what: I agree. As long as Sylvia's okay with it, it's fine with me. I can kick your ass at this with one hand tied behind my back."

"Ah, you must be loving hot dogs."

"I'm going to send you a case, smart-ass, so you can see how good the product is."

"Please do. I'll send you the address."

I'm outside the shamper, sitting on the steps. Once Luke left, I had a meeting with the men and told them the new timeline. They eagerly agreed to put in more hours. Thank God. Otherwise, we'd be screwed.

Can we do everything that needs to be done in five weeks? Renovate, sell packages, get the social media presence up to par so that we open with a bang?

Maybe. Maybe not.

"How are things going?" I ask him.

"They're fine."

There's tension in his voice. Stone's generally calm, even under pressure. *Especially* under pressure. Last time I saw him, when we were with our mother, something was off with him then, too.

"What's up? Something going on with Mom that you want to talk about?"

He sighs. The sounds of people talking fade away, and I hear a car door slam. "There's something you should know."

A piggycorn steps out from the bushes surrounding the shamper. It's Tallulah, the little one Rowe can't get enough of. *What's she doing over here?*

"What is it?" I ask my brother.

"Promise you won't get mad."

"Definitely not."

"I've been talking to Dad."

Every cell in my body turns to ice. "What?"

"Yeah, and you should talk to him."

"No."

He exhales heavily. "Some of the things we've been told . . . Look, they're not true, okay?"

I explode, "It's not true that he abandoned our family and had nothing to do with us? That's not true?"

"It's more complicated than that."

"It's not more complicated, Stone. It's pretty simple, actually. When we needed that man the most, he left us, turned his back on his family." I close my eyes and pinch the corners with my thumb and forefinger. "I can't believe you're talking to him. You hate him more than I do."

"Well, I don't. Not anymore." He pauses. "You should hear him out."

"I have nothing to say to that man, and I'm disappointed that you do."

"Just throwing it out the window, are you? Not even gonna give it a chance? Wake up, Pane. Life isn't always as black and white as you make it. Things happen. People change. You can't shut everybody out all the time and pretend like things don't matter to you. Life doesn't work that way."

"It's worked that way fine for me."

"And what has that gotten you? You don't date anybody seriously. When was the last time you felt love in your heart, or something like it? And I'm not talking about for Natalie or even for me. When was the last time you let someone in?"

Tallulah walks up, sniffing the ground but keeping one eye on me. I shake my head. When *was* the last time I felt anything?

At the bar, with Rowe. That night, I felt something. It was also the same night I realized she can't be abandoned again.

"We're not talking about me," I growl.

"Right. Just shut down. Pretend that you're happy leading a lonely, miserable life."

"What would you have me become, a man-whore like you?"

"At least then you'd feel something instead of walling yourself up in a hotel and pretending like the company is all you care about."

My heart deflates. "Look, I don't want anything to do with our dad. You want to talk to him, fine. But leave me out of it."

After a short pause, he says in a cold voice, "I'll talk to Sylvia about moving up the timeline."

"Thanks."

We hang up, not even saying goodbye. I drop my hands to my knees and close my eyes, breathing deep.

Something wet and soft touches my hand. When I look up, Tallulah's sniffing the phone and gazing up at me with sympathetic dark eyes.

"You weren't meant to overhear that."

She wags her tail and snorts. I smile slightly in spite of myself.

"It's easy to see why Rowe likes you," I admit as the piggycorn pushes up my hand with her horn, a not-so-subtle request to be petted.

I run a hand down her neck, and she nuzzles my shin; then she sits back on her haunches and snorts.

And snorts.

And snorts.

I dismiss her, but the piggycorn stands and paws at my leg with her hoof. When I pet her, thinking that's what she wants, she shakes her body, flinging off my hand.

Then she paws me again.

It's as if she's trying to tell me something.

"Is everything okay?"

Oh my God. I'm clearly delusional if I think this pig is trying to communicate with me. It's a *pig*.

Tallulah backs up, snorting harder, and turns in quick circles, kicking up her hind legs. Just for shits and giggles, I ask, "What's wrong, Tallulah? Is Timmy stuck in the well?" to quasi-quote every episode of the ancient show *Lassie* in existence.

The piggycorn snorts harder, backing up toward the house. Yes, she definitely wants my attention, and now she's got it.

I rise and feel my shoulders pinch. "Has something happened to Rowe?"

The piggycorn snorts again.

Worry knots up my insides. If anything's happened to her . . . I grit my teeth. The need to protect fills me up. It's the same emotion that slammed into me last night when Luke mouthed off about Rowe.

I don't know what took over me then, and I don't know what's taking over me now, except the desire to keep that little sunbeam safe.

Then I say words I never thought I'd utter to a horned swine:

"Take me to her."

Chapter 23

ROWE

We have two fewer weeks to get everything done. Saving the farm already seemed impossible. Well, *more* possible with Pane in charge. But now that Luke's stolen time from us, I'm worried we won't be able to save the place at all.

Even though, after Luke had left the house, Pane assured me we'd be fine.

Will we?

I wander aimlessly across the meadow, unable to sit, unable to eat, unable to think. The earth brightens under my feet, lighting up my footprints and illuminating my entire body. When I was young, I loved coming out here, dropping to the ground, and making angels of light like you would snow angels.

Pro tip: Light angels are much cooler.

But now all I do is pass my hand over the grass, admire how it glows, and then feel a pang of sadness that the magic ends before it touches the house. The river of power dries up at the scrubby bushes that surround the home. After that, the land is barren.

Still wandering, I move past the meadow and head to the road. Before I can stop myself, I'm in the trees, dodging branches and keeping to the tree line until what I'm searching for pops into view.

There, sitting all alone in a pasture, is a small barn.

There are new signs nailed to it, handwritten in sloppy paint as if the person who penned them couldn't be bothered.

Well, *I'm* bothered by their words. More than bothered. A ripple of anger surges down my spine as I scan them.

MAD UNICORN.
BEWARE.
NO TRESPASSING.
ENTER AT YOUR OWN RISK.

I ignore them all and step right up to the barn door. Late-summer humidity clings to my skin, making my palms slick. I wipe them on my jeans, grab hold of the handle, and tug. The door quietly groans open.

Inside, it's warm, and the smell of hay fills the air. Moonlight floods in through the open door, throwing light on the concrete that stretches out before me. But that's not the only illumination in the stable. In the very back, a night-light shines from a socket in the wall.

"Stella," I whisper. "You awake?"

The last stall begins to glow, and a smile breaks across my face. "Hey, girl."

The first part of Stella that appears as she steps up to the open half door is her horn. Golden light erupts from the spirals, and the whole thing shines like a candle submerged in the darkest depths of Sally Ray's black soul.

Stella nickers impatiently as I approach. "You look good."

She shuffles, and the sound of metal scraping against the floor draws my attention. With the light cast from her horn, it's not hard to make out the cuff that's secured to her hind leg, just over her hoof, and is attached at the other end to a plate on the wall.

"I'm so sorry," I whisper.

Her dark eyes are sad as she lowers her head. I slide a hand under her cheek and press my forehead to her nose.

She smells of earth, hay, and sorrow. It's that last emotion that makes anger flare bright and hot in my core. But before it's able to take a firm hold of me, it melts away like snow on a sunny afternoon and is replaced by love—pure, limitless love.

It's the kind of gift that only a unicorn can give.

"One day," I whisper. "One day I'll get you out of here." I throw my arms around her. "I promise."

As I hug her, the smell of roses fills my nose. I open one eye and jump back as a stem shoots out from a crack in the board lining the stable. More do the same, and the stems grow, unfurling into delicate green leaves, which reveal pink buds that grow at an accelerated pace until they open up into red-petaled roses. The blooms sprout by the dozens, snaking through the boards in the walls, falling from the ceiling, rising up from the ground to wind gently around my ankles.

Their perfume fills the air as big, crimson-bloomed flowers blanket the walls, ceiling, and floor.

I grin at Stella. "Thank you for that beautiful gift."

I give her another hug just as a voice breaks the peace.

"Dammit, Sally Ray, how many times have I told you to make sure that door's shut?"

"Oh, *can it*, Luke. You know that stupid uni ain't going nowhere. Nobody wants her."

Oh, crap.

"Nobody but Rowe," Luke says snidely.

"Speaking of . . ." Sally Ray and Luke are getting closer. I go very still, pushing myself up against Stella. "What happened last night at the poker game?"

"Nothing, that's what," Luke spits. "Nothing worth mentioning."

"Uh-huh," she says, sounding like she doesn't believe him.

"I'm telling you, we've got nothing to worry about. That farm's going to be ours, and so will whatever magic that place has left. We take the farm, breed the unis on that land—we get the magic back. Our plan is gonna work, Sally."

What? They're going to take the farm hoping to get close enough to the ley lines that their unicorns will have magic again? Well, I've got news for them: If the piggycorns don't have magic, there's no way the unis will get it back just by moving closer to the source.

Those jerks.

They want to take the farm that's been in my family for generations. No way will I let that happen.

Outside the barn, I can hear the clank of keys on a key ring and the clomp of boots on grass.

"That Wadley place took my best worker." Sally cusses. "I tried offering Ron triple the pay, but he still won't come back." There's a pause. "You get that drone yet?"

"It's coming," Luke tells her. "Now, I'll take this side," he says. "You make sure the other side's locked up, too."

"Why do I have to walk around to the other side?"

"Because I'm tired. Someone's got to make sure the Wadleys don't succeed in buying back that property. You think it's easy to come up with ways to break Rowe's spirit?"

Sally Ray laughs, as if hurting me is some kind of fun game to her. "I got to admit, honey, buying the furniture was a good idea. And using that foreclosure clause? It was brilliant. I tell you what . . ." There are sounds like she's kissing him. "When we get back inside, I'm gonna show you how proud I am of you."

More kissing. Gross.

"I tell *you* what," he says, his voice sounding low and horny. "When we get back inside, I'm going to let you."

They are two peas in a pod—horrible, despicable people.

While they're kissing, and as quietly as possible, I dart away from Stella, out of view of the door that I stupidly left open, and head deeper into the barn toward the far end.

The door's shut tight, and Sally'll see that as soon as she comes around. Now I'm in the dark, and there's no way Luke will spot me.

The kissing stops, and it sounds like he smacks her ass. Then his inky-black silhouette comes into view.

Luke starts to close the door and stops. "Roses? What the hell? The only person Stella makes roses for is Rowe."

Double crap.

He studies them for a moment. "Hmm, probably just a fluke. You don't have to check the far door, Sally."

"Good," she mumbles from beside him.

Luke pauses and I'm deathly still. *What is going on?* He starts to close the door, and I exhale.

But my relief is short lived, because from out of nowhere, the opposite door—the one closest to me—slides open and light slices through the darkness.

They tricked me! Luke sent Sally to open the door anyway!

And now there's nowhere for me to go, nowhere for me to hide. I'll be caught. I'll be arrested. I'll lose my farm.

Just as a beam of moonlight hits the toe of my cowboy boot, a hand clamps around my mouth and I'm dragged back.

A flash of adrenaline surges to my limbs until the scent of juniper hits me. I take hold of the hand that's gently cradling my lips.

"Shh, little Sunbeam," Pane murmurs in my ear. "Not a word, or they'll find us."

He's pulled me into a corner of the barn, out of sight as Luke and Sally Ray study the roses that line the walls and sprout from the ceiling.

"You here, Rowe?" Sally asks. "You come to see your bestie, Stella?"

Pane relaxes his hand on my mouth, but now I notice that he's holding on to my waist, holding me so close that I'm flush against him. My shoulder blades dig into his chest. My rear end is flush with his crotch.

Memories of our kiss ping-pong around in my mind, and when his thumb begins making little circles on my waist, I wonder if he's remembering the kiss, too.

Luke rips some of the roses from the ceiling and drops them on the floor. He shines his phone's light in the stall and sweeps it around.

"Nah, she's not here. Probably just a fluke. This old unicorn's so crazy, she may have made them just for the hell of it."

Luke gets his hand too close to Stella, and she bites at it.

He reels back as she stamps the floor in anger. "Crazy-ass unicorn." He stares at Stella for a moment before swinging his attention to Sally Ray, who also sweeps her light across the stalls.

"Looks empty," she says.

"Yeah. Let's go."

After several long moments, they cross back to the doors and slide them shut. I exhale as the sounds of their footsteps grow fainter and fainter.

Stella's horn starts to glow again, throwing light around the barn. I turn around to find myself nose to nose with Pane.

Like, literally. I back up a step and say, "Thank you. You saved me from being caught."

He folds his arms and cocks his chin. "Is *that* what you call *trespassing*?"

I scoff. "In case you haven't noticed, you're doing it, too."

"That's only because Tallulah told me that you were in danger."

"Tallulah?"

He points behind him, and sure enough, sitting on the floor, giving me her best piggycorn smile, is Tallulah.

I drop my head in my hands. "She must've seen me head toward the road. We sometimes come out here together to visit Stella."

He nods in her direction. "And I assume this is Stella?"

"Yes, come meet her." I head out of the nook we were hiding in and pass the night-light. "She's afraid of the dark," I explain. "If she wasn't, Sally Ray and Luke would leave her in darkness all the time."

The unicorn pulls back as Pane steps up. "It's okay. He's a friend," I explain gently.

Stella gives him a good once-over before slowly extending her neck. "Pane, meet Stella, the last unicorn with magic."

The hotel heir studies her with the quiet respect an alpha male reserves for another creature. "How do you know her?"

I exhale heavily and give her a friendly pat. "She used to be mine. That's until Sally offered to buy her to help with some of Dad's medical expenses. The deal was that I'd eventually get her back, but Sally didn't keep her end—and Stella, turns out, doesn't like Sally or Luke. She bites and kicks them and anyone they attempt to sell her to. They can't get rid of her. So they put her in here, in solitary confinement."

My heart breaks all over again, and I release a shaky breath.

He whispers, "I'm sorry."

"It's okay," I reply. "One day she'll be mine again." Stella paws the floor impatiently, and I can't help but chuckle. "She wants you to pet her."

Pane lets her smell his hand, and then he runs a palm over her neck. "She's . . ." His eyes widen as he drinks her in. "What's that feeling?"

A smile breaks out across my face. "She can give you any emotion. She gives me love."

He frowns. "I'm feeling . . ." He shakes his head. "It's impossible to describe."

"It's your emotion for you to have. You don't have to share it."

His body stills and I watch him, understanding the awe that he's experiencing. I've seen this before when people first meet Stella. They're overcome with emotion. Some have described it as feeling as if their hearts are too big for their chests.

That might be what Pane's feeling now.

Wonder fills his voice. "I've never seen such a creature."

"I told you that there's nothing like meeting a unicorn for the first time."

He glances at the ceiling and the walls. "She made all these roses for you?"

I grin. "She does that for people she likes."

He cocks his head and studies me. It feels like Pane's peeling back the layers of my mind, peeking at the parts that remember how his lips felt, or how luscious it was to experience his fingers curling into my waist.

The urge to run and hide overcomes me.

But thanks to the love that Stella's pouring into my heart, I find the strength to return Pane's open stare.

He smiles. "Thank you for letting me meet her."

"Now we're even. I saved you, and you have now saved me."

He steps toward me and looks down, forcing me to tip my chin up to meet his gaze. I let myself stare at him. He truly is beautiful—a blend of masculine strength and quiet determination, all of which mingle in his features: his strong jaw, piercing eyes. Pane Maddox is a work of art.

And as he watches me, a knot closes my throat. I don't know what's happening. We've been around each other for days, and everything's been perfectly normal. Maybe it's because of Stella's magic. *Duh.* Of course it's because of her magic. Her magic is making the air charged. It's pulling us like magnets toward one another.

This scares the hell out of me.

So of course I pivot with, "So, you figured out how Luke cheats."

This breaks the tension, and Pane rocks back on his heels. "Yes, sure did."

I lightly touch the bruise and he flinches, so I draw my hand away. "And he punched you because of it?"

"Something like that."

"Story, please."

He tells me what happened, and I know the shock is evident on my face when I say, "He did *not* use unicorn mane."

"He did."

"What a jerk." Anger curdles in my veins at the thought of Luke not only cheating but also doing it maliciously, against people like Ron and Isaac—good people. "Well, here's the unicorn whose mane he stole from."

Pane rubs a hand down Stella's nose. "Stella."

"Stella," I confirm.

"So where did the unicorns come from, exactly? How did the ley lines become . . . I don't know"—he scrubs a hand up the back of his neck—"activated?"

"Ah, that. Well, about fifty years ago Mystic Meadows was a logging community. When the industry started to die, the town council decided to find something else that would bring in money. They were going to do a German-themed town, but when they started building, something woke up the ley lines, I guess." I shrug. "No one really knows exactly what caused it, but soon after that the first unicorns were discovered, and then my grandparents found the piggycorns, and the rest"—I splay my hands—"is history. My parents bought the house and farm from them, and had me."

"So it was a happy accident," he murmurs, studying me as if looking for cracks in my facade.

"Right." I don't want to talk about the farm, though, not after what happened today. So I nudge him. "Back to Luke's cheating. How'd you find out about the mane?"

"Now, that *is* strange," Pane says in a low voice.

"Oh, there's something stranger than sticking unicorn hair in your pants?"

He smirks. "The mint in my drink showed me."

My brows stitch tight. "What?"

"The magic came into the drink." He rests both hands on the lip of the open Dutch door and considers something. "But there's not magic in town."

"There isn't." I pull my hair over one shoulder and start braiding. "But the day that you worked the chain saw, the magic helped you out, too. By lifting a log."

He drops his hands and faces me. "And you weren't going to tell me that I only won because magic helped?"

The annoyance in his voice makes me grind out, "In case you haven't noticed, we've been busy. Besides, Coleman Barrier didn't know, and that's what counts."

He winks. "I'm joking. It's fine that you didn't tell me. I'm just surprised that it happened."

"Me too."

When Stella nudges him, he pets her again. "What do you think's going on?"

"I think the land realizes that you're going to save the farm, so it's helping you however it can," I joke.

"I agree," he replies, serious.

Our gazes latch again, and my heart expands, inflating inside my chest. This feeling, this longing, this *something* between us, it's impossible to ignore.

But I must.

After a moment of quiet, he says, "My dad."

This is a change in topic. "What about him?"

Pane pats Stella's neck but keeps his gaze trained on me. "That's why I want to win the Maddox Group. I want to be a better man than my father has been."

Oh.

A tiny seed of possibility sprouts in my gut. This is the seed of friendship, of openness, of the fact that Pane Maddox just told me the one thing he said earlier I wasn't privy to.

This is a gemstone—a rare, precious piece of information that's not to be mocked or ignored.

And it's taking a lot for him to say this, because his voice is raw, as if telling me this is like scraping the truth right out of his throat. I'm not sure how to respond, because my dad wasn't someone I wanted to be better than. He was someone I wanted to make proud.

"Ever since I was a kid," Pane explains, "I told myself that when I got the company, I would be better than him. I wouldn't abandon my family, using the name to get what I want. I would be a Maddox who left a legacy, one that inspired instead of destroyed."

My heart shatters into a million pieces before the vacuum of my chest yanks it all back together.

This is the suffering that Pane Maddox has endured, and I understand it. I understand *him.* He was abandoned, too, and so he wants to be better than the man who destroyed his life.

I turn toward him and he pivots to me. We each take a step in as if we're tethered to opposite ends of a rope that's being pulled tight.

I touch his arm and he immediately responds, tucking a strand of hair behind my ear. I lick my lips and say, "For what it's worth—"

"Rowe, I know you're in there!"

My eyes widen as Sally Ray's voice sounds from outside the barn door.

"And when I find you," she continues, "I'm gonna have you arrested for trespassing."

Chapter 24

ROWE

We are dead meat.

Before I can think, Pane unlocks Stella's door, picks up Tallulah, and ushers us both inside.

Days ago, I would've argued with him. I would've wanted to head into a different stall, but now I'm letting him pull me in, shocked that Pane is actually—*willingly*—picking up Tallulah and guiding the three of us to the back of the unicorn's stall.

"Those roses were a dead giveaway," Sally Ray sneers as she shoves the barn door open.

Silvery light floods into the barn. Even in the darkest corners, there's enough illumination that Sally will find us this time. I swallow past a knot in my throat as I realize that we're done for.

"First, I'm gonna sniff out your ass and have you arrested," Sally declares, her boots thudding heavy on the floor. "Then I'm gonna take your farm, and when I do, I'm gonna have every last piggy slaughtered and turned into bacon."

She cackles like a maniac.

I start to charge forward, but Pane hooks his arm around my shoulder and pulls me back against him.

Tallulah sits on the floor, somewhere by my feet. I hope she didn't understand Sally. I don't know any animal psychologists who could treat her for the trauma of hearing she'll be turned into bacon.

But the pressure of Pane's arm captures my attention because it's resting just above my breasts, and once again, I'm pushed against him, my butt to his crotch.

Oh, wow.

He's got an erection, and it's pressing into the curve of my ass cheeks.

Pane shifts, probably because his pants are uncomfortable, quietly turning me around so that now my chest is against his. But his erection isn't gone. It's now digging into my stomach. And none of this helps my nipples, which are tight and pinched, scraping against the fabric of my bra.

Sally snaps on her phone light and starts whipping it over the stable. The light gets ever closer, and there's nowhere to hide. No place to go. Sweat trickles down my back. It sprouts on my forehead. She will see us, and we will be arrested.

My fingers dig into Pane's arm, silently telling him that we're screwed. In response, his hands circle my waist.

Somehow I don't think his body is saying, *You're right, Sally's totally going to find us.*

I look up at him, and his lips drop to within an inch of mine.

My heart blooms with the feeling of love that Stella has seeded inside me. I don't know what Pane's feeling. It could be that. It could be the need to run. But as I tip my face up to his, his lips drop even more.

Why am I thinking about making out when imminent doom is approaching?

But I can't help it. The cottony scent of his breath washes over me, wrapping me up and making my core tighten.

Behind me, Sally's light creeps ever closer. We'll be found for sure. Sally will call the cops. We'll be charged with trespassing. She'll make bacon. Ugh. I can't even think about it.

All those thoughts and more, like ones I'm trying to ignore about Pane's generous erection, fill my head.

The roses rustle and I stiffen. Are they pulling back? But no, I look up just as vines shoot out next to us, growing at turbo speed, creating a lattice that stretches and pulls around us. In the blink of an eye, they've created a thorny wall, forming a tight web between the three of us and Stella.

We've been camouflaged, hidden safely inside something akin to a hunting blind that Sally can't see into.

Inside the lattice, it's pitch black. All I can hear is Sally's muffled mumbling—something about stupid roses and how she's gonna get me. Then her feet slowly make their way back to the front of the barn.

Oh, wow. She's giving up!

I hope.

As the sounds of her footsteps become more and more distant, I'm suddenly intimately aware that Pane's nose is pressed against mine, and that his lips are hovering less than an inch away.

He rubs his thumbs against my waist, and his voice is low and husky. "You should really stop putting us in situations where you want to kiss me."

It's a joke; I know it is. But it's more than that. It's an open challenge. An open invitation.

I lick my lips. The sound is deafening in this rose cocoon. "What about rule number four?"

"What about it?"

"You created it."

His lips graze the tip of my nose. "Who said anything about breaking it?"

"No one." My core thrums. My groin throbs. "But it seems like . . ."

His lips brush my cheek, sending a shiver cartwheeling down my back. "Like what?"

"Like we might be about to do some breaking."

Pane exhales, and his breath rolls over my flesh like smoke on a river. "And would that be bad?"

"It's a rule."

One that I really, really want to break right now. In fact, all I want to do is rip off my clothes and throw Pane on the floor.

The urge is nearly overwhelming.

But neither of us budge, and Pane keeps brushing his lips over my cheeks, my jaw, my nose, leaving trails of fire burning across my skin.

My knees nearly buckle when he murmurs, "We should go."

But the roses don't budge, and neither do we. A thousand thoughts ping in my head.

He's leaving town in a few weeks.

He's a great kisser.

You should jump him, Rowe.

That last one came out in Clarice Sinclair's voice, which is all kinds of wrong.

His lips keep scraping across my cheek, dipping closer and closer to my mouth. I tip my face up to his, and his mouth slides over mine.

It's just a kiss, the little devil on my shoulder suggests. *What could be the harm?*

The angel on my other shoulder shakes her head in dismay. *Obviously, she'll be abandoned again, and then we'll have to endure* all *the heartbreak. How long will the pain last this time?*

Screw it.

His mouth starts to cross over mine, and this time I'm ready. I angle my lips up, and Pane's mouth seals with mine. An explosion of sensation flares inside my core, shooting fireworks all the way to the ends of my fingers.

Pane's tongue lashes against mine. He tastes earthy and wonderful, like sweat and hard work.

When he moans into my mouth, just hearing the sound—that little pleasure from such a grunty man—makes my knees quiver.

I can't get enough of him.

His hands dig into my waist. My fingers rake through his hair. Pressure builds in my pelvis and I press myself against him, grinding him into the wall. His erection presses harder into me, which turns me on even more, and I grind harder.

Memories of our first kiss flood my mind. If that one was fire, then this one is a towering inferno that reaches all the way to outer space.

He slides a palm down the front of my jeans, cupping my pelvis.

My God, he's gripping me hard, his fingers tightening at my opening.

A gasp rips from me. Even through my jeans, the pleasure rocks me. I want more. I want all of it. He holds me harder, and I grind myself against him like a rabid raccoon needing a fix. I'm on the verge of climaxing by simply being touched outside my jeans.

While Pane keeps the pressure on my pelvis and I'm grinding against him like a horny squirrel, his other hand moves up my waist, and this time, I'm going to let him feel me up. I'm ready. My breasts ache. My nipples long to be touched by someone other than myself.

That's when it hits me. For the past four years, I've been living a half-life, shoving away emotion, but now my heart is thumping in my chest and my rib cage is shrink-wrapped around it.

Maybe that's not right. Maybe my rib cage isn't shrinking. Perhaps my heart's expanding like a balloon, swelling inside my chest cavity, pressing against its bony cage, forcing me to feel things I haven't experienced in . . . forever.

Things like my heart.

Wait. That can't be right.

But I *am* feeling it. My heart is thumping and beating, waking up in a way that makes me realize it's been asleep. It never occurred to me that it's been shut down ever since Luke slashed it to pieces.

But it has been, and now it's wide open for business, whether I'm ready or not.

And I'm not ready.

Just as Pane slides his hand up the outer rim of my breast, the rose wall rips apart, exposing us and bringing with it a shock of night air.

I leap away like I've been caught making out in a car parked by the lake. Pane doesn't move.

Stella's standing where she always does. She glances at the roses as if they're a minor inconvenience and tosses her head back.

Stella. Her power.

That's what caused all this. That's why I was so worked up. That's why Pane kissed me. It's because of Stella's power.

Whew. Thank goodness I know that. Otherwise, this could have been embarrassing. You know, me thinking that this is real and all.

The sound of our panting fills the stable. I look over at Pane. He swallows hard. "Sunbeam . . ."

He's going to say what I was thinking—about how this is all Stella's fault. I'll save him the trouble. "We should get going."

His eyes flare briefly before his face settles into his normal broody expression. "Yeah. Before Sally comes back."

We leave in silence. When we return to the house and he's about to walk off to his shamper, I stop him with, "You know, there's a guest bedroom downstairs. It's yours if you want it."

Moonlight splashes across Pane's face, highlighting his tight brows. He cocks his head as if he's about to say something, then seems to change his mind. "I'll get my things."

He gets his clothes and I show him the bedroom, giving him a quick good night. Too quick for me to throw myself at him, too quick for my eyes to linger on his lips (even though they try to). Then I scamper off to my bedroom and fall into a very lonely and restless sleep.

Chapter 25

PANE

Rowe spends the next week running away from me. Every time I enter a room, she exits faster than a jewel thief escaping the scene of the crime in a Ferrari.

It's killing me. I want to talk about what happened, about that kiss. Whenever I close my eyes, I still feel the burn of her on my lips. But Rowe doesn't want to have anything to do with me.

She thinks I'll be just like all the other men who've abandoned her.

Maybe she's right. Maybe I will be. Maybe as soon as all this is over, I'll feel the pull to leave, to return to my life.

Where will that leave her?

What does it matter if she won't talk about it? We can't even kiss, because when we do, she runs like a chaos goblin in the other direction.

Rowe is like a wild animal I'm slowly coaxing to eat out of my hand—extremely distrustful, prowling at the dark edges of the perimeter. But eventually she'll come around.

At least, I hope so.

Because the ache in my heart from being with her day in and day out, without doing anything about it, is excruciating. I've never experienced anything like it.

The guys notice, too—about Rowe, not about my heart.

So much so that it's become a running joke between Ron, Isaac, and McCauley. They place bets on how fast she can escape a room if I'm in it.

"Rowe, can you take a look at this?" I call out.

Ron and Isaac built the front desk using old doors Ron found in the barn. He had the notion to turn them into a counter, but skirted around telling me, hemming and hawing. Finally, I pointed out everything he'd fixed at the house, and Ron confided in me about his idea. I told him to run with it.

So both men sanded, polished, and finally nailed the slabs together. It's beautiful, a breathtaking piece.

Rowe's going to love it.

Isaac wipes the counter with a rag. "I give her three seconds before she scatters like a caught fox."

"Nah. More like five." Ron eyes the counter to make sure it's square. "She's gonna like it."

"I say thirty seconds for her to fawn over the piece, throw a 'looks good' at Pane, and then hightail it back to painting," McCauley says as he pulls up drop cloths from the floor.

Isaac winks at me. "Whatever caused this thing between the two of y'all, you may need to do it again to get it out of your system."

"Classy, Isaac—and nothing happened."

"Nothing happened to what?"

Rowe appears in the doorway. She wipes the back of her hand across her cheek, where a line of slate-colored paint is smudged.

"Uh, nothing," Isaac mutters.

She smirks. "Doesn't sound like nothing."

I shoot him a scathing look. "It's that nothing happened to this beautiful front desk. What do you think? Ron and Isaac built it."

"I supervised," McCauley jokes.

She steps into the room, making sure to give me a wide berth, and whistles. "Wow. Y'all did great. It's elegant and original."

"Just like this place," I murmur.

The only sign she shows of hearing me is a twitch of her lips.

"Pane would like a kiss on the cheek in thanks," McCauley teases. The other two burst into laughter.

I'm going to kill those guys as soon as she's gone.

Rowe turns beet red and glances out the window. "Oh, looks like the deliveryman is here. I'd better see what he wants."

She darts from the room and out the front door.

McCauley opens his palm. "Pay up. I had to get her out of here somehow. She was taking too long."

"Don't pay him a dime," I snap.

"Yeah, you're no better than Luke," Ron tells him.

"Bring them in," Rowe says from the front. "You can put the boxes there."

I frown. I didn't order anything. Haven't needed to. The plans are coming along great. We'll have everything finished before the deadline. Appointments are being booked, and Ron's in charge of the night walks. Everything will start at the grand opening, which is still weeks away.

And if bookings hold, there's no way this farm won't be valued at less than a million. I'll have Stone beat, which means the Maddox Group will be mine.

A sense of elation should fill me, but the only sensation in my body is a pit opening in my stomach.

Must be indigestion.

When I step into the foyer, the deliveryman is unloading four large boxes off a hand truck. "Be right back. I've got more."

"What's this?"

Rowe shrugs. "It's all for you."

"I didn't order anything."

A sexy smirk smears across her lips. "As long as your name is Donalpane Maddox, then they're for you."

A groan escapes my lips. "They're from Stone."

"Your brother?"

"My brother."

I don't even have to open the first box to guess what's inside. But once I do, I find a case of gourmet hot dogs.

"Wow, Pane. I didn't know you liked hot dogs so much," Ron says from over my shoulder.

"I don't. It's a joke."

The deliveryman drops four more boxes in the foyer and leaves. This is well over four hundred sausages.

Rowe's brow furrows. "What are we supposed to do with them?"

Isaac and McCauley exchange a look before saying at the same time, "Cookout!"

Rowe groans. "We'll have to invite everyone we know to get rid of all these."

I grab a pack from the box and display it proudly. "We could feed them to the piggycorns. Where's Tallulah?"

Rowe snatches the dogs from my hand. "That's cannibalism. You can't do that."

"Says they're all beef." Ron uses his finger to underline the words on the package. "It's not cannibalism."

Rowe exhales so hard her nostrils flare.

I grin at her as I yank the tape off another box. "You heard the men. Invite everyone you know. We're having a party."

"You want another hot dog?" Ron asks as he mans the grill.

I've already eaten three, so I pat my very full stomach. "No, thanks."

He wipes his hands down an apron that reads GRILL POWER before eyeing the crowd. Half of Mystic Meadows showed up, and they came out in color. One look around the property, and I don't see folks wearing drab grays and dingy white shirts like I did when we first went to town. These citizens are wearing blues and reds, corals and yellows.

Most of the people, I don't know, but that doesn't matter to the good folks of Mystic Meadows. They greeted me as if I were their neighbor, their brother, their best friend.

I have to admit, sometimes it feels like I've known these people for a long time—longer even than I've known the staff at my hotels.

"This is the life," Ron says whimsically as he turns the hot dogs.

I can't help but smile. "Is it?"

"Oh yeah. Grilling out, watching your kids run around while your wife hands you a beer and thanks you for all the hard work you've done."

I take a pull of my own beer. "Do you have kids, Ron?"

"Nah, but when I do, you can bet I'm going to be the best stay-at-home dad ever."

"That's if Jennifer decides to trust you alone with them." Isaac comes up from behind and slaps Ron on the back. "Last I heard, Ron left the iron on and the house almost burned down."

"That was three months ago," he counters, stuffing a potato chip in his mouth. "A lifetime in dog years. I'm completely trustworthy."

Isaac chuckles and grabs a cooked hot dog before dropping it in a bun and slathering mustard and pickles on top. He adds chips to his plate and takes a bite.

"Thanks for this, Pane." He eyes the pasture. The sun's beginning to sink, and it casts a golden glow across the grass. "Look at how beautiful this place is and how relaxed you are."

I lean against a balustrade. It's about as relaxed as I can get.

"You look like you belong here," he adds. "Like you're part of Mystic Meadows."

"Yeah, like you're Mystic Meadows' very rich uncle," McCauley says, winking at me before handing Ron a fresh beer.

The guys laugh, and my gaze wanders to Rowe, who's standing with Cristina and Clarice Sinclair, who's here instead of pouring drinks.

McCauley asks the question I'm thinking: "Who's manning the bar tonight?"

Isaac swallows a bite of hot dog and places a fist in front of his mouth, answering, "I'm about to leave in a bit." He eyes me. "You coming for poker night?"

"No, I've got some things to do around here."

"The place looks good," he tells me proudly. "So does town. People are taking notice of what you're doing and cleaning up their storefronts."

My brow lifts. "They are?"

"Yeah, you should see downtown," Ron says. "There's something . . . almost magical going on. The whole strip looks different."

I don't know what to say.

McCauley drops his empty plate in an open trash can. "It's the Pane Maddox effect."

"Working on everybody except Rowe." Isaac lifts his beer to me. "May the curse be broken soon."

I take another sip of my own beer. "You mean the whole Rowe's-bad-luck thing?"

He shrugs. "That, plus if you two figure out your deal, then maybe the town will stop talking about you."

Tallulah bounds up to the porch, her little tail swishing from side to side. She spots me and makes her way over, wiggling happily as she brushes her body against my leg, starting with her shoulder and ending at her hindquarters. I bend over and pet her, tugging playfully on the pink tuft atop her head.

She must be hungry, so I drop a hot dog in her food bowl. The pig snorts in thanks.

"Hey." Ron points to the piggycorn. "Isn't that supposed to be one of your rules? You don't feed the animals? I heard it from Jennifer, who heard it from Clarice."

I brush burnt hot dog marks from my hands. "I have no idea what you're talking about." Then, to Isaac, I say, "The whole town's gossiping about Rowe and me?"

He nods toward Rowe. "Well, she hasn't dated anyone since Luke, uh . . ."

"Dumped her publicly for Sally," Ron finishes.

I frown and feel a crease slice between my brows. "That was a long time ago."

"Yeah," Ron starts. "But what he did to her after—"

Isaac shoots him a fierce look.

Now my curiosity's piqued. "What'd he do?"

Ron takes the hot dogs off the grill and sets them on a disposable foil platter. "Might as well tell him. We already started."

"*You* already started," Isaac corrects. "I was keeping my mouth shut."

"Fine. I started."

"Then you finish."

When he doesn't say anything, McCauley folds his arms and settles onto the balustrade. "Go on, Ron. Put your money where your mouth is."

"All right, but you know I hate gossip."

Isaac and McCauley burst into laughter. "Right you do," the bartender jokes.

Ron rolls his eyes. "Anyway. Most of this is rumor, but Jennifer heard it from Rowe, who told her because they're friends."

"Heard what?" I ask.

Ron pauses, and Isaac gestures at him to keep going. "Don't stop now. Tell the man the whole thing."

Ron grimaces. "Well, when Rowe first came back with Luke, everybody liked him."

"Her dad referred to him as *son*," McCauley adds.

"But Luke had them all fooled," Ron explains, wiping his hands on his apron. "At first he was great, helping around the farm, doing everything that was needed."

"People were still buying piggycorns then," Isaac adds. "The Wadleys had a deal with Sally Ray across the street. She'd send business their way, and both families profited. The farm wasn't run-down then, either. Rowe's dad worked hard to keep it up and profitable."

I'm putting pieces together. "So her mom wasn't hands-on."

"Not with day-to-day activities. That was all her dad. And then Luke came in, and he took over a lot of those roles," Isaac explains.

"Ron, are the hot dogs done?" A short woman with long, dark hair steps up onto the porch. She grabs a beer from the cooler and notices how eerily quiet all of us have gone. Her eyes narrow in suspicion. "Are y'all gossiping?" When no one answers, she nods. "Y'all are gossiping. Don't let me interrupt." Her gaze lands on me, and she extends her hand, knuckles up. "I'm Jennifer. You must be Pane. You've been keeping my husband working late."

I take the hand she offers. "Yeah, I'm sorry about that."

"We won't be late tonight, honey," he tells her.

"You better not be, or you'll be sleeping in the spare room." She kisses Isaac on the cheek. "Great to see you, Isaac, McCauley. Ron"—she eyes him warily—"I'll see you later."

"Yes, ma'am." He sighs as she walks off, her rear end swishing from side to side. When she's out of earshot, he whispers, "She likes to tie me up. It's the hottest thing ever."

"Please." Isaac rolls his eyes. "Do not put images in my head of you with a black ball in your mouth. I would like to enjoy any future sex I might have."

Ron takes off the apron. "She's gone, right?"

McCauley's gaze tracks Jennifer. "She's not coming back."

"Good. We can get back to Luke."

"Right." Isaac opens a bottle of water and takes a big swig. "It was about six months in, and Rowe's dad was going downhill fast. That's when Luke up and announces that he's leaving her."

"For Sally Ray," Ron informs me pointedly.

McCauley grabs a dog and drops it into a bun. "But that wasn't the worst of it."

My eyes flare. "There's more?"

"Oh, there's more," he confesses.

When no one speaks, Isaac points his water at Ron. "Go on. Go ahead and be the person who has to stop Pane from storming across the street and destroying Luke."

I take the last sip of my beer and drop it in the recycling bin. "Guys, you're not understanding what's going on between me and Rowe."

The men pause before bursting into laughter. Isaac wipes tears from his eyes. "Do you even know how you look at her?"

"Like love is a dove in your heart," Ron says.

"What the hell does that mean?" McCauley asks.

"You know, he looks at her all lovey-dovey."

Isaac slaps my shoulder. "Don't worry, she looks at you that way, too."

"*When* she looks at you," McCauley says.

Another pause before the three break up into laughter.

Annoyed, I grind out, "Are you going to tell me or what?"

Ron exhales a breath, shaky from chuckling. When he speaks, it's just above a whisper. "Rowe got pregnant."

The world stops spinning, and red fills my vision. She got pregnant? With Luke's baby? Did he force her to— Stop, Pane. Just *stop*.

I let out a slow, steadying breath. "Then what happened?"

Isaac looks around to make sure no one's listening to us. "From what I heard, she lost the baby."

Ron drops his voice. "But that's not the worst of it. The worst was that—"

"What're y'all gossiping about?"

Rowe has magically appeared in front of us, hair pulled back in a French braid, her cheeks red, and her face scrubbed clean. She's wearing wedge sandals and a strapless sundress that drifts softly around her knees when she walks.

My mouth goes dry at the sight of her.

"We're not gossiping," Ron says. "Who says we're gossiping?"

"Nothing up here but us hot dogs," Isaac adds. "Oh, look, there's someone I've been wanting to talk to."

"Me too," McCauley says.

They scurry off, leaving me and Ron. Ron abandons me with, "This cooking is really getting hard. I need to focus. Sorry, Pane, but you'll have to excuse me."

Rowe smiles softly at me. "Come on. There's someone I want you to meet."

Meet? There's someone she wants me to meet? She hasn't spoken to me of her own free will in days, and now she's introducing me to someone?

She reaches out and tugs on my fingers, and that's when I know she must be tipsy, because she has also avoided touching me since the kiss.

She leads me to a tall man in his early thirties with dreadlocked hair pulled into a man bun. He has a sculpted beard and wears a linen shirt that's open to his navel. Braided leather necklaces hang halfway down his chest.

He looks like a sex god, and I instantly feel the bite of competition hitting my veins like adrenaline.

Rowe motions to the man. "Donner Wright, meet Pane Maddox."

"Nice to meet you, man," Donner says, shaking my hand. "Rowe tells me that you're responsible for the renovation." His gaze sweeps up and down her in way that makes my blood turn to burning lava. "The farm looks great."

"It's shaping up," I say coldly.

Rowe glares at me but smiles at Donner, which really pisses me off. "Donner runs the off-grid yurt community outside of town. He says some of the men out there have been looking for a project to help with."

"Yeah." He runs a hand down his sandy beard. "We need supplies, like lumber. We'll take scraps—and the men are willing to be free labor for it."

"Off-grid community? How's that work?"

He chuckles, placing a hand to his flat belly. Skin keeps peeking through his unbuttoned shirt—and Rowe keeps glancing at his chest.

"Well . . ." He runs a hand over his head. Rowe studies his every movement. I can practically see the drool dripping from her mouth. "We've been trying to figure out a way to bring in electricity that's not intrusive to the natural surroundings."

"So no solar panels."

"Right, or wind. We've just been living without, but the whole point of the community is to live sustainably, and one of the things we want is environmentally friendly power. It's just taking a while for us to get it."

Rowe keeps staring at this man's chest. It's burning me up. Driving me nuts. She keeps looking, and he keeps smiling at me and at her. It's maddening.

All I want to do is button up his shirt and send the man packing, but I need bodies to get this project complete.

I fold my arms, nod hard. "Do your guys have building experience?"

"Oh yeah, I do for sure. I'll bring a few that I know do, too."

Great. He's a sex god *and* a man who can use a hammer. Perfect. Just what I need.

I attempt to tame the scowl that I know is smeared across my face. Rowe keeps pumping her eyebrows at me, silently telling me to put away my mean face.

I do what I can to school it and extend my hand. "We look forward to you helping. There's only one thing . . ."

Donner shakes my hand, smiling with his set of perfect sex-god teeth. "What's that?"

"We have a dress code. No open shirts."

With that, I walk away.

Chapter 26

ROWE

"What was *that* back there?"

"What was *what*?" Pane asks, acting like he doesn't know what I'm talking about, when I know for a fact he knows damn well what I'm referring to.

He's stalking away from the party, toward the gazebo, and I'm hot on his heels. "No open shirts? Why did you say that to Donner? He wants to help."

Pane whirls around, stops. Taps his fingers against his belt. Opens his mouth. Closes it. Opens it again. "Unbuttoned shirts are a safety hazard."

"A *safety* hazard."

"That's right. Nails can get caught in them. You wind up hammering yourself to a board. Next thing you know, you're decapitated."

Is he joking? "Are you even listening to yourself right now? We're in desperate need of making our deadline, and you're worried about a man with an open shirt."

He flings a hand back toward our guests. "Did you even see *how* open it was? Wait, what am I saying? Of course you did. You were staring at his chest."

My jaw drops. "I was not staring at Donner's chest. I mean, I may have noticed it because I'm pretty sure he oils his pecs, but I was not 'staring.'"

"See? You *were* staring. How can I take you anywhere?"

What is going on? Have I fallen into a different dimension?

Pane studies me, his stupidly handsome face all hard, scowled lines.

I squint at him. "Are you . . . are you *jealous*? Of Donner? A man who clearly smokes marijuana every night and drums while standing in a circle of naked women?"

"Sounds like you're speaking from experience."

"Oh, I *cannot* with you right now." He stares at me, a look of disgust on his face. "Donner wants to help you—help *us*. That's what he's interested in. Do you think I'm interested in him? So that you know, he's not my type."

Pane saunters up to me and stares down into my eyes. Emotion flickers across his face—pain, longing. My heart knots up.

"Who *is* your type?" he whispers.

You, I want to say. No, I don't want to *say* it. I want to *scream it.* I want to scream, *You, Pane, are my type. You are the grunty, broody, sometimes-likable man I've been dreaming of.*

But I just can't do it. Kissing him pushed too many buttons inside me. It made me think too much. Made me *feel* too much. Made me *want* too much.

If I take one more emotional step forward, I'll be lost.

"Who is my type?" I repeat his question, sounding robotic even to myself.

He rolls his eyes and shakes his head. "Rowe, look, I know things have been weird between us since—"

"Then don't make them be weird."

He blinks. "What?"

"Don't make them weird." My heart clogs up my throat. My body throbs just thinking about that kiss, how my fingers tangled in his hair, how his tongue swept into my mouth, making me moan. There was nothing weird about it. Everything about it was right.

He takes a step forward, blocking the setting sun so that all I see is him. My stomach quivers.

When he speaks, his voice is earnest, emotional. "Don't push me away. Let me in."

He's asking me to do this, to put down my guard, to stop running from him every time I see him. Granted, I'm not feeling like running right now. It's the beer, for sure. I'm thinking of how silky his hair is, how soft and demanding his lips are.

Maybe . . . maybe I could let him in just a teensy bit.

"Okay," I say.

He flexes his shoulders. "'Okay,' what?"

"Okay, I'm going to show you my secret."

"These are starfizz berries."

From the look on Pane's face, this isn't the type of letting-him-in he expected. But this is a lot for me.

"No one knows about this. Not even my mom."

Behind a thicket of trees, fenced in so that the piggycorns can't reach them, are four long rows of hedges. Waxy green leaves sprout from squatty bushes that sit heavy with unripe plum-colored berries.

I open the gate and step through, explaining, my voice high, my body a rubber band ball of nerves, and I think it shows, because I speed through my speech. "They used to grow here, in Mystic Meadows—and according to my dad, were found on Sally Ray's land fifty years ago. Her grandfather used to feed them to his unicorns, but he got so busy breeding the creatures that he stopped growing the berries and outsourced them to a farm in South America, where they grow superfast."

"Huh," is all Pane says.

So I keep blabbering on, trying to convince either him or me that this is cool. "But what's interesting is that the piggycorns showed up about the same time he outsourced the berries, so they've never eaten berries that have grown on magical land."

"So you think that, what? This will give the piggycorns powers?"

I laugh. "I wish, but no. I'm just trying to cut out the middleman and save some money."

His gaze washes over the hedges. "But you could also sell them to Sally Ray and anyone else who owns unicorns, and at a cheaper price because they're not imported. It's a second source of income for you, and if they do have magical properties . . ."

I lightly shove him. "They don't have magical properties. They're just starfizz berries, the piggies' favorite food."

Pane sweeps a hand over them and pauses. "I don't know. They're humming."

"What?"

I rest my hand on the hedge and nearly jump back. The bush vibrates. The leaves quake. There's power pumping through the branches and stems. *No, Rowe. Can't get my hopes up.* But what if . . . what if the berries do have magical properties? What could that mean? What if eating fresh berries could help the piggycorns? Give them . . . ? *No.* The piggies don't have magic, and they never will. I'm only doing this to save money.

Pane tugs on a waxy leaf. "How much longer until they're ready?"

My heart ping-pongs in my chest from excitement. "Some of the berries are nearly ripe. Only a few more days, really."

"And what will you do with them?"

"See if the pigs will eat them. This is a trial run. I'll make it bigger next year, contacting unicorn owners to see if they want the feed. I'll be able to sell it cheaper than what's currently imported."

A slow smile curves on his lips. "Rowe Wadley."

"What?" Is he angry? He could be. Sometimes it's hard to know.

"You're amazing."

A grin splits my face. "You like this?"

"*Like* this? No. I'm *amazed* at you. I had no idea that this existed."

His gaze settles on me, and my body heats up from the inside. *This,* I ache to say, *is me opening up. Please take it. Please take this, because that's all I can give you. All that I'm not afraid to give you.*

He's right beside me now, standing close. Too close. Alarm bells blare in my head. My skin feels like it's going to launch right off my bones. The air crackles with the intensity I've felt before.

Does he want to kiss me? I want him to.

"Pane, I—"

"Rowe—"

We each speak at the same time. The leaves rustle, bringing with them the smell of smoke from the grill. In the distance, people are talking, chatting, enjoying the party that we left.

Pane rubs his bottom lip with his thumb. "You first."

Great. Now I have to say something. "Well, I—"

His phone rings. Perfect timing.

"You'd better answer that."

He shakes his head. "It can wait."

When it chirps again, I step back. "It might be important."

Pane slides a hand down his pocket and whips out his phone. He frowns at the screen and answers with, "I got your present."

It must be his brother.

Pane's silent for a beat, but then his jaw flexes and his eyes become hard. "What are you talking about?" He listens for another moment, and when he speaks, his voice drips with worry. "What do you mean, Natalie's missing?"

Chapter 27

PANE

I can't throw clothes into a bag fast enough. My mind's working a mile a minute. Natalie never came home from school. No one can get a hold of Greta. Did she kidnap my sister? Is she holding her for ransom?

I curl my hand into a fist.

"It's going to be okay," Rowe says quietly. "You're going to find her."

I've chartered a flight and am heading to the airport. Rowe's driving me. My mouth tastes like iron, and my body's tight with worry. My chest squeezes my heart so hard it feels like my rib cage might crack.

And people noticed, too. As soon as we returned to the party, everyone could tell something was wrong. Guests scattered, heading home.

Some asked what was wrong, but I didn't say a word. Strangers don't need to know private Maddox business.

Rowe hands me my toothbrush. "Here."

"Thanks." I zip up the case. "I think that's it."

"Okay, then let's go."

She starts to move, but I take her arm, letting my thumb caress her silky skin. "Rowe."

Her brows shoot up. "Yeah?"

"I'm coming back."

"Of course." She smiles tightly. "I know."

But she doesn't. I'm leaving, and I know she's afraid I'll never return. "No, I'm serious. As soon as we find Natalie, I'll be back to finish this."

"I know."

But she says it flippantly, as if I'm lying. Dammit, this woman. How can I convey that I won't abandon her? That I'm not leaving?

The more I say it, the more she looks at me like I'm spewing helium and my words will disappear as soon as they touch the air.

But I'm not leaving. I am coming back.

I'm building something here, and it's not just the spa. It's more.

The realization nearly knocks me over.

Holy shit.

I don't want to leave when this is over. I don't want to leave Rowe.

I just have to convince this scared little bird of a woman that I'm not going anywhere.

"We'd better leave for the airport," she tells me, while all I can do is watch in shock as she walks away.

Shock that I've realized this, that the thought is in me. That I'm not thinking about what's going on in Tokyo or Paris, or even New York. I'm concerned about this small town nestled in northern Georgia.

I numbly follow her outside and to the vehicle. She's talking about how everything's going to be okay. My heart races from this tidal wave of feeling that's overcoming me. It threatens to strangle the air from my throat, to floor me right here and force me to accept this.

It feels like I can't breathe, and when I inhale, a new emotion floods my bloodstream: calm acceptance.

Rowe opens the front door. "Pane, you okay?"

No, I want to tell her. *I'm not okay. I'm nuts about you. I'm absolutely batshit crazy about you, and I'm not going to run away like everyone else has.*

"Yeah, I'm fine."

My phone rings again. My heart nearly explodes. Hopefully, it's Stone calling to say they've found Nat. Dear God, I hope that's who it is.

But it's Isaac. Why's he calling? I'm tempted to push the call through to voicemail, but I need to tell him that he'll be leading the project come tomorrow. Just until I return.

"Hey, man," I say. "Listen, there's—"

But a whiny cry interrupts me. "Paaaaannnne, when are you coming to the baaaar?"

I come to such an abrupt halt that I almost fall back. "Natalie?"

"Who else?"

"What the— Where are you?"

She sighs like it's the stupidest question in the world. "I'm at Sparkle Bar! Where else would I be?"

Chapter 28

ROWE

"Deuces wild, boys!" A small girl with a ball of curly, red hair throws up her arms. "Who's in?"

Beside me, Pane sighs in dismay. "I may or may not have taught my sister how to play poker."

Natalie Maddox has taken up residence at a corner table in Sparkle Bar, and is surrounded by Isaac, Ron, and McCauley.

In front of her sits a pile of cash.

This is *so* not legal. A minor in a bar is even more illegal than trespassing.

At least, I think it is.

I slowly turn my head toward Pane. His expression is a mixture of disbelief and disgust. It's like his usual scowl can't figure out what it wants to be.

"This is your sister?"

"That's Natalie," he answers grimly.

Natalie looks like she arrived straight from school, as she's wearing a navy skirt and a blazer with a crest sewn over the right breast. She's got her legs tucked underneath her, and is leaning over the table, eyeing her cards *and* the other players like she's trying to find the weakest link.

She seems to have zeroed in on Ron.

Isaac glances over from his spot at the table, sees Pane, and does a double take. "Be right back," he says, scooting out his chair and striding quickly over to us.

"She showed up about an hour ago," he explains to the hotel heir, who storms toward his sister. I can practically see the anger wafting off him in thick waves. Isaac must sense it, too. "Go easy on her."

He shoots the bartender a hard look before his feet come to a screeching halt at the table.

Natalie looks up and sees Pane, and a grin breaks out across her face. She unfolds from her seat and runs over, throwing her arms around him.

"What took you so long?"

And just as quickly as his anger flared, it melts. Pane hugs Natalie, curling so that his chin touches the top of her head. He squeezes his eyes shut, and for the first time in the last hour, relief washes over his face.

My heart does this little throbby-achy thing as I watch his worry, fear, and angst dissolve.

Natalie pulls away and grins up at her big brother. "I told the boys that if they mess with the bull, they get the horns!"

"She's killing us," Ron says.

"This kid's a shark," McCauley grumbles in a friendly voice.

"Apparently," Isaac explains, "the three of us left the party about the same time. Couldn't find y'all when we did, but we headed over here to play our Wednesday game. About five minutes after we arrived, she showed up."

Pane's eyes flare with fear. "How did you get here?"

"I took an Uber from the airport."

His voice hits the ceiling. "The airport?"

"Yeah. How else was I going to get here? I can't Uber from New York."

Pane closes his eyes. It looks like he's mentally counting to one thousand. When he opens them, the sage green is dark, inky, angry.

"How did you get to Mystic Meadows?" he asks in a restrained voice.

"Oh, that?" She waves a hand. "I used an app to change my voice so that it sounded like Mom's. Then I called the pilot and told him our destination. Since I didn't know where you lived, I asked the Uber driver to take me to the busiest place in town."

Anger fills his eyes as Pane glances down at her. "You're in trouble, young lady. I don't even know where to start—the voice app? Stealing a plane? Taking an Uber in a strange town? Natalie, you could have been killed, kidnapped!"

Her gaze drops to her feet, and when she speaks, it's a whimper. "But I missed you and wanted to see you."

My heart cracks in two right there. This poor kid, who's been missing her older brother, moved the earth in order to see him.

"She missed you," I whisper to Pane.

He looks at me and shakes his head. "Natalie, promise me that you'll never do that again—any of it. Mom's got the entire NYPD looking for you."

She grimaces. "I'm sorry."

"Stay here, and don't move. I'm going to let Mom and Stone know that you're okay. He's on his way to New York right now to help find you."

Natalie drags her top teeth over her bottom lip. "Am I in *big* trouble?"

He backs away and stops. "Mom will decide that." Her face falls. Pane sees this, and his shoulders slump. "I'm glad you're all right." When she doesn't look up, he bends at the waist until they're eye level. "Hey."

Her lids slowly lift. "Yes?"

"I love you, and I'm relieved that you're safe."

A cheeky smile spreads across her face. "What else?"

"And I'm glad you're here."

"I knew you would be," she announces, throwing her arms around his neck.

He lifts her into the air and holds her tight. When his gaze flickers up, it finds me. My heart convulses at the sight of big, mean Pane Maddox melting like a Popsicle for his younger sister.

"Natalie, there's someone I want you to meet."

Now my heart's thundering because Pane hasn't taken those knee-quaking green eyes off me for several long luxurious seconds, making me feel like I'm the only person who exists in his great big world filled with hotels and important people.

My throat shrivels. For some reason, this feels very heavy, very large, like a momentous occasion.

He lowers her, and Natalie's feet lightly touch the floor. "This is Rowe Wadley. We've been working together."

Natalie sizes me up. Sharp green eyes that match her brother's silently pick me apart. After several seconds, she pulls away from him and approaches me.

"So this is Princess Pain-in-the-Butt?"

My gaze snaps to Pane, who suddenly looks very guilty. I fold my arms. "What's that?"

He coughs into his hand. "It's nothing. *Natalie*," he emphasizes, "Rowe owns piggycorns."

She flaps her hands up and down with glee. "Piggycorns! You own them! Pane's told me so much about the creatures. I want one. I want three! I want to see them."

At this point, I can't help but giggle at her glee. It's absolutely deliciously contagious. "You're welcome to meet them."

"Natalie, you coming back to play?" McCauley calls out.

"Coming!" She starts to move off, but then runs up to Pane and hugs him again. "I'm so glad to see you."

Then she grabs me by the hand and drags me to the table. "Come on. Let's play poker!"

I laugh as she pulls up an empty chair. "All right. How do you play?"

Natalie wins just about every hand, even beating her older brother. Pane plays with a grim expression on his face. He's angry about Natalie running off. But once we're deep in the game, he asks her about school, who her friends are now, if William somebody is still pulling her hair every chance he gets. If so, Pane threatens to make William disappear.

At that, Natalie laughs.

I do, too, though I wonder if, deep down, Pane is serious.

He probably is.

Watching them together softens something in me. When Pane brings back empanadas and Natalie ends up with some on her cheek, my heart just about explodes when he dabs a napkin to her face and cleans it off.

After playing for an hour, Pane tells her that it's time to go home. The plane has returned to New York, and his mom is arriving tomorrow to retrieve her.

"On a scale of one to ten, how mad is Mom?" she asks when we're in the truck.

"She's glad you're safe," he says.

"So that means she's at an eleven on the anger scale."

There's a stretch of silence before Pane says, "You're going to be grounded. You knew that would happen."

"I hoped maybe we could skip that part."

He sighs. "You disabled Greta's phone so that no one could reach her. What did you think would happen?"

"That I would stay here with you for the next month. There's a boarding school only an hour away."

Pane taps his strong fingers against the steering wheel. "I'm not . . ." He doesn't finish his sentence, but I know what he's going to say: *I'm not going to stay here.* Those are the words that almost slipped from his mouth.

But instead, he replies, "Mom would never let you leave New York. You know that."

"One can always hope," she says brightly. "And as for Greta, it's her book club night. She always has her phone turned off anyway so that she and her friends can discuss their sex books."

"Natalie," Pane snaps. "What are you . . . How do you know . . . Never mind. Don't say that word ever again."

I can almost hear the grin in her voice. "You mean *sex*?"

I bite the back of my hand to keep from laughing.

Pane, however, is not laughing. He looks like he's about to have a heart attack. "You're too young to use the word, let alone know what it means."

"Please, Pane. I know all about how babies are made."

"Can we please just end this conversation?"

Before either of them can embarrass themselves—or me, for that matter—I pipe up, "Oh, look. We're here."

"Thank God," he mumbles.

I glance at him, but his gaze remains laser-beam focused on the road. His jaw flexes and unflexes, and it takes everything in me not to openly stare at the straight line. His entire profile, all of it, looks like it was painstakingly chiseled and then splashed with a golden glow.

My goodness, but he is gorgeous.

"Piggycorns," Natalie squeals. "Stop the truck, Pane. I want to meet them."

He stops just inside the gate. Natalie practically catapults from the cabin, racing to their enclosure. The piggies smell a new friend, and they stampede to meet her. They run in a pile, bumping and shoving, falling and sliding, until they reach the fence.

They stand on their back legs, noses up, openly begging to be pet. The piggies in back, the ones who were a bit slower, push forward, wedging themselves into all the nooks and crannies the others have left open, pawing until they find a spot and joining the whines of the ones who reached the fence first.

A dozen pigs paw and snort, each of them clambering for Natalie's attention. She breaks into a fit of giggles.

"I love them!"

She reaches in, touching a horn here, a chin there. The piggies drink up the attention, jumping and pawing like a pack of puppies.

"Can I go in with them?" she asks me.

Pane slams his door shut and I turn to him. "She wants to go in with them."

He nods, brooding, and I open the gate. Natalie walks in and sinks to her knees. Piggies climb into her lap, lick her chin, wag their happy little tails at the attention. Meanwhile, Natalie laughs and laughs, loving it.

I sidle up next to Pane. Dark, annoyed energy is wafting off him in big, thick chunks.

"You know, I should be charging you for this."

He looks over and one side of his mouth ticks up half an inch. For as relieved as he is that Natalie's been found, he's pissed off that she pulled the stunt that she did, and rightly so.

He folds his arms. "How much would you charge?"

"Oh, I don't know. How much do you think Princess Pain-in-the-Butt would like to rake in?"

He points at me. "I can explain."

"Can you? I would love to hear all about her. I'm especially intrigued about the part where your sister pegged *me* for this princess. It makes me think that you have a nickname for me."

"First of all, it was originally Princess Pain-in-the-Neck, but somewhere along the line, Nat changed it. It's a story that I made up." He rubs a hand down his tired face. "I tell her a story every night before bedtime, you know that. When I arrived here, everything was so last minute that I didn't have a book ready. Or I did, but my phone was confiscated by my mother. So I made one up."

"Uh-huh," I reply, doing my best to sound ticked.

"Secondly"—he leans a hand on the truck's hood—"when I first showed up, you have to admit . . . you were a real pain the ass."

"And you have to admit that you were more than just slightly arrogant. In fact, if someone had asked me to describe you, I probably would've named you Prince Arrogant Ass."

He tips his head back and laughs. When his gaze drops back down to mine, his eyes brim with mirth. "I suppose I deserve that."

"You sure do."

He extends his hand, palm up. "I think we've come a long way, don't you?"

I slide my hand over his, shivering through the sparks that ignite on my flesh when we touch. "I guess we've come a long way."

"You *guess*?" he teases.

I shrug. "I mean, maybe."

His hand tightens on mine. "I think it's more than a *maybe*."

"Maybe."

"I *know* it's more than maybe."

A nearby tree extends a branch and shoves me toward Pane. It does the same to him, closing the space between us.

Our gazes snap tight, and thoughts of Pane being worried for his sister seize hold of me. The worry, the love he has for her—all of it clouds my brain. I've never seen him so emotional, and it's . . . it's moved me.

"Are you two going to kiss?"

I jump back. Natalie's standing inside the fence, holding a pig to her chest as the others paw at her legs, vying for attention.

Pane takes a step away, and with him, all the mystical energy dissolves. "Let's get you cleaned up and ready for bed."

"Wait." I grab his arm. "There's something we should do first."

"What's that?" Natalie asks.

I quirk a brow. "Have you ever made a light angel?"

Chapter 29

ROWE

The three of us spend the next thirty minutes lying in the magical grass, pumping our arms and legs to make angels that illuminate the ground around us.

It may be the best thirty minutes of my life.

Even Pane finds joy in it, laughing and gently offering Natalie technique suggestions. Because what else are big brothers for?

At one point, he sits up and nods toward the house. "Look at that."

"What?"

A breeze blows, and the grass lights up like a river. The magic winds its way closer to the house than I've ever seen.

"What's going on?" I murmur.

"It's healing." Pane rises and gestures for me to take his hand. I slip my palm over his and let him lift me to standing.

We lock gazes for a beat, and then he says to Natalie, "Ready for bed?"

She stops swishing her arms and legs, but the grass surrounding her still glows ethereally, making her look like a true angel.

"I guess so." She pops up. "Will you keep telling me the story of Princess—"

"We're starting a new tale tonight," he interrupts.

I bite back a laugh, and the three of us head toward the house. On our way I note the lack of trash from the party, and inside, the kitchen is clean and all the leftovers have been put away. My heart swells, because this is what folks in my town do—we help each other. Feeling grateful because I have so much, I snap off the lights, and go upstairs to get some shut-eye.

"Now, when you meet my mom, don't be surprised if she hates you on sight," Natalie says over a plate of steaming biscuits and gravy.

She's elbow-deep in her breakfast, both sides of her lips dotted with specks of white gravy.

"It's not personal," she continues, covering her mouth with a napkin while she chews.

"Don't talk with your mouth full," her brother reminds her as he enters the room. "Good morning." He squeezes my shoulder. "How'd you sleep?"

"Great."

His eyes crinkle as he smiles. "Good." He drags his gaze from me, and it feels like the sun has been hidden by a cloud. "How'd you sleep, Nat?"

"Awesome!" She throws up her arms. "I dreamed of piggycorns."

"Yes, your new best friends," he teases. Pane moves to the counter and pours himself a cup of coffee. "And what were you talking about? What's not personal?"

Natalie takes several big gulps of milk to wash down her breakfast before smacking her lips in approval. "That Mom will hate Rowe."

Coffee spews from Pane's mouth, and he sputters through a cough. "Natalie!"

"What? Mom hates everybody."

I purse my lips to hide a smile. "Is that true?"

He cringes. "It's . . ."

Natalie gives him a firm look. "Stone told me that she made you strip out of your clothes just to come here."

Pane shoots her a cold look. "I didn't strip, and don't use that word."

"Strip, strip, strip," she gloats.

A deliciously handsome smile flirts on his lips as he fights a laugh. "Fine. Yes, I had to remove everything I owned."

"Even your underwear?"

I bust a gut, laughing, and Pane's cheeks turn red. "Not that. Anyway, Sylvia Maddox is a foreboding presence, Rowe. But she's not awful."

"Don't say I didn't warn you." Natalie points her fork at me. "I mean, this is the same woman who wouldn't let her children take their fathers' last names. She's a Maddox. We're all Maddoxes. But I bet your mom's nice, isn't she, Rowe? Probably smells like sugar cookies and gives warm hugs."

"She actually smells like patchouli, but she does give good hugs."

"See? I knew it."

Natalie takes the last bite of biscuit and scoots her chair back, scraping it against the floor. "Now, who's ready to get to work? We have a farm to save."

Apparently, Pane told Natalie pretty much everything about the place, so she knew exactly what needed to be done, and demanded a nail gun.

"How about a paintbrush?" he suggests.

"Fine." She opens her palm. "But I expect real paint on it."

"Oh, there will be real paint."

We work inside most of the morning and go outside to help the guys after lunch. Donner shows up with several men from the yurt community, and they set about painting the exterior of the house. They also make a sign.

"Wadley Farm and Spa," I muse, taking a look at the scrolling black letters etched into the wood.

Pane comes over, rubbing the back of his neck. "What do you think?"

I press my hands to my heart. "I love it."

When I drop my hand to my side, it brushes against the back of his. We freeze, watching as Donner tediously paints. "Glad you like it, because it can't be changed now."

My hand is still touching Pane's, his is still touching mine, and a frenzy of feeling snakes its way up my arm and straight to my heart.

I don't dare breathe. I don't dare move. My fingers twitch, and our hands move to join until Natalie's screeching yanks us around.

The piggies stampede through the yard with Pane's little sister lying spread-eagle atop them.

I frown. "Is she crowd-surfing the piggycorns?"

Pane nods. "It does look that way."

As they fly past, Natalie points up. "Look at that weird bird!"

I follow her finger and see a bird fluttering high in the sky. It *is* flapping its wings in a weird, kinda jaunty way. Must be injured.

Pane's shoulder touches mine as he leans in. "You know she's going to want to stay."

"But she's got to go home."

He glances down at his phone. "Yeah. We're meeting Mom in two hours. You ready?"

No. "Yes. Absolutely."

Chapter 30

ROWE

"So you're Rowe Wadley," Sylvia Maddox declares after descending the steps of her private jet.

Private. Jet.

Pane's family owns a jet.

A jet.

A jet.

Did I mention they own a jet?

My family literally owns nothing—not even the place where we live. And he owns a jet.

My stomach falls at the sight of the sleek plane with the Maddox Group logo scrolled on the tail. It was one thing to know that Pane comes from stupid-crazy money. It's another to witness this wealth in the flesh.

And Sylvia Maddox drips wealth.

She's wearing all white, even her shoes. Her black hair has an elegant silver streak that starts at her forehead and winds its way behind an ear. It's very classy.

She's draped an ivory suit jacket over the shoulders of her blouse, and manages to walk effortlessly down the steps without the jacket slipping even once.

She's mesmerizing.

I'm glad I had the sense to put on a nice pair of jeans, a blouse, and newish pumps. Otherwise, I would've felt underdressed.

Even now, Pane's wearing nice jeans, and he pressed his shirt. There's no looking like a slouch for Sylvia Maddox, and I understand exactly why Pane was pissed off the first time we met, when he had to meet Sylvia after the piggycorns ruined his suit.

When she takes my hand, she studies me with sharp green eyes—eyes that match Pane's and Natalie's.

Just being in her presence makes me want to shrink into a tiny brittle ball. To shrivel up like one of the souls in Disney's *The Little Mermaid*, becoming a dried-up husk of who I really am.

Pane slides a hand along my back. I jump, I'm so startled by it. My gaze slashes to him. I'm sure Sylvia catches my what-the-hell expression. But Pane's face remains neutral, as if he's been touching my back for ages.

His fingers squeeze in a protective yet gentle reminder that he's here, that he's not going anywhere.

Yesterday I would've run screaming from his touch. But today things are different. Watching him with Natalie crumbled the rest of the icy walls that had encased my heart.

It's questionable, how I feel about this.

Sylvia's gaze flicks to the arm Pane has around my back. She opens her mouth to say something, but Natalie jumps out of the truck and runs to her. "Mom!"

She sucks in her cheeks, jaw tightening. "You are in trouble, young lady."

Though the words are stern, Sylvia does give her daughter a hug. However, her arms are so straight that they remind me of pool noodles. It's like Sylvia doesn't know how to offer love.

Good grief, if I'd pulled what brilliant little Natalie did (yes, she's clearly way too bright for her age), my mother would've hugged me tight before spanking the heck out of me and grounding me for the rest of my life.

But instead, after hugging Natalie, Sylvia drops her like a hot potato and snaps, "In the plane."

"But, Mom, they have a boarding school here. It's only an hour away—"

Sylvia glances at her with disdain. "Your brother will be home soon enough. You won't be coming here."

Wow. Talk about being bitch-slapped. Her tone, her words—all of it is rough.

As Natalie tromps up the steps in disappointment, Sylvia turns her attention to her son. "How are things going? Though I probably shouldn't ask you too much."

"They're well."

"I expect you to be ready in a few weeks."

"I will be," he tells her.

She tugs the jacket on her shoulders, pulling it higher. "Good. So you've been making it on your own okay?"

He glances at me and smiles. "I've been making it great. I couldn't have done it without Rowe."

Sylvia places all her attention on me, and fire practically shoots from her eyes as her gaze sweeps over me from head to toe. I know this look. This is the look of someone who wants to make you feel inferior.

She pulls her lips back into a cold smile. "Ah, Rowe. Thank you for helping my son. That's wonderful of you."

Her tone is resentful. Sylvia Maddox, CEO and president of a multibillion-dollar hotel business, is *resentful* that I'm here, and she wants me to know I don't belong.

I've got news for her: I belong well enough for Pane to put his hand on my back.

"You're welcome," I say, smiling through the irritation grinding in my stomach. "Your son's amazing. I can see how he'd be great with the hotels."

"Yes," she says, hissing the *sssss*. "He is great with our international business. It's much bigger than a small mountain town with a gimmick."

Now it's on, lady. "Oh? You've visited Mystic Meadows?"

"I've seen it. It's very worn."

"Not anymore." I nudge Pane. "Because of this guy, people are giving the whole town a facelift."

Her eyes go as wide as saucers at that. "Is this true, Pane?"

He shifts his weight like he's impatient to leave. "Seems the renovation is contagious."

"Renovation?"

"You'll see it on judging day. I don't want to say too much. I'm still competing against my brother."

Sylvia regards him. Then her frigid gaze lands on me. She and Pane may share the same eye color, but his eyes are warm. Hers are filled with ice.

"Yes, about your brother." She sighs dramatically. "There's something I need to discuss with you. In private."

She wedges herself between me and Pane, taking the arm he had on my back and pulling him down the tarmac.

As Sylvia walks off, she literally lifts her nose in the air.

Is she for real? Is this little rich woman jealous of me? Does she think I'm some sort of competition?

They talk in private for a few moments while I study the plane, wondering what it's like on the inside and deciding that it's best not to know. You know, since it isn't mine and all.

After a minute, Pane's voice rises in the air. "I just don't want to talk to him right now."

When I glance over, his mother is replying in a low voice. He nods.

They break apart and head this way. He calls up at the jet, "Natalie!"

A few seconds later, his sister appears in the doorway, hope alighting on her face. "I can stay?"

"No. I need a hug. Rowe does, too."

Her face falls at the realization that she does have to leave. Then she rushes down the steps, hugs Pane around his middle before releasing him and hugging me.

"Please send me a piggycorn for Christmas."

"I'll do my best," I whisper.

Then she breaks free and races back up. I look over to find Sylvia staring at me with contempt burned onto her face.

She laboriously drags her gaze from me to her son. "I'll see you in a few weeks, Pane."

"Bye, Mom."

"Bye," she says with a smile. Then she turns to me. "Rowe."

That's all the goodbye I get from Sylvia Maddox before she disappears into the jet.

Chapter 31

ROWE

The moment we get home, I know something's wrong. The house is dark. The workers are gone. The crickets are chirping.

But something's off.

It's in the air. It's thick and weird, like the magic is frazzled, short-circuiting.

When Pane kills the engine, he turns to me. "Stay here."

"I'm not staying here."

His bottom lip dips in a frown. "But something's off."

"I know. That's why I'm getting out."

He mumbles something about me being stubborn, but doesn't argue when I exit the truck.

Soon as I'm outside, a blanket of foreboding hits me right in the chest. The piggycorns are standing inside their fence, but they're not leaping over one another and sliding across the grass on their rear ends to greet us. They're standing in a neat line, looking straight ahead.

Something is definitely wrong, and whatever it is, it's outside.

Pane must sense it, too, because his next words are, "You should go into the house."

"I'm not doing that. This is my property."

He sighs with resignation. "Do you have to be so resistant all the time?"

I shoot him a weary grin. "It's why you like me so much."

An emotion I can't place flickers in his eyes. "Come on. Stay close."

The first thing we notice is that the fence behind the house has been trampled. Pane curses. "We just put this up."

Dread pools in my stomach as my gaze trails the fence. It's not just been trampled. It's broken into bits as if a herd of buffalo stormed through here on their way to—

"Oh my God! The starfizz berries!"

No no no no no! Please don't let them be damaged.

I run off into the dark. Pane calls after me, but my heart is in my throat, and all I can think about is my plan B—the berries I've tended and worried over, giving them all my focus and energy, raising them from seeds—*please, please let them be okay.*

My legs are heavy as I race across the farm. They don't want to work. They don't want to go where I'm forcing them, but they must.

The world blurs as my vision narrows to a pinprick-sized tunnel. Blood whooshes in my ears. It's all I can hear. I'm barely aware that behind me, Pane is calling my name. I don't have time for him now. This is about my home. Not his. This was never his. He doesn't care about it like I do. He can't, because he's leaving.

My shaky legs take me right past the ruined fence, past the gazebo, past the meadow, and right to—

"No!"

I collapse onto a patch of broken earth and take in the sight. The fence around the berries has been torn away. Chicken wire has been slashed and ripped from the wooden braces, curling into the air like the ends of Christmas ribbons.

And in the center of it all, the berries that only needed a few more days lay destroyed, trampled to juice that now soaks into the earth.

It's so stupid. There's no reason for me to cry. Pane's saving the farm. He's turning it into a spa. Realistically, I don't even need these berries. I don't need any of it.

We have his vision.

But it feels like a part of me has been ripped out and tossed to the ground, trampled just like these hedges have been—hedges I nursed from seedlings.

Pane comes up behind me and grabs my shoulders. "Rowe, it's going to be—"

"No, it's not!"

I rise up and whirl around, facing him. The moist earth soaked through my pants, leaving my knees cold and wet. I smack away clumps of dirt that cling to my jeans, sending them flying across the yard.

"It's not going to be okay, Pane! You're going to fix my house, but then *you leave*. You're going to fly off in your jet and leave me behind. You're going to abandon all of us." I'm flinging my arms around like a thirteen-year-old having the hissy fit to end all hissy fits. "And if this spa doesn't work, if I don't know how to manage it or, God forbid, I run it into the ground, then at least I have—or *had*—these berries. I had them, and they were going to be mine. Something just for me, a way to survive. But now I don't even have that. I don't have anything. All I'll have are a few kisses from *the* Pane Maddox. But kissing won't save me, Pane. It won't save anything. Not when my life is in ruins."

Everything I've felt for the past few weeks word-vomits from my mouth. My fears, my worries, my angst—all of it ejects from me in that moment, and damn, but it feels good to finally say all of it, to tell him everything that I feel.

And guess what? I'm not done.

"And I like you, and I love kissing you, and I want there to be more, but there can't be because you won't be here in a few weeks, and I can't endure being abandoned again. My heart can't take it. I just . . . even if I try to *not* care about it, I still do. It matters because—" I place my hands to my head. "I sound like such a crazy woman right now." I drop my hands back down. "If you think I'm nuts and want to return to the shamper, then I won't blame you, because I even sound nuts to me."

I exhale a super-shaky breath that starts all the way in my chest and staggers from my throat.

"But I just . . . can't do it . . . I don't have it in me to care about someone so much that my heart hurts, to experience that feeling of being boundless, limitless, because I'm high on the euphoria of someone else. I can't live in that and be destroyed again. Not by you."

Tears stream down my cheeks and chin, splashing onto my blouse. My eyes are so full of them that Pane's a blurry mess. When I blink, even more tears splash onto my clothes.

He steps forward. His expression is completely unreadable. He's going to run. I don't blame him. I would run from me, too. I'm a mess—a broken, dirty mess.

He cups my face with his hands and swipes at the tears with his thumbs. When he speaks, his voice is a velvety rumble in his chest that makes my knees become rubber bands. "Are you done?"

"No. Yes. I think so. Maybe." I exhale again, this time stronger. "Yes. I'm definitely done."

"Good. Because I know what did this."

That's all he's got to say? I just poured my heart out to him—well, *vomited* it all out—and all he has to say is *I know what did this*?

Perhaps he's trying to find a way to save my dignity.

It's more than I would do for someone else who just made a gigantic fool of themselves and is crying with wet, sloppy knees.

Maybe I should cut my losses and pretend I never said any of what I did. Seems that's what Pane's doing. Okay, I should *definitely* cut my losses.

I shake out my arms, trying to get some of the blood back into them. It all went to my stupid mouth, apparently. "What did this?"

His jaw flexes. "Let me show you."

Chapter 32

PANE

"Why are we at Luke and Sally's?" Rowe asks through a sniffle when we arrive at their front door.

"Because those were unicorn prints back at the fence. They let the unicorns do this."

Her jaw drops. "What? How?"

My body tightens in anger. It takes everything I've got to keep it cool and together. "Remember earlier today when Nat saw that strange bird?"

"Yeah."

"It wasn't a bird. It was a drone. I didn't put the two together until I saw the tracks."

"Oh my God, and Luke said something about a drone when we were, you know . . ." She cocks her head toward the pasture.

"I know," is all I can manage right now.

Sunbeam's cheeks are tearstained. Her nose is red. Her eyes are swollen, and her lips look good enough to devour.

I want to devour all of her.

But first, I want to destroy Luke for what he's done, tear him to pieces, show him that real men do not sabotage a woman's livelihood.

I push the bell and hear it ring on the inside of the two-story Southern-style home, complete with Greek columns on the porch.

Luke throws open the door, takes one look at the two of us, and guards his face. "Now just—"

And that's when I punch him, aiming for a spot just above where his hands are shielding—his nose.

The sound of cracking bone fills the air, and Luke reels back into the house, falling onto his ass on the wooden floor.

Behind me, Rowe gasps.

My knuckles throb, and I shake out my hand. It's tempting to pounce on him and punch until there's nothing left to punch.

"Ow, ow!" Luke howls in pain. Blood seeps between his fingers, splashing in fat drops onto the floor. "You son of a bitch! You broke my nose!"

"What's going on?" Sally Ray calls from inside the belly of the home.

I take a step and bend down. Luke cowers like I'm going to punch him again.

I shove my finger in his face. "That's for destroying Rowe's property."

"You're crazy!" He spits while keeping his nose cupped in his hand. "You're full of shit. Sally Ray, call the cops!"

Sally Ray enters the hall, sees Luke, and screams, dropping a plate she was wiping dry with a towel. It hits the floor and splinters into a thousand pieces as she slides to her knees and cradles his head.

She's screaming at me to leave, screaming at Rowe to get me out of there. Telling Rowe that she will pay for this.

Her cries become muffled like I'm underwater. All I can see is red, all I feel is fury as I point another finger at Luke.

"You never deserved Rowe. You don't even know who she is."

As soon as the words begin to pour from my mouth, emotion closes my throat. I push through it like I'm clearing a pipe, one that's been clogged with brush and rubbish for years, all of it clumping together until its plunged away, freeing the water trapped behind it. But what's coming out of me now is the farthest thing from water. It's a tender emotion, something small and sacred. Something worth tending to and fighting for.

I claw my way through the words, restraining the emotions surging inside me. "Rowe is the goddess of this land, the one person this earth responds to, its lifeblood and source. You are nothing. You're not even worthy of looking at her."

Luke stares at me blankly. Sally Ray tips her head toward me as well, looking shocked that I'd dare say anything like that.

From behind me, I can even feel Rowe's energy change. Or maybe it's the magic in this earth. It's impossible to know the difference sometimes, where she ends and the magic begins.

Because this place is her. Rowe is a part of this land as much as it's a part of her. She doesn't see it, but I do. Anyone with eyes can.

Sally starts screaming hysterically, this time at an eardrum-popping octave as she threatens lawsuits and police.

I slowly tilt my head toward her. "You will leave Rowe alone. You will not contact the police. If you do, I will make one phone call to my lawyer, and he will see to it that within less than a week, this place will belong to the state. Do you understand?"

Sally puffs out her red cheeks. "Listen here, you—"

Luke waves her off with the hand that's not covering his nose. "We understand," he garbles out.

Rowe grabs my sleeve, tugging me back, silently telling me that it's time to go.

I take one more look at Luke as he whimpers in Sally's arms. He's done trying to destroy Rowe. I have no doubt.

Sunbeam tugs me again and I relent, letting her pull me off the porch.

Anger coils in my gut as I storm back across the road. My knuckles throb, and I flick my hand to alleviate some of the discomfort.

"Pane, are you—"

And then I whirl around and kiss her. Deeply. With everything I have, pouring every emotion I've been keeping to myself for weeks into this. Into her.

My tongue parts her lips, and she moans.

I'm instantly rock hard for Rowe.

For nobody but her.

Her fingers tangle in my hair, and it's my turn to moan. I tug her close, pressing my hard cock against her stomach. She whimpers in response.

Around me, the tree branches shiver as if they're cheering us on. I can almost hear them whisper, *Never thought this would happen!*

Don't stop.

Go all the way!

Tell her everything.

Let her know how you feel.

When we part, she says, "Pane—"

"No."

She blinks. "What?"

"I listened to you talk for a good two minutes back there, giving me every excuse, and that's what you're about to do again. No more excuses, Rowe. I don't want them. I can't hear them. Because here's the truth . . ." Her gaze drops. This won't do. "Look at me."

She closes her eyes, completely ignoring me. "Pane—"

"You don't even know what I'm going to say," I explode.

Her jaw drops and she pulls back. "Of course I do."

I fold my arms. "Then what's about to come out of my mouth?"

"That you're leaving. This won't last. It can't be more than just a fling."

"Wrong."

She sucks in a breath, and it's shaky. I've unbalanced her, knocked that little sunbeam right off the stable pedestal she'd been standing on, the one drifting in the middle of an ocean where her heart can't be reached.

It takes a moment, but I wait for her to whisper meekly, "Then what are you going to say?"

"Rowe." I take her face. I love taking her by the cheeks and staring into her soft brown eyes. There is no better place on earth. "I'm going to say that you have undone everything about who I thought I was. You walked into my life and upended all parts of it. This wasn't supposed to be anything other than a project that I worked on for two months and used to claim my inheritance. But it's become more than that."

"What's it become?" she asks, so shyly that I nearly dissolve into laughter.

The smile on my face is so wide my cheeks ache. "It's become *you*. Every part of me wants you. And no, not just physically. I need you. I breathe you. You have lodged yourself into my core, and if you left today, if I let you leave without knowing how I feel, I would be destroyed.

"You have destroyed me, and I am here for every single part of it. So I'm asking you, Sunbeam. Will you, for once in your life, let someone else take care of you? You don't have to do this on your own, and I don't want to leave you. I want to be with you more than I've ever wanted to be with anyone, and I think you feel the same way."

She doesn't blink. She doesn't run.

So I take a breath and keep on. "And if you let me in, then I will spend every moment I can proving that I'm not the other men you've known. I'm not going to walk away from you."

She has hearts in her eyes. They shine bright for two seconds before disappearing. "But what about—"

"I'm not walking away." I kiss her lips and press my forehead to hers. "Everything else, we can talk about later."

"Why later?"

I rock back on my heels, knocked over by her. All of her. Just her. Good God, I'm pouring my heart out, and all she can focus on is the details? *This woman.* "Because right now, I'm taking you into that house and doing things to you that I've been wanting to do since I first met you."

Her brows cock. "Oh?"

"Yes. You can say no. You *can*. And I'll be devastated. But I can wait. For you, I can wait—"

She throws her arms around my neck and presses her lips to mine, sliding in her tongue and making my cock strain against my jeans.

When we part for air, we're both breathless. She curls her hands around my collar and tugs me close. "Pane Maddox, if I have to wait one more minute for you, then . . ."

"You'll what? Explode?"

"Yes. I will."

I kiss her again, smiling against her teeth. "Then let's get you inside."

Chapter 33

ROWE

We crash inside the house, kicking shoes off, unbuttoning shirts. Me unbuttoning his, actually—the few buttons that it has. I push Pane's shirt up over his neck, breaking the kiss only long enough for him to yank it off and toss it onto the floor.

My God, his body. His abs are so hard, and they quiver when I run a finger down them.

He grabs my hand and says through a kiss, "No tickling."

"Is that your weakness?" I joke. "The thing that will bring down the great Pane Maddox?"

"There is nothing that will bring me down."

The confidence in this one is dizzying.

Pane moves to kick the front door shut with his foot, but I hear a small stampede making their way up the steps. "Wait."

I break the kiss and look through the doorway to find all the piggies are out of the fence. What in the world?

A tree branch waves to me.

Of course it does.

The piggies race to the front door. Their faces practically glow with glee. *Finally!* I'm sure they're thinking. *They're letting us in.*

They spill into the foyer, sliding on their butts and bumping into one another.

Pane takes one look at them. One look at me. "Screw it." He plants a breathy kiss on my lips. "They can stay in the house tonight."

When they're all inside, *then* he kicks the door shut.

The house shudders briefly, and I notice that no vines sprout up from under the floorboards. No windows are opened by branches.

The house is eerily quiet, as if it's holding its breath in anticipation of what comes next.

"You sure about the piggies?" I tease a few of the dark hairs sprouting on his chest with my finger. "This is breaking one of your rules."

"I'm pretty sure you and I are about to break every single rule we *never* made," he murmurs in my hair.

Fair enough.

He carries me upstairs as if I weigh nothing more than a feather, enters my bedroom, kicks *that* door shut, too, and places me on the bed so that I'm sitting on the edge of it. Moonlight spears the blinds, illuminating both of us. He kneels between my legs and kisses me until I'm moaning.

He chuckles into my mouth. "That good, huh?"

I entwine my arms around his neck. "You are the best kisser."

He is. I could dive into one of his kisses and live there forever. Pane smiles, and in my chest, a thousand butterflies take flight.

He rubs the back of his hand against my cheek, and when he smiles, the corners of his eyes crinkle. I catch his hand and lift it to my lips, kissing each red knuckle.

"You didn't have to punch Luke."

He frowns. "Yes, I did, and tomorrow I'm calling the police. They *are* going to pay for the damages."

"You told *them* not to call."

He winks. "Because I hoped that we'd be busy tonight."

I toss my head back and laugh. "You are so bad."

"Which is why you want me," he murmurs against my mouth.

"Which is why I want you." I pull back. "But if you call the police, then they'll report that you assaulted Luke."

Pane shrugs. "I don't care. I've got money and lawyers. No charges will stick."

"You are terrible."

"No, I'm not, or else you wouldn't be here," he whispers between kisses.

He's right about that. This feeling, what's buried deep inside me, is pushing to get out. It's not just that Pane is crazy sexy and I want him.

This is so much more than that. I can feel my heart when he's around, something I haven't experienced in *years*. I never want this feeling to end, and I know it's right. Pane is right for me. No matter how wrong we are on paper, we are so right together.

He kisses me again, deeply, and I melt.

When we part, Pane brushes my hair off my neck. "I meant what I said. This isn't just a project, and I'm not going to walk away from you in a few weeks."

I talk past the lump that's threatening to squeeze my throat shut. "I know."

Once the words are out of my mouth, my body can breathe. My throat opens and my lungs fill with air. Just saying the words makes me realize they're true.

They are so true, and I believe him.

He sits back and glides his hands up my legs to grab me by the hips and tug me to the edge of the bed.

My hands make their way down his naked chest, reveling in the feel of every dip and valley of his muscles—of which there are many.

It would be stupid not to admire him. So I take my time with his flesh, running my fingers over his freckled shoulders, down the dark hairs that lightly coat the center of his chest, all the way down to his abs. His stomach flutters when I touch him.

"No tickling," he warns again.

"Now you asked for it."

I tickle him once before both my hands are in one of his and are being held hostage over my head. To even the playing field, I wrap my legs around his waist and pull him into me.

Pane's erection is hard against his jeans, straining the fabric. He's pressed against the throbbing spot between my legs. All of me wants him.

I wiggle my hands out of his hold and pull him tight, until there's no space between us.

I grind against him like a horny rabbit. My body has no shame when it comes to just how much it wants this man, *and* wants him to know it.

I'm on fire for Pane. Every piece of me wants him. My girlie parts are swollen with need, and my panties are soaked.

The dry humping—or desert-cameling, as Cristina and I jokingly referred to it in high school—is intense. Do not underestimate how close a good old desert-cameling can bring you to the brink of orgasm.

"I'm going to explode if we keep this up," he croaks.

His eyes are lusty, his pupils obliterated. I scoot back on the bed and he glances up. "I like your bedroom. It smells like you—wildflowers."

"And sunshine," I joke.

He crawls over to me and I start unbuttoning my shirt, but he takes my hand.

"I've waited a long time for this. I want to savor every moment," Pane growls.

I think I just got pregnant.

He pulls me up until we're both on our knees atop the mattress. As he nuzzles his way down my neck, the stubble on his face scraping against my skin, his fingers easily slide the buttons on my shirt from their holes.

Pane peels the shirt off, leaving me bare except for my bra. He brushes his lips over my exposed shoulder and slips a finger under one strap. "Your bra is yellow like the sun."

His amusement amuses me. "Maybe I was hoping you'd see it."

Pane palms the satiny fabric, and my nipples ache, dying for his touch. He grins sheepishly. "I approve."

A giggle erupts in my throat as he eases me back onto the bed, takes the bra's front clasp between his teeth, and unlocks it.

My jaw drops as my bra pops open, exposing my breasts. "I've been dying to taste them," he murmurs before pulling a nipple into his mouth. I arch my back in pleasure, relishing the feel of his tongue rolling over my pebbled skin.

When he drops that breast and sucks the other nipple into his mouth, a groan escapes my lips. "*Pane.* You can suck harder."

He laughs onto my flesh. "I love a woman who knows what she wants."

He tenderly bites my nipple, sending a wave of pleasure rolling over me. I tangle my fingers in his hair and whisper, "Pane."

"Say my name. Moan it. That's what I want to hear." He kisses his way down my stomach to the button on my jeans, which he takes in his teeth and undoes with his mouth.

I'm so wet that my panties are drenched. This man. He is the hottest thing ever. "That's a neat trick."

"I thought you'd think so. I've been saving it for you."

"I find that hard to believe."

He sits up and I slip out of my bra and undo his belt, pulling it through the loops and tossing it onto the floor. The outline of his cock is huge, and I swallow, desperate to see what he looks like.

I start to unbutton his jeans, but he stops me with a kiss. He slips a hand up my neck and into my hair, crushing me against him. Pane's gentle, but demanding, exactly how I would picture him in bed.

When we part, he murmurs, "You first."

"Okay," I whisper breathlessly. *Whatever you say. My brain has up and left the building.*

He gently lays me back on my pillows, and he tugs my jeans off. The fact that he doesn't use his teeth *is* a bit disappointing until once they're off and he slips his lips around the string that connects the front and back of my panties. He tugs one side down with his lips and curls his fingers around the other side, pulling.

Once they're off, he climbs on top of me, kissing me deeply as his fingers dip between my legs. He teases my clit, and I gasp.

I grab his face and pull him harder into the kiss. My body's on fire. I'm aching, throbbing, and all I want is relief.

I thrust against his finger and he chuckles, "Patience, beautiful Sunbeam."

My heart lodges in my throat. He thinks I'm beautiful?

He kisses his way down my body, taking his time to pull my nipples into his mouth and gently bite them.

Then he settles himself between my legs. "I've been waiting a long time to taste you."

I'm nearly undone.

He eases a finger inside me, and my walls clench around him, hard. He takes my clit in his mouth, rolling his tongue over the bead. A staggered breath escapes me.

"Tell me what you like," he purrs.

My brain is fogged up from all the hormones. "Huh?"

"Tell me what will make you come."

"Oh, um . . ."

"You know what you like, Sunbeam. I have confidence in you. Tell me."

"Okay." It takes a minute for me to verbalize leading him through the motions and trying to remember that he's not a vibrator, but I instruct him.

"Use two fingers," I say.

He slowly works another finger into me, pumping as he feverishly licks my clit. Pressure builds down below. I'm thinking too much. Worried too much about tomorrow. About the fact that he'll be leaving. The pressure begins to fall.

"Stop thinking," he growls, "and feel. I'm not going anywhere."

How does he know what I'm thinking? I relax and whisper, "Just keep doing what you're doing."

He does until the pressure builds again. My walls clench, and when I'm shattered into a gazillion pieces, I cry out his name, floating on the high of the orgasm until I'm brought back to earth.

"That's my Sunbeam," he whispers, kissing my crazy-sensitive clit before he rises onto his knees and pushes off his jeans and underwear. His cock springs free and I lick my lips.

Oh my God. It is the most beautiful, massive thing I've ever seen. Pane is built like a god. Chest hair sprinkles his pecs, his abs are too many to count, and it all leads down to a tapered waist and one glorious cock.

I'm so spent. All I can do is stare hungrily as he swipes moisture off the head and pumps his hand down the shaft.

I touch him, running a finger down the silky body. Pane drops his head back and moans.

When I move to take him in my hand, Pane stops me. "Tonight is all about you. We can focus on me later, in an hour at our next go round. But I'm so full, all I want is you."

My throat goes dry. No one's ever said that to me. The attention is embarrassing, so my instinct is to drop my head.

Pane hooks a finger under my chin and lifts my face until I'm looking at him. "I want you to feel more pleasure tonight than you ever have before."

"I already have."

"We're just getting started."

We kiss, and I tug him down on top of me, relishing the pleasure of his weight as his body lines up with mine. Parts of my brain fire off every crazy thought possible.

I can't believe Pane Maddox is making love to me. I can't believe I'm letting him. I can't believe that I've fallen for this grunty, cocky jerk.

Wait. He's not a grunty, cocky jerk.

He's everything.

And he is.

He slowly slips inside me and curses. "Sunbeam, you feel better than I ever imagined."

"So do you," I reply honestly.

He waits for me to stretch around him. Then he moves slowly, taking his time. There's nothing feverish about this. This is lovemaking at its core.

I stare up at him. He stares down at me, whispering my name and kissing me as he slowly moves in and out.

It's a beautiful moment that makes my breath catch.

And then I realize we've been so swept up that we forgot protection. "Wait."

He kisses my neck. "I'm not too big for you. Trust me, I've done this before."

"You are so full of yourself."

He lifts his head and shoots me the smirk that highlights how truly beautiful he is.

"Protection?"

He blinks. "Shit." His brow furrows.

"I'm on the pill."

"I'm good to go," he tells me. "If you're asking."

"I'm not asking."

"Good. I'm not asking you, either. Now, may I please continue?"

I bury my face in his shoulder in embarrassment. "Yes."

He takes my hand, threading his fingers through mine and lifting it over my head, gently pinning me. This isn't about domination. This is Pane's way of pouring out his heart without words, of telling me how much he cares about me through this action, of making love to me in a way that I've never experienced before.

My heart is open. It's so open that it aches. I ache for him, and only him.

Pane murmurs my name as he slowly thrusts, and we find our rhythm together as we lose ourselves in one another. And when he comes, I shatter with him, relishing in how he fills me to my core.

When we're done, he pulls me over to lie on top of him and he kisses me on the forehead. I close my eyes, and as I start to drift off, I swear I hear him whisper, "You are mine, Sunbeam."

Chapter 34

ROWE

Over the next weeks, Pane and I make love on every possible surface—beds, tables, dressers, couches, chairs, kitchen counters.

Don't worry, he turns all the roosters around so they don't see.

We even sneak away from the guys working on the house, locking ourselves in the laundry room, frantically yanking aside panties and underwear to fill the need that's overtaken both of us.

It's a need like nothing I've ever known. It's like I spent a lifetime on a deserted island, my only food being coconuts, and now I've been rescued and have a feast before me.

I can't get enough of him, and he can't seem to get enough of me, either.

There are only a few days left before the opening, the foreclosure, and the judging. It's all happening on the same day, and the hope is that the judging comes first, valuating the business higher than Stone's venture. If so, Pane will make sure I can keep the property.

But I don't know exactly how that's going to happen.

Yet if there's one thing I've learned during this time, it's to trust Pane Maddox.

And trust him, I do.

The man has even learned how to make biscuits.

"You got the coffee ready?" I ask, sliding into the kitchen.

He glances up from the stove, where he's frying eggs in a pan, and scoffs. "Do *I* have coffee made? I've run five miles and made breakfast. Do you think I have coffee made?"

I laugh and slip into his arms, kissing those luscious lips. "I think you've done everything. Oh! I have to feed the pigs."

I start to pull away, but Pane pulls me back to him, kissing me again. "Already done."

I gasp. "No!"

"See for yourself."

I pull away and spot the piggies' bowls by the door. They're filled with something small that's been chopped up. "Is that . . . Are those hot dogs?"

Pane winks. "Breakfast of champions."

"But that's—"

He tuts. "It's not cannibalism. They're all-beef, remember?"

He has a point, and before there's a chance to rib him for breaking one of his rules, the feeding-the-animals one—a stampede of piggies spills into the kitchen as they tumble over one another and rump-skate to their bowls.

I chuckle. "They must've heard me mention them."

Pane slides the fried eggs onto a plate and smiles warmly. "They must've. Ready to eat?"

"Yes, sir, I am."

I spend most of the day grinning—at Pane, to myself, at Pane. There's a lot of smiling that goes on between us, and brushing of hands, and general excuses to spend two minutes in each other's presence. I'm not running anymore, and I don't want to. I'm drowning in Pane Maddox, and it's the best feeling ever.

After dinner, and after we've cleaned up the kitchen, Pane nuzzles his mouth to my ear. "There's something I want to show you."

Intrigued, I murmur, "Show me?"

"Outside."

"What could this be?"

He swipes a thumb over the top of my lips. "Come find out."

I follow him outside, where he points to the land. A breeze flutters over the grass, causing a low hum of light to breathe to life. It unfolds from the meadow, ending in a trail that leads all the way to the house.

Shock rocks me. I bring my hands to my face. "What is this?"

Pane casually leans against the balustrade, eyeing me with a look that I can't place. "You remember what I said to Luke?"

"About not calling the police?"

He scowls. "No. About you being connected to this land."

I do remember it. Those words crashed into my heart at a gazillion miles per hour, gutting me. "Yes," I whisper.

He reaches out and tucks a strand of hair behind my ear. Then he nods toward the land. "When I first arrived, the glow stopped at the meadow. Now it comes all the way to the house."

I frown. "I don't understand."

Pane tugs me down the steps. He doesn't have to tug hard, because I eagerly follow him. We walk to just shy of the meadow, where the magic is now bleeding into the bare earth, where the grass doesn't grow because the ground is blocked from the sun by the trees closest to the house.

"Close your eyes."

I reel back. "What?"

"Just do it, Sunbeam."

At the sound of my nickname on his lips, a sizzle spirals down my spine. I do as he says, and the next thing I know, he's holding my hand and touching my waist. Then he sways me side to side in a dance.

Just when I'm wondering what this has to do with anything, warmth starts at my feet and works its way up my legs to my torso. It spreads through my chest, bleeding out into my limbs.

Pane presses his body to mine, still swaying gently. "You can open your eyes now."

I do as he says and gasp. Underneath us, a thick patch of grass has sprouted from the earth, winding its way past my feet and reaching for my ankles.

There's never been grass in this spot—ever. Not just that, but it's pulsing with light that's coming from deep in the ground. Drifting up from it are small glowing globes that uncurl into white butterflies that slowly flap their wings as they surround us and lift off, disappearing into the night sky.

As I watch, hundreds of globes transform before flying up, up, *up*, and the grass continues to spread. The shrubs that frame the old farmhouse, scraggly and sad, have new life breathed into them. Thick waxy leaves sprout from the branches, and bright-white gardenias blossom, filling the night with their sweet scent.

I reach for a blossom and run my fingers over its soft petals. "For years these bushes have barely blossomed."

"And now they're in full bloom," he says.

I turn back to him, searching for answers. "Pane."

A gentle smile spreads across his face. "It's not me. This is all you. This earth is connected to you. I saw it that first night. You seemed to glow when you looked out over the meadow."

I blink, slowly beginning to understand what he's saying. This land, maybe because I've lived here all my life, is tied to me, and because my heart was broken for so long, the land was broken, too.

Sure, vines could wind their way inside the house and fetch me my dad's boots, but for years, the house has been surrounded by a patch of dirt as if . . . as if the magic was broken.

But now it's healing in the same way I am.

Tears choke up my throat. "Pane." I throw my arms around his shoulders and bury my face in the softness of his corded, sturdy neck. "Thank you."

As he holds me tightly, I inhale his scent, letting the smell of him—the sandalwood and dry gin—fill my senses until I'm practically drunk.

"No," he argues. "*Thank you.* For everything."

We hold each other for several long seconds, and I swipe away the tears that spring from my eyes. If only my dad could see this, he would be so proud. He died when I was going through everything with Luke, but now I'm healing. I am healed.

All thanks to Pane Maddox.

I slip from his arms and glance up in wonder as light butterflies dance around his head. I extend a finger and one alights on the tip, slowly opening and closing its wings. Its energy is a low hum against my skin, a familiar and comforting feeling that fills my heart with joy.

I don't want this feeling to stop. Ever. But part of me knows that all good things must come to an end.

Chapter 35

ROWE

"What happened with Luke?" Pane asks later that night when we're in bed.

I'm lying on his chest, tracing the lines of his abs. I tip my head up to look at him. "Oh, we've reached *that* stage in our relationship, have we?"

He glances down, frowns. "What stage?"

"The stage where you reveal your deepest wounds."

Pane's frown intensifies. "You already know mine."

My heart contracts, and I feel bad for bringing it up. I drop my head, and he hooks a finger under my chin, lifting my face until our gazes lock.

"Okay, maybe I do have one or two more."

"Of course you do. We all do."

He releases my chin and I snuggle back onto his chest, where I resume admiring him. I comb my fingers over his pecs. They have just the right amount of chest hair—enough for me to know he's a man, but not so much that I get swallowed whole.

"What happened with Luke is that I got pregnant."

Beneath me, he stills. "I see."

But he doesn't. He doesn't know the half of it. "I didn't know until after he'd left me for Sally Ray. I must've missed taking some of my pills before we broke up. I mean, the whole time was so stressful, what with my dad being sick and everything. I was trying to help my mom and dad, and Luke was acting weird. I knew something was going on, but I didn't know what.

"Then Luke left just before my dad took a turn for the worse. We'd just found out that his cancer was inoperable. It had spread too far. At the time I was furious at Luke. How could he leave me? How could he cheat with Sally? How could he have done that? I was heartbroken on so many levels—for my dad, my mom, myself."

I glance up at Pane's perfect jawline before continuing, "I was miserable. But I still did my best to be present while my dad went into hospice. I must not've done a good job, because my mom took me aside and reminded me that my dad wouldn't be around much longer. She said it was best that Luke left instead of staying and leading all of us on. Deep down, I knew she was right. But it was still a bitter pill to swallow."

Pane's lips brush the top of my head. "I'm sorry."

I sit up and prop my head on my fist. "I'm not. I'm glad he's gone. But anyway. Yes, I found out that I was pregnant, and when I told him"—my stomach twists—"he said that I was lying."

Pane's eyes become as dark as midnight as his jaw clenches and unclenches. "I wish I'd broken more than his nose." He starts to get up. "Let me change that."

I tug him back down and press my lips to his. "The best revenge is not letting him take this farm."

"It's not quite good enough."

"It is for me." I slump back onto the bed and lie on my side, facing him. "Do you want to hear the rest?"

"Do I have to?"

"Don't worry. You'll have your time in the hot seat."

Pane pinches his eyes shut with his fingers and sighs. "Let's hear it."

I brush his hand away from his face, and he slowly blinks his eyes open. When I'm satisfied that his anger has died down enough for him to listen, I keep on.

"Luke wouldn't take my calls, and as far as I knew, we were having a baby. So I went to Sally Ray's to confront him, to try to get him to see the truth." Pane brushes hair from my cheek. It's a sweet, comforting gesture, but surprisingly I don't need any comfort.

I exhale and keep on. "Luke came to the door and said that I was pathetic. But he wasn't done. The pregnancy was a lie, he told me. I was just trying to win him back. I pleaded, *begged* him, swore that it was the truth, but he laughed in my face. He slammed Sally Ray's door and flicked out the porch light while I was still standing there."

The memory washes over me. Used to be that I would've experienced the heartache all over again by just talking about it. But now I don't feel anything, because every moment in my life has led me to this one, to being with Pane.

"He shut the light off and left me standing there. It was the most humiliating experience of my life." I lift my eyes and meet Pane's scorching expression. He looks like he wants to rip Luke's head off. I squeeze his hand. "But all that bad brought me here, to you, so I'm grateful for it."

"And the baby?"

"I lost it not long after. Probably from all the stress. I never told my mom. It was too hard."

"So you retreated into yourself," he murmurs.

"Yeah, I guess you could say that I did."

Pane takes my hand and pulls me back on top of him. His heart drums beneath my ear, and his chest slowly rises and falls as he quietly breathes.

He smooths a hand down my hair. "He never deserved you."

"No, he didn't." I kiss his chest. "They deserve each other."

"They do."

I lift my head and rest my chin on top of my folded hands. "Your turn. What's your horror story?"

He traces a finger along my cheekbone, studying me as if he's about to sculpt me to life. "At the end of college, I dated a girl from Georgia, surprisingly, who told me that she was pregnant."

"What?" This is worth sitting up for. I pull the sheet with me, keeping my breasts covered as I straddle him, admiring his naked chest all the way to the ridges of his nibble-worthy hip bones. "My goodness."

Pane's gaze is as cold as diamonds as he stares into the dark, but it softens when his eyes land on me. "My mother hated her."

"*Not* Sylvia."

He chuckles. "Yes, Sylvia. She said that if I wanted to be a dad and stay with my girlfriend, I'd be cut off from the family."

"What? That's brutal." How could his mother be so ruthless to her own flesh and blood?

"That's Sylvia Maddox," he replies, as if hearing my silent question. "She will protect the Maddox brand no matter what, and me knocking up my college girlfriend wasn't in the cards."

"Oh. So then what happened?"

Pane sweeps my bangs to one side of my head, keeping his eyes focused there briefly before looking me in the eyes. "I told my mother that I didn't want to be a Maddox, that I was giving it all up. When I told my girlfriend, she confessed that she wasn't pregnant. Said that she'd lied. If I didn't have money, then she didn't want me."

My heart cracks in two. Who could be so evil? Sylvia being ruthless was one thing, but for a person to only date Pane because of his wealth, to lie about a baby—to attempt to trap him into marriage—and then dump him when he gave everything up? What sort of person does that?

And then suddenly, I understand him. I get why he only dated women in his social circle, why he pegged me for a fortune hunter: Because the last woman he loved *was* a fortune hunter. Money was all that mattered to her—not this beautiful man.

I run my fingers through his silky locks, and he closes his eyes at my touch. As I'm stretching forward, my grip on the sheet loosens. It begins to slip, but I gather it back up, wadding it at my throat.

When Pane opens his eyes, I say, "Just so you know, I would never be with you for your money."

He smiles sadly. "It's what I like best about you."

"I know. Because I'd be dating you for your *jet*, instead."

His eyes flare in surprise, and before I have a chance to stop him, he flings the sheet away from me, exposing my breasts.

I gasp at the cold that sweeps over my flesh, making it prickle. My nipples harden from the chill and Pane sits up, taking one of them in his mouth.

I drop my head back and moan with pleasure. Underneath me, his cock hardens.

When he lets my pebbled nipple fall from his mouth, he says in a husky voice, "You're going to pay for that."

I laugh. "Please, punish me."

Chapter 36

PANE

I'm going to win the Maddox Group, and then I'm going to stay. There are big plans for Mystic Meadows swimming in my head, plans that involve building a resort in the mountains. Which will bring tourism to the town that will, in turn, feed into Rowe's farm.

A farm she will win back.

So no, I'm not leaving. Rowe is my future. This place is my future. These people are my future. All of it is my future.

I see that now.

And I'll never stop seeing it.

How much of this does Rowe know? None.

I'm holding this close to my chest until after I win. When I'm announced as the newest CEO of the Maddox Group, that's when it'll be time to share my vision with her, and not a moment earlier.

"Pane!"

I look up from the banister I'm polishing one last time. Rowe's just walked in from the outdoors, and she's grinning at me.

My heart convulses at the sight of her. What Sunbeam has brought into my life has changed me from the inside out. I didn't know it was possible to feel so much, to be filled with such happiness, such joy.

Rowe Wadley has been the most unexpected surprise in my life, and I love her.

Love her.

It's not put into words until this very moment as she smiles widely at me, her expression open, her eyes warm as she drinks me in.

And I'm falling. *Have* fallen. *Did* fall for her.

"Come on. I want to get a picture."

She takes my hand and we head outside, where Cristina, Isaac, Ron, McCauley, and Donner, along with the guys from his yurt community, meander in front of the house. The piggycorns race by, tails wagging, hindquarters bouncing. They run in a packed tidal wave, nipping and tugging ears, heads butting shoulders.

My heart swells at the sight of them.

Will wonders never cease?

"Pane, go stand over there," Rowe instructs.

She sets up her phone and hits the timer button. Then she runs over and slides up beside me. I put my arm around her as she yells, "Say, cheese!"

In unison, we all say, "Cheese!"

The photo snaps and we break apart.

Isaac comes over and shakes my hand. "Big day tomorrow."

"We're ready." I turn to Cristina. "You all booked?"

"All booked," she announces proudly with a wink at Rowe. "My first client is one of the Collins boys. Don't worry, I told him I don't do full body. He's only getting a back massage."

Rowe grimaces. "Thank goodness." To me, she says, "We're booked solid for the next two weeks, but I don't see how this is going to change anything."

"Just trust me."

She pushes onto her tiptoes and kisses my cheek. "Okay. I trust you."

"Good."

Ron steps up. "We're doing one final round of poker tonight in celebration. You coming?"

My gaze darts to Rowe, who now rests her elbow on my shoulder. "Why are you looking at me?"

"Because I want to make sure it's okay with you to say yes."

She narrows her eyes playfully. "Will you be back at a reasonable hour?"

"And if I say no?"

She leans in and whispers so that no one else can hear, "Then you'll be getting a spanking."

"Oh, I'll definitely be home late, then."

Her eyes flare, probably because I referred to the farm as *home*. It is home. It's become my home more than any other place that I've ever lived.

A small smile plays on her full lips. "See you *home* later, then."

I press a kiss to her cheek and whisper, "Wait up."

"Oh, I will," she replies with a giggle, leaving me to walk up the steps of the house with Cristina. When Rowe reaches the door, she glances over her shoulder and smiles.

The wind whips through her hair, and when I glance into the sky, steel-gray clouds scroll past.

"Looks like a storm's coming," Isaac murmurs.

No storm could stop the sensation in my heart, because from where I'm standing, it feels like a ray of sunshine is erupting from my chest, filling me with boundless joy.

I am home.

"I was going to do this tomorrow, but it's going to be so busy that there won't be time," I say.

"Do what?" Ron asks between bites of potato chips.

"This."

I pull my wallet from my back pocket and pull out three checks—one for Isaac, one for Ron, and one for McCauley. One by one, I slap the checks on the table and slide them over to each man.

"For all your hard work. Thank you."

Ron flips over the check in front of him, does a double take, and reels back in his chair. Isaac's hand shoots out and grabs the chair, pushing it forward until the front legs hit the floor.

"Is this a joke?" Ron asks. "I thought you didn't have access to any of your money."

I quash the grin that starts spreading across my face. "I was able to get this for you. Sorry it's not more."

"Not more? It's twenty grand," Ron sputters.

"What?" Isaac flips over his check. His eyes nearly pop from his skull. "*Is* this a joke?"

"Not a joke. I told the three of you before you started that you'd be compensated."

"I figured the hot dogs were compensation." McCauley scratches the dark scruff on his chin. "I never thought you'd pay us like this."

"This is small thanks to the three of you for believing in the farm and for giving your time and energy—and for working two jobs." I nod toward Isaac and McCauley. "For sacrificing."

"Hey, man," the bartender says, "in Mystic Meadows, people are more than people. We're each other's family. Rowe is family. We'd do anything to help her."

"And you, with money like this," McCauley jokes.

I rub the back of my neck as laughter rumbles from my chest. Of all the work I've ever done—building hotels, overlooking construction projects—this has been the most significant. It has touched me the most, meant more to me than I can express.

These guys mean a lot, too.

They each thank me.

"You all deserve it. Thank you for all the work you did."

We settle into a comfortable silence and Isaac deals the next hand. "So, what time you leaving tomorrow?" he asks.

"Who says I'm leaving?"

"Well, aren't you?"

I look up from my hand to see the three of them staring at me. I shrug. "What?"

"We just figured you'd be gone," Ron clarifies, eyeing the check that sits face down on the table.

"Did you place bets on when I'd leave?"

"No." Isaac scowls, insulted. "Well, maybe."

McCauley keeps an eye on his hand. "He's staying."

Isaac's eyes widen. "Are you staying?"

"You gonna break Rowe's curse?" Ron accordion-closes the cards in his hand. "Are you?"

"There isn't a curse," I counter.

"Oh, there's a curse," Clarice says, showing up to clear the glasses.

"What gives, Clarice?" Ron says. "You're not supposed to take our drinks so soon."

Clarice puts a glass of water in front of him. "Storm's moving."

As she says it, all our phones buzz, and a computerized voice warns us that severe weather is heading our way.

I open the weather app and check the radar. There's a line of red heading straight for us. "Looks nasty."

"Tornadoes," McCauley says ominously. "That's what's coming."

My head whips up. "Is it even tornado season?"

"It's not." Clarice starts to move off, giving us her back. "But that doesn't matter in the South. From the look of the radar, we got just enough time to get home. Y'all be safe."

Isaac rises. "I'll drive you, Clarice. Leave the John Deere."

I slip the phone into my pocket, ignoring the tightening in my chest. "Has this area been hit by a tornado before?"

"A few years back," McCauley tells me as he pulls his car keys from his pocket. "And the worst part is that storms like to hit the same areas over and over again. Get home and into the basement."

Basement? There's not a basement at the farm. As the men and Clarice move to leave, I dial Rowe to warn her.

There's no answer.

Fear grips me by the throat. I have to get home *now*, before the line of storms hits.

Chapter 37

ROWE

The cell phone lines are down. I've tried calling Pane several times, but the call won't go through.

I only pray that he's safe.

"Come on, let's go," I say to the piggycorns. "Outside, to the shelter. Now!"

The drove races toward the back of the house, skidding across the wooden floorboards. Outside, the wind sweeps fiercely across the house. Branches bang on the roof. The glass in the windows contracts and shudders, flirting with breaking.

The piggycorns scrabble over the kitchen floor, their hooves trying to gain purchase as they slide into one another, bunching up in a group in front of the back door.

I count. "Where's Tallulah?"

They look up at me in question, worry blazing in their dark eyes. I rush back to the foyer. "Tallulah!"

She's not in the living room, which is the new reception area, or Mom's office, where she loves to curl up under the desk.

I take the stairs two at a time. "Tallulah!"

I toss open bedroom doors, frantically searching. She's not in my room or the bathroom. She's not here.

Where is she?

I rush back downstairs to where the rest of the drove sits by the door. There's not the usual ear-pulling or hoof-nipping. They're on edge. Worried.

"Come on. We'll find her."

I grab Buster the Cat from the counter and rush the piggycorns outside and down the porch steps. The sun has set, and I can barely see the horizon as debris flies through the air. Leaves slap against my face. Grit fills my eyes.

The worst storms always occur at night. Always. When you can't see is when the worst things happen.

My hair blows in my eyes. I shove it away from my face. "Tallulah!"

There's no reply. No little piggy grunting in a bush, hiding from me. Nothing.

And where is Pane? The bar isn't safe if a tornado hits. The place will be ripped up from the ground, tossed into the air, and flipped upside down.

I can't focus on that. I can't think the worst. He's safe. Pane is safe. He's all right.

"Tallulah!" I call into the night that's quickly coming.

Branches slash at my arms as I push the piggies around to the side of the house and tug on the storm-shelter door. It doesn't give at first, but after I put my back into it, the heavy steel begins to move, its hinges groaning in protest.

The smell of warm earth and moisture hits me in the face, for the shelter is nothing more than a hole dug out of a hill. But it has a light and it'll keep us safe.

I try to usher the pigs in, but they hesitate. So I place Buster the Cat on the floor and pull the string that's attached to the single light bulb in the center of the room. When the piggies can see the interior, they slowly amble inside, sniffing and snorting as they go.

I slam the door shut and take a moment to study my cramped surroundings.

There's little in the room except for brittle shelves that have been here since Jesus walked the earth, and some wooden boxes of starfizz berries that are slowly drying out.

Pane and I saved what we could from the hedges that the unicorns destroyed, and we stored them in here. The piggies immediately smell the berries and move for them.

When facing the choice of grumpy pigs or pigs with full bellies, I'll take pigs with full bellies anytime of the day.

I push the crates toward them and let them feed. Which reminds me—maybe Tallulah's nearby.

I press my shoulder against the heavy steel door, grunting in frustration as it slowly gives, inch by inch. When it's open a couple of feet, the wind catches it and yanks the door from my hands, throwing it open. When I step out to grab it, the wind grabs hold of me, too, almost throwing me from the shelter.

"Tallulah! Pane!"

The sky's become a steely gray. I can still see some, but soon I won't be able to see at all. It'll be me alone with pigs until the storm blows over.

Fighting the screaming wind, I step back into the shelter, my heart thundering against my ribs. I'm alone. Truly alone. It's the one thing in life that I thought that I wanted—to be alone so that I could take care of myself. Now I realize how foolish that was.

I hate it. I can't stand it. Here I am, facing down a line of tornadoes heading straight for us, and I don't want any of it. I don't want one piece of this. All I want is to be wrapped up safely in Pane's arms, surrounded by my piggies.

If this is what it means to prove I can take care of myself—facing unimaginable destruction all alone—then I don't want it.

I need someone, and it's okay to admit that.

From my jeans pocket, I pull out my phone. There's no service, no way to contact Pane and make sure that he's okay. *God, please let him be okay. I don't ask for much, so please give me this.*

No idea if he heard my request, but as I shut the shelter door behind me and slide down to the floor, my heart tightens.

Never in my life did I think it was possible to care about someone so much, to love them as much as I do Pane.

The piggycorns surround me, sensing my sadness.

I lower my head as they blot their wet snouts to my face. We've lost Tallulah, and I pray that Pane is safe. The only thing that could save my favorite little girl is a miracle.

I pull my knees up to my chin and exhale. *Please, please let them be safe.*

We sit in silence for a few moments, the only sounds being the crunch of dried starfizz berries, the soft grunts of piggycorns eating, and the muffled whir of the screaming wind beyond the door.

Then a noise outside grabs my attention. It sounds like yelling. Then something snaps. Then more yelling. I glance up as the heavy metal door scrapes open.

The wind howls. Trees thrash violently. And in from the shadows steps Pane. He's windblown; his hair sticks up in all directions, and his shirt is smudged with dirt and ripped in several places. But under one arm, he carries Tallulah, and behind him, he's leading in Stella.

Chapter 38

PANE

Rowe jumps up from the floor, where she's surrounded by pigs. She throws her arms around my neck and holds me tight. "Thank goodness you're safe. I was so worried."

I hug her with Tallulah tucked under my arm. "Not even a tornado could keep me from you," I joke, but *not* joke. "I brought a friend that you might be missing."

She takes Tallulah and hugs her close. "Where did you find her?"

"She ran up to the truck when I pulled in."

"And Stella?"

The unicorn neighs nervously. "Was with Tallulah."

Rowe balks. "What?"

Stella steps into the shelter, dragging her chain behind her.

Rowe runs a hand down her leg. "She must've gotten scared and pulled it from the wall. But whatever. It doesn't matter how, just that she's here. Come in. *Come in.* It's a tight squeeze, but we can do it."

Rowe coaxes the unicorn inside, and I grab the door to shut it. The screaming wind changes in pitch. The sound becomes deafening, resembling a freight train.

The hairs on the back of my neck stiffen.

The tornado is here.

Tree branches and leaves fill the air. Twigs scrape against my arms when I grab the door. Tiny shards of leaves wedge themselves into my eyes, blinding me. It's impossible to see, and all I can hear is the blaring tornado as it bears down on the farm, and I pray that, God willing, the storm jumps over the Wadleys and spares us.

Through the grit filling my eyes, I manage to see enough to find the knob and pull the door tight.

The silence inside the room is somehow more terrifying than the howling outside. Rowe puts Tallulah on the floor and moves to me. I wrap my arm around her, hugging her close as we both listen to the storm.

Beside us, Stella blows out air. The unicorn takes up most of the room. The rest of us are wedged together, but the piggies don't seem to mind.

They've found the starfizz berries and are keeping their mouths occupied.

I wipe debris from my eyes and look down to see Rowe smiling at me. "Thank you," she whispers. "For getting Tallulah and Stella."

My arm tightens around her. "You're welcome."

Above, I hear a crash. Even though the noise is muffled, it sounds and feels like the earth is being ripped apart. The shelter trembles and shivers like the wind is doing its best to grab hold of it and yank it right out of the ground.

Concrete spills from the seams in the ceiling, sprinkling my hair and shoulders. The single bulb in the center of the compact space flickers.

Rowe holds her breath.

This could be it. We could die here. The top of the cellar could be ripped right off and all of us sucked into the storm.

I will not die without having told Rowe how I feel about her.

My grip on her tightens just as she wraps her arms around my waist and buries her face in my chest. I pull her in, inhaling her sweet scent, and cradle her head.

"If we die here—"

"We're not going to die," she says, sounding muffled and not very sure of herself.

"You need to know how I feel."

Her head pops up. "Are you seriously doing a deathbed confession right now?"

I scowl. "These could be our last moments."

"Are you trying to jinx it?"

"No, I'm trying to tell you how I feel," I snap.

"Starting a conversation like we're going to die here is—"

"Will you just be quiet and listen?"

She pulls back and glares at me. "Fine."

This woman. I swear, if the tornado doesn't kill me, she just might. I cup her hand to my chest and stare into her eyes.

"Rowe Wadley . . ." The shelter shakes again, and she flinches. Her gaze darts around, then lands back on me. "Before I met you, I was on autopilot. My life was about the company." A bitter laugh escapes me. "What I thought was important, I now see is immaterial. You have shown me that life is worth so much more. Don't look so surprised. This place, this town, you—you have all become my home. You *are* my home, Rowe Wadley. You are my life."

She blinks. "What?"

I nod. "You are my world. The people of this town are my world. This farm—"

"These animals?"

Oh, God. Even in the middle of dying, she's cracking a joke. "Yes, they mean the world to me, too. I want you to know that when this is over, I'm not going anywhere."

She peers into my eyes, really searching—for a lie, for the telltale sign that I'll abandon her. But what she doesn't realize is that I don't want to go anywhere. I don't want to spend my life out of a suitcase, packing up and going to the next hotel. I don't want to do that ever again.

"Pane—"

The structure shudders, and the light flickers—once, twice—before blinking out.

Thrown into darkness, all I can hear is the sound of breathing before Rowe's hands slip from mine.

"Stella?" she says.

The unicorn snorts.

"Stella?" Rowe repeats calmly. "It's going to be okay. Just light your horn."

Right. I'd forgotten that the unicorn is afraid of the dark.

I place a hand on Stella's shoulder and feel her muscle quiver under my palm. She stamps her foot and backs up, breathing even harder.

Maybe touching her wasn't the best thing.

"Calm down, girl," Rowe says.

The air in the shelter shifts. Outside, the storm's still raging, but in here, the scent of terror is thick. It's like a cold blanket has cloaked itself over the room.

The unicorn stamps her foot and blows some more. She knocks into a shelf, and it crashes to the floor behind us. Piggycorns squeal and Buster the Cat hisses as they all dart over my feet, running for cover.

The unicorn neighs. Rowe keeps pleading with her, but Stella bumps into more shelves, and more concrete dust falls from the ceiling, peppering us.

Meanwhile, it sounds like the world outside is being torn apart, tree by tree.

Stella pounds the floor, and one of the piggycorns shrieks. The unicorn will trample all of us to death.

"I've got to get her out of here," I say over the sounds of Stella's panic attack.

"But she'll die," Rowe argues.

"She'll hurt us if she keeps on! Rowe, we have to."

More shelves fall and are pounded by hooves. Wood sprays into the air, splattering against my clothes. Piggycorns squeal. Stella neighs so loudly that it sounds like shrieking.

Everything's coming undone.

If I can just open the door, maybe she'll run out.

Just as I reach it, a light slowly flares to life and Stella goes quiet.

"Pane," Rowe whispers.

I turn around to face them. The first thing I see is Stella standing calmly on top of splintered and broken shelves that now litter the floor.

Above us, the bare bulb dimly glows. Outside the wind has died down. The storm's passed, leaving in its wake a deafening silence. But inside, the hum of electricity fills the cramped room that smells of farm animals.

And in the corner, cowering just behind Rowe, stand all the piggycorns, including Tallulah, the runt.

She looks proudly up at Stella, and Stella looks back down at her.

Because Tallulah's horn is glowing.

It's glowing just like the light in the cellar.

Chapter 39

ROWE

Holy cow.

Tallulah's horn is lit up. As I stare in wonder, trying to put puzzle pieces together, the other piggycorns' horns light up, and as they brighten, so does the bulb hanging from the ceiling. It shines as if the piggycorns are what's causing it to glow.

I blink as I realize the piggycorns *are* causing it to glow.

Pane points to them. "They're doing it."

"How?"

He looks around until his gaze lands on the starfizz berries. "I think that may be the culprit."

"No."

"Yes."

"But how?"

He walks over and runs a hand over the dried berries. "The ley lines."

"What?"

He scoops up a handful and lets them fall through his fingers back into the crate. "You said that they used to grow here, right?"

"Uh-huh."

He studies the crate of dried dark-purple husks. "And you also said that they stopped growing berries here around the same time as the piggycorns showed up."

"Yeah."

Pane thinks for a moment, and when he speaks, it's with the energy of someone who's solved a long-puzzling mystery. "And you also said that the power began to dwindle at the same time."

Now I'm on board, completely following his logic. "You're saying . . ." I try to keep the excitement from my voice, because there are a lot of probables and a lot of places where this whole idea could be wrong. But it might not be. We might be very, very right.

I start over. "You're saying that the magic began in the ley lines, but it flourished because of these berries."

"Yes," he proclaims. "Yes! The berries are the key. Mystic Meadows didn't lose its magic because the unicorns were overbred, though maybe that had something to do with it. Your town was drained dry because the land needs these, and it needs these to grow here, near the ley lines."

"The ley lines," I murmur, really not knowing what else to say.

He scoops up another handful and lets the small round globes fall through the spaces between his fingers. "These are the key, and you, Rowe Wadley—brilliant, beautiful you—figured it out!"

I roll my eyes. "Kind of by accident."

Pane strokes my cheek and gazes down at me, eyes brimming with emotion. "The best kind of discovery is that which is unexpected."

My heart does this little flutter thing because it feels like he's talking about more than starfizz berries.

The light bulb buzzes and he looks up. "I mean, you're seeing what I am, right? That the piggycorns are creating electricity?"

"I think so," I murmur. "Are we sure?"

My gaze flicks to the piggies, and as if they understood my doubt, their horns flare brighter and so does the single bulb dangling from the ceiling.

A grin breaks across Pane's face. "They have magic."

The realization slowly soaks into me, and I throw my arms into the air, yelling, "They have magic! The piggycorns have magic!"

My heart nearly explodes with happiness. All these years, people scoffed at my piggycorns. They were called useless. Worthless. A waste of existence.

But they are not a waste. They are very much not so. They have magic, the likes of which no one has ever suspected.

Least of all me.

Pane pulls me into a hug and murmurs in my ear, "I knew they had powers all along. I knew they could do it."

I laugh, pulling away to stare into those sage eyes. "No, you didn't."

"Now, why would you ever think that?"

"Because you hated them."

He presses his lips to mine and I melt. "*Used to* is not now."

I pull back and grin. I could stare at his beautiful face for the absolute rest of my life and be happy. Nothing could change that. But there's a competition to win, a spa to open, a farm to buy back.

"What do you say we get out of here and see how things look?"

He nods. "Yeah, before we've got a pile of heaping manure to clean up."

I laugh, trying to keep my spirits high, because from the way the wind was howling, there's at least one tree down, and I pray that's the worst of it.

Chapter 40

ROWE

That is not the worst of it.

It's gone.

All of it.

Where the house stood, there's a pile of rubble—splintered wood, shattered glass, crumbled shingles. If all the planks and tiles and walls were glued back together, there would be a house.

But that's not what I'm looking at. I'm looking at a pile of garbage.

My heart cracks in two as, the next morning, I take stock of what's left. Pane, the piggies, Buster the Cat, and Stella are safe and sound. That's what matters. That's what *should* matter. But right now, my entire life has been obliterated.

What are we going to do?

My phone rings and it's Mom. I can't even begin to tell her what's happened, but I can't ignore the call, either.

"Hey, Mom."

"Honey, are you okay?"

I force myself to talk around my shrunken throat. My gaze lifts, searching out Pane, but he left to go into town. He was on the phone all morning, trying to get men out here to clean up. Turns out there was a lot of storm damage in the area, and the work crews are all busy.

Not once did Pane say anything about the competition. His heart must be just as broken as mine.

"Yeah, Mom. Yep. I'm fine. We survived."

"Did the storms do any damage? Clarice Sinclair said they ripped up part of her yard, but she didn't know how you're doing."

I can't bear to tell her the truth. She had so much hope these past couple of months. She believed in me so hard and put her trust in me because I'd put mine in Pane.

To tell her that we've lost everything will destroy her. It's destroyed me. There's an abyss in the pit of my stomach that will never be filled now.

"We're all safe," I squeak out, doing everything to keep my voice from breaking. "Mom"—I exhale a staggered breath—"can I call you back?"

"Sure, honey. Sure. I can't wait to hear how great things go when Pane wins today. The spa's fully booked, right?"

"Right," I say lamely.

Oh, God. The competition. The spa. Saving the farm. There will be none of it now. *None of it.* It's over before it even began. That dream has been eviscerated.

The farm won't be resurrected. It will go into foreclosure.

What will I do?

My heart doesn't just break for me. It throbs for Pane. For six weeks he worked on this place, giving it everything he had—and now his wish, this business . . . they're both dead before earning the chance to fly.

It's so awful that I can barely breathe. "Listen, Mom, I've got to go."

"Sure, honey. I know it's a busy day for you. Keep me posted. Fingers crossed."

"Fingers crossed," I repeat weakly before hanging up.

There's so much that's a mess that I don't even know where to start. And I can't even begin to know how to deal with today.

The sound of Pane's truck rumbling down the drive grabs my attention. At the same time, Buster the Cat runs out from under a line of bushes and attempts to wrap his body around my legs like a pretzel.

I reach down and pick him up. "It's okay, Buster. I'll find you some food soon. Maybe you can eat starfizz berries, too."

It's literally the only food we have.

Pane exits the truck holding two coffees. "Power's out all over town, but the coffee shop has a generator."

He glances over at Dancing Trails. Somehow they managed to escape the eye of the storm.

Of course they did.

Pane hands me a coffee and I sniff. It's a mocha.

I bite back the sob that swells in my throat. "What do we do?"

He brushes a strand of hair away from my face. "It's going to be okay. It's all gonna be fine."

"No, it's not. You've lost the competition. I've lost the farm." My face scrunches up in sadness. "I'm so sorry."

He knuckles away a tear that streaks down my face, and when he looks down at me, emotion brims in his eyes. "I've already won everything I need."

His words make my heart quiver. "But the house—"

"Houses can be rebuilt."

"But the foreclosure?"

There, he's silent, because he knows as well as I do that we don't have a chance.

Before he can argue, or agree with me, or say anything at all, Clarice Sinclair rumbles down the road, honking her horn. Behind her are at least a dozen vehicles. They all swing into the driveway and I watch in horror as people I've known my whole life fill up our small gravel drive.

They're here to see Pane win. But now he won't.

They slowly get out of their cars and drift listlessly toward what's left of the house. Their expressions are filled with shock and sheer disbelief.

Cristina runs up and throws her arms around me. "It's gonna be okay."

I manage to keep the tears in check.

Ron appears and pulls his hat off his head, squashing it between his hands. "It was gonna be so great."

Isaac squeezes Pane's shoulder. "I can't believe it, man."

McCauley pulls up in his work truck and just stares.

It's all any of us can do. Just stare.

The scent of defeat is heavy in the air. Some folks start picking up boards, but there's no place to put them.

I'm so shocked that I don't know what to do first—cry or collapse.

It's while Cristina's still hugging me that Luke's truck rolls into the driveway. Oh, God. He's here to see if I have the money to keep the house from going into foreclosure.

It's so insane that I want to laugh. There's no money. Pane has lost the competition, and whatever chance I could have had to somehow win back the farm is gone.

Caput.

Done.

Right behind Luke, fast on his heels, is a limousine.

Acid churns in my stomach, rolling up into my throat. It takes all my willpower to swallow down the urge to vomit.

Please, let's just get this over with.

Luke parks and kills his engine. But it's not Luke who everyone's watching. All eyes are on the limo as it comes to a stop.

The driver, wearing a black suit, exits the vehicle and opens the rear passenger door. Sylvia Maddox emerges, once again wearing all white from head to foot. She takes a step and surveys the damage. Her brows pinch, and a look of surprise sweeps over her face before it is quickly schooled.

She knows that Pane's lost. There's no way for him to recover from this.

From the other side of the limo comes a short man wearing a tweed suit and wire-rimmed glasses. He's carrying a clipboard in one hand and surveying the land with a confused expression. It's like he's thinking, *Isn't there supposed to be a house here?*

"The valuator," Pane tells me, putting an arm around my shoulders. "He judges what the business is worth."

A bitter scoff escapes my lips. "What business?"

But Pane just squeezes me, offering what comfort he can, before releasing his grip to greet his mother.

"Pane." Sylvia air-kisses his cheeks. "I heard about the storms. Rowe"—she nods to me—"I'm sorry for what happened."

"Thank you," I tell her.

Luke is out of his truck and watching. He's got a load of paperwork in his hands, and he's eyeing the house like a snake about to sink its fangs into a rabbit.

Mrs. Maddox's gaze sweeps across the yard as she slowly takes in the rubble. "Stone's business has already been valuated. Your brother has done well."

"I'm not surprised," Pane tells her.

She shakes her head. "As much as I'd like to extend the contest, you both signed a contract. Your brother has worked hard, just as you have. Given the circumstances, I'm afraid that there's no choice but to award the president and CEO position to—"

"Wait." Pane flings out his hands. "Just wait."

His mother rolls her eyes. "You can't save this."

"Yes, I can," he insists in a tone that makes her pause. "Just watch me." He then turns his back on her, cups his hands over his mouth, and yells, "Donner! Donner Wright!"

There's a brief silence before the answer comes. "Here!"

Donner slips out of the tangle of people and approaches us, looking as oiled up as ever.

Pane gestures to his mother. "Sylvia Maddox, meet Donner Wright. He runs the off-grid yurt community."

Donner's glistening pecs glint in the sunlight as he approaches with a grim smile. "Pleasure."

Sylvia shakes his hand with the tips of her fingers.

"Donner helped with the renovation," Pane explains.

"Wonderful." Sylvia gives him a tight-lipped smile. "Pane, none of this changes the fact that—"

"This property is in foreclosure," Luke announces, deciding to take this moment to step up and let everyone be graced with his presence. "In accordance with the terms of the loan, if the land owner does not have the funds to pay a substantial amount of the mortgage that is owed, then the property returns to the bank and will go to auction." Luke's smug gaze lands on me. "Do you have the funds, Rowe Wadley?"

Anger rakes over my chest. *Does it look like I have the funds?* I want to spit. I'm silent for a moment, feeling the weight of the crowd staring at me.

It's a fight for me to get the words out. "No, I don't."

Sylvia Maddox stares openly at me. She must think I'm such a loser. This woman will never approve of me, not with how messy my life is.

Luke starts to shove a piece of paper under my nose, but Pane steps between us. "Wait. This isn't over."

"It's not?" Luke says sarcastically, scratching his head. "It looks *over* to me. Rowe just admitted that she doesn't have the money. If she doesn't have it, then the property returns to the bank. End of story."

A thought occurs to me and hope flares in my chest. "What about home owner's insurance?"

Luke shakes his head. "Your mother canceled the policy."

"How do you know?"

"She told me," he sneers. "She couldn't pay the mortgage, so she stopped the insurance."

"Donner," Pane says.

Why is he so focused on Donner? What is going on?

"Pane, I'm sorry." Sylvia starts to walk off. "I have no choice but to award the company to your—"

"Wait, Mom. *Wait.*" He grabs her by the arm and pulls her back into the crowd, who watches the scene with their gazes ping-ponging from Luke to Pane, to Donner, to Sylvia, and now back to Pane.

Pane's gaze flicks to Donner. "You need electricity, right? You want clean power. Isn't that so?"

Donner scrubs his cheek, looking uncertain. He's probably wondering where this is going.

I was until that very moment. Now a tingle cartwheels down the back of my neck as I realize Pane's plan.

His gaze snaps to me, and I rush to the crumpled fence, where Tallulah's foraging for roots. I hoist her into my arms and carry her back to Pane. It also just so happens that I've got starfizz berries in my back pocket.

You know, 'cause you never know when you're going to need to feed a pig some starfizz berries.

At least, that's what I thought earlier this morning when I shoved them in there.

"Everyone, follow me," Pane says. "Mom, you come, too. You too," he commands the valuator.

His mother sighs, but she, along with the rest of the crowd, follows Pane to the gazebo, which surprisingly, is still standing.

He points to the string of lights. "The yurt community outside of Mystic Meadows and plenty of other off-grid communities want power, but they don't want solar panels or wind. They need something that doesn't intrude on their lives but is also a clean source of energy. Enter, the piggycorn."

I pose with Tallulah like a model on *The Price Is Right*, swishing this way and that.

People laugh nervously. I'm sure they're thinking Pane's lost his mind.

Luke guffaws. "He's done lost his mind."

Don't say I didn't tell you so.

But the townsfolk have no idea what's coming. Hope bubbles in my stomach as I feed Tallulah a handful of berries. Her tongue slides over my palm as she snuffles up the last of the treats.

Pane points to the lights. "Tallulah, make them glow."

Does she understand him? I have no idea. But as she finishes chewing the berries, her horn begins to shine. She snorts happily, content with the feed, and as her happiness grows, her horn shines brighter, and then the gazebo lights flare to life.

The crowd gasps. People murmur in delight. They're surprised. Elated. Amazed.

It's not just the gazebo lights that flare, either. The streetlamp on Luke's side of the road flickers, and people's cars power up as headlights blink on and radios sing to life.

Donner's jaw drops. "Can one pig light a whole village?"

Pane's face breaks into a handsome smile. "I believe so."

"I'll give you fifty thousand for her."

My eyes nearly pop out of my head in disbelief. "What?"

"We need her." Donner places his hands on his hips. "Everyone will chip in. If that's not enough, we can go to sixty."

Pane squeezes my hand as he walks past me and speaks to the valuator. "There are communities all over the country who want something like this. There are private homes that would pay, too. I predict that by the end of the week, we'll be sold out of piggycorns. The demand for them will only continue to grow, and we"—he drapes an arm over my shoulders—"can supply piggycorns to people all over the world."

Luke's face is beet red, his cheeks puffed out. He glares at me. Stares at Pane. Watches the valuator worriedly.

The valuator cocks his head back and forth. "This is an interesting business. What do you think, Mrs. Maddox?"

Fascination sparks in her green eyes. "Pane, this is your competition entry?"

"This is it."

She nods to the valuator. "Estimate the worth."

My stomach does flip-flops. The crowd is silent while the valuator gets to work plugging numbers into a calculator that's attached to his clipboard, then writing down whatever it is he's penning onto sheets and sheets of paper. After a while Tallulah becomes restless, and I set her on the ground.

After about ten minutes of pure agony, he gives a final nod and whispers something into Sylvia's ear.

She listens intently. "Are you sure?"

"I'm sure."

Then Sylvia Maddox, current president and CEO of the Maddox Group, fixes her penetrating gaze on her son. "Pane."

"Yes?"

The air buzzes with intensity. I've got all my fingers and toes crossed, praying that he wins.

A slow smile breaks across her face. "Congratulations, son. You've won."

Chapter 41

ROWE

The crowd erupts into cheers. Pane throws his arms around me, pulling me into a hug that lifts my feet from the ground.

There's so much commotion that I barely hear Luke shouting, "That still doesn't stop the foreclosure. The bank will take this property."

Pane lowers me to the gazebo floor and shakes his head. "No, it won't."

Luke folds his arms. "What do you mean, the bank won't take it?"

The limousine driver hands a briefcase to Sylvia, which she opens, revealing hundreds of bills. Pane's mother throws a disdainful look to Luke.

Then Sylvia Maddox says something that floors me. "Since Rowe's business won the competition, she receives one hundred thousand dollars in compensation."

My knees become jelly, and I start to slip toward the ground. "Is that true? Is this a joke?"

Pane pulls me back up to standing and stares down at me with so much emotion in his eyes that my heart slams into my rib cage. "Sunbeam, I never told you because I didn't want to give you false hope. But yes, you just won back your farm."

I can barely breathe. This is literally the best day of my life. My hands shake as I take hold of the briefcase. It's more money than I've ever seen in one place.

A staggered breath escapes my lungs. It's a long time before I'm able to drag my gaze away from all the cash. But when I do, a spark of courage and pride fills my chest. I lift my head high and ask Luke, "Will the bank take a cashier's check?"

Chapter 42

ROWE

As soon as the words leave my mouth, Pane pulls me into a hug, kisses the top of my head, and whispers, "Congratulations. You just saved your farm."

There's still so much to work out: How will I part with my precious piggycorns? How many will it take to light up a community? How am I going to manage growing starfizz berries *and* raising piggycorns? But I've got Pane beside me, and that's all that matters.

And right then my heart expands. I feel like the Grinch in *How the Grinch Stole Christmas*, when his heart breaks the bands encasing it. My heart overflows with love. Nothing—not one thing—can yank this feeling away.

While I've got my face pressed into Pane's chest, inhaling his amazing scent, I hear murmurs and gasps around me.

He strokes my head and whispers, tickling the hair surrounding my ear, "Look up, little Sunbeam."

When I do, my heart nearly pops out of my chest. I blink, wipe my eyes to make sure I'm really seeing what I'm seeing.

A patch of earth in front of the house, about twenty feet long, glows with light, illuminating the grass all the way to the tip of each blade. But unlike all the other times when I've seen this happen, this time there's no catalyst. The wind isn't blowing; the air is still. But even so, the earth buzzes with energy.

As I watch, vines unwind from the ground and shoot into the sky. They stretch like long, elegant fingers, jutting way up before stopping their ascent. They hang in the air for a brief second, swaying lightly in the breeze, before curling their tips back down and plunging into the rubble like a swimmer diving off a cliff.

From underneath the pile of debris, the clang of snapping and popping fills the air. It sounds like bones cracking and glass shattering all over again.

"Is the house going to fall into a hole?" someone whispers.

"No. It's being fixed," I hear myself realize.

Shingles rise into the air, lifted by the vining ropes that stretch unnaturally from the earth. More vines dive down into the mess and resurface, bringing with them panes of glass and cracked planks of wood.

Orbs of magic lift from the ground like sprites. They surround the rubble that's risen from the dead and, quick as lightning, spin in a blur. The air around the house seems to exhale, and as it breathes, the shattered and destroyed planks of wood and shards of glass swirl with it. Planks click and clack as they snap back the way they were. Glass grinds and shingles scrape as they are stitched, becoming whole once more.

"Holy cow," Cristina says, her voice overflowing with awe. "Rowe, what did you do?"

I shake my head, unable to put into words what I'm feeling, watching in disbelief as the broken and destroyed house—the wood splintered to dust and the glass ground into powder—spins, creating a vortex that whips the air around us. My shirt flutters. My legs shake as the house spins and spins, until it finally lands with an earth-shaking *thump*.

The very world stills as we stare in silence at the house—*my* house, the Wadley farm—as it stands tall and proud in the middle of the yard.

And then, just like when Pane bested Coleman Barrier's chain saw challenge, what feels like the entire population of Mystic Meadows erupts into applause. The power of it hits me in the solar plexus, choking me up.

Honestly, I'm not sure if it's the love of this town or the love of the earth for me, but I'm overcome with emotions.

And all is right in the world.

There is a party at Sparkle Bar, of all places, to celebrate Pane's win, me gaining back the farm, and the house being rebuilt. Not only has the whole town shown up, but Pane's brother arrived, too. His mother has even stayed.

Pane has changed into a three-piece suit that Sylvia brought, and he now looks like the powerful CEO and president of an international company.

He makes me proud.

I've changed into my best dress (I wore it to Jennifer and Ron's wedding several years ago). Music plays, people celebrate, and Pane Maddox is man of the hour.

Someone notified the press of the contest, and news crews have shown up as well. They've been pelting Sylvia with questions, but soon enough it'll be Pane's turn.

I push up onto my tiptoes and place my elbow on Pane's shoulder. He's been talking to Isaac and Ron, but at the intrusion, he turns my way and wraps an arm around my waist.

"Sorry to interrupt, gentlemen."

"It's no interruption," Isaac confesses. "I was just congratulating Pane."

"And I"—Pane kisses my cheek—"have been dodging every reporter possible."

I toss my head back and laugh. "Looks like you've done a good job. They're with your mother now."

He lifts his whiskey glass toward her. "Sylvia always knows what to say. I'll let her have at it."

"Brother!" A tall man with a very clear resemblance to Pane—wide shoulders and a thick neck, but lighter hair—strides up in a dark suit and crystal-blue tie.

Pane glances up and his face breaks into such a wide smile that the pulse in my neck begins fluttering. I slip my elbow off his shoulder and sink back to my heels as the brothers embrace.

When they part, Stone holds Pane at arm's length. "Congratulations! It's well deserved, though I almost had you beat. I would've gotten away with it, if it hadn't been for those meddling piggycorns," he jokes, referencing a line from every *Scooby-Doo* episode. Ever. "I told you piggycorns were a big deal."

"Yes, brother. You practically handed me victory. I almost owe you my win," Pane says with amusement lighting his eyes and laughter filling his voice. When the laughs fade, his gaze flashes in my direction. "Stone, this is Rowe Wadley."

Stone takes my hand and smiles at me warmly. "Ah, I finally get to meet you—the piggycorn whisperer."

I laugh as we shake. "The piggycorn whisperer? That's a new one."

"Didn't you know?" He winks. "That's what Pane's been calling you. Says he couldn't have done any of this without you, and I can't help but agree, because it's well known that animals hate him. Or that *he* hates animals."

"Don't listen to him," Pane chides. "I've never said that—"

I tug him by the lapels and pull him in. "That you, what? *Don't* hate animals? What a fibber! You *hated* all the piggies when you first arrived."

Stone folds his arms, giving his brother a scrutinizing look. "Is that true? You actually told her you hated them?"

Pane takes my hands, which are still curled in his suit jacket. "Do I hate them now? That's the real question."

"Now he feeds them," I inform Stone smugly. "With your hot dogs."

"That's cannibalism," Stone decries.

"They're all-beef," Pane and I chant in unison.

Stone laughs. "So, not cannibalism. Great to know. Come on." He claps his hands and rubs them together. "Let's celebrate your win."

I start to walk off with them, but Sylvia Maddox catches my eye. She lifts her brows like she wants to speak with me. "You go ahead," I tell Pane. "I'll catch up."

He frowns. "You sure?"

"I'm sure."

I watch them walk over to the bar, admiring how happy Stone is for Pane. It doesn't surprise me that he's not jealous. From everything Pane's told me about his brother, they are so committed to one another that a little bit of jealousy couldn't sour their love.

It's really admirable.

Warmth bleeds through my chest as my gaze flicks back over to Sylvia. She's untangled herself from the reporters and is making her way over. The woman looks like a sore thumb in the middle of the excruciatingly tacky Sparkle Bar, a place that resembles a field of rainbows vomiting more fields of rainbows—with stuffed buck heads to top it off.

As Pane steps up to the bar, reporters surround him, shoving a camera and microphone in his face. He smiles pleasantly, talking with an ease I couldn't muster no matter how hard I tried.

"Congratulations," Sylvia says as she walks up. "You should be very proud."

"I am," I tell her, referring more to my pride in her son than anything I hold close to myself. "I'm very proud of him."

She twists in Pane's direction. "He's going to be very busy now that he's won the company. I'll need him back in New York immediately. From there, he'll fly to the West Coast and then make his way to Japan. After that, it's Europe. He'll be gone for months, introducing himself and making sure the company gets off on the right foot under his direction."

My stomach convulses. Gone for months? Pane never said anything about that.

Sylvia inspects her manicure and says coolly, "I know you expected him to help get your little piggycorn business up and running, but I'm afraid my son will be much too busy."

Too busy?

She nods at the reporters. "There will be more interviews like this, of course. It's fun doing it here, in Mystic Meadows, where all this started. It's cute, really. But this isn't real life. Real life for a Maddox occurs in the boardroom, in a hotel."

In a hotel.

Of course I know that. Pane's lived in a hotel his whole life. But he said he doesn't want that, that I'm his future.

But it's not really true, is it? The company is his future, and that doesn't exist here. The hotels are in different cities, across the country, around the world.

What's actually in Mystic Meadows for Pane Maddox?

"Has my son ever told you about his father?"

I'd almost forgotten that Sylvia was here. "I'm sorry?" I clear my throat, hoping that will remove some of the cobwebs hazing up my brain. "Um. Yes, he has told me something about him."

"Has he told you that the man married me for my money?"

"No, not exactly." What did Pane say about his dad? "He just said that he . . ." The word *abandoned* doesn't seem like a nice way to phrase what I know. "He left, Pane said."

Sylvia takes a calculated step toward me, sizing me up with eyes that radiate arrogance and affluence. "He married me for my money, and when he realized that he wouldn't get any of it, he left, abandoned our children. He was a fortune hunter. I've always told Pane to be leery of such people."

Heat flushes my neck. Is it hot in here? It *feels* hot in here. I fan my face with one hand. "I can understand that. Mrs. Maddox, I can assure you that I'm not interested in—"

"My son's money?" She tips her head back and laughs. "Of course you are, dear. Anyone would be. That's a given. My point is that even if you two wind up together, do you *not* see how different you are?" She points one exquisitely lacquered fingernail to the decorations in the bar. "You are from this place. He is not. Once Pane takes up his new position, he won't be returning to Mystic Meadows, no matter what he's promised you."

She lays a cold hand on my shoulder. "I'm trying to stop you from being hurt more than you need to be, because my son is not the sort of person who lives in North Georgia. He is a Maddox, and the Maddox life is one of luxury and service." She delicately lifts one of her eyebrows; no doubt it's a look that has weakened many a board member's knees. "Do you see luxury anywhere here?"

No, I don't. There's no luxury here. What do I have to offer Pane other than mud and biscuits?

Nothing. Oh, myself, of course. But how long will it be before the shine of *me* wears off? Before Pane realizes that *little Sunbeam* can't compete with his world? It probably won't take long. In a few months, he'll wake up and realize I don't fit.

My gaze lifts to scan the bar. He's on the other side, talking to a reporter, giving an interview while wearing a three-piece suit. The dress I'm wearing is a Vera Wang knockoff. It's made of cheap imitation silk and has itchy straps.

Pane turns and sees me. He smiles, but all I can feel is a pressure building. The pressure of not being good enough, of not meshing with his life.

Sylvia's right: We are different. I run a pig farm; he runs hotels. At some point our differences will become blaringly obvious, and he'll leave.

I'll be abandoned again.

Realization crashes down on me. It feels like there's a baseball in my chest. One that grows, expanding, filling up, and cutting off the air that tries to thread its way into my lungs.

I can't think. Can't breathe.

"Excuse me," I whisper to Sylvia.

I push my way through the hot, crowded bar packed with people, throwing myself against the door and spilling outside.

The cool air caresses the film of sweat that coats my arms, and I shiver. I rake my fingers through my hair and inhale several deep gulps of oxygen. Air rushes into my lungs, and the claustrophobia that was setting in disappears.

I press my back to Sparkle Bar's brick exterior and take my time inhaling and exhaling, trying to right myself and wrap my mind around what comes next.

What *does* come next?

The door slams open and Pane runs out. He stops, spins around, sees me, and comes over, his hands immediately sliding up my cheeks.

"What's wrong? Did my mother say something to you?"

In his eyes, all I see is concern. Worry bleeds across his face, twisting his features. It's the worry of a man who cares about me, who thinks we have a future.

I shake my head and push myself off the bricks, sliding out of his touch.

"Rowe?"

"What are we doing, Pane?"

The concern melts into confusion. "What do you mean?"

I rub the back of my thumb across my forehead. "I mean, you're all expensive hotels, and now you're president of the Maddox Group—*president*—while I'm stuck here in Georgia as a piggycorn farmer."

"That's *Miss* Piggycorn Farmer to you," he jokes.

"I'm serious."

He slides his hands into his pockets. "My mother said something."

"Does it matter?"

"Yes, it matters. Rowe, I've meant everything that I've said. I'm not leav—"

"I know, I know. *I know* what you *say*. But yes, Pane, you *are* leaving. You have to. Now that you're president, there are people you have to see. Things you have to do. What, are you going to fire up a laptop and work between chores? Maybe between feeding hot dogs to Tallulah?"

His head falls back and he stares into the sky. After a moment, he lifts his head and levels his gaze on me. "Yes, I will have to go away for a little while. But I'll be ba—"

"To do what?" I interrupt.

"To help you." He approaches. "I'm not done with this town. I have plans. I want to build a hotel."

I cock my head. "By yourself? Or with board approval?"

"It's not like that, Rowe."

"It is, Pane."

He reaches for me and I pull away. The look of hurt on his face almost wrecks me, but then I remember the times I've been abandoned. Luke promised to stay. My dad tried to stay. But they both left, and I can't help but think that things like this come in threes. Even if it is irrational for me to believe this way, it's true. Those men left, and so will Pane.

He will. He just doesn't know it yet.

So it's up to me to remind him of how all this has been play. It hasn't been real.

"For weeks you and I have lived in a tiny little bubble." I form a cup with my hands to demonstrate. "A bubble that only exists here, in Mystic Meadows. But now we're facing real life. We're not in fantasyland anymore. You don't belong in my world, and I don't . . ."

My voice falls away and he nods. "And you don't belong in mine?"

"Exactly."

Agony, *excruciating* agony, flickers across his face as I let my hands drop to my sides. Pane closes his eyes briefly, and when he opens them, his features have gone cold, his expression stony. "Rowe, think this through. I'm telling you that—"

"I have thought it through."

"No, you haven't."

"Yes, I have."

There's a breath of silence before his spine snaps straight. "Okay," he says slowly. "If this is what you want—"

"It is," I say quickly, so quickly that there isn't time to change my mind. "It's what's best."

There's a moment where we stare at each other, and then he retreats, spreading his arms wide. "I'll do whatever you want. If you want me out of your life, little Sunbeam . . ."

My heart breaks when he says it.

"Then I'm gone."

When I don't say anything, he gives a stiff nod and walks back into the bar, leaving me all alone.

Chapter 43

PANE

One month later

"Come in."

I look up from my computer as the office door opens and Natalie skips in, her mouth dropping, her eyes going as big as volleyballs as she takes in my new surroundings.

The office is nice—there's lots of polished wood, undercabinet lighting, crystal decor I didn't pick out. Not to mention the view of the city skyline.

She lets out a wolf whistle. Where does a ten-year-old learn how to do that? "Fancy, shmancy. You clean up good, kid."

A laugh rumbles from my chest. "Thank you. So do you. How's school?"

She plops down in one of the chairs in front of my desk. "Oh, you know. I drew pictures of kids and made them pay twenty bucks for their portrait." My little sister pulls a stack of folded bills from her pocket. "I'm rich!"

"Looks like it."

Nat flaps her hands against the armrests. "You got a great view."

I spin around and check out the skyline. My heart stutters once, twice, goes empty. Once, weeks ago, it would have expanded to feel love at this sight. That's because I would've known that waiting for me at the end of this day, this trip, back in Georgia, was Rowe. But she's not waiting for me.

So I feel nothing. "I do have a great view."

"Then why don't you look pleased about it?"

"I'm pleased."

She exhales a loud gust, lips flapping as spit and air spew out of her mouth. "You don't look it. Pane, you haven't smiled since we played with piggycorns."

"I didn't play with piggycorns—and, Nat, I have a lot of work to do."

She jumps up. "Greta's outside, anyway. I just wanted to say hello."

"Hello."

Before she goes, my sister points to a cube-shaped box sitting on my desk. "What's that?"

I eye the label and my heart throbs in pain. But all I say is "It's nothing."

"Doesn't look like nothing."

Before I have a chance to stop her, Natalie lifts the box's flap and narrows her eyes as she pulls out a glass bottle. It's shaped like a woman, curvy and sensual, and the name Rowe is typed in flirty, swirly letters across the front.

She lifts off the cap and sniffs. "Is this—"

I open my hand. "Give it to me."

My sister gently lays the bottle in my palm. "I was just curious."

I toss it into the trash. It lands with a deafening thunk in the quiet room. "Is there anything else I can do for you, Natalie?"

She glumly rises. "No."

"Then I'll talk to you at bedtime."

My sister starts to walk out of the room. Stops. Turns around. "You can do one thing."

"What's that?"

"Try to smile, big brother."

I clench my jaw until she's out of the room, and it's then, and only then, when I'm alone, that my mouth trembles.

Just when the hold that I have on my emotions begins to disintegrate, I remind myself that Rowe did me a favor. We were too different, our worlds too unlike each other's.

Then I grab the empty box and toss it on top of the perfume bottle that holds Rowe's scent—the custom fragrance I had specifically made for her as a gift. Sunbeam would have loved it.

After staring at the trash can for a second longer, I swallow my feelings and get back to work.

Chapter 44

ROWE

"This little one is going to a great home." Donner lifts the tailgate of his truck and slams it shut. "The community in Colorado will love her."

I smile at the piggycorn in the kennel. She lifts her nose to the air and sniffs. "Thanks, Donner."

He grins, looking up at me from under his lashes. "You've got a great business here."

"Appreciate it."

He keeps smiling and my heart sinks. "Listen, Rowe . . ." He scratches his chin sheepishly. "I was wondering if you'd like to go out with—"

"I can't, Donner. I'm just not . . . I can't."

He lifts his hands in a surrender gesture. "No worries. Can't blame a guy for asking."

No, I guess I couldn't. "Let me know when she arrives. I'll call the community and go over everything about her feed."

"Will do." He slaps the tailgate. "See you soon, Rowe."

"See ya."

In the past few weeks since Pane's been gone, it's been a whirlwind. Calls have come in from across the country about the piggycorns. Donner's community was the first to have one, and with them, we've been able to work out some of the logistics, like how much starfizz berries they have to eat in order to make electricity. Turns out, not much.

Which is good for me, as it gives the new seedlings time to grow.

Donner drives off, and from behind me, I hear the screen door open and the sound of shoes slapping against the stairs on their way down.

"Did I just hear correctly?" Cristina says, sidling up beside me. "Did Donner Wright just ask you out on a date?"

I sigh. "He did."

"And you said no."

"I said no."

She thumbs toward his truck. "You rebuked the sex god?"

"You sound like—"

I stop myself before his name can slip out.

"Like who?" she prods. "Pane?"

"Don't say his name." I pick up a box that was delivered and walk it up the stairs.

Cristina trails behind me. "Why not? Why can't I say his name?"

Because it's too hard, I long to tell her. Just thinking about him makes a wound open in my chest—a raw, seeping wound, one that won't heal.

Since he's been gone, I've been going through the motions, keeping my chin up and my head down in my work.

But it's been hard. I've started cyberstalking Pane, which doesn't help anything. However, I do know that he's set up in New York, taking the reins and running the company.

A truck drives by, blasting the horn. I turn around to see Cristina waving to the Collins boys. "From what I hear, Rhett Collins is still looking for a girlfriend. If you want a purely sexual rebound, I'm sure he'd be great."

I roll my eyes. "No thanks." Time to get Cristina off me and back on to her. No offense to my best friend, but talking about Pane Maddox isn't helping anything. "How was your client this morning?"

"If you think I'm going to just drop this conversation, you're wrong." She takes the box from me and I follow her into the house, where she sets it on the front desk. "But since you asked, my client was great."

We kept Pane's business plan since everything was set up. Cristina's been busy with clients. At night, Ron takes folks on a tour of the garden. The area bed-and-breakfasts are filled to overflowing with new tourists. Luckily, the tornado that hit the house didn't destroy anything in town. It basically plowed through the countryside. Mine was the only house that was hit, thank goodness, and when the magic righted the home, all the new additions remained.

So the town of Mystic Meadows has spit-polished itself to gleaming, and the mayor has even announced that we're going to have a Christmas festival.

Yeah, things have changed since the Pane Maddox effect took place. That's what folks call it—the Pane Maddox effect. Though Pane would have called it the Rowe Wadley effect.

Either way, he would be proud.

"Have you called him?" Cristina asks.

I shake my head. "No, and he hasn't called me, either."

She follows me into the kitchen, where I slip out of my shoes and open the fridge, grabbing a pitcher of water and filling a glass.

She slides onto a stool at the breakfast bar and drops her chin into her folded hands. "And why should he call you, when you're the one who did the dumping?"

"Look, I did it—"

"For the best, yeah, I know. So you keep telling me. Then why do you look so miserable?"

I speak between gulps of water. "I'm not miserable."

"You're not? Could've fooled me, with the way you mope around the house, sighing all the time. And don't think that I don't know that you've been cyberstalking him."

"You broke into my phone," I accuse.

She huffs. "You can't call it *breaking in* when you gave me your passcode years ago."

"That's besides the point," I mutter.

"Look." She sits up straight and takes the glass of water that I offer. "Call him. You two were great. I know his mother said that you were wrong for each other, but since when do you listen to what anyone else says, anyway?" Before I can muster an answer, she continues, "I know you want to do it all on your own. I get it. But there are some things in life that should never be done alone."

"Like what?"

"Like living."

I laugh painfully. "Living?"

"Yeah. Do you think that if I had what you and Pane did—correction, *do*—that I would give it up?"

"There are other—"

"Rich billionaire fish in the sea?"

I shoot my best friend a pointed look. "It's not about the money."

"Yes, it is. That's why you dumped him. Rowe Wadley, you left Pane Maddox because he had too much money, because with it, that meant you wouldn't have to do anything alone. You'd have to rely on someone."

"And what about when he left?" I snap. "What would happen to me then?"

She shrugs. "He already left because you made him, and look how miserable you are."

My heart convulses because Cristina's right. I am miserable. I am miserable and lonely and in mourning for giving up the one person I wanted to keep.

She rises, knocks back her water, and takes the glass to the sink. "I bet if you called him, he'd answer."

Without another word, she leaves the room, leaving me to thoughts that do nothing but paralyze me in place.

Chapter 45

PANE

These halls are cold to me now. Once, what feels like a lifetime ago, I would've swept through the grand entrance of a hotel and been electrified by the buzz of life—from the chatter at the front desk to the couples gracing the restaurant tables, to the teenagers charging devices by the grand fireplace.

All of it used to feel so real, so full. This was the center of existence for me.

But now it just seems so empty.

Without Rowe, everything is empty. As much as I've thrown myself into work and tried to ignore the pain, I'm hollowed out inside. Food tastes like cardboard. Experiences that should make me happy wind up leaving me emptier.

This is not what I expected being CEO would feel like.

And I've tried. Oh, I've tried. I give it all my heart every day, but everything just seems . . . barren.

There's nothing left inside me now. Nothing that feels or *wants* to feel. Running a business means going through the motions. So that's what I'm doing. Keeping things profitable. Working hard. Rising early and, at night, burning the midnight oil.

I'm doing exactly what's expected of me.

"You're late." Stone shoots a look at the watch on my wrist. "I thought you'd forgotten."

I flip the Rolex to gaze at its face. It was one of the first things I retrieved when I arrived at the hotel. My clothes, my watch, my phone.

None of it matters anymore.

"Didn't forget," I say. "Let's eat."

As the maître d' walks us to a table, my gaze skims the restaurant. The tablecloths are crisp. The waitstaff looks sharp in dark shirts and slacks. The diners smile over glasses of sparkling water.

Everything looks perfect.

It is. I should take pride in that. But I do not.

Stone glances at me from over his shoulder. "I've invited someone to join us."

"Who? Please don't tell me you're setting me up."

He chuckles. "There's no one on earth who I hate enough that I'd force them to spend time with you."

I scowl.

"See? Exactly. Case in point. You're barely fit company for yourself, much less anyone else. And here I thought winning the Maddox Group would make you happy. You're more miserable than ever."

"I'm not miserable," I murmur.

"Keep telling yourself that."

We're led to a table in the very back. As the maître d' shows us our seats and steps away, he reveals a man who's already been seated.

He wears a brown jacket over a camel-colored cashmere turtleneck. Even though I haven't seen him in years, I would recognize my father anywhere.

"What's this?" I grind out.

Stone pats the air, trying to calm me down and gently remind me that we're not allowed to make a scene. Or *I'm* not. My brother can do whatever he damn well pleases.

"Pane, allow me to introduce—"

I shoot him a look that could burn the hair off the top of his head. "It may have been years, but I know Frank."

My father studies me quietly while I stand beside my chair, frozen. Stone pulls it out for me. "For God's sake. Just sit down."

My entire body is stiff from the shock of this. Every limb feels heavy as I lumber into the chair and sit across from my dad.

He watches me with eyes full of questions. I drag my gaze away, refusing to look at him.

Stone's phone rings. He slides it from his pocket and gives the screen a nonchalant glance. "I've got to take this. You two get started. Order me a water and the rib eye."

"Wait." But it's too late. My brother's already gone, slipping into the crowd of waiters as they approach their tables.

How convenient. Perfect that Stone would receive an important call and have no choice but to abandon me with our father.

I scoff. This is unbelievable.

My dad watches me like I'm a tiger just escaped from its cage. That's how I feel. Like my skin's too tight to contain me, like I'm on the prowl, searching out anything smaller and weaker, something I can sink my teeth into and destroy.

How could Stone have done this?

As much as I'd love to walk away, in the corner of my vision, waitstaff convenes, slyly looking over their shoulders at me and whispering to one another.

Great. I'm on display.

Someone's probably getting video of this. Capturing the newest CEO on the verge of a complete meltdown.

Making a scene is not the right choice here.

"Look, I don't know why Stone set this up, but there's no point in it. I have nothing to say to you."

He folds his hands on the table, and I take a moment to study him. He looks the same as he did when we were children, except his hair is now white. It's also thinner, and his jaw is weaker. He has that same quiet confidence that I remember, and when he smiles slightly, all those times when he declared the platitude of the day, the cliché of the hour, flood back to me, and I remember how much I loved him.

And how quickly he destroyed our family.

I don't know why I'm here. I adjust in my seat, leaning forward and smiling so that none of the waitstaff or managers sense that anything's wrong.

"I'll stay for fifteen minutes, but there's nothing you can say that will change anything. You left us, walked out on our lives, and not once, in all these years, have you tried to reach out to me. But here you are, now that Stone and I have established ourselves within the company. What do you want? Money? Have you spent everything our mother gave you?"

He frowns. "Your mother never gave me money."

A laugh explodes from my throat. "Oh, that's rich." I repeat his words with so much bitterness that a sour flavor bleeds across my tongue.

"It's true."

The waiter arrives and I order Stone's rib eye, as well as a water and salad for myself, wanting to get the hell out of here as quickly as possible.

"Look, Pane," my father says when the waiter's gone, "I know what you think of me."

Fury burns a hole in the bottom of my stomach. "How could you possibly know what I think?"

"Because I know what I would think if my dad had abandoned me like I did to you."

"At least you admit that you abandoned us," I growl.

He folds his hands and stares down at them. "Your mother made me."

When he doesn't move, I say, "What are you talking about?"

He opens his mouth, but pauses, seeming to weigh his words. "I never wanted to leave, but your mother had this idea that I was a threat to the family business. So she divorced me, got a restraining order, and threatened that if I ever came within an inch of either you or your brother, she'd have me arrested and thrown in prison for the rest of my life."

I freeze. "What?"

He's still staring at his hands. "Your mother wanted children to keep the family legacy, but she never wanted a husband to share it with. Why do you think she never took my last name and you didn't, either?"

He takes a sip of water. "Sylvia was cold, sure. I knew that. It was how her father had treated her. But I thought that when she had children, things would change, that she'd soften somehow. But she didn't. She saw me as a threat, as competition for your love and affection. I had no choice, Pane. When I tried to fight her, her lawyers always won. She had millions to throw around. I got nothing, and I wanted nothing from her except you and your brother."

There's so much that rings like truth in what he's saying. It sounds like my mother perfectly. For God's sake, she had Stone and I compete against one another for the company. Was she purposefully attempting to drive a wedge between the two of us?

I study my father's features, but all I see is honesty and regret in his face. "Why now? Why are you reaching out to us now?"

He sighs, his shoulders sagging. "I ran into your brother on the street a few months ago. He immediately recognized me, and about punched me in the face." He chuckles. "I asked him to talk to me for five minutes, to let me explain. We went into a coffee shop—and I tell you what, I've never spoken so fast in five minutes in all my life."

He smiles. "I told him what I told you. That she kept you from me, on purpose. I wanted to be in your lives, but your mother saw to it—because of her jealousy, because of her need to control—that I wasn't allowed anywhere near either of you." He tears a hunk of bread from a loaf in the center of the table. "I hear the second guy got it worse than me."

Natalie's father also has nothing to do with her. My mother is controlling, but this?

This . . . the cogs of time in my mind whirl backward to the moment she told me I could either be with Ilana or I could be a Maddox. They spin again, stopping more recently, when I was told that Stone and I were going to compete. She said our numbers were similar, but was that true? As far as I knew, I had a lead over my brother—a good solid lead when it came to managing a well-oiled, profit-pumping hotel.

The position should've been mine by default.

But no, Mom had to play her little game. Her little games that have cost me time, happiness—

My gaze locks on to my dad's. "If you'd never run into Stone, then—"

He nods, and says what I expect: "Then I would've let her continue to poison your minds against me. I knew that's what Sylvia had done. Me coming to either of you wouldn't have changed how you felt. You would've believed that I left you of my own free will. That's what Stone thought. Your brother believed that until he gave me a shot." He shakes his head as emotion floods his eyes. "If there's one thing that I regret—and there are many—I regret that I didn't fight harder, that I didn't let myself be ruined trying to make the two of you see that I loved you, that you were my moon and stars. Every morning and every night, I think about you both. You're the first people on my mind in the morning and the last when I say my prayers at night." He shakes his head. "Don't let the precious ones get away, I've realized. Don't let someone else dictate your own happiness, because often what people want is for their own misery to be mirrored in the eyes of others. They don't want people to strive and succeed. They want the population to be sad and lonely, as heartless as they are. Because that's what makes them happy, not the joy of others."

It's those words, the very last ones that he says, that hit me in the chest like a sledgehammer, cracking and splintering the ice that's grown up around my heart these past few weeks.

The worst part? I let it. I embraced it, allowed it to mold me into someone who thought only about work, and who lived by the mantra that I didn't deserve love.

What a lie. I deserve love as much as anyone, and I deserve a mother who isn't selfish and scheming.

I rise. "Thank you for this."

My dad stands, too, looking confused. "Did I say something wrong? If you don't want to see me again, I understand."

In one quick movement, I move around the table and embrace him. My father is surprised, unsure what to do at first, but then his arms slowly encircle me, and he whispers, "My son."

Chapter 46

PANE

My mother bursts into my office, white heels clacking against the marble floor. "What do you mean, you're resigning?"

I close my laptop and shove my chair back. "I'm not *resigning*."

Relief washes over her face.

"I've *resigned*."

She stops in front of my desk and drops the printed letter I emailed only minutes earlier. It floats down and lands atop my computer.

"You can't be serious, Pane. This must be a joke."

"I assure you, it's very serious."

The fury in her face freezes in realization. My mother scoffs. "Is this about that woman? Rowe, was it? If it is, Pane, I did you a favor."

I stand and slip my computer into its carrying case. "It's about *her*. It's about *Dad*. It's about everything."

"Your father—"

"You kept him from me," I explode. "For over half my life, you lied about him."

"Who's to say that I lied?" She tosses her arms into the air. "Have you met him?" When I don't answer, she rocks back. "I see. So you've talked to Frank. Well, I can tell you that he's filling your mind with poison."

"No, Mom. You're the one who's filled my mind with poison"—I shove my finger toward her—"and I'm done with it. I'm going to make sure Natalie doesn't suffer the same fate Stone and I did, cut off from a dad who loved us."

Her face turns bright red. "You have no right."

I lean in and see the fear brightening her eyes. The great Sylvia Maddox, the woman who's led the company for years, is terrified of losing control over the very people she claims to love.

"Goodbye, Mom. Good luck."

As I leave my office for the last time, she shouts, "You'll regret this, Pane. Without the Maddox Group, you're nothing."

I pull the door open, stop, and turn around. "No, I'm not."

Chapter 47

ROWE

It's been a couple of weeks since I've been in downtown proper, so I go for a drive through Mystic Meadows. What I see stops me cold.

The grime, the faded exteriors, the dull, lifeless film that coated Mystic Meadows for *years*—gone. It's like someone took a celestial sponge and scrubbed the town clean, swiping away every trace of decay and disappointment.

For so long, people tried to fight back against the fading magic. Pressure-washing their storefronts. Slapping on new coats of paint. Stringing up extra lights to chase away the gloom. But no matter what they did, the sparkle never stuck.

Until now.

Now the town *gleams.* The buildings, once faded and tired, practically glow in the sunlight, their facades vibrant and crisp. The trees seem taller, fuller, their emerald leaves rustling like they've finally shaken off years of exhaustion. Even the sky is bluer—not just blue, but a rich, deep sapphire that stretches endlessly overhead, the kind of sky that makes you want to believe in things you once thought impossible.

And the air . . .

It's *alive.*

The scent of freshly brewed coffee drifts from the café, richer and warmer than I've ever smelled it. The buttery sweetness of pastries lingers in the breeze. Even the earth beneath my boots feels different—softer, warmer, like the very land is humming beneath my feet.

And now the river sparkles.

No longer a sluggish ribbon of murky sludge, it shimmers under the afternoon sun, liquid silver threaded with flecks of iridescence. It's the kind of water you want to touch, just to see if the magic clings to your skin.

But it's not just about how things look.

It's about how they *feel.*

There's a hum in the air, a quiet, pulsing energy that vibrates through every breath I take. It's in the wind. In the pavement beneath my boots. In the way people walk—heads higher, shoulders looser, laughter spilling from their lips like a melody the town had forgotten.

I think of what Pane said, that the starfizz berries worked with the ley lines, strengthening the magic that had been dormant for so long. It wasn't just the town that needed them; the magic itself needed something to anchor it. A symbiotic relationship. One couldn't exist wholly without the other.

I know this firsthand. My family's farm has always held *some* magic, but it was small, quiet, nearly forgotten. Nothing like *this.* Nothing like the way it breathes through Mystic Meadows now.

The people are different, too.

Gone are the drab, lifeless clothes, the muted tones that once let them fade into the background. Now, color *explodes* everywhere—bright skirts, patterned shirts, vibrant scarves fluttering in the wind. People smile freely, their movements lighter, as if some invisible weight has been lifted from their shoulders.

It's joy, pure and unmistakable, and it's everywhere.

"Hey, Rowe!"

I glance over to see Coleman Barrier waving at me as he opens a clapboard sign advertising discounts on hammers.

Coleman Barrier, the human splinter, is waving. At me.

I return the gesture and yell out, "Good to see you, Coleman!"

"Same here! We're all proud of your farm."

So am I, so much so that I can't stop smiling as I make my way home.

By the time I reach the farm, I feel the change here, too. The land welcomes me back, buzzing with the same quiet magic that now fills the town.

I pull into the driveway, kill the engine, and step out, drinking it all in. The farm stretches before me, vibrant and alive, *mine* in a way it hasn't been in *years*. I let out a breath and smile.

For the first time in ages, Mystic Meadows—and the people in it—feel like they've finally woken up.

"Have you heard?" Cristina says into the phone, her voice on supersonic speed.

"Heard what?"

I take a bite out of a carrot before handing the rest to the piggycorn at my feet. Currently, we're sitting in the gazebo, enjoying the fall air. The humidity's finally receding, and the temperature has dropped at night, washing the air with a coolness that's invigorating.

"About the resort," she says.

"What resort?"

"The resort going up in the mountains."

"No, I haven't heard anything about it, but it'll be great for our business." Saying that should make me feel awesome, but instead it only amplifies the hollowness inside me, the words echoing in my chest, reminding me of just how lonely I am. Nothing has been the same since Pane left. I've tried to ignore it, to push aside the ache that eats away at me, but it's persistent, gnawing, reminding me that I'm so very, very alone. That I had happiness within reach, but I decided to push it away. "So that's a good thing—a new resort."

"So you *don't* know," she tells me flatly.

"Yes, I do. You just told me."

"But you don't know who's building it."

"Why would I know who's building it? I only just found out about it."

"Hold on. Are you ready?"

It's the tone of her voice that tips me off, and I know without having to ask who is building in Mystic Meadows.

"It's Pane," I say.

"It is!" she shrieks. "He was in town today, apparently, talking to people about it—Ron and Isaac, I guess. Clarice told me."

My stomach somersaults in on itself, falling into a black hole from which there is no escape. I'm elated, surprised, angry. Why is he building here? Has he returned to torment me?

No, no. Of course he's not here to torment me.

He's keeping his promise. Even though I spurned him. Pane has returned. He's come back.

He's come back.

That's when guilt crashes down on me. I broke things off with him because we were too different, because deep down I knew he would abandon me. It's always better to be in control, to *hurt* first instead of *being* hurt first.

As I walk back to the house with the piggycorn following me, Cristina goes on about Pane, about the project, how the town is overjoyed that he's come back.

They're overjoyed.

I'm even more devastated.

How can I face him after what I did?

My heart throbs in agony as I step inside the house. It pulses with frustration as I push the door closed behind me. It screams in torment as I spy my dad's old boots.

Somehow they survived the tornado. I thought they'd been lost, but when the house fixed itself, it delivered the boots in their usual spot just inside the back door.

I slip into the cracked leather, tired and dusty from years of hard work.

I take one step.

Snap.

The sole of the right boot has broken in two. After years of wear, after years of belonging to my dad and then me, its time has ended.

It's funny, the things that register and the times when they do. I slide my foot out, pick up the boots, and walk them to the trash.

I stop just in front of it.

"You there, Rowe? Rowe, are you there?"

"Let me call you back," I tell my best friend.

I stamp on the trash can's pedal, and the lid lifts. The blackness waits for the boots to fall in, and as it looms, my heart convulses. Throwing these away feels like I'm throwing away part of myself. No, not part of me—part of my dad. It feels like if I lose these, then I've lost myself.

How silly is that? It's just a pair of old boots.

Even though things change—years pass, people die, surroundings alter—the one thing that remains is you and how you deal with those changes.

And I'm tired of expecting the worst and waiting to be abandoned. No more. I'm ready to fall, and hopefully Pane will catch me, because I love him. With all my heart, with all my soul, I love that man, and he needs to know it.

"Goodbye, Dad. See you on the flip side."

Then I drop the shoes in the trash.

Maybe I can catch Pane before it's too late.

Chapter 48

ROWE

I throw on a jacket and slide through the house in my socked feet. I slip on shoes, open the front door, and throw myself through it.

I blink. Stare. Blink again.

Fairy lights are strung up in my front yard. The pigs are out and playing. They're making a circle around someone who's bent down to pet them.

"Pane?"

He glances up, and even with the shadows slicing over his jaw, I would know that silhouette anywhere.

He straightens and I can't believe it.

He's wearing overalls.

Overalls.

My heart contracts with joy because that is the one piece of clothing that, months ago, he never would've put on.

But now he's wearing them for me and only me.

I race down the stairs, and before he can say two words, I throw myself into his arms, which open just in time to catch me. He staggers back, and at first I'm certain he's not going to return my hug, but then he wraps his arms around me and lifts me into the air.

"It's you," is all I can say as I push my nose into the crook of his neck. "It's really you."

He spins me around and then slowly lowers me to the ground. "I can leave if you want me to."

"No." I pull back to look up into those eyes, eyes that make me want to swim in a field of the greenest grass, to dip myself in a jade stone that's been liquefied. "No. I was wrong. I was so wrong."

He cocks his head. "Wrong about what, little Sunbeam?"

My heart expands at my nickname. Before every ounce of courage I've mustered drains out of me, I grab it like I'm holding on to life itself.

"What I said about how different we are—it's true. That's all true. Nothing will change that. But sometimes it's the differences that make everything right. Pane, I didn't give you a chance before. I told you to leave before you were allowed to prove that you wouldn't go. You said that you'd stay, and I should have listened. But my dad had said he would be okay, and Luke had told me he loved me, and both of those turned out to be lies."

It all sounds so stupid now that I'm saying it. I rub a hand back and forth over my forehead, as if erasing myself will help me live down some of this humiliation. But I refuse to disappear. It's time for me to shine.

So I continue, "I know how silly all of that must sound. My dad didn't plan on dying. It wasn't his choice to go. But it stuck with me—and the only way I could prove that it didn't bother me when someone left was if I didn't need them in the first place. If I did everything by myself and never needed anyone, then I couldn't be hurt."

I force myself to look up from his Adam's apple and into his eyes. I don't know what I expected—him to be scowling, him looking passive. But he's neither of those. Pane smiles down on me, looking at me with eyes so full of love that my heart jump-starts to life.

It's time to leap even further. I'm not done here. There's a lot of groveling that needs to happen. "I've never said this first before, but, Pane, you should know that"—deep breath, take the plunge—"I love you, and if that makes you run, I'm sorry. But you have to know."

He blinks and shakes his head.

"What?"

"That was a lot to digest," he explains. "I thought I'd just get a simple *hey, what are you doing here, I'm kicking you out again,* but that was more than I expected."

My throat shrivels to the size of a pinhead. I've said too much, scared him off. I start to back off, and Pane grabs me by the arm, pulls me to him, and crushes his lips against mine.

I melt and let myself drown in him. I don't ever want to come up for air. I want to stay like this, fall into him, kiss him until I'm so dizzy that I've forgotten my own name.

Every part of me aches for Pane, right down to my toes. If this kiss never ends, I still won't have had enough of him—because I want everything he's got to give, and in return I want to give him everything that I have to offer. Without limits, without fear, without holding back.

When we come up for air, Pane takes my face in his hands. "Sunbeam, I've loved you since the moment we met, since you screamed at me not to hit your piggycorns. I've loved you, and even though I tried to deny it, told myself that I needed to focus on the competition, it was impossible to ignore the feeling that took over me from the moment I first laid eyes on you." He sighs and brushes hair from my eyes. "I couldn't love you any more if I tried."

I frown. "Is that a compliment? Or are you saying that you can't love me more? Or you don't want to love me mo—"

"Shut up." He cups my face and kisses me again, harder, until I can't think. When we part, he presses his forehead to mine. "I love you. I love you. *I love you.* And please don't ever doubt me again."

Breathless, I reply, "I won't. I won't ever doubt you again."

"Good." He sweeps his nose against mine and says, "Also, I'm building a resort."

A huge grin takes over my face. My cheeks ache, I'm smiling so hard. "I heard. Does that mean you're going to need a place to stay while you build it?"

He quirks a brow. "Would you happen to have a shamper available?"

I toss my head back and twine my arms around his neck. "I think we can do better than that."

"Oh? There's a piggycorn bed available?"

I kiss him. "Even better than that."

"A bedroom?"

"One, more specifically."

"There's one free in the house?" he says, playing along.

We kiss again, and when we break apart, I tell him, "Mine. My bedroom is available. If you want it."

He frowns. "And where will you sleep?"

"I was thinking beside you."

Pane pretends to consider this. "Only if you promise one thing."

"What's that?"

"To let me love you."

I push up onto my tiptoes and kiss him. "I think that can be arranged."

Epilogue

Six months later

There's a saying in my little town just outside Mystic Meadows, Georgia: *Bad luck begets more bad luck. And if you're Rowe Wadley, you won't just* attract *bad luck—you* are *bad luck.*

Or at least, that's what they used to say.

I glance out over Wadley Farms and my heart swells. The piggycorns prance beneath the towering oaks, their tiny hooves tapping against the grass. Wherever they step, soft golden light pulses in rhythmic waves, bathing the yard in a dreamlike glow. The air is rich with the scent of honeysuckles and fresh earth, and for the first time in my life, I feel like luck is finally mine.

"You ready, honey?"

I turn at the sound of Mom's voice. She stands in the doorway, elegant in a pale-pink dress with a matching jacket, a look of warmth and pride in her eyes.

I press a hand to my waist, smoothing the soft ivory fabric of my dress, nerves and excitement tangling in my chest. "How do I look?"

Mom's lips tremble just a little as she blinks fast, like she's holding back happy tears. "Like a beautiful bride."

A lump rises in my throat, but before I can respond, Bill steps up beside me, offering his arm. "Your dad would be proud," he murmurs, his voice gruff with emotion.

I nod, swallowing hard, and let him lead me outside.

The farm is transformed. Twinkling fairy lights hang from every branch, but it's the piggycorns who bring them to life, their magic sending a soft shimmer through each glowing bulb. Stella is among them—my Stella, returned to me after I bought the farm from the bank. Sally Ray and Luke practically tripped over themselves to take my money and run, but I didn't care. Stella was mine again, and she was home.

The wooden gazebo ahead is wrapped in white roses, the scent mingling with the crisp night air. And standing at the center, waiting for me, is Pane.

My heartbeat stutters.

He's never looked more broodingly handsome, his suit crisp, his dark hair just messy enough to remind me of all the times I've run my fingers through it. But it's his smile that undoes me—the slow, knowing one that says, *I see you. I choose you. I love you.*

My cheeks burn as I realize all our friends are here. The whole town turned out, along with Pane's family. His father, his brother, his sister.

Not Sylvia, though. The rift between them is still too deep, and she hadn't been able to bring herself to come. But she made one concession—Natalie is attending a prep school only an hour away now, which means we see her on weekends. She's an incredible kid. And somehow she has an unspoken bond with the piggycorns.

After all, they do let her crowd-surf on top of them.

Pane's brother, Stone, left the Maddox Group, too. He and Pane are now business partners, determined to build something all their own. And they're already off to an incredible start: Their resort, built right here on the magical land of Mystic Meadows, opens next year.

Turns out, when you've got an enchanted landscape, piggycorn yoga, and a spa infused with actual magic, people will flock to book a session.

Bill releases my arm as I step up to Pane, and Pane bends down, voice husky as he murmurs, "You look beautiful, Sunbeam. And you smell so good."

I giggle, my heart fluttering. I'm wearing the perfume he had created just for me. "You like it? I might know someone who can have a one-of-a-kind scent made just for you."

His eyes narrow playfully. "Really?"

"Really."

"You'll have to reveal your secret," he whispers, but before I can reply, Ron clears his throat from where he stands, officiating.

We turn, but all I can think is that I'm marrying Pane Maddox. The love of my life. My partner. My home.

The ceremony passes in a blur of laughter, vows, and the steady warmth of Pane's hands in mine. Then, suddenly, we're married.

The celebration explodes around us—music, dancing, piggycorns twirling between the guests. Pane and I spin together beneath the strings of glowing lights, lost in each other.

By the time the night grows late and my feet ache from dancing, Pane pulls me close, his arm tight around my waist. He leans down, his lips brushing my ear. "Watch," he murmurs.

I tilt my head up just as fireworks burst above us, painting the sky in ribbons of gold, pink, and violet. The piggycorns respond with joy, prancing around the crowd with their horns lifted, their soft glow shimmering like stardust.

I sink into Pane's arms, my back against his chest, his warmth surrounding me. He drops his lips to my ear, voice low and sure. "I love you, Mrs. Maddox."

A shiver of happiness runs through me. "I love you, too."

For a moment, I let myself feel it—all of it. The wedding, the magic, the piggycorns.

Life could literally get no better than this.

Or so I think.

A bush near my feet rustles. My nose wrinkles. "What's that?"

Pane presses a quick kiss to my temple before bending down to part the leaves. He stills. And then . . . he laughs.

"You're never going to believe this."

I crouch beside him, peering past the waxy branches. My breath catches.

A tiny, delicate lamb stands in the shadows, its wool soft and curled like fresh clouds. It takes a timid step forward, blinking up at me with impossibly big eyes.

And then, the light catches it.

A slender, golden horn, barely longer than my pinkie finger, protrudes from its forehead.

I gasp. "Is that—"

"A lambicorn," Pane confirms, scooping the tiny creature into his arms with a grin that makes my heart stumble.

I press a hand to my chest as he lifts the baby toward me. Carefully, I stroke its soft coat, wonder blooming in my chest. "Welcome to the family, little lambi."

Pane shifts closer, wrapping his arms around both of us, his lips brushing my forehead before his fingers skim over the lambicorn's tiny horn.

"Yes, little one," he murmurs, voice thick with something deep and sure. "Welcome."

Book Club Questions

1. How does Rowe Wadley's self-perception as being "bad luck" influence her actions and decisions throughout the story? How does it compare to Pane Maddox's privileged yet detached view of the world?
2. Discuss the significance of the piggycorns in the story. What do they symbolize for Rowe, and how do they contrast with the unicorns?
3. Pane and Rowe have very different lifestyles and personalities. What do you think draws them together despite these differences?
4. What themes of resilience and resourcefulness do you see in Rowe's efforts to save the farm? How does her character reflect the challenges of small-town life?
5. Pane Maddox is forced to step out of his privileged life and work from scratch. How does this challenge change his character throughout the story?
6. The story is set in Mystic Meadows, Georgia, with magical elements like piggycorns and ley lines. How does the setting enhance the narrative?
7. The story alternates perspectives between Rowe and Pane. How does this dual narration add depth to the story?
8. Stella, the unicorn, represents a blend of magic, grace, and power within the story. How does her presence reflect the

broader themes of authenticity versus commercialism in Mystic Meadows? What does Stella's role reveal about the characters' values, especially Rowe's and Sally Ray's differing approaches to their farms?

9. The destruction caused by the tornado forces the characters to confront their deepest fears and vulnerabilities. How does this event reshape their priorities and relationships, particularly Rowe's connection to the farm and Pane's understanding of community and belonging?
10. Do you think Pane lets Rowe go too easily? Or do you think he believes that her old wounds are surfacing and he can't compete against them?

Acknowledgments

Books are not written in a vacuum, and this one is no exception. First, I want to thank God for all that He has done for me and my family.

Thank you to Bambi Crivello, Jean Hovey, and Stephanie Jones—without the three of you, piggycorns never would've come into existence. Our plotting sessions are always the highlight of my year, and you forcing me to write a romance, and *only* a romance, has been a game changer in my life.

To the Moxies—thank you for all your support and being a sounding board when I needed one. Thank you to Skye Warren, who helped me sculpt a path that has led to this book existing.

Big thanks to my agent, Jill Marsal. Your decision to answer an email from an unknown writer and for believing in me has been amazing.

Huge thanks to Maria Gomez for acquiring a little book that featured magical creatures. Your support of my vision has meant the world to me.

Another huge thanks to my editor, Lindsey Faber. I've truly been gifted with the Dream Team at Montlake, and I'm appreciative of all your support and encouragement.

Thank you to all my early readers—Eryn, Sarah, and Alex. I appreciate you taking the time out of your busy schedules to read my books and answer my questions. A special thanks to Eryn, for always being willing to chat out a sticky plot point and for answering all my texts. I owe you many, many more whoopie pies.

I would be remiss if I didn't mention Mark and my girls. For years, you've all been so patient when I've said, "Let me just finish this chapter!" Your support is my lifeblood, and big love to all of you.

Lastly, but most of all: Thank you, readers! I wouldn't be here without your love and support.

About the Author

Photo © 2022 Christy Stahlnaker

Amy Boyles is the author of the Sweet Tea Witches mysteries, the Bless Your Witch series, and the Magical Renovation Mystery series, among many other novels. A resident of northern Alabama, Amy loves antique shopping, cooking for her family, and watching K-dramas. When she's not chauffeuring her two kids to after-school activities, she can be found reading a good romance. For more information, visit www.amyboyles.com.